THE DEEP AND SHINING DARK

BOOK 1 OF THE MAREK SERIES

JULIET KEMP

THE DEEP AND SHINING DARK

BOOK 1 OF THE MAREK SERIES

Elsewhen Press

The Deep and Shining Dark
First published in Great Britain by Elsewhen Press, 2018
An imprint of Alnpete Limited

Copyright © Juliet Kemp, 2018. All rights reserved
The right of Juliet Kemp to be identified as the author of this work has been asserted in accordance with sections 77 and 78 of the Copyright, Designs and Patents Act 1988. No part of this publication may be reproduced, stored in a retrieval system or transmitted in any form, or by any means (electronic, mechanical, telepathic, magical, or otherwise) without the prior written permission of the copyright owner.

Elsewhen Press, PO Box 757, Dartford, Kent DA2 7TQ
www.elsewhen.press
British Library Cataloguing in Publication Data.
A catalogue record for this book is available from the British Library.
ISBN 978-1-911409-24-3 Print edition
ISBN 978-1-911409-34-2 eBook edition

Condition of Sale
This book is sold subject to the condition that it shall not, by way of trade or otherwise, be lent, re-sold, hired out or otherwise circulated in any form of binding or cover other than that in which it is published and without a similar condition including this condition being imposed on the subsequent purchaser.

This book is copyright under the Berne Convention.
Elsewhen Press & Planet-Clock Design are trademarks of Alnpete Limited

Printed and bound by CPI Group (UK) Ltd, Croydon, CR0 4YY

This book is a work of fiction. All names, characters, places, trading organisations, governing councils and events are either a product of the author's fertile imagination or are used fictitiously. Any resemblance to actual events, governments, companies, places or people (living, dead, or spirit) is purely coincidental. No angels were harmed in the making of this book.

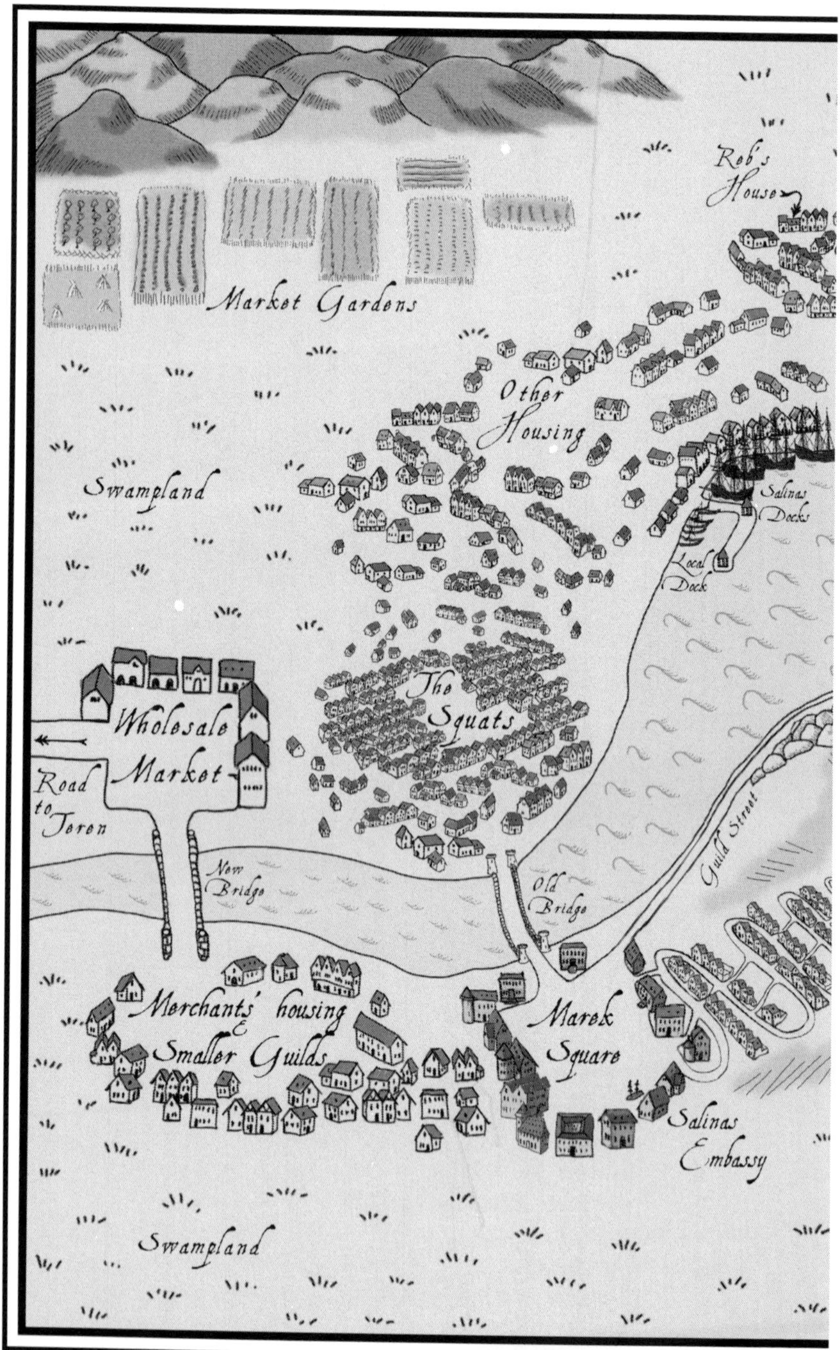

Rob's House
Market Gardens
Other Housing
Swampland
Salinas Docks
Local Dock
The Squats
Wholesale Market
Road to Jeren
New Bridge
Old Bridge
Guild Street
Merchants' housing & Smaller Guilds
Marek Square
Salinas Embassy
Swampland

Swamp Fishers' Village
Housing & Shops
Tanneries
Old Market
Oval Sea
Ferry
Cliff
Cliff path
Statues of Beckett & Marek
Leandra
Park
The Council Chamber
Shops
Goat Herders' Village
Marekhill
Marek

ONE

Jonas t'Riseri sat on the river wall, a warm pastry in his hand, idly watching Marek's early morning water traffic. Downriver to his right, on this side of the river, the ferry was pulling out from the foot of Marekhill, its bow coming round to point towards the Old Market on the other side. Nearly opposite him, a fishing-boat was coming back from the early shift into the small local dock, catch shining silver-blue at the back of its deck; and in the larger section of the docks, little boats darted in and out among the masts of the sea-going Salinas ships.

He grimaced and looked away. He didn't want to think about Salina right now.

To his left, the shallow curve of the Old Bridge was already busy with folk – servants and shopkeepers – headed from well-off south Marek to the wholesale market north of the river, and returning the other way with loaded trolleys and lighter purses. Carts and carriages took the more direct New Bridge, a few streets further upstream; but for anything that could be carried on foot, especially if you were delivering to the narrow streets of the older parts of the city, or Marekhill itself where carriages and carts were forbidden, human-power was still quicker, and most folk preferred to avoid the dusty, vehicle-crowded routes to, from, and over the New Bridge.

Jonas spotted Tam, one of the messengers he'd met when he first reached Marek, and now a good friend, coming over the rise of the bridge, bare feet skimming across the paving. Messengers were light on their feet; you had to be. Jonas raised a hand as Tam ducked around a porter with a trolley of vegetables and came level with him where the bridge met the river wall.

"Go safe!" Tam called over without stopping; the messengers' traditional greeting.

Tam, and someone else – Jonas couldn't quite see their

face, but there was something odd, something wrong, about the way they moved. The stranger had to duck under the low doorway that short Tam wasn't bothered by. Both of them walking towards Jonas...

Jonas blinked, and the flicker was gone, the dim room – had that been evening light from its doorway? – in his mental eye replaced by the bright sunlight of the real morning in front of him. He scowled, the edges of his good mood fading. He'd been having more than one a day, the last couple of days. Definitely more than usual. Not that his flickers were 'usual' at all, not for anyone else, and they shouldn't be for him either. He didn't want them, and he couldn't go home with them. That was why he was here in Marek, famous for its magic, finding out how to get rid of them for good. The Salinas did not have – mustn't have – magic. He had to fix it; but he'd got here and discovered that there wasn't a sorcerer on every street corner any more. Marek's sorcerers had almost all been wiped out by a plague a couple of years previously. There were a couple left still, he'd found that out too, but the problem with talking to a sorcerer about his flickers was that it meant, well... talking to a sorcerer, about his flickers. In the season he'd been here, he hadn't quite brought himself to do it. And then every so often he'd have a longer patch between flickers and think, well, maybe it was just going of its own accord...

He'd get round to it eventually. There was time enough yet. He distracted himself with another big bite of his pastry. The rich crackly leaves of the outside dissolved in his mouth, and he relished the sweet fruit inside. Berries from Exuria, at this time of year, which meant they'd be brought in by Salinas ships... Against his will, he looked rightwards again, following the flow of the water moving steadily below him, out towards the mouth of the estuary and into the Oval Sea. The curve of the river blocked his view any further, but in his mind's eye he looked around the Marekhill cliffs, past the swamps at the estuary's mouth, and across the Oval Sea towards Salina, invisibly distant. Though, at this time of year, nearly all of his people would be out at sea rather than at home in the villages.

Behind him an infusion-seller was pushing a clanking

barrow and calling their wares. Jonas swallowed the last crumbs of the pastry and counted his coins. Not enough. Time to go looking for the next job. He hopped down off the wall, then hesitated. The Old Market was good for messages this time of day. He had a penny for the ferry over from the far end of Guildstreet, at the foot of the cliff end of Marekhill, and that was quicker than going over the bridge and round the port, but he hated the ferry. It wasn't a proper ship. And anyway, a penny was a penny. He headed towards the bridge. He'd go the long way. Maybe he'd pick up a job on the way; he wouldn't get that on the ferry.

The flicker was still nagging at the back of his brain as he threaded his way through the crowds on the bridge. Who was it that Tam was going to introduce to him?

His flickers were aggravating, mostly, rather than useful; though he'd won money on a boat race more than once, and he never played dice with people he liked, or not more than once. He sighed. He really did need to get on and track down one of those sorcerers. His mother had been very clear on the matter. *Go to Marek*, she'd said, barely able to meet his eye, when she'd realised what he was telling her. *They have sorcerers there. Go to Marek and fix it.*

He couldn't just keep letting time slip by, however busy he was earning a living and making friends and exploring this fascinating new city. And however much he hated the idea of talking to a sorcerer.

He was over the bridge now, passing through the wholesale market that stretched in both directions along the river, sandwiched between the riverbank and the squats that rose behind the big market square. Fish and meat and vegetables and grains all in their separate areas, and all of them thronged with people. One of the vegetable sellers beckoned Jonas over; Jonas spread his hands to sign 'busy'. Wholesalers always wanted to send you out towards the yard where the carts waited, just outside the city bounds, and you could never get anything on the way back again.

To his left, carts were loading up to wheel out onto the main road that led through the marshes towards Teren. To his right, there were three smaller roads and half a dozen alleyways. Jonas swerved towards the alley furthest right;

always easier to dodge around folk on foot than carts. And that one cut down towards the northern riverbank. River wasn't sea, but he still liked to be near the water when he could. And the path went through the docks, where ships were moored in tight ranks, and almost all of them Salinas.

It was too early though today for most anyone to be up, when they were safely in port. The only Salina he saw was a harassed-looking quartermaster overseeing burly dockers removing huge sacks of grain from the ship's deck. Jonas didn't recognise her, and she was too busy to notice him. Most times someone would, though; Jonas' fair hair stood out among the darker Teren dockers, even if it wasn't as white-blond as most of his compatriots. What stood out even more was a Salina in Mareker tunic and trousers, working on land, and when he wanted a few free drinks, Jonas went down to the drinking dens along the edge of the port, and waited for one of the sailors to ask his story. Sometimes he'd wind up taking someone home for the night, too, one of his age-mates on her first solo tour, or an older woman taken by his cheerful smile. That was fun, too. But he couldn't explain why he was here; couldn't talk about his little *problem*.

Automatically, he looked up at the masts. He slowed, and his eyes widened. Every Salinas ship was flying the New Year flag. And, now he came to look at them, there were a lot more masts than usual. Almost as if they were coming up to... It couldn't possibly be New Year already, could it? Could he have lost track of the calendar that badly, here where they named their year the other way around? He started counting weeks on his fingers; swore; counted again.

Shitsticks. How could he have left it this long? Half a year, his mother had said; half a year to sort it out, and then he could grab a lift home just after the New Year, when everyone set off for Salina before the bad weather set in and they ceased trading for the season. And here he was, could only be a couple of days from New Year, and he'd got nowhere. How could time have passed that quickly?

Today. He had to find a damn sorcerer, *today*, and sort this thing out. That was all there was to it.

☉ ☉

Reb handed the messenger a penny tip, shut the front door after them, and unwrapped the parcel from the grocer. A bag of floor-sweepings, and another of powdered eggshell. Floor-sweepings from a busy shop were about the best thing going for getting the feel of the city. All those feet, in and out, bringing dirt with them from every corner of the place. Eggshell was just a substrate, but Reb hated powdering it herself. The local grocery was sufficiently busy for her purposes, and the grocer considered bagging his floor-sweepings and powdering his eggshells to be well-worth the honesty-charms she exchanged with him for it.

Not that many people bothered with honesty-charms any more. She'd turned a lot of folk away, just after the plague, wrapped up in her grief and guilt. With no one else to go to any more – it was hardly the sort of work that brat Cato would do, even if respectable shopkeepers were prepared to go to his part of the squats – people had found ways to do without magic.

When she'd started working again, there was still enough business to keep her afloat, and she hadn't raised her rates, but it seemed like she hadn't that many repeat customers these days. She remembered, once, being friendly with her customers. Those who still came to her didn't seem so chatty these days.

That suited her fine.

She took her parcel into the inner workroom, automatically bolting the door behind her. Her jars of ingredients were lined up on shelves above the workbench. As she took down the eggshell and sweepings jars to top them up, she ran her eyes over the shelves, gauging the levels of each ingredient. She'd pay a visit to Christie's later. Mid-Year was coming up, and going by last year, even now sorcery was less popular that would still mean a boost in trade – beforehand, for protection during the festival time, and afterwards, for fixing any little problems that people might have acquired while they were celebrating. She stared at the shelves. Once, she would have been run off her feet already, and complaining of it with her colleagues. Once, she had *had* colleagues.

She shook her head, sheering away from the thought. Soot she was fine for and could scrape off her own hearth anyway; a couple of the herb jars were low but culinary from the grocery did just as well as the stuff Christie sold, and with a lower markup. Shame she hadn't known he'd be sending the eggshell and floor-sweepings, or she could have sent a message for the herbs too. Dried ants she was low on, and hair-clippings; it was worth paying Christie's markup on hair-clippings for the guarantee that they'd been anonymised already. The anonymisation process didn't need magic, but it was tedious. The big question, of course, in the long run, was whether Christie was going to carry on stocking any of it. Christie had always been a source of all unusual things, not just magic ingredients – but. Well. Two years on, how long would Christie continue providing something for only two people? If Cato even bought from Christie's; perhaps it was just her. Who knew what Cato got up to. (She should know. She should still be keeping track. Should.)

And if that did happen, what could she keep doing, with just what she could get from regular shops and suppliers?

How much did she care, any more? Fewer folk were coming to her, after all. There were only two sorcerers left. Maybe magic was just… fading away from Marek. She ought to care. Once, she would have cared. A lot had changed since then.

She found herself glancing upwards, to the small leather case on the top shelf that contained her blood-magic instruments, relic of the days before she came to Marek; then she looked away. Blood-magic was illegal here. She'd promised Zareth when she apprenticed. Then she'd broken that promise, in desperation, during the plague, and it hadn't made a blind bit of difference.

She sighed, and pushed the heel of her hand into that painful point in her forehead that always seemed to be there these days, trying to concentrate again on what she was doing. She had what she needed for the simple charms that were all she had commissioned for today. (Or any other day. No one wanted anything more complicated, even if she had the heart for it.) And plenty of time to manage them; even if that charm for the grocer had taken far longer than she'd expected the other day. She was getting more and more out of practice. She should get on with it.

Half an hour later, she was swearing without restraint. Two crucibles lay in shattered pieces on the bench, and the shards of the third were scattered across the room. Blood was oozing down her cheek from where a piece had shot straight at her, and she dabbed at it with her sleeve while she swore some more.

This couldn't possibly just be her making mistakes. Even when she was learning Marek-style magic, when she'd first come to Marek and apprenticed to Zareth, she'd never been clumsy enough to screw up three different charms in succession at all, never mind this badly. Something else was going on. Something was getting in the way of her pulling down the magic.

She bent, slowly, to pick up the pieces of crucible from the floor. If only there was someone else to talk to about this. If only she wasn't on her own. Her throat tightened in a grief that hadn't abated in the last two years.

Of course; there was always Cato.

She scowled. She wasn't at that point yet. First of all, she could try something even more basic. Something that didn't involve flying crockery if it went wrong. She took down a handful of jars, then looked at them for a moment, chewing at her lip. Carefully, she took a pinch of each and dropped it onto the edge of the table, in a neat row of tiny piles. She re-stoppered the jars and put them in their places behind the protective ledges of the shelves. She cupped her left hand and reached towards the first pile with her right, then stopped, eyeing the remains of the crucibles. Instead, she crouched down on the floor, drew a neat chalk circle on the boards, then reached again towards the piles.

Eggshell, scattered over the circle. Floor-sweepings, towards the six compass directions. The eggshell shifted a little, and she cocked her head to one side. A pinch of rosemary, and another of powdered rowan-bark, drawing a circle within the chalk. She watched, intently. Nothing happened.

She chewed at a fingernail. Once upon a time, in another

place, she would have put a drop of blood into the circle, to connect with the flow of magic. But Marek magic wasn't supposed to need that. She pulled her finger away from her mouth, and looked at it. Her own hair, and her own nail, that wasn't blood magic, but it was hers, and she was a sorcerer. It would be enough sympathetic magic to boost the spell.

Still watching the circle she reached out, without looking, for the scissors on her table, and snipped off a nail-paring and a couple of inches of hair. She crouched back down again, and gently tossed them into the circle.

Chaos. She jumped back instinctively, even though the circle was containing it. The components of the spell were whirling around one another, without any rhythm that she could see, flying up and down and around within a dome with the chalk circle as its base. Reb watched, hoping that maybe it was just more complicated than she was used to, that if she looked hard enough she'd see something there, that it was simply a more complex pattern than anything she'd worked with of late – but as the minutes ticked by, nothing resolved.

Her throat was dry. Magic was chaos, yes, at its root; but not *here*. Outside Marek, when you wanted to tap into the flow of magic, to pull it down, to tame it, you used blood, or you made a deal with a nonhuman, and you took the risks of both of those. Here, in Marek, there was the cityangel, bound to the city since its founding, some three hundred years ago, who tamed the chaos. That was why Marek was how it was; that was why Marek was (had been, *had* been, and her throat tightened again) the city of sorcerers, all these years. The cityangel was always there; and the cityangel wouldn't allow anything like this. And yet, here this was.

She looked again at the miniature whirlwind, beginning now to settle as the components burnt out. Was it possible that something could have happened – and if it was, *how* could it be so – to the cityangel?

☉ ☉

Reb shook her head, slowly at first, then more forcefully, as the last of the dust within the circle settled to the ground. No. It wasn't, couldn't be, possible that anything had happened to the cityangel. That was absurd nonsense. Marek and the cityangel had been bound together since the city was founded; long enough that for most folk it was just a myth. Marek's reputation for magic might be common knowledge; the link between that and the cityangel was known only to sorcerers, by now. It couldn't be anything wrong with the cityangel. She would have known. It had to be her, something she was doing wrong.

Maybe it was just a sign that she should, finally, give up. Just stop trying. Maybe Marek just wasn't supposed to be a city of sorcerers any more. Maybe the plague had a purpose. It might have spared her, but maybe she should have given up anyway, buried it along with everyone she'd known. She laced her fingers together, and tried to pretend that they weren't shaking.

The knock on the front door startled her. She stood up hurriedly, her right knee creaking slightly, and went back through to the main room.

"Yes?" she called as she bolted the workroom door behind her.

The front door creaked open, and a skinny lad poked his head around it. His pale hair, tied back in multiple braids, screamed Salinas, though his skin was only a shade or two lighter, and his features only a little more pointed, than the average Teren. Reb frowned – the Salinas famously had nothing to do with magic, so why would one of them come to her? Was it some kind of dare? Then he came right round the door, and she saw that he wore a messenger's red armband. Her eyebrows went up – she wasn't sure she'd ever seen a messenger who wasn't Mareker-born, and while Marek had inhabitants from all around the Oval Sea, the Salinas almost never settled anywhere other than their own islands.

"Afternoon," he said cheerfully.

"Afternoon," she said.

"You were expecting Asa. They had a message go long, asked me to take over. I'm Jonas."

That was right. She remembered, now, asking that messenger to come back. For those deliveries that she'd been expecting she'd have ready by then. Dammit.

"What did you want?" he prompted her, after a moment.

Reb scowled. "Well, what I did want was a bunch of deliveries, but unfortunately that won't be happening. Can I send you to Christie's, instead? And then I'll have some notes for when you come back."

"For certain," he said politely. "Have you a list?"

"Not written," Reb started, but he was shaking his head.

"No need. I'll remember it."

"Well then. A jar each of dried ants, and of hair-clippings – make sure they're the anonymised ones, not the ones he sells for processing yourself. And a quarter-jar of amaranth horn." Christie was expensive, but reliably ethical, which the cheaper providers of amaranth horn weren't at all. "And tell Christie I'll be around to see him myself later this afternoon." She turned to the dresser and dug out one of the coin rolls she kept for messenger errands. "Here. That should see you right."

"For certain," Jonas said again, and slid himself back out of the door.

Reb found paper, pen, and ink, and wrote notes for the commissions she'd be late on now – which was infuriating. She was *never* late. After than she swept up the workroom. Jonas wasn't back when she was done, which meant that there wasn't anything she could reasonably use to avoid thinking about what had happened.

Maybe she'd messed up. But – well. She was certain that she had done everything correctly. She'd been doing that spell for twenty years. And the idea that she'd suddenly stopped being a sorcerer was both patently absurd, and contradicted by the effect her hair-clipping and nail-clipping had had on the spell. That had to be her own magic acting as mediator.

The idea that Marek, or the cityangel, or both together, didn't *want* her to be a sorcerer any more, and that was affecting her magic – that wasn't outside the bounds of possibility. Part of her hated the idea with a visceral distress that churned her stomach and left her nauseated. The other part was just weary.

She could just leave it. Hope it fixed itself. Hide her head in the sand. She'd been good at that, the last couple of years.

Or she could hie herself to the squats to find that little shit Cato, and hope he was sober and prepared to talk. (He would talk. If she told him what she feared, he would talk. When it came right down to it, they were both still sorcerers.)

Neither idea was particularly appealing, and she was still trying to think of an alternative when a knock on the door made her jump again.

When she opened the door, Jonas was barely out of breath.

"You're fast," she said, taking back the parcel and her change. He'd already taken his fee out of it, but she took another coin out and handed it back to him. He nodded his thanks.

"That's me," Jonas said. "Fastest runner in Marek."

She flicked an eyebrow. "Do those who grew up here agree?"

Jonas shrugged. "They have the home ground advantage. But I'm catching up. I like moving fast. Reminds me of sailing." The Salinas were the only ones who sailed the depths of the Oval Sea. They spent most of their lives at sea, carrying trade goods for every city and nation that gave onto it.

"What're you doing in Marek, anyway?" she asked.

"Oh, you know. Looking around. New experiences, get to know a place a bit better than you do when you're just trading. Interesting, being on dry land for a while."

His eyes were too wide and innocent. What he said might be true, but it wasn't the whole truth. But then, who didn't have secrets? It was none of her business, after all; she was just making conversation.

"Hey," he said suddenly. "You're a – a sorcerer, no?"

He seemed a little nervous. No wonder, given the Salinas attitude to magic.

"Yes," Reb agreed.

"Is that something you, like, *choose*?"

"Well." Reb considered the question.

"If you don't mind my asking," he added hastily, looking as though he thought she might throw a spell at him for the enquiry.

"No, that's – no, it's fine. It's a talent, sorcery. Not everyone has it. I suppose not everyone who has it has to use it." Not that she could imagine herself having made any other decision, back when she'd discovered it in herself, when she still lived in the Teren village where she'd grown up.

"So you could stop."

Reb felt suddenly weary. "I could. It would still be there. But I could – do something else." Could she? "Like you could choose – are choosing, I suppose – not to sail."

"I'm going back. Soon," Jonas said, immediately, automatically, but there was an arrested look in his eyes.

"Can you, like, see the future?" he asked, after a moment.

She laughed. "I only wish I could. No, that's only for fairy-stories, I'm afraid."

He nodded, looking almost stricken. What on earth did he think sorcerers *were*? Of course, though any Marek child knew exactly what sorcerers could and couldn't do, Salinas children were presumably told only to stay away from it.

"There's seers will tell you your future in the cards or your hand," Reb offered, "but…"

"But that's just trickery, I know that," Jonas said, brushing it aside. "That's not what…"

He stopped suddenly, and Reb wondered again what he was really after. This didn't quite seem like just a casual chat.

"There's stories about the cityangel," Reb said, calling it suddenly to mind. "That the cityangel can give visions to those who need them, if Marek needs that. Eli Beckett saw visions, so the story goes, or they'd have turned back before they even got here. And Xanthe Leandra – you've seen the statue by the south side of the Old Bridge? She was supposed to have been given a vision of the invaders. Though I can't think you'd please the Leandra these days by suggesting it might happen again." She laughed, then shrugged. Jonas was watching her intently. "Mark you, I don't think there's many would really believe in the cityangel now, even if they recite their charms and the rest."

She could feel what had happened earlier itching at the back of her throat. It was true enough. It was only sorcerers, really, knew different, and really now that meant her, and Cato. People believed in magic – hard not to, when you could see the results – but they didn't know the why of it.

"Salina don't believe in such things, either, do you?"

"Believe in them?" Jonas said, a little scornfully, though there was still something else lurking in his expression. "Spirits? Of course we *believe* in them. Hard not to, when we see them, often enough, out there." He gestured towards the wall, in the direction of the estuary and the open sea.

Reb blinked. She hadn't thought the Salinas would know about spirits. Most Marekers treated them as half a story – spirits didn't come into Marek, as a rule. The cityangel scaring them off, was the prevailing theory. But of course there'd be spirits out at sea, water-spirits, like the earth-spirits she'd grown up with in Teren, though those weren't always treated as whole-truth, either, by folk who hadn't met one.

"We just don't have anything to do with them. Unreliable." Jonas grinned suddenly at her. "Like magic generally, saving your presence."

Well; it was true enough today, Reb thought, feeling her face twitch, before she summoned up a smile for Jonas.

"Never heard tell of cityangels, though, other than here."

"It's only Marek has a cityangel," Reb said automatically, then shook her head. She didn't want to be in this conversation any more. "But I must get on."

She handed him the notes and another couple of coins. "Deliver these, if you could?"

He nodded, pocketing the coins and pulling a stick of charcoal out to scrawl his initials across the seals of the notes before she ushered him to the door. He hesitated on the threshold for a moment, and she thought he was about to ask something else; then he was off down the road like a hare. She shrugged, and turned to shut the door behind her.

There couldn't be any problem with the cityangel. The cityangel just *was*; that was the deal that Rufus Marek and Eli Beckett had made, three hundred years ago, the deal that bound Marek-the-city and the cityangel together, that created Marek's magic. The cityangel must be fine. There must be another explanation.

Dammit. There was no way around it. She really was going to have to go to that grotty squat of Cato's and talk to him. She scowled, and sighed, rubbing at her eyes. Tomorrow, though. Tomorrow would be soon enough, and maybe she'd feel up to it by then.

TWO

The Reader banged their staff on the polished ironwood floor of the Council Chamber, signalling the end of the session, and a buzz of conversation arose around Marcia as the Chamber began to empty.

"Well," her mother Madeleine said, her irritation visible even beneath her formal face-paint. "That was a waste of time."

Whether Madeleine meant the expedition itself, or this meeting to announce its failure, or indeed both, Marcia was unsure. It wasn't like the failure was news to either of them; as funder of the expedition, House Fereno had had a report from the captain yesterday morning, before the Council had been convened.

Marcia glanced down at where the expedition's captain, scrubbed and pressed for the occasion but still bearing the signs of the retreat down the mountain, was taking her leave of the Reader. Perhaps she ought to go down and speak to the woman again, reassure her of the House's appreciation even if the outcome had not been what they wanted. It had been under Marcia's control, this expedition; the captain was working for her directly and arguably deserved that. On the other hand, Madeleine would surely point out that such public acknowledgement would remind the other Houses that House Fereno had sponsored this and it was thus Fereno's failure.

The captain bowed stiffly to the Reader and turned to limp out, making the point moot. Marcia could hardly run after her; that was certainly below the dignity of Fereno-Heir. She gritted her teeth. It was infuriating that this first solo venture had gone so badly; but she had known the risk and judged it worthwhile. It *had* been worthwhile, even if it hadn't paid off as she'd hoped, with a full overland trading route. Knowing that there wasn't any such was useful in itself. She just hoped that Madeleine saw it that way.

"Come, then," Madeleine said, and rose to leave their wooden pew, in the second of the concentric partial rings that rose around the central circle.

The Chamber managed to be both imposing and oddly intimate. The corridor into it ran under the banked seats, coming out by the front of the stage with its dais. The wall behind the stage carried the coats of arms of each of the Houses arranged around the central pair of the arms of Marek itself and the arms of Teren. The rows of seats stretched upwards in a three-quarters-circle, facing the stage, each row sufficiently higher than the one in front that no one's view would be impeded. Right at the back was the newer wood of the Guild pew, added ten years ago when the Guild representatives were finally, after decades of wrangling, admitted to the Council. The argument over where the Guild arms should be displayed was still ongoing.

At the opposite side of the circle, grumpy Gavin Leandra-Head, was levering himself up from his place at the opposite side of the circle. He was, of course, alone – Leandra still had no Heir. Marcia's mind skipped neatly, well-practised, over the rest of that thought.

Since being confirmed as Fereno-Heir two years previously, Marcia had become more than sufficiently familiar with the Chamber. Before that, even, she remembered sitting with her twin up in the visitors' balconies above the circle, when they were kids; knowing that one day she would be Heir, and then Head, down in these carved pews. And then they'd become teenagers, and her sister Catya had become her brother Cato, and everything else that had happened that year they were sixteen; but right enough, here she was. She bit back a sigh. What she hadn't expected was how little she actually had to *do*.

Cato wouldn't have been surprised. Cato had always been the cynical one. Maybe that was why he'd left.

When her mother was Marcia's age, her father, Marcia and Cato's grandfather, had nearly reached the end of his twenty-five years, and was preparing to retire. Madeleine was already taking over more and more of the running of the House. As a child, even in her early teens, Marcia had expected the same treatment. Then, the same year the Guilds finally won representation, the Council had voted to abolish the twenty-five year limit and allow the Head to retire when they saw fit. And now, Madeleine clearly had no desire to hand over her power any time soon. Nor did any of her age-mates. Madeleine *had* been more prepared than some of the other Heads to let Marcia take responsibility, but even that might change after this debacle.

She scowled at her mother's back as they began to leave the Chamber. The expedition had been Marcia's idea, after the Salinas put their trading and carriage prices up again. There had, once, been an overland trading route between mainland Teren and neighbouring Exuria, up and through the mountain passes. Its increasing unreliability (for which read, 'tendency for large rocks to fall on people at regular intervals'), just over three hundred years ago, had been what drove Rufus Marek and Eli Beckett's expedition into the swamps, seeking a route around the mountains. What they'd found was the outlet to the Oval Sea, which had seemed to them nearly as good and possibly better – after all, who else might be there across the sea? Could Teren now trade directly with Exuria's overseas partners?

Just as Marek and Beckett were considering how to go about turning their swamp-going barges into something sea-worthy, along came the Salinas, with their ships, their extensive trading partnerships around the Oval Sea, and their very reasonable carrier prices. Prices which would make trading profitable, and which made independent voyages look much less appealing to finance, especially when the Salinas smilingly made clear their opposition to any such trips and the steps they were willing to take to express that opposition.

Thus the founding of Marek, initially as a city and chief trading-port of Teren (though fairly soon, as the original Thirteen Houses traded and grew wealthy, it had become a semi-independent city-state). A proper road was built through the swamp, and the mountain routes were abandoned. Sea trade was cheaper and more reliable by far, even allowing for the Salinas' cut. The Salinas themselves notionally lived on islands, but for the duration of the trading season, which lasted most of the year, the vast majority of them lived on their ships, trading goods, transporting people, carrying information both official and otherwise. They'd held the monopoly of the Oval Sea since long before Marek was founded, mostly by being good at it, and only very occasionally by sinking other ships who thought to challenge that monopoly.

But things changed, and the third rate-hike in a row – however justified by the appalling weather in the last year – had led Marcia to suggest that it was worth exploring the mountains again. If Fereno found a route and got a head start… Unfortunately, as the captain had explained quite bluntly to them in private yesterday, and in more polished terms to the Council today, there was no such route. For a few small high-value items, perhaps the route might be worth it – Marcia fully intended to follow that up – but for the bulky produce that was a significant chunk of Marek's economy and Teren's survival, sea remained the only reliable option. Even most of the high-value items created by the Guilds would be too large to pass safely and reliably over the route the captain had described. Marcia scowled again. Maybe it was time to try another round of negotiations with the Salinas ambassador. Although the ambassador would find out this result quickly enough, and that would hardly leave Marcia in the best of negotiating positions. If Madeleine would even be prepared to give her negotiating power after this.

On the other hand, this was the time for it; in a couple of days it would be Mid-Year, and after Mid-Year came the trading hiatus, when Marek grumbled slowly to a standstill, the Salinas sailing off to their islands to ride out the storm season, the few carts and wagons whose owners had not already departed standing empty in the yards outside the city, until the weather turned again in a month or two, and the Salinas ships and their cargos returned.

Marcia hated Mid-Year; but not because of that.

She shook her head, flicking the memory away before it arrived. She had to establish another plan *now*, before Madeleine herself thought of something and took it over.

"Mother," she started, not sure yet where she was going. "Given this information, I have a few ideas about where we can go from here…"

Madeleine flapped a hand at her, clearly not really paying attention. "Later, Marcia."

Marcia gritted her teeth. Obviously they weren't going to have a detailed discussion here, where everyone could hear them, but Madeleine could perhaps be a *little* less dismissive.

They were in the middle of the foyer now, heading towards the large carved doors to the outside. They stood open, blue late summer sky showing above the heads of those passing through them. Gavin Leandra stepped in front of them, and Marcia nearly ran into her mother as Madeleine stopped and inclined her head.

"Fereno," he said, his scowl not moving.

"Leandra," Madeleine said, with a smile.

"A word, if I could?"

Marcia controlled her expression only with some effort. A couple of other House representatives in her line of vision didn't bother doing that. Leandra and Fereno, enemies for generations, did not, as a rule, engage in private conversation. Marcia thought it was absurd, in all honesty; Marek would do better if the Houses were, in general, more supportive of one another. During her discussions with the Salinas ambassador the year before, she'd encountered the proverb 'a rising tide lifts all boats', and it had struck her quite forcibly. However. She wouldn't have bet that any of the current Heads agreed with her, and she most certainly would have bet, until this moment, that both Madeleine and Leandra-Head did not.

Madeleine inclined her head, still smiling, and Leandra led them away to one of the side alcoves, offering some degree of privacy. Although merely the fact that they were having a private conversation would rouse the gossip-mongers. What was Gavin Leandra up to? What was *Madeleine* up to?

"The child too?" Leandra asked, indicating Marcia with the top of his stick without looking at her.

"She is Heir. Hardly a child."

"Which one is it, then?"

Madeleine's lips compressed. "This is Marcia." *As well you know*, she could have answered.

"Ah yes. The other one – left. I recall."

Cato had been cut off, in fact, when he left, but mentioning that explicitly would be a step too far in this particular dance.

"And how is your own son, then?" Madeleine enquired sweetly.

Leandra's lips tightened in turn. There was plenty of rumour about why Daril b'Leandra still hadn't been named Heir and taken his proper House-name. Daril b'Leandra himself was, at least as of the last few years, a notorious hell-raiser with appalling morals and no conscience, so any of the rumours were feasible. But for Leandra's son not to be Heir was, whatever Leandra might pretend, of deep embarrassment to the old man.

Marcia and Daril had history. She preferred not to think about it.

"The trade routes," Leandra said, abruptly, abandoning the game.

"We are back where we started," Madeleine said crisply. "As you knew yesterday, I have no doubt."

He didn't react to the implied accusation of spying.

Marcia's eyebrows drew slightly together. This sounded like the continuation of a conversation, not the start of one. Why was Leandra interested in *her* project, and why had Madeleine not spoken to her about it before?

"I suggest a meeting. I have information that may be of use to us both," Leandra said.

"Tomorrow afternoon?"

Leandra shook his head. "No, that won't work. Day after tomorrow."

"Very well. At House Fereno."

Leandra hesitated, then nodded. Madeleine inclined her head in farewell, then swept past him and out, trailing Marcia after her.

Marcia felt her jaw clench again. So, once again Madeleine was keeping her out of things. To think that she'd once expected that being named Heir would involve some actual knowledge and power; rather than just following her mother around until she *died*. Or until Marcia died. One or the other.

Suddenly, sharply and fiercely, she missed Cato. She hadn't seen him in far too long. She would look him up soon. This afternoon, maybe. Cato would understand; or he'd mock her, gently, which added up to much the same thing in the end.

"I wonder whether Leandra *will* ever name Daril Heir?" Madeleine said as they walked down the wide steps that led down out of the Council building. She waved aside the litter-bearers that clustered in the piazza in front of them. "It's a nice enough day. We'll walk."

Their servants, who'd been waiting in the shade under the Chamber portico, fell in behind them. The streets of Marek were safe enough, especially in broad daylight, but it wouldn't do for the Head and Heir of House Fereno to wander the streets unescorted, not when they were in full Council regalia. The stiff robe was over-warm for the current weather, although it had been rather worse in full summer a month or so previously.

Madeleine liked to have an escort anyway, even when she wasn't in her formal best. Madeleine liked everyone to be aware of who she was. Marcia preferred walking the city alone, as anonymous as she could manage to be.

It was hardly a long walk back to their House. The Council Chamber was the highest building in Marek; the only thing above it was the park that capped Marekhill, with the statue of Rufus Marek and Eli Beckett right on its peak, looking down over the city. The far side of the hill fell away steeply, with no buildings on it bar a few huts and cottages towards the bottom, dwellings for people who herded the hardy goats which colonised the steep slope and supplied much of Marek's milk.

The rest of Marek lay in front of Marcia and Madeleine as they started down the single road which led from the Council down Marekhill to Marek Square and the Old Bridge. It switchbacked across the full width of the side of the hill, with passages running straight downhill, linking each tier of the road. On the top two tiers stood the Thirteen Houses, and on the next two, the most prestigious shops, supplying the Houses and anyone else whose money was good enough. Below those were merchants' buildings, the houses of the well-to-do middle class, and dwellings belonging to distant House members who preferred not to live in their House. The road came out at the foot of the hill into Marek Square, around the sides of which stood a cluster of the more prestigious Guildhalls and embassies. As Madeleine and

Marcia walked down towards the turn that would take them onto the first tier of the switchback, Marcia looked out towards Old Bridge, on the far side of Marek Square, and over it to the squats that rose on the other side. Cato was over there, somewhere. She sighed.

"I heard that the old man offered and Daril turned him down." Madeleine was still talking about Daril b'Leandra. Marcia wished she wouldn't.

"What was Leandra talking about just now?" she asked, hoping to turn the conversation.

"Oh – he put some money into the expedition," Madeleine said, off-hand. "Silent partner."

"What? Mother, you didn't tell me! I thought this was my project?"

Madeleine shrugged. "I gave you a budget. There was no need for you to know where it came from."

A hundred retorts rose in Marcia's mind, but she kept her mouth shut. There was no point in arguing this with Madeleine. She had to focus on her next steps.

Madeleine was still talking. "Leandra mentioned some minor cousin who had some interesting alternatives to the mountain route. I assume that is what he wishes to discuss at this meeting. With these ruinous Salinas rate hikes…"

They were passing House Leandra, whose dark stone had always looked brooding to Marcia, even back when she was sixteen and believed the best of everyone, including Daril b'Leandra.

"Two years of unseasonal storms have taken it out of the Salinas fleet," Marcia pointed out. "It's not entirely unreasonable of them, even if we don't like it." Move on, move on, get her ideas established… "But I was thinking of trying further negotiations with them. I suppose suggesting that we are continuing to investigate alternatives will be helpful. And there are those small high-value possibilities the captain mentioned. That might give us a little leverage, too."

"Yes, yes," Madeleine said, clearly not paying much attention. "A fine plan."

Five Houses further along, at the end of this tier of the road, they approached House Fereno. Its warm golden stone always cheered Marcia. House Fereno was the farthest north, its northern windows overlooking the river. Beyond it, the road switchbacked to start its second tier across Marekhill, and a small path led to the steps down the cliffside to the ferry over to the Old Market. A porter had just reached the top of the path, a box of fruit on her back.

One of the servants hurried up the front steps ahead of them, to push open the big wooden front door. Inside, the blue and grey tiles of the entrance floor shone in the early afternoon light that came in through the window above the door. Stairs at the back of the hall rose towards the library and offices on the first floor; and to left and right the doors to the dining room and the main reception room stood open.

"Well, Marcia, I must be off," Madeleine said, shrugging out of her Council robe and handing it to a servant. "I want a full analysis of the expedition by this evening, and I expect you at dinner tonight. We have visitors from Teren, and that tedious academic friend of Cousin Cara's. Formal dress." She turned, dismissing Marcia, and swept away into the reception room, her secretary and two of the household staff following behind her.

Marcia sighed, and turned for the library.

☉ ☉

Daril b'Leandra sat in bed, tackling his breakfast infusion – rosemary, with a little citrus, ideal for revitalising oneself first thing, even when 'first thing' meant rather after noon – and bread rolls. Roberts, his man, had drawn the drapes when he brought in the tray, and Daril could see out of the wide windows, down the roofs of Marekhill to the open space of Marek Square giving onto the Old Bridge. The early afternoon sun sparkled off the river. When he came of age, he had toyed with the idea of taking rooms that looked out over the back of the hill and the park, just to annoy his father, but when it came to it, even for that pleasure he couldn't bear the idea of not having the city under his eye.

In his mind's eye he could see the lines of power tangling and twisting across the city; Houses and merchants and docks all linked together. He yawned suddenly, his jaw cracking. It had been a busy day or two, and it should all have been over two nights ago. A new cityangel, a co-operative one, should have been safely in place, and ready to move onto the next stage of their plans. Instead, they were unexpectedly only halfway through, and Urso, now he'd recovered from his absurd swoon – and how it could possibly have taken him a full day, Daril did not know – was insisting that he hadn't the power to go any further alone. Which meant a trip to the squats, and tonight; they couldn't just leave things as they were for any longer. Really it should have been last night, but by the time Urso accepted his lack of competence it was too late.

Daril tore a roll apart with unnecessary force. He had less than no desire to visit the squats, but Urso was very clear the man they wanted to see wouldn't so much as listen to Urso on his own.

It was sorely tempting just to send a few heavy-duty folk to take care of the situation; but you could never rely on that sort of thing with a sorcerer. He scowled. Still. The man could doubtless be persuaded, one way or another.

Roberts re-entered the room, and coughed softly.

"Your father is just returned from the Council," he said. "He wishes to see you at your earliest convenience."

Daril sighed, nodded, and drained the rest of the infusion.

Roberts provided washing-water and towel, but Daril didn't need his help to dress in indoor wrap and shirt. That at least should be unobjectionable – his father didn't hold with modern fashions. Gavin Leandra didn't hold with much of anything.

His father's room was in the other wing of the house. Like his own, it looked out over Marekhill and down towards Old Bridge. Gavin, too, liked to be able to look over the city; but he had power over what he surveyed. Unlike Daril. For now, at least. Daril bared his teeth at the thought, then smoothed his expression out before he knocked on the door.

"Ah, it's you. Only just up, are you? Well, I suppose I was the same at your age."

Gavin Leandra seemed in an unusually good mood. Normally this would be the prelude to a few minutes on the shocking morals and behaviour of Daril and his friends, as the embodiment of modern youth. Daril had tried, once, a long time ago, to argue that they were dissipated partly because they had so little else to do. His father had listened, expressionless, then tasked Daril with three books in Old Teren to translate and *consequences* if he failed to do so in the time Gavin Leandra considered acceptable. Daril had done the translation. His father hadn't so much as cracked a smile.

Of course, last night's activities had hardly been in the category of pointless dissipation – watching Urso sweat through incantation after incantation might have been, as it happened, pointless, but it was far too tedious to be dissipation – but that was hardly something he could tell Gavin.

Sunlight was streaming in through the big windows that dominated the room, but the heavy, ancient furniture sucked up the light and left an impression of looming darkness. Daril's father himself added to that. He was a man of medium height, his greying dark hair cut short in the style that had been popular in his own youth and which he had never bothered to revisit. He was a little plump, now, around the middle, and his chin had become two chins. He rarely smiled, and his green eyes were hard and thoughtful, contemplating his only son.

"The mountain expedition has returned," Gavin said, abruptly, turning and walking to the windows. The light was bright, and Daril could see him only in silhouette.

"The mountain expedition?" Daril asked.

"By the angel, boy, do you never even read a news-sheet?"

By the angel, indeed. Ha. As it happened, Daril knew all about the expedition, that it had failed, and what might be happening next; because Urso, who was a trader of sorts when he wasn't practising secret sorcery, was up to his neck in the whole business. Not to mention its implications for their joint project. But none of that was anything he chose to share with his father.

What he didn't know was why his father was interested in it.

"House Fereno funded an expedition to discover whether any new routes have opened over the mountains, that might permit direct trade with Exuria," Gavin said. "It transpires that there are not."

"Why is House Fereno's business of interest to us?" Daril asked, with a shrug.

"Leandra was a silent partner," Gavin said.

"We allied with *Fereno*?" Daril asked. He didn't have to fake his incredulity. How had Urso not known about this?

"Fereno had the word out that they were looking for investment. Fereno – well, we have had our disagreements, over the centuries."

Now that was an understatement, Daril reflected. And that was without even getting into his own recent – well, ten years since, now – involvement with House Fereno. He tried not to grit his teeth.

"But they have always had a nose for an investment opportunity. There is – was – the scope for significant financial benefit to us if that expedition had succeeded. And now there is a further option."

Blood and angel, was the old man getting dragged into Urso's scheme?

"I know we have disagreed, you and I," Gavin said.

Another understatement.

"But truly, Daril, I believe it is time and past time that House Leandra had an Heir again."

Daril blinked. What?

"I wish you to join with me in pursuing this new opportunity. Prove to me," the old man's tone was almost pleading, Daril realised, "prove to me that you *do* have the ability to be Head, in due course, and I will invest you as Heir."

"Prove... What's finally brought this on, Father?" Daril demanded, playing for time.

The Heir-ship. *Now*. He could almost cry. He'd *given up* on the Heirship, given up on the old man ever getting over his fury and antipathy to his only son. He'd tried proving himself, he'd tried going to the other extreme, he'd tried pleasing the old man, and he'd tried annoying him, and none of it had ever *worked*.

Why now, now when he had finally given up and was about to grasp another form of power, *now* was when Gavin

Leandra decided it was time to make his grand gesture?

Why now, when he was poised to rip out the whole devil-rotted system, when in a matter of days it would no longer matter to him?

He almost choked on the irony of it. If his father had offered this a year, even three months ago, he would have jumped at it. He wouldn't have set any of his current plan into motion. And his father wouldn't be pursuing this scheme of Urso's and asking him to prove his worth on it, because the scheme wouldn't exist either. He couldn't tell whether what was rising in him now was fury or laughter or desperation. Or all three.

His father walked away from the window, stopping by the side of the desk and resting his hand heavily on it, his head bent down, for a moment, as if he needed help to support himself. Then he sighed, and thumped his stick on the floor, standing upright, back straight as usual.

"I am not getting any younger. I need to be *certain* that you are fit to inherit the House. But there is, now, an alternative."

What?

"A cousin." Gavin grimaced. "You are my only son, but this business with Fereno... Urso Leanvit. We have been working together, and he had some suggestions in case this expedition came up short. Truly, his work has impressed me."

Daril bit back a hysterical bark of laughter. He knew exactly what Urso had been doing in his work with Gavin, and what his end-game was. He was torn between satisfaction that it was working so well, and fury that Gavin was treating Urso as a potential Heir.

Gavin was still talking. "I would – Daril, I believe you have the ability, if you wish. You are my only son. If you can *prove* to me that you are fit to inherit the House, then I will name you Heir. If not, well, I will offer the same opportunity to Urso." His chin was up, his expression a curious mix of determination and distress.

Daril's jaw clenched. "You want me to prove that I am *fit* to hold power? More fit than some cadet-branch cousin?" Will offer, Gavin had said. Hadn't done it yet. At least that meant that Urso hadn't been keeping this from him. "Father,

I assure you I have more knowledge of *power* than you could imagine…" He stopped, before he let the whole business out into the open.

"Then *prove* it." His father leant forward, his eyes glinting; then sat back. "Or I could disown you. Disbar you from the title, as Fereno did with that twin of her Heir. Or Garat, before your time, when his daughter took her gambling too far."

Daril swallowed. It didn't matter, it didn't *matter*. Everything he was working for was nearly in his grasp. He could say anything he liked right now and it wouldn't *matter*.

Except that his father would be suspicious, and perhaps that in itself would be enough to hole his own plans.

And that was a lie too, even while it was truth. Regardless of anything else: he could not turn this down. However meaningless it might be.

"I would be Heir, Father," he said, finally. His tongue felt thick in his mouth. "I will do my best to demonstrate it to you."

"Very well," Gavin Leandra said, and Daril saw his shoulders relax, just a tiny bit. "This business of Fereno, these ideas of Urso's – they offer this House unparalleled trading opportunities. I will discuss the matter in more detail with you after I have met with Fereno, but for now – your role will be to begin to establish tradition relationship with some of the other nations. Directly. You understand? You will need to be circumspect, of course, at this point. But we are about to change the game, Daril." The old man's eyes were gleaming. "We must be ready to seize our opportunity. Prove that you can do this, my son. Prove that you can lead this House."

Daril nodded, slowly. "I look forward to hearing more about it, Father." The words tasted odd in his mouth.

The gleam in Gavin's eyes receded, and he looked suddenly tired. "Good. Good. Very well. For now, then, you may go."

Daril hesitated for a moment more, then turned and left.

☉ ☉

Marcia put her pen down in the dip in the desk, leant back, and sighed. So much for visiting Cato today. Her analysis of the expedition's results wasn't yet halfway finished, and the afternoon was almost over. But there wouldn't be a Council session tomorrow – indeed, today's had been the last until the Mid-Year formalities. She could go over to Cato's around lunchtime tomorrow, when Cato ought to be at least awake, if perhaps not up.

She looked back down at the paper on the desk, and the brief notes on rough paper next to it that were the captain's formal report, written in a large blocky script. The interview yesterday had yielded more detailed information; the captain had obviously been rather more comfortable with the spoken word than with the written.

She leant back again and chewed at a fingernail. It was clear that the main hope of the expedition – a true new supply route through the mountains, one suitable for significant quantities of goods – had failed. In truth it had always been something of a risk. Marek had been founded, three hundred years before, when the known route through the mountains from Teren to Exuria had been destroyed in a major landslide. Even before that, trade between Teren and Exuria had always been expensive and difficult. Finding the route through the marshland to the Oval Sea, and establishing Marek as a trading port, had been a boon for Teren. And, of course, even more of a boon for the traders that had first made their way to Marek in the footsteps of Eli Beckett and Rufus Marek's original expedition.

But what a landslide took away, further landslides could perhaps give back. It was known that there were goat-tracks up through the mountains, used by the hardy folk who lived up there year-round and who traded on a very small scale with their neighbours over the peak of the mountain. And Marcia had heard rumours, when she visited the wholesale market and talked to some of those coming in from Teren with mountain goods, of a more accessible route. That information had driven her suggestion that House Fereno put resources into exploring such a thing.

Rumour had, as it turned out, played her false. Or mostly false. When pushed, the captain had agreed that it would be possible to trade small goods over the mountains. And small valuable goods were a Marek specialty. On the paper in front of her, Marcia already had a list of Guilds who it might be worth approaching for such a trading party: the Jewellers Guild, of course, for the styles that were particularly popular in Exuria, and House Fereno had well-established links with the Jewellers. Much of the Smiths' and Cutlers' output would be too large to carry on foot, but they might have some smaller goods and weapons that would be more portable. Exuria lacked significant metal deposits, so high quality Marek metal goods made from Teren-sourced metal were valuable. Some of the Broderers' work might also be a good choice, although much of their lace and embroidery was most popular in the Crescent Guilds; and in any case, they weren't a Guild that House Fereno had had much to do with in the past. Marcia leant forwards to make another note that it might be worth cultivating someone in that Guild for the future, if this new attempt went well. She stopped, and thoughtfully regarded the pen she held. It was a recent innovation by a Mareker metalworker, that held ink inside the pen, rather than requiring dipping every few letters. Perhaps that, too, would trade well? She should speak to the metalworker; they had been keen to promote their invention when Marcia had been in the shop and bought this pen. A unique offer like that might be the very thing to make the most of a small-scale trading group. (One could hardly call it a caravan, if it were entirely on foot, could one?)

That was, of course, if Madeleine permitted her to try this. Marcia felt her teeth grind. By now she should have more power than this. By now, Madeleine should be handing things over to her, preparing the way for her own retirement. Instead, there was no sign whatsoever of such a thing. Madeleine had taken over at thirty, just as her own father had. Marcia would be thirty in four years, but Madeleine had already made it clear that, now that her retirement was no longer a legal obligation, she had no intention of retiring at fifty-five to hand over to Marcia.

On the upside, of course, if that had still been required, Marcia should have a child of her own by now, to be brought up ready to take over in their course. Madeleine mentioned that, from time to time, but in the absence of a deadline, well, she could hardly push for it. And in the absence of an heir, Marcia's own ability to push Madeleine to hand over to her was also limited. She had to admit that under the previous arrangements, she would have been under a great deal of pressure to produce a child of her own, one way or another, by now. She scowled down at her fingers. Nevertheless. Since the rules had changed ten years previously, allowing Heads of House to determine their own retirement as they saw fit rather than being limited to twenty-five years of service, it was evident that the current generation intended to hold on to their power for significantly longer. And her own peers were all beginning to show their frustration. It had come up in conversation with Cato, a month or two previously.

"Nisha's fed up," Marcia had said. "And she's not the only one."

"Well, who can blame her? Or you? Or any of you? Waiting around to have some kind of responsibility handed to you? On the other hand, well, I suppose it serves you all right for just waiting around."

"What else do you suggest we do? Evict our parents by force?" Marcia had struggled to keep her temper.

Cato had shrugged, elegant as ever despite his worn and patched clothes. "Give up on the whole sorry business? Council and Guilds and all the rest of it?"

Marcia still couldn't make any sense of that suggestion, and she'd said so at the time. The system worked. Marek was prospering. This was a minor point, surely. Cato had shrugged, again, and turned the conversation to other matters.

Thinking back on it, she wondered whether it was worth speaking to him again. She knew Cato didn't like the current system; but she'd never been wholly clear as to why. It didn't seem like it was for the same reasons that she didn't. He talked of the people over in the squats, the merchants and craftspeople who weren't part of the House or the Guild system, and she never quite understood what he thought should happen instead and how he felt those people were being let down. Perhaps she should ask him again. He'd likely have good ideas, too, about how she should present her proposals to Madeleine.

She sighed, and glanced at the clock. For now, she really needed to concentrate on this if she was to have it finished before the afternoon light finally faded. She hated working by candlelight.

THREE

Jonas leant back against the wall of the Dog's Tail and sipped at his beer. Asa and Tam were both running late. The shutters across the bar's windows – no glass, like he saw in the houses and shops in Marekhill, on this side of the river – were thrown back to let in the warm, slightly close evening air. A storm was coming, unless Jonas missed his guess. He shifted on the bench, aware suddenly of how hot he felt. Hot, and sticky with sweat from running messages. For a sharp moment, he desperately missed the cool evening breeze at sea, could have sworn he smelt a phantom pang of salt. He rubbed at his forehead. If he didn't sort this out, he wouldn't be back there at all, ever. He'd been counting on the belief that once he found a sorcerer, they'd be able to just... fix it. What was magic *for*, after all? The idea that his unwanted talent was *unknown* here hadn't even crossed his mind. But he refused to believe that all was lost. That was just one sorcerer. There might not be many now but there must be *more*. This one not knowing didn't mean no one knew. It didn't. He could still fix this.

But more than anything else right now he didn't want to think about it. He wanted to have a drink with his friends, his Mareker friends, and enjoy being here. He could worry about sorcerers again in the morning. Just like he'd been telling himself for the last half-year, and now suddenly maybe he was wrong. Dammit.

Asa appeared in the doorway and stopped just inside, looking around. Jonas waved a hand, and they nodded at him and made their way over through the messengers, market porters, musicians, and the odd thief (strictly off-duty) who made up the clientele of the Dog's Tail.

"Evening," Jonas said, grinning lazily up at Asa, when they reached the table. "Tam not with you?"

Asa shrugged. "He was until half a street back. Said he'd seen someone, he'd be along in a minute. Did you get ours in while you were waiting?"

Jonas spread his hands. "Didn't know how long you'd be, did I? Wouldn't want it to go stale. More stale."

Asa rolled their eyes and went to the bar, returning a couple of minutes later with three pints.

"Here you go, and don't say I never get you anything. Which reminds me – how'd you get on with the sorcerer?"

"Well, she didn't turn me into a fish," Jonas said, "and she tipped well, so I guess it went fine. Thanks, Asa. I suppose it sounds daft to you, wanting to meet a real live sorcerer."

Asa hadn't handed that job over of their own accord; they'd mentioned to him, when Jonas had run into them around lunchtime, that they were booked by the sorcerer out back of the Old Market, and he'd convinced them to swap him the job. He'd claimed it was tourist interest – he'd never seen a real Marek sorcerer before – which was true enough, and stood Asa a poke of fried potatoes for lunch in thanks.

"You could have just commissioned her," Asa said. "Real actual magic, not just gawping."

Jonas shuddered. "*No* thank you."

And what would removing his flickers have been, if she'd been able to do it, but real magic? He preferred not to consider that further, on the whole.

"Ah, you Salinas are just superstitious," Asa said cheerfully. "I spent half my childhood with my mum sending me to the sorcerer down the street for vile cold remedies. His room proper reeked, it did, and he was worse himself. Not sure it was any great loss when the plague got *him*."

Jonas remembered the first time he'd ever asked his mother about magic, when he was a child himself. He'd realised by then what his flickers were, and that other people didn't have them; realised in time to avoid telling anyone about them. But he'd wondered, enough to ask, about magic. His mother's face had shuttered off immediately.

"No," she had said firmly. "Salinas do not do magic. Magic and the sea do not mix."

He hadn't been able to stop his flickers from happening, though he'd tried. And, in the end, he hadn't been able to hide them from his mother, either. He thought again of those New Year flags. He was running out of time, if he didn't want to stay another year, and what would his mother think of that? He scowled into his beer.

"Few years back," Asa said, "no way you could have been in Marek for half a year and not seen a sorcerer. Loads of them. Well. A fair few, anyway. Now it's just her, and that bloke lives in the dodgy part of the squats. I wouldn't recommend going gawping round at him. He'd magic your bollocks off soon as look at you."

"Thanks for the warning," Jonas said drily, suddenly awash with relief. There *was* another sorcerer, and maybe he would know something. He would. He had to. It sounded like he wouldn't be able to get away with idle enquiries, there, though. He'd have to – what, to admit to it? Outright? To commission this sorcerer properly? He swallowed. Tomorrow. He'd think about it tomorrow.

"What was it like, though, growing up on a ship?" Asa asked. "I mean, other than that you didn't have sorcerers round the corner. I mean, I suppose you didn't have anything round the corner, right?"

"I didn't exactly grow up on a ship," Jonas said. "My mother's a captain, right enough, but I was only away with her eight months in the ten, and it wasn't every year, not quite."

"Eight months in ten is growing up on a ship, even if it wasn't quite every year," Asa said. "What happened the other two months, then?"

"That's New Year – what you call Mid-Year, when the seas are too rough to be sailing," Jonas said. "We all go back to Salina. People swap crews, if they've a mind to, and folk who've stayed back that year or who've come of age join them, and folk retire or stop home for a while." He remembered the intensity of those two months, so many people on the islands that usually only held a fraction of them, so many relationships being negotiated and re-negotiated in a way that as a child he'd only barely understood.

"Come of age?" Asa asked. "But I thought you said you sailed as a kid."

"I did. Not everyone does. Some stay home to raise kids. Some leave their kids with other families. My father was going to stay home, but they died when I was very young.

Mama took me to sea with her, when I was little, rather than leave me with my aunt or uncle. Though she did that once or twice, for some voyages. I'm not the only one, sure, but most kids grow up on the islands." He'd preferred the ship, though; the years he'd been left behind had felt like abandonment.

"Huh," Asa said. "It's neat, though, that you got to see so many places. I've never been out of Marek."

They sighed, then sat back and stretched their arms out above their head, their vest rising to show a stripe of brown stomach and the curve of their hipbones, then rubbed their fingers on their trousers, scrubbing off the traces of charcoal from the day's messages.

"Long day?" he asked. "What did you do instead of that booking this afternoon?"

"All the way up the Hill and back, half a dozen times," they said, grimacing. "Carrying messages from some grumpy merchant to some equally grumpy noble, right up at the top." They waved upwards. "Stairs, too, even to the back door."

"Worth it?"

"Not bad," Asa admitted. "Dunno what they were dealing, but they both cheered right up in the end, tipped me too. I earnt it, though, can't say I didn't."

Their short dark hair, spiky with sweat, showed the truth of their claim. "Few years back," they said, with a sigh, "I could have spent some of it on a nice charm to soothe my feet, but I guess I got out of the habit, after the plague. Just her out the Old Market left now, and it's not like I want to be traipsing across town again after a long day. Ah well. Times change, I guess. Look, there's Tam."

They nodded at the door. Tam was making his way over to their table. Just behind him was a tall person, moving slightly oddly, just ducking under the low doorjamb. Jonas swallowed against sudden nausea. His flicker, that morning. This was what he'd seen.

"Evening," Tam said breezily as he reached the table. "This is – what did you say your name was?"

"I didn't," the person standing beside him said. They – Jonas was pretty sure that 'they' would be correct, from everything about them – were staring, head slightly tipped to one side.

Tam shrugged very slightly, and carried on. "We had a race yesterday morning. Not sure who won, eh, but it was good fun. Saw them down the way, thought hey, they should come for a drink with us. And look, two beers here already! Ta. Sit down," he nodded at his friend.

Jonas opened his mouth to claim one of the beers as his, then thought better of it and nudged the mug towards the stranger.

After a moment of standing awkwardly, Tam's friend sat down and stared at Jonas and Asa.

The newcomer had pale skin, much paler than anyone Jonas had seen before, and they were nearly bald, with a fine white fuzz all over their head, as though their hair was just growing in from some accident. They were tall, and angular, and held themself rigidly upright on the wooden bench. They were dishevelled, with the look of someone who hadn't been sleeping indoors or eating properly.

And – storm and fire – they weren't human.

After Reb's reference to the cityangel this afternoon, Jonas wasn't sure any more what they knew here about spirits. For a people who didn't go in for sorcery, the Salinas were surprisingly familiar with spirits, although close encounters were frowned upon. Still, you couldn't spend that long on the sea without coming across the odd elemental or sea-being. Once Jonas had seen a demon, from a distance, flickering red and green and gold in the middle of a waterspout. They'd taken the ship the very long way around that one, sweating the whole time that the demon would move in their direction. But Tam hadn't said anything to suggest that his friend was spirit, and it looked a lot like they were trying to pass.

Flicker or no flicker, it was none of his business, Jonas told himself. If Tam chose to pick up randoms off the street, that was Tam's affair, and up to Tam to manage it.

The decision didn't last. A little while later, while Asa was trying to talk to the spirit – who still hadn't admitted to a name, and who didn't seem particularly well-versed in human communication – Tam leant over, looking worried, and whispered to Jonas.

"I'm a bit worried about them, mate. Yesterday, they were a bit wild-eyed, sure, but not like this. Dunno what to do, though. You can't just –" he waved an arm, and Jonas wasn't sure what he'd meant. Leave someone out on the street, maybe? "Reckon they could do with a roof over their head, right, but you know there's no space in my gaff." He looked hopefully at Jonas, and the implied request might as well have been written over his head in letters of fire.

"Not much in mine either," Jonas said, slowly, reluctantly, wishing that he could ignore the whole thing, "but – yeah, alright. For a night, just, right." It was warm tonight. He could sleep up on the roof; he wasn't about to share a room with a spirit. But Tam had helped him out when he first got here, and had been a good friend ever since. He owed Tam a favour or two.

Tam beamed cheerfully. "You're a star, mate."

He squinted over at the spirit, and his eyebrows creased together a little.

"I've got to say, though, mate," he confided to Jonas, "they kind of give me the creeps a bit, you know what I mean? I'm sure they're sound enough, and they sure run well, but..." His voice trailed off and he shrugged. "Still, we've all been there, right, not at our best, you know what I mean? You gotta help each other out, right?"

He nodded, as though he'd settled something to his satisfaction, and raised his glass to clink it against Jonas'. Jonas tried to ignore the sinking of his stomach as he downed the last of his beer.

A little later, as Jonas watched Tam and Asa walk off down the road towards Tam's gaff, he suppressed the thought that the real reason Tam hadn't wanted to help out his new 'friend' was the hope that Asa would be coming back with him. Lucky Tam. Though perhaps it wasn't like that; he shouldn't assume. He sighed, and turned to the spirit. They were staring down the road too, their features even more angular in profile. It was something about the nose, Jonas decided, something almost beaklike. Somehow he expected at any moment to see wings erupt from the being's back, spread themselves across the street...

It was like being punched in the stomach. He tasted bile in his mouth. This was no mermaid or elemental or even a land-beastie like the sea-beasties he knew. It was an angel. Storm and fire. What was an angel doing, down in a squat pub in Marek? And how could it be that none of them had recognised it? You shouldn't be able to miss an angel, unless they wanted you to miss them. You shouldn't be able to have a beer with an angel, an angel who had even drunk the beer, though they'd looked more than a bit confused about the whole business, without... Without...

He swallowed, and did his best to keep his knees steady. The angel had turned back and was studying him with those wide, black, confused eyes.

"You are ... unwell?" they asked, doubtfully.

"I am..." Jonas stopped, and took a deep breath. "You're an angel. Aren't you." He meant it to be a question, but it came out flat; he already knew the answer.

The angel dropped their gaze and looked down at their hand, spreading the fingers and turning the hand this way and that. They seemed uncertain, although Jonas couldn't imagine what an angel was uncertain of.

"I was," they said eventually. "I do not know what I am now."

Jonas blinked, and the pieces fell a bit further into place.

"A fallen angel?" he said, and the line sounded somewhere between trite and archaic as he spoke it.

"Fallen?" they said. "I was the cityangel, and I walked among the city as I pleased, and I made things as they should be. And now I am here in this body, and people like you," their gaze on Jonas was neither judging nor otherwise, "can see me whether I wish it or no, and I can do nothing." They blinked, and let their hand drop. "I do not even know how I take care of this body. Or if I need to."

"You're *Marek's* angel?" Jonas asked, scrabbling for understanding.

The angel nodded. "Or I was. Or I still am. But... not."

"You could – do you want to be on this plane, then?" Jonas asked hesitantly. Spirits could be in their own plane or on this one, but most of them spent the main part of their time on their own one. "Couldn't you step through to the other one?"

"I can do *nothing*," the angel said. "I cannot – I am here and I cannot be elsewhere. I do not know why."

They looked almost as if they would cry, if that strange

angular face could cry.

Jonas didn't know that much about angels. An angel belonged to something, took care of that thing. Lore had it that you could see an angel only if the angel wanted it so, and you would know what you were looking at if they did. (Although Jonas had always thought: surely, if the angel *wanted*, they could just look like nothing much? If it was useful to do that?) They were powerful, and they didn't really understand humans even when they looked after human things, and they were highly unpredictable from a human point of view. But they didn't live on the sea, and so the Salinas only knew of them from stories.

So Jonas didn't know much about angels, and he knew even less about angels who might not be angels any more. Which would explain why it had taken him so long to realise what and who he was looking at. But he didn't, he *really* didn't want to take it back to his place now.

There's stories about the cityangel, mind, Reb's voice said in his head.

Reb. That was it. Whatever she might have said about the cityangel, sorcerers surely knew about spirits. He would find her, and turn the angel over to her, and then he'd be done with the whole sorry problem. He could get back to messaging, and hanging out in bars. And trying to sort out the problem of his flickers, he reminded himself, and paused for a moment.

Or... Maybe he could ask the angel some questions, himself. If his flickers were magic, and the angel was magic, and the things Reb had said about visions...

He looked at the angel, standing silent and remote, and thought of them standing in his, Jonas', tiny room. His stomach clenched.

Or he could take them to Reb, and get her to deal with them, and he could come back and ask his questions some other time. Yes. That was clearly a better plan.

"Um," he said, to the angel. "I'm not sure what I can do. I mean, I don't think I can do anything much."

The angel didn't react.

"But I might know someone who can."

The angel still didn't react.

"Will you come with me?" Jonas asked. "To – well, she's not a friend, but she's someone I know, and I think she might be able to help you."

"She cannot help me," the angel said, categorically.

But they nevertheless followed Jonas as he turned to go back down the street, away from his nice cosy room in the nice cosy squats, and down towards the bridge to Reb's rooms. He just hoped that she was in; and that she'd be prepared to take his unwanted guest off his hands.

☺ ☺

It took a minute or so of knocking, during which time it suddenly occurred to Jonas to wonder nervously what sort of hours sorcerers kept, before Reb opened her door. She was dressed, but she looked as if they were a very unwelcome interruption.

"Oh," she said, after staring at him for a moment. "It's you. Did I... ?" She frowned, blinking slowly, her eyes not on him at all for a moment, then they snapped back. "No. I didn't. I'm sorry if you thought I needed you, but I've no more messages to run today. *Is* it even still today? Do you normally work this late?"

Messengers worked any hours there was work to be done, for the right money, but she was right enough that this was very late to be out. Jonas shook his head. "It's not that. Not work. I have – well, it's not a problem exactly, and it's not me either..."

The crease between Reb's eyebrows deepened, and she was shaking her head slightly, already beginning to turn away, as Jonas scrambled for words.

"She cannot help me," the angel said from behind his shoulder.

Reb's eyes snapped over to the angel, and her eyebrows shot up. She blinked a couple of times, rubbed the bridge of her nose, then pulled the door a bit wider.

"You'd better come in. Both of you. Before you wake the whole neighbourhood." She didn't sound, or look, enthusiastic.

Jonas wondered for a moment whether he could just shove the angel inside in front of him and then run for it. But no, he had to make some attempt at an explanation first. It wasn't like the angel seemed particularly competent to manage on their own; and then, if the angel might have answers for Jonas, he needed to keep an eye on where they went.

Inside Reb's cramped front room there were a handful of chairs to one side, cooking equipment against another wall, and two doors side by side at the back. One of them was firmly bolted, the other stood a little open, and Jonas could see the corner of a bed beyond it. The three of them stood in the middle of the front room for a moment, all looking at one another. No one seemed willing to speak. Then Reb sighed, and sat down heavily on a battered armchair.

"Sit," she gestured at the other chairs. "You are welcome here," she added, formally. "Not entirely within my good judgement, but you are nevertheless welcome."

The angel seemed to lose a little tension, but they didn't sit down.

"*Sit*," Reb said irritably. "Both of you. You make me tense just looking at you."

Jonas perched on the edge of the furthest wooden chair from Reb's armchair. His skin felt itchy with nerves. The angel folded its legs and dropped untidily to the floor.

"Humans sit on chairs, usually," Reb said to the angel. "If you're trying to play human."

"Not always," Jonas said, feeling suddenly argumentative. "Plenty of people where I live got no chairs. Not that many chairs shipboard, either."

Reb looked over at him. "Right enough," she said. "Sit where you like, then." She leaned back a bit and sighed again. "So. Is someone going to tell me what's going on here? What is a spirit doing wandering around Marek, and what is a Salinas messenger doing with a spirit? I thought you didn't hold with them."

Jonas had to bite his tongue not to say that he didn't hold with them, not one bit. If he wanted something from the angel, insulting them was hardly going to help.

"What sort of spirit even are you, come to that?" Reb continued, turning to the angel. "And what do you want?

Spirits aren't really my speciality."

Well, at least Jonas had been partly right that she would recognise the angel. Obviously she hadn't yet come to the whole of it.

"He said he'd take me to see you," the angel said. They stared at Reb for a long moment. "I know you," they said, sounding suddenly relieved. "I knew you well, before this happened."

Reb was frowning deeply again, then she blinked, twice, and her eyes went wide.

"Took you long enough," Jonas muttered. Reb glared at him.

"You're Marek's angel," she said flatly, after a moment.

"I am," the angel said, then, less certainly, "I was."

"Shit. That explains, then, maybe..." Reb was chewing at one knuckle. "Well. What happened?"

The angel shrugged. Their angular face looked lost. "I do not know. I was, and then I was not. I am stuck in this," they gestured down at themself, "and all my connections with my city, my people, *my city*, are gone. Gone. And I cannot even *leave*."

"You can't go back?" To the other plane, Jonas interpreted her as meaning. The same question he'd asked.

"I am *here*, am I not?" The angel sounded slightly irritable. "Believe me, if I could return I would." They paused for a moment. "That is – I cannot go back within Marek. I will not go outside Marek and try. I belong here. I want my city back. I want to be myself again." Their expression changed, grew more set. "I must be myself again."

Reb had moved on to chewing at her thumbnail. "That's – a bit of a tall ask, without knowing what happened. And if you can't step back through... When did this happen?"

The angel looked at her blankly.

"Today?" Reb asked. "Yesterday? Last week?"

"Week?" the angel asked.

Reb sighed. "Can you count in days? In nighttimes?"

"There have been two nights since it happened, and then this night tonight," the angel said.

Reb frowned. "Two nights. Yes, that fits. But *why*? And *how*? Do you remember anything that might explain this?"

"I... cannot... No," the angel said slowly, wonderingly. "So much time, and I cannot quite remember..."

There was a long silence. Jonas could hear the clock above the fireplace ticking and, outside, two pairs of feet passing and a murmured conversation.

"I think perhaps there was something," the angel said. "I think perhaps that was why I was walking the streets, when it happened."

Reb sighed. "At least I know now what's happened to the damn magic. But it wasn't – *you* might have known something was off before that, but it wasn't, at least I didn't notice..." She trailed off, chewing at her lip.

"Can you help?" the angel said, hopefully. "I want to go back. I want to be, I must be, myself again. I must be Marek again. Can you help?"

"*Should* I help?" Reb countered. "There must have been a reason why this has happened. Maybe you weren't doing your job. Maybe what was going wrong, before, maybe that's your fault and that's why you've been kicked out."

"No!" the angel said vehemently, coming to their feet in a tangle of arms and legs. "Never."

"But how do I *know*?" Reb said, then sat back again. "I don't and I can't, is what. And as well as that, I don't – I'm not who you need."

The angel just stared at her. The air in the room seemed suddenly still and thick.

"But – you're a sorcerer," Jonas said. Neither Reb nor the angel broke their gaze to look at him. "It's not like you're on every street corner any more. If not you, who else?"

Reb took a sudden breath, and the angel dropped their eyes to study the floor. The pressure in the room lightened very slightly.

"Well," she said with a grimace. "As it happens. There is one other left. Lad called Cato, lives over in the squats. You know him?"

Jonas shook his head. But this must be the one Asa had spoken of. The dodgy one.

Reb pursed her lips. "He's shady in a lot of ways – well, in all ways, really. He and I don't exactly get on, but for this... Well. He's done a bit of work with spirits, which is more than I have. I don't just mean to be unhelpful, you understand. It's not my area. I don't even know if I *could* do anything, even if I understood more about what happened. Cato's a competent enough sorcerer when he's sober." She grimaced. "Which at this time of night he undoubtedly won't be. Tomorrow, it'll have to be."

The angel's shoulders drooped. Reb was worrying at her knuckle again.

"I am *really* not comfortable with this," she said after a moment, "but without knowing more about it... You can stay," she nodded at the angel, "until the morning. Around lunchtime Cato should be useful again." She looked at Jonas. "Thank you. I suppose."

It was a clear dismissal.

Well then. That was that. Home, and not before time, and this problem off his hands. He began to shift his weight to get up, and then cold fire shot through his skull and he heard Reb's voice again. *There's stories about the cityangel.* He knew, cold-certain, like a flicker – although it wasn't a flicker, it didn't have quite the trappings of one, that if he left now, he wouldn't come back. Or if he did, the angel would be gone, if this Cato was any good, or they would just have disappeared, or... He'd hooked this fish; now he had to play it, or lose this chance for good.

He shifted his weight back again, and Reb frowned.

"I found the angel," Jonas said. "I want to see them safe to this Cato. I know the squats better than you anyway."

"It is my *city*," the angel said, sounding irritable. "I know..." They trailed off. "It was my city," they said, and the sorrow behind the statement made Jonas' guts ache.

"I know fine well where Cato lives," Reb said, rolling her eyes. "Go home."

Angels and fishes, wouldn't that be better. Get out from this weird situation. Go back to... trying to find out what his flickers were, and get rid of them, and hadn't he been doing that ever so well so far? It wasn't just the cityangel, either. Cato. The only other sorcerer in Marek. The only other chance he knew of. If he stuck it out here, he could speak to Cato tomorrow, or at least *meet* the man, have an introduction of sorts.

He wanted to go *home*; and he didn't allow himself to think about whether he was thinking of his cosy room back in the squats, or a hammock on a rolling ship. But.

"It is a matter of *honour*," Jonas said, in desperation, counting on Reb having the customary Mareker lack of knowledge about Salinas customs. (And it wasn't wholly untrue, not if you squinted at it right.)

Reb rubbed at her head, then threw up her hands. "Whatever. Fine. It's late and I cannot be doing with arguing any more. Tomorrow you can escort us to Cato's and we'll sort this all out and satisfy your *honour*."

She got up and opened a cupboard, throwing a few blankets out onto the floor. "You can both sleep on the floor here."

Jonas thought longingly of his bed. But this was an *opportunity*, thrown in his lap. He had to hold it.

"I do not sleep," the angel said.

"In this body you do," Reb said.

"I have not yet," the angel contradicted her, and Reb swung round to face them, rolling her eyes.

"No wonder you look so bloody strung out then. Well, it's up to you, but I recommend you lie down with a blanket and see what happens. And another thing – what's your name?"

They stared at her for a moment, dark eyes wide, then said, "I am Marek."

"Yes, well, you can't go round calling yourself Marek," Reb said. "Try something else."

The angel looked almost panicked.

"Eli," Reb suggested. "For Eli Beckett. Marek-related, if that's how you think of yourself, and Eli's neutral."

Jonas wondered suddenly if the angel had been there, when Eli Beckett and Rufus Marek and their team found the island that would become Marek, and if it had been there when Marek died before they could start back again, and which if any of the myths and stories about Beckett and Marek he'd heard in his months here were true, and what they had been like, these mythic historical people that the angel had known, had made a deal with...

"Beckett," he said, staring at the ex-angel, rocked with a sudden sense of correctness. "It's Beckett."

Reb looked sharply at him.

"Beckett," the angel agreed, and smiled, sudden sweetness passing over their face. "I remember Beckett."

Hearing that, Reb's face held a sudden hunger, then she rubbed her hand over her eyes again and turned away. "Well. Time to sleep, Beckett."

Beckett may have claimed that they didn't sleep, but by the time Jonas himself was settled in his blanket, and Reb had vanished into the other room, the one without the heavy door, they were already snoring. They looked somehow more human in sleep. Jonas rolled onto his back, and set himself to working out a private way of discussing his flickers with Beckett. But his eyes drifted shut despite himself, and he was asleep.

FOUR

When Jonas woke up the next morning, sunlight was leaking through the cracks in the shutters, casting slivers of light across the floorboards. It was unsettling. He couldn't remember the last time he'd slept past dawn. And then sounds round here that he could hear from the street outside were different from in the squats.

Beckett was already awake. Or at least, they were upright, eyes open, sitting awkwardly in the middle of the floor. As Jonas sat up and stretched, one of the inner doors rattled, and Reb came out of what was presumably her bedroom. The other door, the one with the bolts, Jonas would bet money that was where she did her magic. He was just as glad for the bolts.

Reb nodded grumpily at both of them, and set about making an infusion on the stove.

Well, that put paid to any idea of asking Beckett about his flickers just now.

"Open one of the shutters and let me know when Ceri comes past with her pastry-cart," Reb said, without looking round from the stove.

"So," Jonas said, when they were all drinking tea and eating pastries, unable to bear the silence any longer. "Is it true that Marek doesn't have any other spirits? Cos I've not seen one all the time I've been here."

Beckett raised a shoulder in an approximation of a shrug. "In general my race choose not to come into my dominion unless directly invited. Spirits are not particularly sociable, in the main. Unlike humans."

"But you said Cato talks to spirits, and works with them, and so on," Jonas said, looking over at Reb. "And he's in Marek."

"That is a spirit invited in briefly to speak with a particular human," Beckett said. "It is not the same as a permanent resident, nor even an independent visitor."

"Not that spirits are often permanently in one place, or on this plane," Reb said.

"Never," Beckett said. "We would never remain permanently on this plane." They looked, if it were possible, even more uncomfortable.

"Spirits don't have to involve themselves with the human plane at all," Reb said into the awkward silence, "and when they do, they don't have to involve themselves with humans. That's mostly angels and demons – though those are human terms themselves. Angels are helpful to humans. Demons largely aren't, or at least are doing it for their own reasons, which might include helping you for a while, but it's not a moral statement. Angels have made a moral choice to work with us on our plane, though not at the cost of damage to themself, in general. Demons will make deals, but otherwise they're not too bothered with their effects. I believe there's plenty of other spirits who just aren't interested in humans, or in this plane, or both."

"We don't deal with spirits, Salinas don't," Jonas said. "But we see them sometimes, out on the waves. They don't seem that interested in us, the ones we see." Which fitted into Reb's description of types, he supposed.

"No spirits, no magic," Reb said. "Safe, in a way, I suppose."

"Magic, spirits, it's all the same, right? Spirits are all about magic," Jonas said.

Reb spread a hand and tilted it from side to side. "Yes and no. Sorcery involves in some sense accessing the spirit plane, that is true. By blood sacrifice, or by working with a spirit. Oftentimes, blood is easier than finding and negotiating with a spirit. But Marek is different. Marek's cityangel is here, all the time. They act as a mediator, I suppose you could say, for any sorcerer working within city limits. That's why Marek's magic doesn't involve blood, unlike everywhere else; and why it's more powerful, and more reliable. But. The cityangel may permit access to the power of the spirit plane, but the sorcery itself must still then be done, and that's the same as anywhere else." She shrugged. "But what I don't know anything about is how spirits go about their business, or indeed how and why Marek is as it is. Not my field. Never was."

"But it is this Cato's field?" Jonas asked.

Reb nodded, her lips tight. There was a silence.

"I wish to speak to Cato," Beckett said.

"Well then," Jonas said brightly. "Now we've all had our breakfast, we can go find Cato, and hopefully he'll be sober. Right?"

Reb glared at both of them, then stalked over to finish her pastry by the window.

"Sod this," she said, after another period of uncomfortable silence. "Let's go. If Cato's asleep we'll wake him up, and if he's still drunk I'll sober the little shit up myself. Come on."

☉ ☉

Reb stalked irritably through the streets, Jonas and Beckett trailing behind her. Jonas wondered, uncomfortably, how obvious it was that Reb was a sorcerer, and what in the name of the sea-beasts they looked like, the three of them. Something unnerving was prickling under his skin, something like but not quite like his flickers. And how was he going to ask Cato about his flickers, in front of Reb and Beckett? He wasn't, was how. He'd have to come back, once he knew where to come.

The sense of foreboding wasn't going away. He couldn't tell if it was cousin to the flickers, or if it was just normal – reasonable – discomfort at this weird situation.

The squats took up several streets north of Old Bridge, a series of blocky three- and four-storey apartment buildings that consisted mostly of single rooms, sized for individuals or for families, with a few slightly larger two-room apartments. There were shared ground-floor water-closets that emptied via pipes into cesspits on the edge of the city, and a couple of large bathhouses at the south-east edge of the area. The buildings were owned and maintained by the city, and they were free to live in. Apparently, Jonas had been told, the squats had been the solution, a couple of hundred years previously, to a surge in unemployment combined with a lack of affordable housing in the city for what Asa described as "the folk who made it run – messengers and servants and shop-folk and marketers and so on, you see?". Given the position of Marek, hemmed in with mountains, sea, and swamp, land was limited. The Council had set the unemployed to building the apartments, paying them a stipend for doing so, and then made the apartments available to whoever needed them. Free or no, anyone who could afford rent elsewhere preferred to do so – the squats were clean but very basic – but it was a system that seemed to work.

Jonas' own room, in the same building as Asa and Tam, was close to the river side of the squats, a couple of streets north of the most coveted apartments, the ones right on the edge that looked out from the densely built squat streets over the river and up to Marekhill. Cato, it seemed, lived a few more streets north, where the mostly-legal subculture of messengers and day servants and the odd highly respectable fence gave way to dealers, thieves, thugs-for-hire, and those who sold things to them. And, apparently, dubious sorcerers.

Reb took the turns without pausing, and ignored the curious gazes from the knots of people hanging out by open front doors, chewing or smoking.

"You been here before, then?" Jonas asked.

"Yes." She didn't elaborate.

They turned another corner, and Reb stopped in front of a closed door.

Reb swung round and hissed something unintelligible over Jonas' shoulder, and he recoiled as someone behind him swore and backed away again. Half a year in Marek and you'd think he'd know enough to be paying attention. He'd never come to this area though; Asa and Tam had warned him off early on.

No one answered Reb's knock. After a moment, she put her hand to the door and pushed; muttered under her breath then pushed again. Jonas' ears popped, and the door swung open onto a narrow corridor and stairs leading up. Reb ignored the doors off the corridor and headed straight for the stairs.

"Reb?" Jonas said tentatively, after the first flight. "You recognised Beckett nearly straight off. Cato'll surely know even quicker, if he knows about spirits. Should they maybe stay outside the door? Just until we get a feel for Cato's, ah, position?"

They'd reached a landing at the top of the second flight of

stairs. It was dark and musty-smelling, lit only by the city-provided emergency glows. Reb muttered something uncomplimentary about Cato's position, but nodded grudgingly as they reached a door with a C scrawled on it in red paint.

"You're right. Beckett, stay out here while we test the waters."

Beckett nodded.

Reb knocked; then, when nothing happened, knocked louder. As the pause lengthened, she rocked back on her heels, tapping her thumb against her index finger.

"Can't you just…" Jonas suggested, waving a hand at her, after another few moments.

"Of course I could," Reb said. "He'll have wards up, of course, yes, I could deal with those too. I hardly think he's likely to be inclined to help us if we break his door down when he's asleep, though, do you?"

Jonas hunched slightly into himself at her tone.

Reb hammered on the door again, loud enough this time that an annoyed shout came from a door further down the corridor. There was still no reply from inside.

Jonas' back began to itch, and his head was throbbing. He pinched at the bridge of his nose, then… *he was inside an untidy room, a multicoloured patch of space he couldn't quite focus on in front of him and reaching towards Beckett, already engulfing them, Reb slumped against a wall in his peripheral vision, dread coiling over his skin…*

Beckett was looking at him, head slightly tilted, as he came back to himself, suppressing a gasp. Reb didn't seem to have noticed anything. She was running her fingers over the door lightly, head cocked to one side like she was listening, and frowning.

"What is it?" Beckett asked.

Reb shook her head. "It's warded from the outside, not from the inside."

"So he's not in there?" Jonas said. His breath was still coming a little short from the flicker. "You said he was likely to be out drinking last night – maybe he's just not back yet." In some gutter somewhere, perhaps.

Reb shook her head again. "This isn't that sort of ward. It's all done up tight. The sort of thing you do when you'll be away for a while, not when you're going out for the evening."

"He's gone away?" Jonas said.

"Well, except that seems tremendously unlikely," Reb said. "He's a sorcerer. We don't leave Marek, not as a rule. Cato's never left the city since I've known him." She rolled her eyes. "He barely leaves the squats unless he's working."

"He could be visiting elsewhere in the city, couldn't he? Or working, come to that."

"I suppose," Reb said. "But why would he bother? It's not just out for the day wards. Why would he stay somewhere else when his room is here? Marek's not that large. And his workroom is here." Her fingers were still tapping against the door. "I wouldn't... well. It's odd, that's what I'm saying. And I can't help but find it particularly odd when the sorcerer who knows about spirits goes missing just when this thing has happened to Beckett."

Beckett had moved closer to the door now, head to one side. They looked almost as if they were smelling the air.

"There has been another spirit here," they said, abruptly. Their face settled into a scowl. "Another spirit. In my city."

"You're sure?" Reb said, then shook her head. "Stupid question."

Beckett, still scowling at the door, didn't reply. Reb chewed at her lip, then seemed to come to a decision.

"Right. I really shouldn't be doing this, but, given what we're here for, and that there's been another spirit here... Stand back."

She laid one hand on the door, muttering under her breath. Jonas couldn't hear the words, but the rhythm caught at the nape of his neck. Reb dipped her other hand into the bag at her belt, withdrew a pinch of something, and threw it against the doorframe, left, right, top. The pressure at the back of Jonas' neck popped, and the door swung open. He followed Reb over the threshold.

The room was in a state of massive disarray. Clothes and papers were strewn across the floor, with half-eaten food in various states of decay on every surface. The only remotely tidy part was a small table in one corner with two shelves of small jars above it, and a bowl, mirror, and feather nib placed on the table. It was immediately obvious that Cato wasn't there; there was nowhere in the room for a full grown human to hide. The room reeked of smoke and herbs that Jonas couldn't immediately put a name to; with an overlay of rotting food, and human urine coming from the half-full chamber pot in the corner.

His back prickled, and *he stood in this room, looking at a dark-haired, brown-skinned Mareker with a bony face, a little shorter than himself, talking animatedly and gesturing at the jars and the table.* He blinked and looked around, but Reb still hadn't noticed. At least this flicker hadn't been like the last one. That must surely be Cato that he'd seen; so he would get to talk to Cato about his flickers at some point, even if he wasn't here right now? Not for the first time, Jonas wished that his flickers came with a time stamp.

Reb was turning around slowly with a dissatisfied expression. "You might as well come in," she called to Beckett.

Beckett stepped just inside the door and stopped, looking slowly around the room. "Cato is not here," they said.

"You got it," Reb said. "So there was a spirit here, and now Cato's gone."

"And wherever he was off to, apparently he didn't have time to clear up properly," Jonas said, wrinkling his nose. In his experience all Marekers were less tidy than he was brought up to – not much room on board ship. But this was something else again, and it had the look of a habitual state, not the disarray caused by someone searching.

"He's left some of his kit," Reb said. "But... not all of it. Not the essentials. Those are all gone." She was looking closely at the table. "What he's left out, here... If I had to bet, I'd bet that he was talking to a spirit, before he left. The feather nib, and the mirror... He wouldn't pack this mirror to carry, and if he used the nib, it's used up now..."

Jonas blinked at her, uncertain if she wanted a response. Not that he had the first clue what she was talking about.

"He spoke to a spirit?" Beckett was prowling around the room, still almost sniffing. "I can tell that it was here, but if he spoke to it..."

Reb looked over at them and nodded slowly. "Yeah. That occurred to me as well. You've left a space, up there, haven't you?"

Beckett's lips had drawn back a little from their clenched teeth. "It is *my* space."

Reb was looking around again, chewing on her thumbnail. "Fishscales," she swore suddenly. "I suppose I'll have to."

She went to pick up the bowl on the table, then obviously thought better of it and dug into her pockets, pulling out little bags of this and that. Carefully, she mixed a pinch from each of them into her cupped hand, muttering something Jonas couldn't hear as she did so, then gently blew it over the table and shelves. Jonas' neck prickled again as the dusting of scraps settled across table, bowl, feather, and floor.

"You should probably stand back a bit," she said absently, mixing up another collection of bits and scattering it around her. "I don't like working with someone else's things – and Cato would have my guts – but we need to know. I don't like the feel of this." She glanced up, and said sharply, "Stand back, I said!"

Jonas retreated to the door. Beckett didn't move.

"You too," Reb said without looking round. "I told you, I don't like the feel of any of this. You're why we're here. Let's not find out the hard way if that's related to whatever happened to Cato. Especially not if he really was talking to a spirit before he left. Or before he was made to go, perhaps, but – well. Let's see what I can find out."

Beckett, face expressionless again, stepped backwards to join Jonas. Reb scattered the latest mixture around her on the floor, then, hesitantly, picked up Cato's bowl with her sleeves tugged down over her fingertips. She made another mixture, this time in the bowl, shaking rather than stirring it, and carefully stowing her little packets away after she had taken what she needed from each one. Finally, she tipped the mixture out of the bowl onto the table, set the bowl down very carefully, and picked up the feather, again with the edges of her fingers.

"Sorry," Jonas heard her say under her breath, then she started to draw patterns in the dust on the table top.

Jonas could feel the pressure building in his head, but this time nothing popped. It just kept building, as Reb kept drawing patterns. He shook his head and swallowed, trying to disperse it, without any effect. Reb had stopped drawing now, and was staring down at the table and the bowl and the patterns. Jonas' head felt almost unbearably tight, and he clenched his teeth against the urge to say something, or do something, to break it.

Then, with a noise that was almost a thunderclap inside his head, the pressure vanished, just as Reb sailed backwards across the room. She landed, hard, against the wall, and crumpled to the floor. In front of the table was a ripple in the air, blue and green with swirls of red. It intensified and grew, the red streaks getting wider and brighter.

Jonas' ears were ringing, the noise growing louder as the ripple grew bigger. Reb was slumped unmoving on the floor, Beckett stood to his left. The ripple was growing, moving, reaching out towards Beckett... That was here, wasn't it? Here and now? He'd seen this thing in his flicker, seen it pulling Beckett in...

The ripple had nearly reached Beckett, and Beckett wasn't moving. Jonas wasn't sure if Beckett was even seeing what he was seeing. Did that mean it wasn't really there? The colours intensified, the air looking hot and strange, and Beckett was starting to move as it reached towards him...

He should run. He should run *right now*.

Instead, without conscious decision, he stepped between Beckett and the ripple. With another thunderclap, the ripple disappeared.

☉ ☉

Jonas' ears were still ringing, but under that he could hear that the room was silent. None of them moved for a moment. Then Reb groaned, and Jonas ran over to her.

"I'll live," she said, pushing away his offered hand and slowly unfolding herself from the floor. "I think. Fishscales and demons, that hurt."

"What in flame was that?" Jonas asked.

"More to the point, what did you do to it?" Reb asked.

"I didn't do anything!" Jonas protested.

"But it stopped." She looked at him, narrow-eyed.

"It did not wish to touch me," Beckett said, from behind them. "It was a ward, perhaps?"

Was that the truth? Jonas blinked, trying to remember. It had been moving towards Beckett, and Jonas had stepped in front of it. But had he imagined that moment of the ripple bouncing off him, folding back in on itself? He would much rather believe that it had all been Beckett. And surely the cityangel wouldn't lie. He'd imagined it being anything to do with him; he must have.

He swallowed. He still felt a bit sick.

Reb was looking over at Beckett, shaking her head. "I don't know what the hell that was, but it wasn't a ward. I think Cato was talking to a spirit, and that, whatever it was, was left behind. Which is – well. A bit worrying, let's say. What in the hells is going on here?"

"An excellent question."

Jonas blinked, startled, and all three of them turned to the door. A short dark-haired woman, older than Jonas himself but younger than Reb, stood in the doorway. Her cloak and the trousers showing under it looked expensive; and Jonas had been in Marek long enough to recognise her clipped accent. What was someone from Marekhill doing over here in the squats? And the arse-end of the squats at that?

"What *is* going on here? Where is my brother, and what are you three doing in his rooms?"

Brother? This Cato was her *brother*? Some dodgy sorcerer had grown up Marekhill?

"I said," the woman said impatiently, stepping over the threshold, "what is going on here? Where's Cato? What are you doing in his room?"

Belatedly, Jonas looked round for an exit route. He wasn't at all sure he wanted to hang around arguing with some Marekhill type. One against three might be poor odds – unless she had backup waiting outside, which in this part of town she really ought to, though the sorcerer's sister was perhaps very safe – but if she was to swear a writ against them they wouldn't stand a chance.

Surely Cato must have had more than one way out of this

place? But the only obvious options were the door, which meant getting past the woman, and the third-floor window, which was certainly possible but not with the other two in tow. Of course, he could just ditch them; he didn't exactly owe them anything.

But he still hadn't talked to Beckett about his flickers. And if Cato wasn't here, Jonas had no link to him, and he was the only other person who might be able to help. This Marekhill woman was Cato's sister, which was surely another way to find him, even if she didn't know where he was right at this moment.

Beckett was calmly watching what was going on. Reb's hands were hanging apparently idle, but Jonas could see the balanced, wary, tension in her stance; and a slight frown, as if she were trying to remember something.

The woman came to a stop in front of Reb. Reb blinked, dismissing whatever it was, and spread her hands.

"We have no idea where Cato is, and we have done nothing to him, I swear. We came looking for him too."

"He owed you something? Or you had need of his services?"

Reb shrugged her shoulders minutely and didn't answer. The woman was glaring at her.

"Did you remove the wards?" she demanded.

"Yes," Reb said. "But they were set from the outside when we got here, not from the inside. He knew he was leaving."

"You broke in?" The woman's eyebrows were raised.

"I had reason," Reb said, folding her arms.

The woman was looking at her narrowly. "You know Cato, then?"

"We've had words," Reb said, neutrally. "Once or twice."

"Cato never has liked other sorcerers. But breaking in – you had no *right*."

Reb opened her mouth, then closed it again and looked more closely at the woman facing her.

"You," she said, voice tight. "*You're* Cato's Marekhill sister? I remember you. Marcia. And to think I thought *he* was a bad 'un."

The woman – Marcia? – flinched, then her chin rose and she stared back at Reb.

"It was a long time ago," she said. "I was young, and I was stupid, and I haven't been anywhere near b'Leandra, or any of his lot, since. Though I don't suppose you'll believe me. You seemed to have the righteous anger thing down pat at the time, and it doesn't look like it's changed much."

"Didn't I have the right?" Reb demanded.

"Yes," Marcia said. "You were right, and they were wrong. I shouldn't have believed him. I made a mistake. I spent a good long while afterwards telling myself all about how swamp-slimed foolish I was. Does that help?" She glared at Reb. "And whatever I may have done a decade ago has no bearing on you breaking into Cato's room, for which you still haven't given me an explanation. Now. Are you going to justify yourselves, or am I going to call the guard?"

☉ ☉

This wasn't what Marcia had expected. She'd come here for Cato, to talk to her brother. And quite possibly, at this time in the morning, to find him an infusion to deal with his hangover. She hadn't expected to be faced with no Cato, and a sorcerer she'd last seen at a point in her life she'd expended a lot of energy in forgetting.

"Guard won't come here," the Salinas boy said.

Marcia looked at him. What was he doing here? His white-blond hair was caught back, Salinas-style, in a twist of rope, but his skin wasn't as shipboard-tanned as most Salinas. And he wore a messenger's armband. Mostly Salinas folk kept to their ships, sailing the Oval Sea then returning to their villages between voyages and around the Mid-Year trading lull. For certain, there were a handful of Salinas families in Marek, mostly around the docks, plus there was the embassy and its staff. But he didn't speak like he'd grown up in Marek and if he was a messenger, he wasn't employed at the embassy.

"She's Marekhill, Jonas," Reb, the sorcerer, said. "They might. Maybe."

She was still eyeing Marcia suspiciously – as if it weren't *Reb* who was the one who'd broken into a warded room.

Jonas made a hmm sound. "Well. You think there's something odd going on, and this Cato's gone. So while you're arguing about guards, I'm going to go down those stairs and see what I can find out about when he was last here." He flicked an eyebrow up. "Can't see any of the rest of you managing that."

He nodded round at them and slipped around Marcia and out of the door before she could stop him. His footsteps clattered down the stairs and the front door banged. She had a sneaking suspicion that he might not be back again.

The situation was slipping out of her control. She had to say something.

"So. You're looking for Cato, and you think there's 'something wrong'. Enough to break into an innocent person's rooms." Room singular, and it wasn't like there was much Cato was innocent of, but anyway. "Perhaps if you tell me why you are concerned about my brother, we could settle this amicably."

People took you at your own value. She kept her chin up, and locked eyes with Reb, waiting. Outside the window, in the street below, she could hear voices.

Reb looked away first.

"Well. He's out, at this time of the morning, which you must admit is unusual," Reb said, and Marcia found herself nodding. "And I have reason to believe that the last sorcery he did in here was to speak to a spirit, and they left a trap."

"That's his *job*," Marcia said impatiently. "And if the trap wasn't for Cato, it's none of your business. It wouldn't have got you if you hadn't been breaking in."

Reb was watching her again, her arms folded. Marcia was accustomed enough to dealing with people who carried power, but Reb's presence was still nearly overwhelming. Even though – Marcia's eyes narrowed slightly – there was something off about her, too. That competence and authority that Marcia remembered from ten years ago was still there. But there was also – something crumpled, a sense of self-doubt, when she turned away, that hadn't been there ten years ago. What had happened to her since then?

Reb ran a frustrated hand through her short brown curls, then gestured around the room. "Do you see anything unusual in here?"

"Why are you *here*?" Marcia demanded. She was missing something. Or Reb wasn't telling her something. Marcia knew the signs well enough.

What was Reb hiding?

"I am Marekangel," the other one said, the odd-looking one that Marcia hadn't been able to place.

Reb threw her head back in – exasperation? Anxiety?

"I was Marekangel," they said again. "Now I am not. I am Beckett. And I must solve this."

Marcia stared at him, her mouth hanging open for a moment before she caught herself and shut it with an audible snap. Her mind whirled. The Thirteen Houses were barred from using magic, either directly, or through someone else. As a result, magic was something that was rarely or never discussed, treated as something for the Guilds – who also tended not to use it, in imitation of the Houses, especially in recent years – and the lower city. And the cityangel, in turn, was a foolish superstitious story. That summer ten years back, Cato had discovered his abilities, and Marcia had been dragged into Daril b'Leandra's disastrous plans. All of them defying the ban on magic, and for long enough that Marcia knew, now as then, that the Houses were wrong, that magic and the cityangel alike were truths.

Cato had decided he wanted magic more than the House. Marcia had realised how foolish Daril had been, and how foolish she had been in turn to follow him, and she'd wanted nothing more to do with any of it. She'd stood by Cato when their mother disowned him, but she'd done her best never to ask about what he did or how; and she'd done her best as well not to think about magic, or the cityangel, since.

Now, apparently, the cityangel was standing in front of her? And Cato was gone. She swallowed. What was happening here?

Reb took a breath. "Well, now that Beckett's gone for the blunt approach," she said. "They're speaking the truth. As far as I can tell. They used to be the cityangel, until a couple of days ago. Now they're not, and they don't know why. I don't know why either."

"And that brings you here?"

"Cato knows more about spirits than I do. I was hoping to consult with him."

"Why do you even care?" Marcia demanded.

"The cityangel makes Marek's magic possible," Reb said bluntly. "Magic that isn't blood magic, more or less, though it's a little more complicated than that. I have a vested interest in sorting this out. As does Cato. Or so I would have thought. We are sorcerers. We are *Marek* sorcerers. We need the cityangel."

"The cityangel?" Marcia asked softly. "Or *a* cityangel?"

"Magic needs *a* cityangel," Beckett said, suddenly, and Marcia and Reb both jumped. "It does not follow that it need be me. But also, I have – I had – the cityangel has – a great deal of power. Within and over Marek. At present, that power is not – attached."

"But, then – what has this all to do with Cato?" Marcia asked. There was a ball of dread in her stomach. "And where is he?"

"There's two sorcerers left in the city," Reb said. "And someone's removed the cityangel. Last night, Cato was talking to a spirit. It's the last thing – the last thing with a magical trace, at least – he did in here. And it left some kind of trap, something I triggered. Beckett seems to have shut it down. The thing is, like I say, Cato deals with spirits, at least sometimes, and I don't. He knows more about them than I do. That's why we brought Beckett here in the first place. So. Beckett is no longer in their place. Cato has been talking to a spirit, and has packed up his stuff and gone. It's a bit much to think that these things are entirely coincidental. Especially given that he's your brother." She stared at Marcia.

"What do you mean?" Marcia demanded.

"You were mixed up in that dangerous nonsense ten years ago. How do I know that you're not up to the same thing again?"

Marcia stood up, pulling herself up to her full height. "I have had nothing to do with anything of the sort between now and then. You know as well as I do that I have no magic of my own. I didn't even discuss magic with Cato," she added, half-despairingly. "And now I wish I had, because maybe then I might *know* something." Damn. She hadn't meant to give that much away.

Reb, narrow-eyed, stared at her for a moment, then shrugged. "I'll believe you, then. For now." She sighed. "In which case I too wish that Cato had told you more."

Marcia's stomach was tight. Spirits – but no, even the very little Cato had ever mentioned about what he did, she knew that not all spirits were bad. Not of necessity. Just because the one, that time… Cato had refused to be involved, back then. He hadn't changed that much in ten years. She knew he hadn't.

Reb was chewing at her lip again, obviously deep in thought.

"But when it comes down to it – this is still not your business," Marcia said. "Cato has done nothing wrong." That any of them knew of, at least.

Reb, clearly frustrated, opened her mouth to reply when they heard footsteps on the stairs. Marcia saw Reb tense at the same moment she did so herself, before Jonas appeared at the door.

"So," Jonas said. "How are you all doing up here?"

"Wonderfully," Marcia said. "Did you find anything out about my brother?"

"Impatient, ne? Fine, fine. Two nights ago he was drinking at the Purple Heart – his local, so the barmaid knows him well. Someone – hired muscle type, she said – came in to talk to him. Trying to be all quiet like. Cato said, very loudly, he wasn't about to be summoned for some Marekhill idiot, next time send the puppetmaster not the puppet. The barmaid says she was bracing for a fight, but the hired muscle just walked out again. Then came back, she reckons an hour, maybe two, later, with a tall, thin bloke in a hooded cloak. Cato clocked him, laughed, and got up and left with them. She reckoned he looked more than a bit surprised. She was pretty sure the new bloke was Marekhill, he walked that way. And he paid Cato's tab happily enough. She didn't get a good look at his face, I'm afraid, but she said he had a sharp sort of nose, under the hood."

Tall, thin, Marekhill. Marcia's stomach flipped. But it was absurd to think… no. There were plenty of men matching that description. But also…

"Cato hated Marekhill folk," she said. "He liked working

here. He says he gets more interesting problems here than he would if he were – more reputable." They'd argued about that a lot, over the years. Marcia had never yet won. "He wouldn't just have gone off with some rich person." Still less if it was… But that was absurd, surely. She had no reason to think it.

Reb had been pacing the room while Jonas was speaking, running her fingers lightly over the dusty furniture and unmade bed. She turned round, a single strand of long dark hair across her palm.

Cato's hair was mid-brown, like Marcia's, though Cato's had a touch of red. And Cato kept his hair close-cropped. This could be from a lover; Cato surely had lovers, though he rarely mentioned anyone to her. But she didn't believe it was.

She looked up again to meet Reb's gaze.

"You seen Daril b'Leandra lately, then?" Reb asked.

"He's Thirteen Houses," Marcia said. "It would be illegal…" She didn't want it to be true. She didn't want Cato to be anywhere near Daril.

"Didn't stop him ten years back," Reb said, ripping straight through her paper-thin argument.

Marcia shook her head, teeth clenched. "I haven't spoken to him, more than for public courtesy, in ten years. But yes, he's still around, if that's what you're asking. And Cato definitely wouldn't have gone anywhere voluntarily with b'Leandra."

He wouldn't. He still remembered that time, too. She was sure he wouldn't. Her stomach felt hollow. If it was him who had come for Cato, was it all her fault for being so stupid ten years ago? It couldn't be. That was all deep history, now. Dead and buried.

"Well," Reb said. "It's a starting place. If b'Leandra was here – maybe Cato isn't the one to blame, in all of this."

Jonas was looking between them. "You reckon it was someone called Daril b'Leandra? He's Marekhill?"

"Leandra is one of the Thirteen Houses," Marcia said.

"You know him?"

"I… It's a long story." She felt unutterably weary.

"Nasty piece of work," Reb said. "Or he was, ten years ago."

Marcia could feel Reb's eyes on her, but when she looked up, Reb's gaze was warmer than it had been, just a little. She laid her hand briefly on Marcia's shoulder, and Marcia relaxed, just a little. Enough to start to think again.

"There's – there's a party tomorrow night," Marcia said, taking a deep breath. "A formal event. Everyone will be there. Including him. Whatever else is going on."

"And you?" Reb asked.

Marcia nodded. "I will – I don't know. I can ask? Talk. Say something. See how he reacts."

Reb's eyebrows went up. "Don't go alone."

"Don't be absurd. Who am I to take?" Marcia said. "I can hardly tell anyone all of this. And in any case, I won't be alone. I will be in a room full of people."

"I want to know what you say to him," Reb said, her voice cold again.

"It was *ten years* ago!" Marcia snapped, suddenly furious. "My *brother* is missing! What reason do you have not to trust me? I just want him safe."

"That's exactly it. I'm saying that we may have different priorities," Reb said. "Something has happened to the cityangel, your brother is talking to spirits, and Daril b'Leandra is involved. I don't know what you'd trade, or agree to, to get your brother out of trouble."

Marcia bared her teeth. "Fine. Well. Are you intending to escort me, then?"

Her tone was harsh, and Reb flushed.

"I don't scrub up well enough," Reb said, with a shrug. "And Beckett is right out."

Marcia wasn't sure she agreed with the scrubbing up remark, but Reb would certainly stand out. Her eyes fell on Jonas. Young, attractive, Jonas. He would stand out a little, too, but in a way that was much more explainable. Marcia flouting convention with some young Salinas visitor, that wouldn't raise anyone's suspicions.

"Jonas?" she said. "Do you want to go to a party?"

FIVE

Marcia's hand shook slightly as she picked up the pot of eyeblack. She put it down, rested her hands on her lap, and took a couple of deep breaths. This was just a party. Just another party, like hundreds of other tedious Marekhill parties she'd been to over the last ten years. Many of which Daril b'Leandra had even been at.

Except that for the last ten years she'd been assiduously avoiding him and his hangers-on. And now, she was... Well. What? What exactly was she intending to do? She could hardly ask a direct question. If he *did* have anything to do with Cato's disappearance she might as well just hire a crier to announce her suspicions to him.

But then, was there any way of avoiding that, really? Even short of a direct question, the fact that she was approaching him at all would give him pause. If he had nothing to do with this, he'd just be surprised; and she wasn't sure how he'd react after that. If he *did* know about it, there was nothing, however indirect, that she could say at all that wouldn't have him drawing conclusions. Ideally she'd get someone else to do it, but who was there that she could take this to? Especially given that as Fereno-Heir she shouldn't be dealing with Reb, even socially. Was there any mileage in the fact that Daril, even if he wasn't Heir, should also most certainly not be engaging with sorcerers? But then, that was back to being obvious.

She bit her lip savagely. She had to find something, some excuse. That was all there was to it. She picked up the eyeblack again and began to apply it delicately, forcing her hand to hold steady. Really, this was just another form of politicking, and she'd been Heir for four years now. She knew all about politicking. She grimaced slightly as she closed the pot and put it down. Of course, that also meant that she should consider the political effect of being seen talking to Daril – ha, then again, perhaps that gave her other options. That conversation after Council with Gavin Leandra could potentially provide cover – even if Daril wasn't Heir, she could imply that she had some interest in making nice with the House now. Would that ring true as a reason for suddenly seeming to want to be on terms with Daril? Or could she get some mileage out of Jonas as a visitor? She tapped her fingers on the table. Perhaps it was best to wait and see when Daril showed up before making a decision.

Gods. She was going to have to talk to Daril. Her stomach churned. She was going to have to talk to Daril, and she was going to have to forget about any of their *history*, at least for now, otherwise she was highly unlikely to manage anything.

She found herself wishing it had been Reb, rather than Jonas, who agreed to come. The idea of Reb's solid presence was somehow comforting and, unlike Jonas, Reb knew about what had happened, which... She shook her head to clear it. An absurd idea. A sorcerer in the middle of a Marekhill party? It would be ridiculous even if Marcia could be seen with a known sorcerer. It was bad enough that it was common knowledge that she was still in touch with Cato. That was – reluctantly – accepted, because half-hidden, and because of the relationship. Reb had neither of those attributes. Of course, Marcia wouldn't *actually* be committing any crime, but the perception of it could be nearly as bad.

And surely it would be worse, not better, that Reb knew about her history with Daril? It wasn't like Reb trusted her, after all. She'd said as much. Marcia swallowed and raised her chin. It didn't matter what Reb thought. She was in this for Cato, and that was all. And if she didn't get on with her face, she wouldn't be ready in time anyway.

Some time later, face painted, hair arranged, and dressed, she sat in her sitting room watching the clock. Where was that wretched messenger? It was going to take more than a minute or two to get him clean and appropriately dressed – she had raided the clothes Cato left behind to get something for him to wear – and at this rate they would be late enough to be rude.

The door opened.

"Jonas t'Risali, madam," a servant announced.

Marcia frowned. Surely Jonas would have the sense to

come to the back door? Marekhill did not officially receive messengers. He must know that. Angels, why hadn't she been more specific?

"Your servant, m'lady," Jonas said, stepping through the door and bowing.

Marcia's eyebrows flew up. The scruffy messenger she'd met the day before was clean, his long hair braided neatly back in a complicated pattern that she thought she'd seen before on the Salinas ambassador at formal events. His loose trousers and bright blue tunic were Salinas-formal, not Marek-formal, with richly-coloured panels of embroidery. Together with his bare face, it emphasised his foreign-ness, as borrowed Marek-formal and face-paint might not have done, but that might work to his advantage.

His lips twitched, and Marcia realised that she'd been gawping. She flushed slightly.

"I thought I might attract less attention visiting like this than if you were to be spiriting some street messenger into your house to be cleaned and dressed."

"Yes," Marcia said, then added, fairly, "I'm sorry. I didn't think that you would have anything suitable. I apologise, I shouldn't have made assumptions."

Jonas shrugged, and sat himself down on a chair at right angles to hers.

"Not unreasonable," he said. "You wouldn't have expected a Mareker living in the squats to be able to dress for a Marekhill party. Why expect me to?"

"I know Cato," Marcia said. "So I should know better. I should at least have asked rather than assuming."

She sighed, and rubbed at her fingers to keep them away from her face paint.

"Cato is fine," she said, hoping to convince herself. "He always lands on his feet, however much trouble he gets into. I just – want to make sure." And to find out what Daril b'Leandra was up to, if anything? That too, maybe. She had a bad feeling about the whole situation.

Jonas looked back at her and quirked a smile. "Brothers, eh?"

She laughed, and the moment eased.

"So," Jonas said. "What do I need to know about tonight?"

Marcia considered. "Do I need to talk about etiquette and so on?"

Jonas shrugged. "My –" he paused for a fraction of a second. "I learnt Marek basics, along with the other trading states. As long as I'll have a little slack for being foreign, I should be well enough."

Marcia desperately wanted to know more about his background now (what had he been about to say?), but she couldn't think of a way to ask that wasn't rude.

"Well. This particular party is in honour of some visiting dignitary from Teren, but more importantly, it's being held *by* House Haran – one of the Thirteen Houses – which means it is socially obligatory. That in turn means it will be full of politicking and social manoeuvring. Lots of behind-the-scenes Council talk."

"Do you have a position in the Council?" Jonas asked.

"I am Fereno-Heir," Marcia said. "I will take over from my mother in due course." Which didn't exactly give her a position *now*, or power, not exactly, but Jonas didn't need to know that. She thrust aside the memory of her meeting with Madeleine that afternoon.

Jonas nodded.

"But at any rate – for a long time, Daril b'Leandra avoided all those things, but he came back on the scene about two years ago. So he'll be there, but I expect he and his cronies will be late." She glanced over at the clock, and stood. "As will we if we do not leave. Come. We'll walk. It's only along the street, and I hate being carried on a fine evening like this."

"Is there anything I should know about Daril?" Jonas asked, as they made their way down to the front door.

Marcia stopped in the middle of arranging her shawl.

"In all honesty," she said, "I don't think I can say anything useful. And perhaps it will be best for you to have minimal expectations. I will say – be careful."

She set her teeth, and reminded herself firmly: it was a decade ago. She was Fereno-Heir now, and her youthful indiscretions were behind her. She could face Daril b'Leandra.

She shivered, and tightened her shawl around her.

☺ ☺

House Haran was on the same level of the Hill as House Fereno, but away from the river side of Marekhill, closer to the Council. All the Houses on this level backed onto the manicured park that occupied the very brow of the hill. Jonas looked up towards it as they walked along the street, torch-bearing servants ahead and behind.

"Doesn't that annoy you all?" he asked. "Not being able to build all the way to the top?"

Marcia laughed. "That was the point," she said, "or so the story goes. When the Houses were first establishing themselves, and wanted to begin building homes suitable to their new status, there was a great deal of arguing over land, especially higher land. After a few deaths, the Council – it was still very new, in those days – agreed to draw a line around the top of the hill and put it out of bounds. Meaning any House on this level could claim parity. There was a bit more fuss over who got here and who got Second, of course." She indicated the level one further down the hill, after the first switchback turn. "Though it is all a very long time ago now."

"Your family is high in standing, then?" Jonas asked.

"Yes," Marcia said. "Highest among equals, of course, you understand," she added with a self-mocking half-bow, and Jonas grinned. "House Fereno has always been strong among the Thirteen."

Below them, Marekhill was dark, the brightly-lit fronts of the buildings all looking down towards Old Bridge, or angled slightly towards the river. Glancing back over her shoulder towards her own house, Marcia saw the edge of the cliff outlined against the stars,, and the bulk of the mountains far off on the other side of the river.

The square courtyard of House Haran was lined with stands of night-blooming flowers, their perfume sweetening the air. The central three-storey building was square and blocky in the old style, much like Marcia's own home. Built on around it were newer wings in various of the styles that had been popular whenever a Head of the House had a little more money over the last couple of hundred years. The effect was a little gaudy in places, Marcia felt. The extensions to House Fereno had always been done in the old style.

And Beckett had seen them all built. Marcia shivered.

Jonas, gazing around the courtyard, was looking a little apprehensive, but he summoned a smile when she glanced over at him.

"Over in the squats, you've half a hundred families in a building that size," he said.

True enough, but somehow she never thought of it when she wasn't over there.

They had reached the door by now, where two servants in green tunics were bowing them in and reaching for Marcia's shawl. She noticed for the first time that Jonas was wearing no over-jacket.

"You don't feel the cold?"

"Cold at night, out on the water. Well, in the winter, anyway. You get used to it."

"Marcia Fereno-Heir and Jonas t'Riseri," the major-domo announced them. Jonas, with a small bow, offered Marcia his arm, and they swept into the big room.

It was already reasonably full. Marcia estimated that they had arrived at a little past the halfway mark. Enough time to settle in before it became hopelessly overcrowded. Tonight would be well-attended, both for the political value of the Teren visitor and because this was part of the lead-up to Mid-Year.

Even ten years after her first entry into society it still always took her a few minutes and a circuit of the room to feel comfortable. Or as comfortable as one ever could in a room full of acquaintances, friends, and enemies, both personal and political, all busily examining and analysing one another's behaviour and speech. Marcia's mother had described it to her once as "exhilarating", and it was one of the rare occasions (increasingly rare, in fact) on which Marcia and Madeleine had been wholly in accord. Navigating these social and political waters was a challenge, and Marcia enjoyed a challenge. She'd been raised to this.

She sighed. She had been raised to it, but Madeleine wasn't letting her *do* it, not when it really counted.

She nodded politely to various people as she and Jonas moved through the room. Tonight, in fact, it might be best to engage in as few conversations as possible. Being seen entertaining a Salinas visitor would raise questions, which might not be such a bad thing given the trading situation. Was this a sign that Fereno was dealing well with the Salinas, after the abortive expedition? Or was this merely a personal connection of Marcia's own? The fewer conversations she engaged in, the less opportunity anyone would have to lean in one direction or the other. The ambiguity would be more useful than any certainties. Especially given that the real reason wasn't one she could admit to.

"This room is mostly for the older generation," she told Jonas. "House Heads and their cronies, the Guild Masters, and so on. Heavily political. We must circulate here to be seen, and I should greet the hosts, but after that we can move to the other room and relax a little." Except for how she was intending to speak to Daril, and could not afford to relax at all, even if she were capable of it.

"Is there anyone I need to know about?" Jonas asked.

"Not yet," Marcia said. "It's fine; I can introduce you. No one will expect you to know anything about anyone." Another advantage of his dress; a clear and immediate indication of his foreign status.

Jonas inclined his head in easy agreement, and she wondered anew how much political practice he had at home.

She spotted the Salinas ambassador, Kia t'Riseri, across the room, making her way towards them. Dammit. She didn't want to discuss the matter of pricing right now – but no, on a second look, it was Jonas, not Marcia, on whom the ambassador was focused. The Salinas wear did stand out.

"Jonas," she said in an undertone, leaning in to him. "Your ambassador approaches. Do you wish me to deal with her? I can think of some excuse for your presence or for our acquaintance if you wish?"

Then she realised that Jonas had been announced, just now, as t'Riseri, as well. That didn't mean family, in Salina, she remembered that, but she couldn't think what it did mean. Did they know each other already? Demons, she should have thought of this.

Jonas gave a bare head-shake. "That ship won't sail. I will manage it."

The ambassador gave a quick nod to Marcia then launched into a rapid-fire flurry of Salinas. Marcia maintained her social smile and tried to pretend that she wasn't both curious and slightly infuriated, as Jonas bowed and spread his hands, smiling as he replied.

"My apologies, Fereno-Heir," Kia said, returning to common dialect. "I have not seen young Jonas since we were last ship-mates, and I did not know he was visiting."

"I didn't want to create a fuss," Jonas said. His smile was only a little forced, but he held himself tensely. Marcia might not have noticed had she not seen him so relaxed on the walk here. "Where would be the point of coming all this way merely to ride on your anchor, ne? I have been having a very interesting stay in Marek, and it is delightful of Sr Marcia," he bowed slightly to Marcia, "to introduce me now to Marekhill society."

"Of course, of course," Kia agreed. "Sr Marcia is no doubt a delightful guide to the city. You are here simply to explore, then?"

"Marek is a fascinating city," Jonas agreed, "and after passing through it so many times as a child, well." He spread his hands, and Marcia wondered if Kia had noticed that he had not, strictly speaking, replied to her question.

"I am glad to hear you are enjoying your stay," Kia said. "Will you be leaving after New Year? Your pardon, Sr Marcia, Mid-Year I should say, given where we are."

Jonas shrugged, but his shoulders had tensed again. "Most likely. I have not decided for certain."

"Well, then you must of course come to visit me so we can catch up properly, before you leave," Kia said. "Welcoming though Marek is, it is always pleasant for me to speak Salinas. And I would be distraught to miss the opportunity to reminisce given our past, t'Riseri. Tomorrow, perhaps? Since there is so little time now before Mid-Year."

Jonas twitched, and Marcia frowned, catching his tension. Something about the use of that shared last name had changed the tone of the invitation. She had no idea what currents were flowing here. She hated that.

"That would be wonderful," Jonas said, after a long moment. He was almost convincing.

"Tomorrow, then," Kia said. "I will look forward to it."

She turned to Marcia.

"While I am discussing social arrangements, I wonder whether I might pay a visit soon to you and your delightful mother? I gather that there is some concern over trading prices."

In other words, she knew about the expedition and its outcome. Well, after the announcement in the Chamber, of course she did. It was her business to know.

"It has been a bad season, indeed?" Marcia said noncommittally.

Kia spread her hands. "Not a matter for discussion now, when our host wishes us to enjoy ourselves. But I am sure we could both benefit from it another time."

"By all means," Marcia said. "I will send a message." Hopefully not by Jonas. She suppressed the twitch of her lips. Although if there was any way to use the link with Jonas, given his apparent closeness to the ambassador... Something to consider later.

Kia t'Riseri had evidently accomplished her aims; she excused herself a couple of moments later.

"You know the Salinas ambassador," Marcia said, turning to Jonas. "She'd clearly have put you up in the highest of style if you'd come straight to her, but you're living out in the squats and scraping farthings together for your dinner."

Jonas hunched a little more, not meeting her eyes. "What would I find out about Marek if I was living up here?"

Marcia flushed slightly, and Jonas looked over at her then away again.

"That's – you live here, you've always lived here. You get to choose."

"Really?" Marcia asked, slightly bitterly.

"I would have been kept in a visitor's cage. It is different."

It might be the truth, but Marcia was damned if it was the whole of the truth. But she wouldn't get more out of him just now.

She shrugged. "As you will. T'Riseri, though? She is family?"

Jonas shook his head. "She belongs to my mother's ship, the Lion. Or did, the last time she sailed."

"She is a family friend, then? Your family is of high status?"

"My mother is well known." Jonas was looking a little awkward

"And so you are obliged to visit…" She stopped herself. "No, my apologies. I should not be interrogating you like this."

Jonas smiled suddenly at her. "Indeed, I understand your interest, and plan only to take advantage of it by returning the favour and interrogating you about the habits of Marekhill."

Marcia smiled back. "Perhaps another time? We do after all have another aim tonight. I should circulate a little more, introduce you to our hosts, and then we can go to find the younger crowd. I have some friends here, and it will be a good bridge to," she hesitated, and hated herself for it, "the other thing."

"Lead on," Jonas said, and took her arm.

☉ ☉

Marcia recognised some bankers from the Crescent Guild cities, with their olive skin, and braided dark hair, but didn't want to speak to them; House Fereno wasn't in need of money at the moment and she didn't want to discuss the current trading situation with them. She always left a conversation with any of them convinced that she'd given away more information than she realised she had. A couple of Guildmasters were in earnest conversation with one of the Crescent Guilders, which was potentially interesting information; were they seeking investment, and if so, could House Fereno make anything of that?

The Warden of the Jewellers Guild, one of the most powerful Guilds in Marek, was obviously doing the rounds. She was a sharp political operator, and had been the driving force behind the deal that finally got Guild representation on the Council, ten years ago. She herself was one of the Guild Council members, and Marcia had a great deal of respect for her. She'd also been in the Chamber earlier, so was aware of the results of that damn expedition. And Jewellers Guild wares were exactly the sort of thing that might be able to go across to Exuria via that goat-track that the expedition captain had mentioned. They exchanged a few polite words, Marcia introduced Jonas, and when Marcia suggested that it might be useful to meet later in the week, the Warden was happy to agree.

The Teren Lord Lieutenant, the party's guest of honour, was standing with Haran-Head towards the back of the room, and she really ought to at least greet her, and indeed Haran-Head as their host. Marek's relationship with Teren was always slightly tense; Marek governed itself in practice, but notionally was a part of Teren, and as such the Lord Lieutenant in theory could make decisions. In practice, the Council was polite to the Lord Lieutenant, and the Lord Lieutenant refrained from attempting to exercise their theoretical power.

"So," Jonas asked a while later, after they had exchanged social niceties with Haran-Head and the Lord Lieutenant and moved on again, "your friends are elsewhere?"

"In the second ballroom," Marcia said. "There'll be livelier music, and less overt politicking. More space. Fewer of our parents watching us."

"You prefer to keep older and younger separate, then?"

Marcia shrugged. "It depends on the situation, but often yes, socially speaking. It's not obligatory, you understand, but as it tends to fall that way anyway, it is easier when hosts plan for it. Why, is it not so with you?"

Jonas hesitated. "No," he said, finally. "Social events are surely to support bonds between all ages, ne? So that all understand one another." He sounded suddenly more Salinas, just as when he was speaking to Kia.

"Yes, well," Marcia said, "you may have the right of it." She sighed. "It's all changed in the last ten years or so, you know. When my mother took office, it was after my grandfather had done his twenty-five years – it was twenty-five years at most by law, you understand. The Council voted that down at the same time that they voted the Guild representation in. So I – and my peers – we are all waiting on the decisions of our House Heads when they choose to step down. Something which none of them seem terribly enthusiastic to do."

She was surprised to find herself putting it that bluntly. Mostly she tried not to think of it quite like that. Surely it was reasonable that Madeleine wanted to wait a little longer before she stepped down. Surely it was reasonable that she wanted Marcia to prove herself a little more?

They were nearly at the doors to the second ballroom, and Marcia could hear the music drifting out.

"Are any of your friends also involved in politics, then?" Jonas asked.

"Not – well. Not really. They're all younger, or not yet named, or…" Suddenly she didn't want to talk about the situation any more. "Here we are. I will find them and introduce you."

She took a breath, raised her chin, and swept through the doors into the smaller ballroom, holding Jonas' arm. Her eyes took a moment to adjust to the slightly lower light in the smaller room. A handful of couples were dancing in the empty space at the back, but most of the room contained little groups of low chairs and tables, all occupied with people leaning in to talk and laugh, or to play dice or cards.

She scanned the room, looking for her own friends, and noting the absence of Daril. She still had no idea how to approach him. A servant with a jug came up to them, produced two glasses from a basket tied at their waist, and filled them. Marcia sipped hers; a decent kick, but nothing outrageous, which was doubtless for the best. Jonas was smiling and nodding thanks to the servant. He did have a nice smile. Nisha was going to be all over him.

Her eye fell on Nisha's dark head in a far corner.

"Ah," she said. "There they are."

These were the friends she'd known from childhood, and yet she couldn't tell them about what she was doing this evening. Her throat felt oddly tight. As they got closer, she saw red-haired Aden, in his customary dark green, stand up and say something that set the half dozen in the group laughing uproariously. Aden took a step back, turned, and saw her. His eyes crinkled cheerfully, the concentric rings painted around them highlighting the movement.

"Marcia! You join us at last. Duty done?"

"For now," Marcia said, smiling round. "This is Jonas t'Riseri, who visits us from Salina."

After initial introductions, Marcia chose a seat where she could see the doors without being too obvious about it; then annoyed herself by tensing up every time she saw someone new about to enter. None of them, yet, were Daril b'Leandra.

Several of her friends were already a fair few glasses down. Dark, pretty Nisha, to Marcia's total lack of surprise, definitely had her eye on Jonas. For a moment she thought Jonas was hooked, but in the end he chose to deflect the implied offer. Nisha seemed unbothered, smiling ruefully but cheerfully enough.

Aden came to perch on the arm of Marcia's chair, telling her a convoluted tail about his latest sailing trip. Halfway through, she saw another group approaching the door – but this time there was a tall, thin man in the middle, his dark hair cut close at the sides with a single long lock tied at the back and falling down his back. She saw his slightly pointed nose as he turned to say something to a woman beside him. Her stomach flipped. Daril b'Leandra. She saw Jonas, watching her, tilt his head very slightly to one side.

She realised, a little too late, that Aden had reached his punchline, and made herself laugh. Aden, unsurprisingly not fooled, followed her gaze.

"Ah," he said. "Our compatriot of Leandra. Does he owe you money, or something, the way you're looking at him, Marcia?"

Marcia forced herself to smile and lean back in her chair.

"Nothing of the sort, Aden," she said easily. "Just that my mother and his father actually exchanged words yesterday, and I got the impression his father might finally consider dealing with the Heirship."

Nisha, overhearing, leant forward. "I'd heard that he's under pressure from the ghastly Gavin to start fitting in a little more. One presumes, as you say, with the Heirship dangled in front of him as incentive." She raised a sardonic eyebrow. "Not that I can imagine Daril ever *fitting in*, as such. Still, he's decorative enough to see around a room, and he and his little satellites behave so much more outrageously than the rest of us that it quite takes the heat off the disapproval from the aunties."

"Reassuring for you, Nisha," Marcia said.

"Of course, Marcia my dear, you are squeaky clean as always and need not worry about such things," Nisha said. She had a flash painted at the corner of her mouth, which emphasised her smirk.

Was Nisha just being snippy, or was she referring to Marcia and Daril's past history? As much as she would know of it. Marcia couldn't remember, now, what she'd told any of them at the time. She tried not to remember much of that year at all.

Getting into a row with Nisha wouldn't help right now, regardless. Nisha was probably just peeved about Jonas.

"Can't blame Daril for being a bit irritable," Aden said, with a roll of his eyes. "At least you've been confirmed, Nisha."

"Yes, and what earthly good does it do me? I don't get to sit in the Council."

"I might get to sit in but I don't exactly get to do anything," Marcia said bitterly, then cursed herself and shut up. She didn't want to talk about that here.

"Daril was talking about this the other night," Nisha said, leaning back. "The way we're all sitting around waiting for our parents to decide to let us in."

Marcia's eyebrows went up. Daril was trying to recruit sympathy, now, was he? Or just those in a similar position? She wanted to ask more, but she didn't want to do it right now.

"Sounds like an interesting person," Jonas said, and Marcia silently blessed him for keeping his mind on what they were here for.

"Oh, really not all that fascinating," Marcia said with a shrug. "Just local gossip."

"I'll introduce you, if you like, Jonas," Nisha said. Her smile was aimed at Marcia, and it had edges. She did remember something, then.

"Perhaps later," Jonas said, and Marcia made a mental note of the potential setup. But not yet.

Time passed. More drinks were sunk. Marcia drank rather

less than she pretended to, and she was fairly certain that Jonas was doing the same. She was equally certain that her friends weren't pretending, nor was anyone else. The noise level went up, and the inhibition levels went down.

Nisha, now sitting on Aden's lap, to his amused tolerance – Aden didn't go for women – brought out a little box and snapped it open. She took a dab of powder from it and licked it slowly off her finger, her expression equal parts distaste and anticipation, then shivered. Aden reached around to take his own dab, then Nisha leant and offered it to Jonas.

"Ah..." He looked uncertain.

"It's pejo," Marcia said, leaning over to him. "It's a stimulant. Keeps you awake, makes you feel good."

"Thank you, but no," Jonas said.

"Oh, go on," Nisha said. "You'll like it. I love it." She rolled her eyes dramatically and laughed.

"Leave him alone, Nisha," Marcia said. "He doesn't have to."

"Oh, you would say that," Nisha said. Her mocking tone had the same undercurrent it had done all evening. "You being all pure and clean, eh?"

This. This was her opening. She narrowed her eyes. "Fine," she said, got up, and took the box from Nisha's hand. "I'll take some, and then you can leave Jonas be, how about that?"

Nisha raised her eyebrows and settled back onto Aden's lap with a little toss of her head. Marcia listed a little drunkenly – mustn't overdo it – as she balanced the box in one hand, and dabbed, angling her hand so in the dim light, Jonas was the only one who could see that her finger stayed clean. She licked at her finger, and pulled a horrified expression. Everyone watching laughed. The sense-memory of the bitterness was bright in her, for a moment. It was a long time since she'd taken pejo. About ten years, in fact. But she still remembered it well enough to fake it.

"Devils and angels, I'd forgotten how vile that stuff tastes," she said, then shivered the same way that Nisha had.

She snapped the box shut and handed it back to Nisha, who passed it on in the other direction. Jonas gave her a shiver of a wink. She just hoped he'd be ready for his cue in a couple of minutes.

The atmosphere in their group changed again over the next few minutes, voices getting louder, eyes brighter, gestures more pronounced. Finally, Marcia managed to get someone to mention Daril's name again.

"Oh, he's just a nasty little shit," she said loudly.

"That's not what you thought back in the day, Marcia, is it now?" Nisha said, laughing.

"Oh-ho! Is that why you're scared to speak to him now?" Aden said.

"Of course, you were off in Teren that summer, weren't you, Aden?" Nisha said. "Marcia was besotted, darling, honestly."

Marcia really didn't want to let Nisha get started on that story. At least not in front of her. Her eyes flicked over to Jonas, and, thank the angel, he took the cue.

"Who?" he asked.

"Daril b'Leandra," Aden replied. "He of the wide berths and dubious reputation. Our Marcia jumps away like a startled cat whenever he's nearby." He was teasing, mostly. Nisha's tone had been... more pointed.

Marcia let her words slur slightly.

"Scared of him? Rubbish. I'm not *scared* of Daril b'Leandra. Just because everyone makes out he has this reputation he walks round like he's all that? *Scared*, ha." Her chin went up and she beckoned regally, drunkenly, to Jonas. "You'd like to meet him, you said earlier. Let's."

Jonas played the baffled outlander perfectly. "Eh, I don't know the man. By all means, Marcia, if you say so." He bowed slightly, radiating bemused amiability.

"Well then," Marcia declared, as if something had been settled, and crooked her arm, inviting Jonas to walk with her. "Let us make introductions. I am sure b'Leandra will be delighted to meet you."

"Marcia..." Aden called after her, sounding suddenly concerned, but they were already halfway across the floor and Marcia didn't turn round.

"Finally," she said, looking up at Jonas. "Took me long enough to find a moment." And that wasn't at all about her not wanting to do this at all, no. "Thank you for setting that up earlier."

Jonas nodded slightly. "Do you need anything of me?" he asked.

There was something in his eyes that she couldn't quite read.

"Pull me away if I pinch your arm," Marcia said. "Otherwise feel free to keep up your whole foreigner-abroad thing."

They were nearly at the other side of the room. Someone next to Daril leant over and said something to him, and he turned to look at them. Marcia's breath hitched slightly.

"I don't know how this is going to go," she confessed – to Jonas? To herself? "I have no idea what I'm going to say."

She wasn't sixteen any more. She was an adult, and Fereno-Heir. She held onto that thought, and to Jonas' reassuring arm, as they reached Daril's table.

☉ ☉

Marcia felt herself sway slightly as they stopped, and told herself it backed up her claim of inebriation. She was glad of Jonas' presence; and of the fact that he gave no indication of how hard she was gripping his arm.

Daril, slouched in his chair, looked up at them. His dark hair, drawn back from his face over the shaved sides of his head, emphasised his pointed features. The light was too dim for her to read anything in his dark eyes.

"Daril!" Marcia said, aiming for cheerfully inebriated, and with no idea how well she was doing.

"Marcia." Daril's small smile widening a little. "It's been a long time."

She couldn't suppress the twitch in her shoulders. For a moment, looking at him, she was catapulted back to sixteen. The first time she'd met Daril had been at some summer drinks afternoon, given by one of Madeleine's friends. Marcia had been dragged along as Heir-presumed. Cato had refused to join them. Daril had been in a similar position as her, Heir-presumed of Leandra at the time, before his falling-out with his father. They hadn't quite been the only two under thirty there, but in retrospect it was inevitable they'd end up talking. Less inevitable that they had talked all afternoon, with no attention to spare for anyone else, to Madeleine's slight disapproval.

Marcia had been besotted from the start. That was the summer Cato had discovered his magic, too. Marcia had been interested, of course she had, but her focus was all on Daril, that summer. Stupid.

"My friend here is a visitor from Salina, and was curious to meet you," she said, pulling herself back to the present day. His eyes were the same. She couldn't quite bring herself to meet them. "Your name came up in conversation."

"For all the best reasons, I am sure," Daril said, and Marcia gritted her teeth. She hated the idea that he would think she had been speaking of him.

"Jonas, this is Daril b'Leandra," she said. "Daril, this is Jonas t'Riseri."

A subtle insult; as a House member, Daril outranked a non-Marek visitor, and Jonas should have been introduced to him, not vice versa.

Daril's smile didn't flicker.

"Welcome to our city, t'Riseri."

Jonas bowed neatly, in the Salinas style. "I am delighted to be here."

"So, Marcia, what have you been doing, all these years?" Daril asked, his attention snapping back to Marcia.

The memory that surfaced now was of the last time she'd seen him. What his planning and persuasion had led them to. Reb saving them all from themselves on that bloody roof…

She couldn't think about that now. She was here for Cato.

"Much of my time is spent with the Council," she said. "Dull but necessary. Although I suppose you wouldn't know." She smiled, wide and false.

From what Nisha and Aden had been saying, he'd finally taken to criticising that situation. Would he repeat that to her?

"Indeed not," Daril agreed. "The current situation has led to the ignoring of all talents and abilities possessed by those of us under forty or so. I am glad if this does not apply to you, but still – a shocking waste, would you not agree?"

For a moment, his gaze was direct and honest, and Marcia struggled with a wave of sympathetic understanding. It *was* absurd that Gavin had been manipulating – attempting to manipulate – Daril for over a decade. It was absurd that Nisha was Heir only in name. *And you are Heir in truth?* a self-mocking voice whispered at the back of her head. She shut down the image of Madeleine sweeping out of Council ahead of her, plans already made.

No. Whatever Daril was arguing, even if there was a kernel of truth in it, she was not on his side. But she couldn't bring herself to disagree out loud, either.

She had hesitated too long. He looked away. "And thus, as you doubtless remember, my time is frittered away in diversions of various sorts, many of which it seems are disapproved of." He sighed theatrically. "I am misunderstood, as ever; I seek only interest and pleasure, and who can criticise that?"

As you remember. She remembered his interest when she bragged about Cato's new abilities. She remembered him telling her not to be silly, that blood magic was perfectly safe, it was only hidebound Marek that forbade it. But for her, he would try the Marek way. She remembered his fury when she introduced him to Cato and Cato told him to get lost. And the determination that replaced that fury.

He wore a sleeveless shirt tonight, but she couldn't see, in this light, whether the scars were still there. She stopped her hand from straying to the thin white line on her own inner arm, and breathed out her anger, swallowing down the retorts that sprang to her lips.

"I am sure your diversions are entirely above criticism," she said, praying that her voice would stay steady. "My brother – you remember my brother? His diversions, now, I frequently find myself criticising."

"Your brother?" Daril said. "Dear me. I was under the impression that House Fereno had repudiated their social dropout altogether. Some time ago."

Marcia's chin went up. "House Fereno may have. I have not."

"Indeed," Daril said.

There was a long, excruciating, pause. Daril looked amused.

She wasn't sure, now, what she'd been hoping for. Some reaction when she mentioned Cato? Had she really expected

Daril to be that obvious? Her stomach felt tight, her anxiety rising. Try again. Try something more personal to them both. Something more specific.

"I suppose Cato's sorts of diversions are unlikely to be of interest to you, any more." She laid a very slight stress on the last two words, and this time she let her hand fall forwards, baring her inner arm, and let her thumb move to that scar.

Daril did react to that. His eyes had been wide and innocent, surrounded by a blue ring of face-paint that made the irises appear bluer and the whites whiter. Just for a moment, they narrowed, and his face tightened. She saw his throat jump. She was getting somewhere, she just needed to push him a little bit harder…

She let her voice go up a few notes in the high tones of someone wired on pejo, fighting nausea as she spoke.

"I mean, I know I could never think of magic again after that time…"

He twitched slightly – surprise? – then settled back in his chair with a slight smile. She'd gone too far. Too obvious. She dug her fingernails into her palm.

"Or of me either, as I recall," he drawled, leaning backwards. "I'm still a little hurt that you never even left a message, Marcia. Is this an attempt at an apology, ten years on?"

She felt herself flush to the hairline and spoke almost at random, desperate suddenly to get away. "As I recall, I was bored. Of you. As indeed I find myself now. Jonas, I am afraid that, as you see, Daril is hardly as fascinating as the rumours might suggest." She flicked her hand at Daril. "Good evening to you."

It was abrupt, too abrupt, and she didn't even know anything for sure about Cato. But she *had* to leave, now, before she screamed, before the memories came back even more strongly.

"Good evening," Jonas nodded.

Gods, he'd barely spoken. Daril would surely know this was just about him and her. She leaned into Jonas again, hoping to suggest that he was her current fling.

"Good evening," Daril said, a laugh lurking under the surface.

She clenched her teeth so hard her jaw hurt. They turned to leave; and he added, "I will convey your regards to your brother."

She felt herself jerk, involuntarily; found herself halfway to turning round, to grabbing him by the throat and to hell with the politics of it all. It was only Jonas' firm grip on her arm, his nails digging in painfully, that kept her moving, away from Daril.

She was not going to let anything happen to her brother. Whatever Daril b'Leandra might have planned. She was *not*.

SIX

The rain started just after Jonas turned away from House Fereno to walk back down Marekhill. They'd stayed for maybe half an hour after the conversation with Daril, before he'd claimed tiredness in the hope of getting Marcia out. She looked nearly as strung out as if she'd really taken those uppers. It was clear what her friends thought they were going off to do, the two of them, but Marcia had ignored the insinuations so he did likewise. Would he have been tempted, if she'd offered, he wondered? Likely not. She was pretty enough, no doubt about that, and they got on well, but he wouldn't care to try more than that. And most certainly not tonight, when she was clearly in some emotional distress.

On the way home, he'd checked that Marcia really had heard what Daril said, and she'd point blank refused to talk about it until they met up with Reb the next day. Her voice had cracked as she said it, but she politely and persistently turned down his expressions of concern and offers of help, so in the end he walked her to the door of House Fereno and left. They barely knew each other, anyway; who was he to try to help her?

The streets were mostly empty now, though his Salinas tunic and trousers garnered a couple of curious glances from other party-goers presumably also wending their way home – or out somewhere else to extend the night a little. He snorted. Of course, it hadn't so much as occurred to Marcia to wonder if *he* would be safe returning to the squats in this getup. Just as well he'd already thought about it himself.

He was a few streets down the Hill before the houses were close enough together that he was easily able to take to the roofs. He found a house with a solid-enough one-storey side extension, from the roof of which he could get up to the taller houses. Doing so without damaging his good clothes did make the task a little harder.

The rain meant the roof-tiles were slippery and the gutters

half-full of water and damp leaves. It was still easier than being up a mast in a storm. And the rain was gentle, reassuring, pattering soft and almost warm on his face.

He found a convenient flattish ridge-top and made his way along it, gathering his impressions of the day as he went. He'd spent the afternoon, after leaving Cato's, running as many messages as he could to make up for the morning already lost, given that he wouldn't be able to do an evening shift. Though evenings were always erratic, to be fair. Housing in the squats might be free but nothing else was. And then Marcia just now had blithely assumed he'd be round at Reb's tomorrow, missing yet more work. He rolled his eyes. Thoughtless rich. No wonder, with a society so divided, in so many ways. It still seemed strange to him. The Salinas sought always to bind people together, in different ways – blood-family, ship, trading fleet, chosen-family – rather than to separate.

He wiped a drip of rain off his nose. At least he wasn't wearing Marek-formal face paint, to run in the wet. It had been odd, seeing a whole hall full of those painted masks. He knew the style already, but he'd never seen so many at once. Not that they disguised everything, there was that. Not as much as you might have thought, at first sight, once you got accustomed. Faces still moved the same way, body language didn't change. You could still read people.

So, then. Reb's, tomorrow. Would he, or not? He could just not go; could get on with his own affairs and leave them to it. No skin off his nose if Marek lacked a cityangel. But he'd had no chance yet to ask Beckett about his flickers. The cityangel – former cityangel – might have the answers that Reb apparently didn't; the answers that would allow him to get rid of his wretched flickers and go back home. And if he let things go now, who knew where the cityangel might disappear to. It was possible, even, though Jonas rather begged leave to doubt it, that Beckett would achieve their aim of returning to their old position, and then Jonas would have no chance at all at getting any information from them.

He slowed as he came to the tall roof of one of the Guild buildings alongside the river's south side. He'd stowed a bundle of street-clothes, wrapped in his ship oilskins, behind a chimney up here. He hadn't fancied walking through the squats in full formal wear. Probably he would have been fine – the squats weren't the hotbed of crime that some of the more excitable Marekhill folk seemed to think – but he stood out enough already as it was.

As he skimmed out of his formal wear and back into a loose shirt and Marek-style trousers, he looked out over the city. Torches shone their dots of light outside the big houses up on Marekhill; further down the hill the houses were dark, but the odd moving torch-flicker showed up well-off groups presumably on their way home. Down around the river and the market on the far side of the river, the only lights were outside the couple of pubs and inns that were still open at this hour; people walking managed in the dark.

Changed now, he wrapped his formal clothes carefully in the oilskin, and tied the package to his belt. Then he climbed up to the top of the roof, and sat on the ridge-pole of the Guild-house.

The rain pattered softly onto the tiles around him, and he pushed tendrils of wet hair back off his forehead.

Kia. He hadn't really thought through the possibility that someone at the party would know him. His mother had told him, before he put ashore, that Kia was the current ambassador, and he'd nodded and ignored the information. He didn't want to be Jonas t'Riseri, staying on Marekhill and being shown around. He wanted to be Jonas, making a living same as anyone else. He couldn't see how he'd have any chance at getting the information he wanted otherwise; not that he'd exactly been making the most of his opportunities. He scowled into the darkness. And then, today, he just hadn't thought about how Marcia's Marekhill party might be the sort of thing that ambassadors attended. He certainly hadn't realised what Marcia's House position meant, in terms of her involvement in Marek politics.

So now Kia knew he was here, and he had a horrible suspicion that she would want to press her point a little harder. Would feel obliged to look out for a t'Riseri, or expect him to be available to support her politicking. And he didn't want to be penned up in the embassy. He wanted to solve his little problem, without any interference from Kia, and get the hell out. But if he didn't show up tomorrow, she'd be even more likely to interfere, to be on the lookout, now she knew he was here.

Of course, if he'd actually got on with solving his little problem a bit sooner, this wouldn't be an issue.

Beckett might yet have an answer. And then there was this Cato, too. If Beckett didn't know anything, maybe Cato would. If Jonas could find him. It sounded like he had knowledge that Reb didn't, or at least didn't want to. Maybe his flickers were more that sort of knowledge. Jonas shivered slightly. Though if Cato's area of expertise was spirits, like Reb had been suggesting, maybe that would be bad news.

The thought took him back to that moment in Cato's room where the *thing* in the air had been reaching towards Beckett, and he'd stepped in front of it. Jonas scowled down at his knees. Beckett had said, afterwards, that it was their doing, that it disappeared. But Jonas was nearly certain that the cityangel was lying. It had been him. It had gone when he moved. And what the hell did that mean? He couldn't think of any explanation that felt remotely comfortable. Coincidence, perhaps. He would surely love to put it down to coincidence, but that would be fear talking, not truth.

He wanted to get rid of his flickers. He wanted to find out what the hell had happened there in that room. He wanted to have absolutely nothing more to do with any of this magical nonsense at all. And, quite clearly, those first two weren't compatible with that last one.

The flicker was just a tiny one this time; Marcia and Reb, nose to nose, shouting at one another. Jonas snorted. Not like that was telling him anything he couldn't have guessed already. If the two of them managed to spend more than a couple of hours together without arguing he'd be surprised. It couldn't have been a *useful* flicker, then, this one? At least it suggested that Marcia wasn't too badly shaken by her talk with Daril. He wished he knew what it was that had happened between those two – and Reb as well, from what she'd said to Marcia, back in Cato's room. Magic, for certain, so maybe he already knew all he wanted to, except neither Marcia nor Daril was a sorcerer, so what on earth had they been playing at?

Jonas sighed. He'd let these people drag him into their problems, and it wasn't getting him any further with *his* problem. Which was becoming fairly urgent.

He stared out across the rooftops towards the river and the docks on the other side of it, hidden now in the darkness. Very faintly, he thought he could hear the slap of wet rope against masts as the ships rocked gently on the water. It was getting urgent – but he'd been here for half a year. Why hadn't he done anything about this before?

He forced himself to face the question, rather than letting himself turn away from it, the way he'd been turning away from the whole problem since he got here. Granted, he'd had no particular desire to meet a sorcerer. Though as it turned out, Reb was hardly the terrifying creature of magic he'd imagined she would be. Just an irritable woman who happened to create magic for a living rather than sail a ship. Or run messages. But – even if he'd been nervous about meeting a sorcerer, if this was as important to him as it had been to his mother, when she sent him here, would he have put it off?

Marek wasn't his home. But he had to admit that he liked it here. He liked the friends he'd made – especially Asa and Tam, who'd taken to him and helped him out right from the start, never-no-mind that he wasn't Mareker. His own people weren't always that way with strangers. And even if they didn't know about his flickers, the matter-of-fact way they were about magic meant that he didn't feel as uncomfortable around them as he did around some of his own compatriots.

A sneaking thought crept into his head. Did he really want to go home? Did he really want to get rid of the flickers?

He shook his head, angry at himself all of a sudden. Of course he did. That was why he was here. That was the whole purpose behind this. Get rid of the flickers, go back to Salina, choose his first ship as an adult. That was what he was supposed to be doing. He was just feeling odd, right now, because it was the middle of the night, and he'd gotten himself tangled up in someone else's problems. He needed to focus on his own goals.

He sighed again, and scrubbed at his face with his hand. It was far too late – he could already see the first glow of dawn on the horizon. He'd been hoping to get a decent morning's work in tomorrow, but there was no way that would work out now. He had to sleep. Which meant it was time to get down off this roof, get over the bridge, and get back to his room. No point in spending any more time moping on rooftops.

But he really was out of cash now, which made tomorrow's breakfast – or lunch, given the time – a problem. He brightened, as a thought struck him. He couldn't avoid Kia now, and he'd agreed to tomorrow. So if he turned up at the embassy just before lunchtime, Kia would be bound to offer to feed him. If he was lucky he'd get in a message on the way; if not he could get a good afternoon's work in with a decent meal under his belt. Too, it gave him an excuse to stay away from Reb's and to let Marcia and Reb fret about Daril and Cato. For sure, he had to visit again, had to talk to Beckett, and see if they were going to give him a way of getting to Cato. But he could do that later, when it suited him. Stick to his own interests, his own goals, that was the thing. Avoid getting pulled into this Mareker nonsense.

He yawned widely enough that his jaw cracked, and started to slide down the roof, bent on home and his bed.

☺ ☺

House Leandra was almost entirely dark as Daril reached it. Only two lights were showing; a crack through the curtain of his own receiving room, where there would be a lamp burning to await his return, and the light which blazed at all hours from his father's room in the opposite wing.

He had left the others carousing. Doubtless they would be at it well past sunrise. For himself, he was finding those evenings increasingly dull, although it wouldn't pay to reveal that just now. And he was exhausted, after the last few days. All he wanted was to get himself to bed and sleep.

The encounter with Marcia had been unexpected. His aim for the evening had been the same as for the last couple of years – circulate, put a few rumours into play, very gently suggest that the status quo could use a shake-up. Nothing overt enough to give anyone reason to suspect his true aims.

Just nudges, moving people's thinking enough that they would be more prepared to support him when the time came. It wasn't even hard; his generation were disillusioned and everyone knew it. He'd even had one or two people he'd not spoken to before approach *him* to sound him out further.

He wasn't about to share his main plans, but having the offspring of the Houses behind him would be useful for consolidation, and to cut away the ground under the feet of the Council, if that was even necessary after the cityangel did its thing. Once they'd sorted out the current problem with that, of course.

Crossing the front courtyard, he frowned. Why *had* Marcia come to speak to him, for the first time in ten years? Well, obviously she suspected he knew where Cato was – but why? And why so quickly? Surely Marcia Fereno-Heir wasn't in the regular habit of poking around the squats. He knew she still met with Cato, but as far as he knew, she didn't visit his room to do so, and Cato hadn't seemed to think they were due to meet up. He'd shrugged off the notion of any commitments he would be missing by accompanying Daril. Though Cato wasn't always *reliable*, it was true.

Daril wondered, briefly, if she knew something of the other thing. But that was surely impossible. According to Urso, now the cityangel was missing it was obvious to even a half-competent sorcerer that something was wrong, but Marcia couldn't even turn a charm.

And it wasn't like there *were* many sorcerers around any more. Cato. Urso, but no one else knew about that. There was that sorcerer down in the Old Market – but no, that was absurd. Marcia would never deal with a sorcerer, and risk the accusation of breaking the Council's laws, especially not now she was Heir. No. It must just be that she was after her brother, and somehow she'd jumped to the conclusion that Daril was involved. He scowled. He *knew* it had been foolish to go down there himself, but Cato hadn't been prepared to budge, and Daril had convinced himself he could get away with it without being recognised. Foolish.

He could have – should have, really – continued just to deny it. But it had been so tempting, and seeing her react and try not to – surely it had been worth it. He smiled, fiercely, as he climbed the steps. She couldn't prove a thing, after all.

The big front door, gilded with the Leandra crest, swung open, and his valet, Roberts, bowed him inside. Daril heard the door bar sliding into place before the man came to help Daril remove his coat.

"I'll undress myself," Daril said, moving towards the stairs. "Go to bed."

The wall-lights were mostly out, the stairs and corridors dark with little islands of flickering light at intervals. Daril barely needed any light at all, though, not here where he'd spent his entire life. His footsteps fell softly on the thick rugs along the centre of the corridor, until he came to his door, a wall-light glowing next to it.

Inside there was warmth from the fire, a couple of candles lit and halfway down their length; and a short, thin, scruffy man slumped in the best armchair by the fire.

"Enjoy your party?" Cato asked.

His cropped hair was a touch less dark than his sister's, the red showing in the reflected firelight, and it clearly saw a comb less often. Cato had, though, taken well to the bathtubs available at the Leandra house. The bags under his eyes were no less prominent in his pale face for his current luxurious living; he'd evidently been semi-nocturnal for too long now. He had a glass in his hand, and the decanter on the side was half-empty.

"What are you doing here?" Daril demanded. Gods. He didn't want to deal with bloody Cato at this hour.

Cato shrugged hugely. "Bored. Tell me gossip. There must be gossip, there always is at these things. Marcia still keeps me up-to-date..." He stopped. Daril could have sworn that he didn't move, didn't change his expression, but Cato's eyebrows went up. "You saw Marcia? No, not just saw her. You *talked* to Marcia?"

"She talked to me," Daril said, and immediately regretted admitting it. Too late now. Cato would know how unusual it was for Marcia to speak to him. "Curiously enough, she was looking for you."

Cato's eyes narrowed. "You told her, didn't you? Well. That wasn't such a great idea."

"Told her what?" Angels, Cato was too sharp. He needed to

back out of this conversation.

"Told her you knew where I was. Bad idea. She's like a little snapper when she gets hold of an idea." He made a gesture with his hand, reminiscent of the famously tenacious semi-carnivorous fish.

Daril tried not to react. Cato had done this when Daril had come to the squats, too – realised more than Daril meant him to, from only a few words. He'd accused Cato of being able to see into his head, and Cato had nearly laughed himself sick before assuring Daril that he was just terribly, terribly obvious.

Which wasn't true. Daril knew it wasn't true. Cato was must just be very observant. Perhaps it had something to do with his work with spirits, and his ability to communicate with them.

Cato was at his most annoying when he was right. Although, Daril reflected darkly, he was moderately annoying all of the time. It was deeply frustrating that they'd needed him at all, and in such a hurry that Daril hadn't been able to think things through as well as he would have liked.

Cato was shaking his head. "You really should have made me your offer up front, without all the cloak and dagger stuff," Cato said. "Then I could have settled Marcia myself."

Daril shrugged. "Couldn't be sure what you'd say. And we were in a hurry." And once they'd come to their agreement, he really hadn't wanted to leave Cato running around loose in the squats for any time at all.

"Anyway, I thought you said you had no commitments? No one would be missing you?"

Cato shrugged. "I didn't. She must just have come visiting."

"In the squats?" Daril demanded, incredulous.

Cato smirked. "Just because you're too precious doesn't mean Marcia is."

She would have been, ten years ago. The last time Daril and Marcia had had anything to do with each other.

"Why wouldn't you get involved, back when – when I knew Marcia?" Daril asked abruptly, turning round.

Marcia had tried to recruit Cato – Daril had asked her to, after she told him that Cato was experimenting with sorcery, and had the ability for it – and Cato had turned her down. Marcia hadn't been able to tell Daril why, either, just shrugged and said he wouldn't, and to leave her alone about it.

Cato slouched back in his chair and looked at her. "Back when you were demon-raising, you mean?"

"You wouldn't then. Now you are. Why?"

Cato shrugged a shoulder. "I was a moralistic child, at the time." He grinned, mockingly. "Obviously, it wore off. Though in that instance, given how it turned out, it was probably just as well for me. Also, this time, you offered me money. Cold hard cash will get you a long way."

Daril squinted across the room at him. It sounded a little too pat, a little too offhand. Then again – ten years ago Cato had been living in House Fereno, acknowledged scion of the House. Now he was living in a grubby squat over the river. It wasn't so unreasonable that his motivations – and his opinions on life – had changed. Was it?

"I suppose things change in ten years," he said, giving up. "But you just said – you still see Marcia?"

Cato looked cautious. "Occasionally. We have a drink together, she complains about our – about family things." The hesitation was only barely noticeable. Cato had a sore spot around Madeleine Fereno-Head, then. Interesting, for someone who was so enthusiastic about claiming that he preferred life outside of the Houses.

"She had a Salinas lad with her," Daril said. "Any idea who that might be?"

Cato shrugged. "Never heard her talk about a Salina. Just someone she picked up, I guess. Was he pretty? Her taste is... erratic."

He smirked, and Daril clenched his fists, fighting the impulse to punch him.

"Maybe you're right, but there was something about him... Oh, never mind."

He walked impatiently over to the window. Outside, the few lights in a pre-dawn Marek twinkled away down the hill, down towards where he could see the faint outline of the Old Bridge. For a moment he could almost hear the river slopping against its piers, before he shook his head again.

"Well. Was there a reason you were waiting for me, or did you just want to annoy me?" he asked, turning back to Cato.

"Well, there was the gossip. But mostly just to annoy you," Cato said. "Prisoners have few other entertainments, after all."

"You're not a prisoner," Daril said impatiently. "You're here of your own free will."

"Ah, but if I wasn't here of my own free will, I'd be here without it," Cato said lightly. "Which by my reckoning makes me a prisoner."

He untangled himself from the chair, and walked to the door before Daril could marshal any argument.

"Goodnight."

Daril stared at the door for a moment after Cato had closed it, then shook his head. It was late. Time to sleep.

But nevertheless he stayed at the window, staring down across sleeping Marek. He was so close. It was so nearly his. Cato was probably right. Telling Marcia had been unnecessary, at best. But then, what could she do? There was hardly time now for her to interfere before everything came together.

He could still wish that they hadn't had to involve Cato. He could wish, come to that, that he had sorcerous ability of his own; but they'd been certain that Urso had enough to expel the cityangel. And he *had* been able to. Daril had felt the charge as it happened.

The problem had come when Urso tried to summon a replacement. Urso had been certain that the hole in itself would be enough to draw a spirit of some kind to fill it. They hadn't, truly, much cared what; as long as they could bargain with it, and enforce their terms. The terms the old one hadn't been prepared to agree to.

But apparently the absence alone wasn't enough; and Urso didn't know enough about spirits to call one, to fix the problem that way. Nothing came. Finally, Urso, gasping and on his knees, had had to stop. He'd only just managed to tie the power off before he passed out. He'd been in bed for a straight day afterwards, incoherent, shaking and sweating. Once he had come round properly, he had been very clear that they needed to fix this, as soon as possible. Marek's magic relied on the cityangel; and in any case, without the cityangel's magic, none of the rest of their plans would work.

Daril's teeth clenched. It was all infuriating. But they just had to fix this, and then all could carry on as he had planned.

Thus, Cato. Who was good, and experienced with spirits, and still alive, unlike any other Marek sorcerer but one. Once Daril had found him in that ghastly slum and explained the situation, he had been most co-operative. In exchange, admittedly, for a serious amount of cash. Cato was confident he could find a suitable spirit for their purposes; had even summoned one on the spot to demonstrate his ability, which – Daril shuddered slightly in recollection – he hadn't been wholly prepared for.

They would fix this little hiccup, and then carry on with the plan. And all those old Heads of House, sitting on their arses in the Chamber long past their appointed time, would be upended.

Which took him back to Marcia. He bit his thumbnail. Could that just be coincidence? Just her concern for her reprobate brother, and the ability to ask a question or two in that ghastly pub?

Throwing up his hands, he pushed himself away from the window. It was late. He could not possibly be thinking clearly any more. Sleep, and tomorrow they would fix this little cityangel problem, and all would be back on track. It would.

SEVEN

Marcia woke up the next morning with a single clear idea. She had to rescue Cato.

They'd found that hair in his room. Daril had been seen there. He had *said*, last night, that he knew where Cato was. Therefore, the obvious conclusion was that Daril had taken Cato away, quite possibly by force; and from that it followed that Marcia must retrieve him.

Of course, what she didn't know was what the hell Daril was up to. That thing Nisha had said, about everyone sitting and waiting for their parents to let them in... It was true, that was the worst thing, and it was something their parents, this generation, had done to them. They'd taken their seats at the traditional time, and then changed everything around to keep themselves in power. The way Madeleine was behaving to her... and even so, she was better off than most of her peers, because she did at least nominally have some power.

But why was *Daril* talking about it? As far as anyone could tell he'd given up on ever becoming Heir to his own House years ago. Had that changed? Was he trying to stir up dissatisfaction? And what did he hope to get out of it if so? He wasn't even Heir; if it all changed back again it made no odds to him. Unless Nisha's other bit of gossip, about Gavin changing his mind, was true. But even then, stirring up trouble would hardly endear Daril to his father.

She remembered, almost against her will, a time back when she was sixteen, waiting for Daril in a teashop. He'd been late, and when he had finally arrived, he had been coldly furious in a way she'd never seen him before. She remembered jumping up anxiously to greet him.

"Are you – is everything well?"

Daril took both her hands. "My father..." He looked around. "Could we – would you mind if we went somewhere else?"

"Of course not," Marcia said, gathering up her bag.

"Let's go up to the top of the Hill. I'd like to talk to you, but we could use a little privacy."

He hadn't said much as they made their way along the crowded streets, walking up towards where the rows of houses (and Houses) gave way to Marekhill Park; but as they emerged into the park itself, and gained a little space around them, he seemed to relax a little.

"Your father…" Marcia said, tentatively. "Did you have an argument?"

Daril barked a humourless laugh. "You could say that." He looked upwards, towards the statue of Marek and Beckett that stood at the top of the hill. "We were discussing the Guilds."

After decades of wrangling, the Guilds were on the cusp of persuading the Council to add ten elected seats to their number; so for the first time, Guild representatives would join the Heads and Heirs as part of the Council. But the final vote was still uncertain. Madeleine, on the side of the reformers, had spent weeks now closeted with one Council member after another, looking increasingly harried.

"Yes?" she said, cautiously.

"Father was – he thinks it is a disaster. He voted against it throughout."

"Mother thinks it is an unfortunate necessity," Marcia volunteered. "She would prefer otherwise but fears the consequences if they are not admitted. And besides, it is a mere ten seats." Which meant that the Guilds were still handily outnumbered by the twenty-six Heads and Heirs of a full Council, although several Houses, including both hers and Daril's, lacked an Heir at the moment.

"I think it is a *good* thing," Daril said, fiercely. "The city is not simply a fiefdom of the Houses, any more. The Guilds are as vital to Marek's success as any of us."

"But without the Houses trading, the Guilds would have no outlet for their wares," Marcia objected.

"That goes both ways," Daril said. "Without the Guilds, what would we be trading? Potatoes and beets and rice and cured meat." He waved a hand. "The true wealth of our trading relationships are based on what the Guilds make. Fine cloth. Jewellery and finished gems. Paper. Marek leather.

That is what we have to offer. And it is hardly fair to continue to exclude them from decisions."

"So you said that to Gavin," Marcia said.

"At length," Daril said. "We... disagreed. Violently."

"I'm sure he'll forgive you after a while," Marcia said, after Daril hadn't said anything more for a moment. "I often argue with Mother. But you will be Heir soon."

"No, I will not," Daril said. His face was set, but Marcia could see him swallow after he spoke.

She blinked at him. "But –"

"The conclusion of our conversation," Daril said, biting the words off, "was that my father is no longer prepared to confirm me as Heir after the elections. Indeed, he reserves the right to never do so, if I do not – shape up, was his expression. By which he means, bow down and agree to all of his demands. I will *not*."

Marcia didn't know what to say. Daril was twenty-one now. It was unthinkable that he not be confirmed this autumn.

"Is he disowning you?" she asked, finally.

"No," Daril said. "That would at least be final. No, he wishes me to have plenty of time to consider my decisions. To *recant*, I believe he said. To think better of my principles." He bared his teeth. "I will do *no such thing*. I swear."

Was Daril right? Was he right enough to stand against his father like that, rather than going along with things until he became Head himself? It didn't seem like something she could ask just at this moment, with Daril looking the way he did.

Instead, she tugged him down onto the grass, and let him put his head in her lap and rant until he was calmer, while she half-listened and half turned the problem over in her head. Gavin thought the Guilds should have nothing to do with government. Madeleine thought the same, but would rather let them in to keep the peace – very literally. Daril thought they should if anything have more power than the Houses. Marcia herself had never truly thought about it before; and the idea of standing against her mother in the way Daril was arguing with Gavin gave her chills. Surely the wellbeing of the House was more important than all of this?

She carded her hands through Daril's hair, and stared out at the city spread below them, and wondered.

It had been a week after that when the final vote succeeded. Gavin Leandra-Head had voted for it, to everyone's surprise. His price had been an amendment that removed the twenty-five-year-limit rule and allowed Heads to choose when – and if – they handed over to their Heirs. The amendment that Marcia's friends were so bitter about now. And two months after that, Daril had tried to summon a spirit, and everything else in Marcia's life had changed.

In her own room, ten years later, she blinked fiercely. Whatever. It was ten years ago now. It didn't matter. What mattered was helping Cato get out of whatever hole he'd fallen into. Whatever hole Daril b'Leandra had pulled him into. She was not going to stand by and let Cato get screwed over by Daril the way she had been. At least Cato would have more sense than to get romantically involved with him. The memory of how stupid she'd been, how much she'd believed in Daril, always gave her a surge of nausea. She swallowed against it, pushed the memory away. It was ten years ago. She'd been a kid. A stupid kid. And Cato wasn't stupid. She couldn't believe that he would willingly get involved with anything Daril was up to. He knew all about what happened last time. He'd refused to get involved back then. He wouldn't change his mind now.

Which meant that Daril had to be forcing him. And she wasn't going to let her brother languish in trouble, in Daril b'Leandra's clutches, if she could get him out.

Not that it was going to be that simple, of course. She could hardly just march over to House Leandra, barge in, and demand that Daril produce Cato. But Reb, surely, would help. She had no love for Daril either. She would visit Reb, and Reb would help. They would rescue Cato together.

Reb had given Marcia her address the day before – a single-floor cottage on a narrow but busy street behind the Old Market. She wore an aggravated look when she opened her door, but it vanished when she saw Marcia.

"Oh! How did last night go?"

Marcia stepped into the house. The front room had wooden floorboards and white-washed walls; basic but clean. Against the right-hand wall there was a small stove. A dresser with crockery stacked on top of it was next to the stove, and a water-basin next to that. Towards the left of the room was a battered armchair, three wooden chairs, and a couple of side-tables. Beckett stood next to a chair, by the wall, their body held stiffly. There were two doors in the back wall, one of which was not just shut, but bolted shut. Did Reb do her sorcery through there?

Reb hesitated for a moment, then sat down in the armchair, and gestured Marcia towards one of the wooden chairs. It creaked a little as she sat down. Beckett turned to look at her, their torso moving as though Beckett wasn't so much inhabiting it as controlling it by force of will.

"Daril knows where Cato is," Marcia said without further preamble, and told them of the conversation. "So. We need to get him out. How are we going to do it?" she finished.

"Well," Reb said slowly. "I suppose what we do now depends on whether we think Daril b'Leandra is behind what has happened to Beckett, and whether that is why your brother is there."

Marcia blinked. "What do you mean? What we do now is, we get Cato the hell out of there."

There was a long pause, then Reb spread her hands. "Marcia. As a sorcerer, I do not hold with folk holding sorcerers against their will. Or indeed, with anyone else being held against their will. That much is true. But – forgive me, but we have no evidence that it is against his will."

Marcia felt sick.

"He wouldn't work with Daril b'Leandra. He wouldn't. They said, the people who saw him, someone came, persuaded him, he didn't want to go... He was *taken*. He wouldn't have *gone*."

"Marcia." Reb looked uncomfortable as she leant forwards. "Cato is a *sorcerer*. I haven't much time for what he does, or his attitude, but he's always been more than competent. I can't see how Daril b'Leandra could hold him against his will. He was seen in the pub, voluntarily leaving with whoever it was. Daril, if you like, I accept that it's likely that it was him. They went back to Cato's rooms, together. The wards were set again, from the outside – he had time to do that."

"You said he didn't take all of his things, his work things." Marcia felt light-headed. Surely Reb couldn't believe...

Reb shrugged. "Not all. Some. But he wouldn't necessarily take everything."

"The room was left, though, he didn't pack up properly, he didn't clear anything up..."

Reb's expression was kind but faintly exasperated. "Marcia. You've visited Cato there before, yes? It's not like he's particularly inclined to being *tidy*, is it, now? The one thing he's likely to be reliable about is the wards, and he dealt with those."

"What about that spirit you were talking about?" Marcia demanded, desperately. "You said – you said he'd summoned a spirit. Or someone had, anyway. Maybe it – maybe it threatened him, maybe it *took* him. Maybe it was working for Daril."

Reb looked down at her hands. "Marcia. Cato works with spirits. Much more than I do. And that's fine. There are spirits and spirits, certainly, but plenty of them are – there's nothing wrong with them. Only a few of them are like that one Daril tried to summon that time." Reb had, at least, the courtesy not to remind Marcia directly of her own involvement. "They're not. And more to the point – *Daril* isn't a sorcerer. He couldn't summon anyone. Last time he worked with others with ability. But you know what happened to anyone with ability two years ago. There's no one else left. It's me, and Cato. I didn't do it. So if anyone summoned a spirit, if anyone's working with a spirit, it's not Daril. It's Cato. And, perhaps, Daril through Cato." She looked up. "I'm sorry, Marcia, but that's what it looks like. That's the simplest explanation."

Marcia was shaking her head already. "But he can't. He wouldn't. He wouldn't work with Daril. He *wouldn't*."

"Cato has always said he would work with anyone who paid his rates," Reb said bluntly.

"Not Daril..." Marcia said, but Reb was already carrying on, talking over her.

"I thought this over, last night. Beckett has to take priority. The cityangel must return; we must return magic to its normal state. I can't prioritise Cato over that. And I definitely can't if it looks like he's working with Daril b'Leandra. It's not my job to rescue him from his own decisions."

"Just because he doesn't stick to your rules," Marcia said, furiously. Her insides were raw. Reb wasn't *listening*. She didn't believe Marcia, didn't believe that she knew Cato better than this. "Just because he makes his own decisions, doesn't belong to your little club..."

"There is no little club any more, remember?" Reb's voice was suddenly raw. "They died, Marcia? You remember? They all died, and why Cato and I didn't, neither of us know. Which," and her shoulders sagged, "is why I have to prioritise. Because if I don't fix it, then it won't get fixed. And then there won't be any sorcery at all here. Or it'll be back to blood, to the way everyone else does it, and trust me, we don't want that." Her eyes softened, and for a moment Marcia was hopeful again. "Marcia, I do understand why you just want Cato out of there. Truly I do. But..."

Marcia shook her head, her lips pressed together.

"I've run around town trying to find out things for you. I made a fool of myself trying to – talking to Daril b'Leandra. And now you're letting me down." She swallowed, trying not to cry. She'd thought she could trust Reb. She'd thought there was something there, some way they could work together. And now...

"You've been trying to find out things for you," Reb said, sharply. "Don't make out like you're entirely altruistic. You want your brother back. I want magic sorted out. Beckett wants back where he belongs. Jonas wants..." she paused, a frown crossing her face. "Where is Jonas, anyway?"

"You want magic back, and you don't give a ha'penny for anything else," Marcia spat. "I wish I'd never bothered trying to help you out. I should have just gone my own damn way to find Cato."

"Marcia, look," Reb took a deep breath. "We're both tired, we're both wound up..."

"Oh, shut up with that lackwitted patronising nonsense. I'm wound up? I'm wound up because my *brother* is stuck in that mausoleum of a house, with Daril forcing him into who-knows-what..."

"Or he's there by choice," Reb said.

Marcia stood up and looked across at Reb. Her cheeks were burning, and she felt like she couldn't breathe properly.

"Very well," she said, tightly. "I will fix this *myself*."

She slammed the door viciously behind her. It didn't help.

☺ ☺

Marcia was fuming as she stormed out of Reb's front room and up the street. Screw her. If no one else cared about Cato, she, his sister, certainly did, and she would damn well sort it out by herself.

Her footsteps slowed as she reached the market square, and she stopped. A big woman with a shopping basket on her arm pushed past her with a glare, muttering something about thoughtless rich folk, and Marcia glared back at her before starting to walk again, towards the jetty at the south end of the market where the ferry came in.

She would sort it out by herself. But what exactly was she going to do? If it were as straightforward as walking into House Leandra, Cato would already have walked out all by himself.

Assuming he wanted to.

Marcia scowled. If he was happy to be there, why hadn't he let her know? Surely he would know that once she thought he was in danger, she would do her best to get him out of it? Surely he would know that she would worry if she found him just *gone* from his rooms like that? Reb had to be wrong. He wasn't there by choice.

Then again – arguably he'd been in danger for years, doing what he did where he did it, and she'd never lifted a finger. But she had offered, back in the beginning, and he'd been at pains to point out that he was there by choice, and that he could look after himself. They'd argued over it, even. But that had been his choice. This time she was certain, whatever Reb might say, that he was there against his will. And she would not let her brother be used by Daril b'Leandra. Not like she had been.

The ferry across to the foot of the Hill was coming in as she reached the jetty. Almost all of the other waiting passengers were servants from households on the Hill, or porters, all with bags and boxes of goods enough to make it worth paying the ha'penny for the ferry rather than walk around and across the bridge. A messenger hung over the railing at the end of the jetty – she must have been given the fare to get her message delivered faster.

The ferry hooted, the ferryman cast off, and Marcia leant on the rail at the front of the deck and looked across at the Hill rising on the other side of the river. Beautiful and aloof, the houses stared out across the river. She could see House Fereno at the top, and the park rising behind it; as the houses spilled down the Hill they increased in number and decreased in size, crowded together in neat rows until the higgledy-piggledy jumble that spread around Marek Square and Old Bridge at the foot of the Hill.

What in the hells *was* she going to do, then? The question span unanswered around her mind all the way across the river. At the other side, the messenger jumped off the boat almost before the gangplank had settled properly on the deck, and was off at speed, running up the twisting path to the top of the Hill. A couple of carriage-porters hanging around hopefully at the pier offered Marcia a lift up the path, but she shook her head. The walk would do her good. Behind her, she heard one of the servants haggling with them for herself and her collection of boxes and bags.

Halfway up the steep, winding path, she paused for a moment to rest. She looked back across to the market and the docks to its west. Ocean-going Salinas ships bobbed alongside tiny fishing boats and marsh barges. Out towards the coast she could see a few fishing vessels tacking to and fro.

She remembered, suddenly, climbing this path with Cato. They'd climbed up and down it often enough, as children, but the time she was thinking of had been just before he left.

They'd been sixteen, and it was the first summer the two of them hadn't spent all their time together. She'd been wound up in Daril; Cato in magic. She'd bragged about Cato's abilities to her lover, and Daril had been fascinated. The nearest they had come to a row was when he suggested – then denied that he had meant to – that he was disappointed that Marcia herself wasn't talented. Of course, if she had been it would have been illegal for her to use, given her standing in the House. Daril thought that was ridiculous. Cato just shrugged and ignored her when she mentioned it. And Cato wasn't in line for Heir, so she had decided, with a little discomfort, perhaps it didn't really matter.

Then Daril had decided to summon a demon, after that day when his father had told him he wouldn't be Heir. Marcia hadn't realised exactly what he was planning, until Cato told her bluntly, once he himself had declined to be involved. That was their other near-row. Marcia had been shocked by the idea, but Daril had reassured her. Plenty of magicians and sorcerers dealt with demons, he'd said. They were only a form of spirit, and even in Marek, with all its restrictions on magic, people dealt with spirits. Even then, Marcia had known that that was an exaggeration, but Daril had waved her questions away. No need to worry. And, love-dazzled and young, she'd allowed him to convince her.

He'd never really explained what he wanted of it. Power? Money? Revenge on his father? Just the challenge of it? He said things that had sounded like an explanation at the time, but when she thought about it after it was all over, she never managed to make sense of it.

He hadn't had the ability himself. But he knew people, and they knew people... And he brought together a collection of people across the city with dribs and drabs of power, and one or two with more than that. (And how many of them, Marcia wondered now, were dead or injured from the plague?) Marcia herself had no ability at all, but she'd been there anyway. She'd just wanted to be involved, to be with Daril...

Remembering, she bit the inside of her lip hard, again. She'd been so *stupid*, so careless.

She remembered the ring of them, holding hands on the roof at House Leandra, the full moon shining down. She remembered the crackle of the air as they began the ritual. She remembered the cringing terror as the demon appeared, staring hungrily round and pushing at its bounds. She remembered seeing Daril trying to greet it, trying to bargain with it, and realising cold in her belly that it was ignoring him. That it was waiting for something. She remembered seeing them all sweating and shaking, as they fought to hold the spell together. She remembered the moment when she realised that they couldn't.

And then she remembered Reb, landing on the roof at a run – where had she even *come* from? – with an older man behind her, shouting something at the demon. Then it was a blur of this and that, of the older man tackling the demon while Reb herded the rest of them downstairs. She'd missed Marcia, huddled in terror behind a chimney-stack. Reb had turned just in time to lasso the demon back from the old man, but not before it had crunched through one of his arms. Marcia had pulled herself together enough to crawl across the roof to the old man, trying to staunch the flow of blood, as Reb battled the demon back. Reb succeeded. Marcia didn't. The demon vanished, back to the other plane, Marcia assumed. The old man had died right there on the roof.

Marcia remembered Daril and Reb facing one another, wild-eyed. Neither of them had spared a glance for her, and, sobbing, she'd run for the door to the stairs, run through the house like the demon was still after her, down the street and back to her own House.

Cato had known, of course. Her mother had thought only that she'd had a bad end to a love affair. And that was true enough. Daril had sent a note; Marcia had burnt it unread, and then there were no more notes. Cato had been casually present whenever she needed him, cracking jokes and refusing to take anything seriously, letting her cry on his shoulder for hours at a time. Cato couldn't be working with Daril now. He would remember that. He would remember how much Marcia hated Daril, and how much Cato hated him on her behalf. He *couldn't* be doing this.

Cato had patiently supported her through dealing with the aftermath of the whole thing; then, just as she was emerging from her haze of curled-up misery, Cato had told Madeleine about his magic, and Madeleine had forbidden him from touching it again. And then Marcia was biting back more tears in Cato's room as he stuffed possessions into a bag, his face set and pale.

Madeleine had disowned him, formally, when she found out. Cato had shrugged and said he didn't care, when Marcia told him. He was settled down in the squats by then. She worried for him, but he shrugged and told her he'd be fine. Which, right enough, he had been, even through the plague. She'd nursed him through that, running backwards and forwards between the squats and House Fereno, consumed by an anxiety she couldn't speak of to her mother while Madeleine watched her with anxious eyes and didn't ask. He'd been fine. Neither of them knew how, and neither of them wanted to talk about it afterwards – why Cato, when so many others died? But he'd survived.

He was her brother. They'd always been there for one another, one way or another. For certain, they were less close now than they had been back then; it was ten years since they'd shared a roof, and in those ten years, Cato had created a niche for himself in the city's underworld and half-world. Marcia had become Fereno-Heir and spent her time dealing with the Council. But they were still there for one another. She trusted Cato. Reb couldn't be right.

She couldn't – she wouldn't – believe that he was doing this voluntarily, whatever it was that Daril was doing. Whatever Reb might say. Maybe he had been talking to a spirit, as she said. But Reb didn't know anything more than that. It might have been a perfectly reasonable thing to do. Or if it wasn't, it might have been that Daril was forcing him, once they were in private.

He was her *brother*. Marcia couldn't – wouldn't – let anything happen to Cato. If Reb wasn't going to help, she would damn well do it herself. She couldn't live with herself if she just let this go.

EIGHT

Reb stared at the door Marcia had just slammed. It reverberated slightly in its frame.

"Well then."

She couldn't think of anything else to say. She sighed and sat down again in the armchair. Its familiar sag comforted her.

"He is her brother," Beckett said. They were still standing by the wall. Reb hadn't yet seen Beckett sit down in an actual seat.

"And what would you know of human emotional ties?" Reb demanded, narrowing her eyes.

"Spirits have ties too, even if they are not human ones. And I have watched over Marek for three hundred years. Marek's humans have many emotional ties. It would hardly be possible for me to remain entirely ignorant of them. Blood ties are often among the strongest. And stronger still, sometimes, in another way, when they break."

Reb's parents were long dead, and she'd never had any siblings, but – yes, Beckett's words rang true. Marcia's bond with Cato might not have broken, but even Reb knew that Cato's mother had disowned him, though she'd long forgotten which of the Houses it was he'd come from. He'd flaunted the fact, for a while, when he first chose sorcery over the status of his birth. He'd claimed it as a badge of his commitment, aimed it at those who looked to treat him as a child still. He'd been barely sixteen. So Marcia was the only link remaining between Cato and the rest of their family. Was she trying to make up for that?

Beckett was still standing patiently by the wall. They moved less than a regular human would; they didn't fidget or sigh.

"Your kind have emotions, then?" Reb asked.

Beckett took a long moment to answer. "Yes," they said. "Emotions, and ties to one another. But not perhaps in the way that you know them. We –" They gestured in frustration as they visibly sought for words. "I do not think I can explain."

"Never mind," Reb said. "I was just curious. We would probably be better addressing ourselves to the problem in hand."

"Which is?" Beckett asked politely.

"Marek has no cityangel. Magic isn't working properly." Reb hesitated. "I know lots of sorcerer lore about how and why magic works, and what the cityangel does with it. But some of it's contradictory, and some of it's unlikely. You're a more reliable source. How does it, how did it, work?"

Beckett's eyes were unfocussed. They seemed to be looking off at something in the distance. "I made a deal with Rufus Marek and Eli Beckett, when they first came to Marek and stopped on what is now Marekhill, and recognised it as a suitable trading location. Power for power."

"Power for power?"

"Humans have power, simply by existing, but only rarely can you use it. Can, or do? I have never been sure. My kind can only access it, as a rule, in certain situations, by making certain limited agreements. Or by – doing other things. Things most of us prefer not to do. The deal gave me access to a city's worth of human life-power, and in exchange I am," Beckett hesitated, then corrected themself, their voice dropping a little, "that is, I was, bound to the city. It seemed fair to all of us."

"So, what, you're *draining* us?" Reb asked, and resisted the urge to back away.

Beckett shook their head. "Humans – you expend power anyway, all the time, simply by existing. This merely means I collect it – I collected it – rather than it drifting away."

"Life-magic," Reb said, slowly. "Blood-magic, but without the blood."

"Indeed," Beckett agreed. "Humans can access their own power with blood, or they can make individual deals with one such as myself. Or one of my kind can use human power," they hesitated, "more directly."

"Demons," Reb said.

Beckett frowned at her in curiosity.

"Spirits who use human power without permission. Which

generally means human blood. We call them demons."

"But they are merely the same kind as I, but acting in a particular way," Beckett said. "They need no separate word."

Reb shrugged. "Maybe so. But that's what we call them. Or those who are prepared to deal with a human offering the blood of others."

Beckett nodded slowly. "I see."

"So," Reb said. "The cityangel – you – is indeed what allows Marek magic to work. What made us a city of sorcerers, without the blood of sorcery elsewhere." A city, once, before the plague. Before there were only her and Cato left. "Why didn't you *help*?" It burst out of her, unintended.

"Help?" Beckett asked.

"If you're bound to Marek. If you were all about mediating magic here. Why did you just let so many of us *die*, in the plague."

Beckett looked down at their hands. "I could not help," they said softly. "I cannot – I have power, I can help Marek be stable, I can pour that power to you again, but I could not interfere in the way you mean." They looked up again. "I tried. When I realised. I did try. For myself, not only when asked. I tried." An aching loss was in their voice, a loss that echoed the ache in Reb's own heart.

Reb remembered asking, remembered spell after spell, remembered finally breaking her word to Zareth and spilling her blood into her bowl, and none of it, nothing she did, working.

She swallowed. "Well. Let's – I don't want to talk about it any more." She looked away, tried to find her way back to the now. "So. Someone removed you, and now Marek magic isn't working. Did they *know* that would happen? Is that what they wanted?"

"I do not know," Beckett said. "Perhaps. But perhaps they sought only to remake the deal I made with Marek and Beckett. Perhaps they expected only to summon me, not to unbind me. Or to unbind me and rebind me, and were as surprised as I was by my fall. Or perhaps they had another candidate in mind. Perhaps they assumed another candidate would appear." They pursed their lips, the first truly human expression Reb had seen on their face. "In truth, I might have expected that too. There is surely," they gestured, shaping something in front of them, "a hole, where I once was. A hole of power."

"So if they were expecting something like that, it didn't work," Reb said. "Which might explain why Cato is now involved."

"You are assuming then that Daril b'Leandra is indeed responsible, and that Cato and he are connected."

Reb shrugged. "Something magical goes wrong. Daril is on Cato's doorstep the next day. Not a huge stretch to connect the two, given how few sorcerers there are around now, and that Cato is the one, of the two of us, who is known to deal with spirits, and whose morals are more flexible. Especially if Daril told Marcia, or at least strongly implied, that Cato is with him now." She frowned. "Though – if we have the timing right, there must be at least one other sorcerer, somewhere in Marek, and I missed them. Someone must have unbound you." Which was a thought both alarming and very slightly hopeful. Might she have missed others? But then, how could she have missed even one? How had she not been paying attention? "Daril has no magical talent. He must be working with someone who does, someone strong enough to break the bond, but someone who for whatever reason could not fill it again, and now wants backup. Enter Cato." She nodded slowly to herself. "Daril having an intense interest in power – well, his House is among the highest in the city, so it doesn't entirely make sense, but he has form for such things, and it's not like greed is unfamiliar."

There was a silence between them.

Did Daril and Cato even intend to solve the problem? Daril must have done this for a reason. Would he even want to replace the cityangel? Was his aim simply to destroy Marek's magic altogether?

If Marek's magic were truly gone, what would it mean for the city? Or for her? Could she, would she have to, just... stop? No longer be a sorcerer? The idea grated inside her like broken glass. But perhaps she'd brought this on herself. She'd let herself slide into the small magics of the day-to-day; she'd stopped thinking about Marek's magic as a whole. She'd stopped thinking, if she was honest, about the reality of the cityangel, or about her responsibilities.

And now it was gone, and there was nothing she could do about it but wait to see if someone else – someone she didn't even start to trust – could fix it.

Or she could return to the old ways.

The thought came from nowhere, and it stunned her for a moment. The old ways; the ways that still operated everywhere that wasn't Marek. The blood magic she'd abandoned when she came here. Hope leapt inside her. Maybe, after all, she could change this, right now. Could restore Beckett, and make it all right again. Could make it not matter that she'd stopped watching over Marek's magic, that she'd let this thing happen in the first place.

If – if – she was prepared to let herself use blood magic again. She swallowed against her suddenly dry throat. She'd promised herself. She'd promised Zareth, too, long ago, when she came to Marek, and he agreed to teach her. But if ever there was a reason sufficient to break that vow (again... but she did her damnedest never to think of anything that had happened during the plague), surely, this was it. And after all, what were the alternatives, now? If she could fix it, if there was even a possibility that she could fix it, how could she not take it?

"Well." She tried to sound decisive, certain, but her voice was shaking just a little. "I don't think I want to wait around and see who Daril and Cato and whoever else Daril has persuaded to join him recruit to fill the gap. If they intend to do that at all. So I suggest we fix it."

"You can put me back?" Beckett said with evident surprise.

"I can *try*," Reb corrected them.

She unbolted the workroom door and let Beckett follow her in. Her skin was tingling slightly as she took down the small leather case. She was doing this to restore her city's magic. That made it right. It would make up for her mistakes.

"Regular Marek-magic doesn't work, because that relies on you to mediate it. And we hardly want to bring another spirit into this affair, do we now? But what doesn't rely on you, or anyone else, to mediate it, is blood-magic." She opened the case. "Let's go."

☉ ☉

Marcia stopped at House Fereno for long enough to dig out a plain, nondescript tunic and wide trousers that she would never normally dream of wearing in public. With a scarf over her hair, at least she wouldn't be obvious from a distance. She couldn't really hope for more than that; either Cato or Daril would be certain to recognise her if they got a good look at her face, and covering it properly would look absurdly suspicious.

She walked briskly down the street towards House Leandra at the other end. There was a slight wind blowing, ruffling her scarf. She could do this. She just had to get in. Even in a half-shut House like Leandra, run by someone as parsimonious as Gavin Leandra, there were always people in and out. People came to the back doors even if they weren't visiting at the front.

There were alleyways between each of the Houses, wide enough to allow access round to the back, for anyone not wishing, or not suitable, to come to the main formal entrance. Coming up to the corner of the House just before House Leandra, she slowed a little, bracing herself and rehearsing her strategy, envisaging herself turning the corner and walking down towards their back gate.

It was just as well that she'd slowed down; she heard someone talking, just around the corner, coming closer from the alleyway towards the main street. She couldn't hear the words, but she could never have mistaken Daril's voice, sharp and excited. She span round to her left, and stepped over to the kerb, as if she were about to cross the street, a second or so before she and Daril would have come face to face.

☉

Beckett hadn't reacted to Reb's declaration, not in any way. Reb wasn't sure if she'd expected them to.

But they didn't stop her when she opened the case. Reb didn't usually allow other people in her workroom. But Beckett should be here for this. In fact, would probably need to be, unless she wanted to take their blood in the other room.

She bolted the door again behind them. You couldn't risk anyone coming in in the middle of any kind of sorcery; still less in the middle of this particular ritual. Blood magic wasn't just risky for the caster; it was illegal in Marek, and highly restricted in Teren, and everywhere around the Oval Sea where it wasn't banned outright.

Outside of Marek, it was also one of the few ways to access anything like real sorcery. That was where Reb had started off, out in the mountains of Teren, before she'd saved enough money to make her way to Marek, and the promise of Marek's sorcery. She'd looked for a teacher, and found Zareth, and Zareth had made her promise not to touch blood magic again.

But Zareth was dead now, and so was anyone else who would have told her not to do this.

☉

Under the guise of checking for traffic along the road – there was a heavy delivery cart coming up the street – Marcia turned round enough to look at Daril and whoever he was talking to. She could see only their backs now, but her heart lurched, then lurched again. Cato was behind him. Even in a hooded cloak, she knew his gait, his slight limp, that one holdover from the wretched plague.

They weren't looking back; as far as she could tell, they hadn't spotted her. The street was busy enough here that one more person wouldn't stand out in the crowd. She stepped back from the kerb, and began to trail them, far enough back that she didn't think she would be obvious. Either of them would probably recognise her if they turned around and she was close, even dressed like this. Cato most certainly would. Though, it was Cato, her brother, and she was here to help him. Would it matter if he saw her?

She didn't care to risk it.

But she was here, following them, and she could see Cato. The sense of *doing* something was intoxicating. What exactly she was going to do, she didn't quite know yet. But there would be something. There had to be something.

Daril was a couple of steps ahead of Cato, his back stiff.

Couldn't Cato make a run for it? Could she just grab him and run? Then she got a better look at them through the crowd in the street, and realised that there was another man there, shorter by a head than both Daril and Cato, walking at Cato's sleeve.

The other man's head turned slightly, and, with a shock, she recognised him, from that rooftop ten years ago. Urso – a cousin of sorts of Daril's, who'd had a small amount of talent. But surely not enough to do whatever it was they were doing here? Although – that, presumably, was why they wanted Cato. She squinted at the three of them. Urso didn't exactly look physically strong, Daril was up ahead not paying attention. Couldn't Cato make a break for it?

Unless Cato really does want to be there.

She thrust the thought away. If Urso was a sorcerer too, maybe he had more on Cato than Marcia thought. That would explain it.

☉

Beckett stood by the closed workroom door and watched Reb take the instruments out of their case and lay them out, ready for use. She expected her fingers to shake, but they were rock steady. She laid the twin steel blades – silver was traditional but not essential, and it did tarnish annoyingly – next to the vials, and took out the wide-mouthed container for the later stages of the spell.

"What will you do?" Beckett asked. "This can hardly be an established protocol."

"Make it up as I go along," Reb said, flippantly, then made herself focus. "I know a little of the protocols for speaking with spirits, though of course you're already here in this case; and a lot more of the protocols for banishing them. Though the last time I did that it was Marek-style magic."

"I remember," Beckett said.

Ten years ago. In her mind's eye, she saw Marcia that night, an overwhelmed, terrified teenager suddenly realising what she'd been involved with. The woman Reb had met yesterday, Marekhill-poised to her fingertips, was nothing at all like that girl.

Marcia hadn't saved Zareth. She'd tried, to give the child

credit, but neither she nor Reb had managed it. Maybe Reb could have, if she hadn't been banishing that damned demon at the time, but if she hadn't done that they'd all have been in even more trouble. And then again, if she hadn't tried to save Zareth, she might have caught Daril b'Leandra; but she hadn't done that either, and she hadn't been able to make anything stick to him afterwards. The other sorcerers of the Group had held her back from throwing herself at Marekhill privilege, arguing that they couldn't risk upsetting the balance between Marekhill and sorcery. Marekhill rules banned sorcery amongst their own, and turned a blind eye to it in the rest of the city. House Leandra would have torn the whole edifice down, Reb's colleagues insisted, if that was needed to defend one of its own. Reb and Zareth had stopped the raising, and there was no sign that Daril b'Leandra was about to repeat the experience, and whilst Zareth's death was a tragedy, taking House Leandra down and sorcery down with it wasn't going to bring him back.

They might even have been right. But Reb wasn't in a state to hear that, back then.

And somewhere in the years since, gradually, Reb had abandoned the magics which were about looking after the city, the magics that had belonged to the Group. She'd limited herself to spells and charms for people in need, and told herself (accurately enough, even) that it was good and useful, and (less accurately) that it was enough. Then there had been the plague, and after she'd emerged from the swamp-thick months of nursing and burying and fruitlessly seeking a solution; after she'd forgiven herself for the trick of biology that brought her through it with nothing more than a winter cough; after that, the idea of returning to true sorcery (alone? With Cato of all people, the only other survivor?) had seemed laughable. Minor charms. That would keep her busy, and damn the rest of it.

Now here she was, with something truly important, and even now she wasn't returning to the work of the Group. She was using a form of magic she'd sworn off when she first came to Marek, barely an adult.

Zareth would know how important this was.

Would he? a tiny voice in the back of her head asked.

Daril was moving fast, and Cato and Urso were struggling a little to keep up. Marcia nearly bumped into people several times, trying to keep them in sight, getting sworn at more than once. Obviously her disguise was more effective than she'd thought. People never swore at her when she looked like Fereno-Heir. She could read some of Daril's emotions from the way he was moving, a frantic excited anxiety that she'd last seen... She swallowed. The last time. Anxiety churned her stomach.

House Fereno was in sight at the end of the street, and Marcia wondered if she saw Cato tense, for just a second. He looked calm otherwise, moving with the laid-back slouch that disguised his limp.

The three of them turned up the narrow alleyway next to House Fereno, which led up towards the Park. After a moment's hesitation, Marcia doubled back and turned down the mouth of the alleyway before the House she was just passing. She was too likely to be seen if she followed them up that quieter street; they'd only have to glance back over a shoulder. But she should be able to catch them again at the top... Coming out at the other end of the alley, a House garden back wall to each side, she was rewarded by the sight of the three of them walking into the scrubland at the edge of the Park.

She hesitated. How could she follow them in the open ground of the Park? As always during the day, there were groups of people strolling in different directions. Where could Daril be headed? She let them go as far as she dared, then came out herself, walking diagonally across their track, ready to turn again in a few moments, like a sailboat tacking. She tried to look like she was sauntering aimlessly, stopping to admire this plant or to stare back down the hill towards the city. But as far as she could see, none of them so much as turned to look behind them.

She realised then where they were going. Where they must be going. The monument, right at the top of the hill. The monument to Marek's founders, Eli Beckett and Rufus Marek, who had done that first deal with the cityangel (with

Beckett); the monument that had Rufus Marek himself buried under it. She could keep going around the hill, spiral up it... And then, maybe, she would get there in time.

And then what?

She would think of something. She had to think of something.

☉

"Well then," Reb said, and picked the knives up. She drew the first knife across the inside of her arm, then swapped it for the first vial. Wordlessly, Beckett held out their arm for the second knife, and the second vial.

Beckett's blood smelt different to hers, sour-sweet.

She took a deep breath. The next stage would be to mix them together in the bowl, and bind them together for the summoning-and-banishment which she was trying to piece together in her head; banish-and-summon Beckett *to* their true place, rather than away from here. Bind them to the gaping hole around Marek.

☉

As Marcia got closer, she saw that the area around the monument was unusually empty; then, saw a couple strolling together up the hill smoothly change their course to head away again, apparently unaware. Cato must be doing something. Even thinking about that, as she got closer, she found herself turning to move away, finding it strangely important that she go down the hill, not up, why up? She had to stop for a moment to persuade herself to go against that urge. It was Cato. It was just Cato. She could ignore it. Cato's manipulations had never worked well on her.

She was sweating by the time she stopped behind a clump of trees a little way from the monument. Daril and Cato and Urso were visible nearly at the top. She leant against a tree with her back to them, and racked her brains. Whatever they were doing here, it had to be to do with the cityangel. Up at the monument, how could it be anything else? But what? Beckett had fallen, from what they and Reb had said, before Cato's disappearance. So the fall must have been Urso, nothing to do with Cato. And they were recruiting Cato – to fix whatever problem the fall had left them with. Such as, for example, not having a cityangel.

She wanted, desperately, to believe that they were going to reinstate Beckett themselves, that Cato was working with Daril voluntarily because Daril had realised it was all a terrible mistake. Cato just saving the situation. But…

But that didn't ring even slightly true.

Had it really been a good idea to walk out on Reb and Beckett like that? Certainly, Reb had been hugely insulting, but… She rolled the beads of her bracelet between her fingers, staring outwards over the river. She wanted, very badly, to fetch Reb up here; but there was no time to do that. She had to save Cato. That was what she was here for. Save him from whatever he was being forced into. He had to be being forced. He couldn't be working with Daril of his own accord. And that meant that whatever it was Daril was planning – she didn't want it to happen. Whatever it was, it was bound to be a bad idea.

She looked round, trying still not to be seen, not to be noticed. Urso and Cato were facing one another, just to one side of the statue; Daril stood slightly to one side. He was staying out of the magic itself this time, then? Maybe he had learnt something last time. Just not enough. Daril gestured to Urso, and Marcia knew. It was now.

The only thing she could think of was to disrupt the ritual. Any way she could. Surely, if she timed it right, surely just that would be enough? And she wasn't entirely on her own. Once Cato knew she was there, he would help her. He would.

She made her way between clumps of trees, moving whenever none of them were looking in her direction. Daril had his back to her. She could only see the edge of Urso' cloak and shoulder past the bulk of the monument. She could see Cato clearly, but he was looking at the monument.

The he looked over, straight at her. His look was, for a fraction of a second, sincerely apologetic, like all those times in their childhood…

Then her head rang as if she'd been hit inside it with a giant bell, despite the fact that no one was near her. Lights flickered across her vision, and the muscles in her legs gave way. She hit the floor, and blacked out.

☉

Reb was lifting the first vial to pour when it happened.

She could never after describe it in words, that seismic shock that reverberated through her skull. It made the physical effects – her flying across the room; the noise of both vials and the bowl shattering; the nasty crack as she landed on her wrist – all feel unimportant.

She never forgot Beckett's face, in that moment. The incomprehensible loss carved deep across it for a fraction of a second before Beckett shuttered it away.

She'd missed her moment. She'd broken her promise, and it hadn't even mattered.

"They did it," Reb whispered hoarsely, as the pain of her arm – broken, she was miserably aware – filtered through. "Daril, Cato. They replaced you."

NINE

Jonas' efforts to sleep late that morning had been sabotaged, initially by Asa, with the room opposite his, banging doors first thing in the morning; then by the sun coming bright through the window. That, he supposed, was the downside of sleeping in a room fully open to the sun. Usually he just got up at daybreak. He really should get curtains; he understood now what land-dwellers saw in them. Except he'd be leaving here soon. Wouldn't he?

He burrowed under his blankets and sought sleep again; but it was patchy and full of dreams that alarmed him yet fled like minnows through his mental fingers as he surfaced towards wakefulness. He woke for good, thick-mouthed and muzzy-headed, in the late morning. Thumbing sleep from the corners of his eyes, he remembered his intention of visiting Kia for that early lunch. It seemed less appealing now than it had in the early watches; but then again, running messages on an empty stomach to get the coin to fill up that stomach didn't appeal much either. And now Asa was out he couldn't even get a loan off them.

And it was still better a time of his choosing than to be watching over his shoulder for Kia.

He hesitated for a moment over dress. Salinas formal was overkill, tempting though it was in the cause of making a point. His shipboard wear would do well enough, except that then it would be near-impossible to find jobs afterwards, even with an armband; he'd look like a sailor and no one would believe he knew the streets. He didn't want to have to come back home yet again, and he was flat broke; he had to do *some* work today. He pulled Marek trousers and shirt, the neatest and cleanest of the lot, out of his chest, and Kia would have to like it. That made a point, too, of course; that he *had* Marek clothes, that he had a job and a place in the city, without her sponsorship.

He dressed rapidly and threw the window wide. Sitting on

the window ledge, he wriggled further and further outwards, feet dangling over the three storeys below, until he could twist round, grab the helpfully uneven brick to one side of the window and the top of the window frame, and pull himself up and onto his feet. From there it was an easy couple of moves to the roof itself, and away towards the Old Bridge and Marek Square. He liked being up here, the air fresher than at street level, the city laid out before him the way it had been from the top of Marekhill the night before. He could see properly, up here.

He had to drop down to street level to cross the bridge, and the smells of the various food carts he passed tugged at his empty stomach. The walk felt longer than usual, and Jonas rubbed more than once at his eyes, stinging still with tiredness, on the way. The embassy was on the far side of Marek Square from the Old Bridge, at the foot of Marekhill, a few roofs away from the Guildhall he'd sat on last night. The young woman who answered the door looked very much like she was about to turn him away until he told her his name, with heavy emphasis on "t'Riseri". She blinked at him, eyes wide.

"Oh, of course. I didn't realise..." She broke off and flapped a hand at him, then ushered him into a waiting room.

Of course. Salinas to everyone in this benighted city. Marek to his own people here, just from the clothes. As if he didn't look Salinas anyway, regardless of what he wore.

The waiting room had a combination of traditional shipboard decor and Marek-style furniture and paintings, presumably to set what would mostly be Mareker visitors at ease. But he didn't have long to look around before Kia arrived.

"Jonas!" Kia said, throwing her arms open as she hurried in. "The way you were yesterday, I quite expected to have to seek you out myself. But here you are. How splendid."

Kia, annoyingly, looked fresh and awake and nothing like Jonas felt.

"Perhaps you could use lunch?" she added.

For that, he could forgive a great deal. She led him to what was clearly her office, a small room deeply reminiscent of the captain's cabin in all the ships he'd been on, but with three good Marek-style chairs and a table between them which the maid, introduced as Xera, was already busily loading food onto. Kia gestured him to a seat, and Jonas let himself relax into it as he reached for a Salinas-style bread wrap. Just for a moment, he indulged himself with the idea that he was back home, on board any one of the ships his mother had captained when he was a child.

It wasn't quite as reassuring as he wanted it to be.

"So," Kia said, after the requisite few moments of silence in courtesy to the food had passed. "You were with Fereno-Heir last night. How on the seas do you know her?"

"We met when she was across in the squats looking for her brother," Jonas said. "She was curious as to what a Salinas lad might be doing in Marek, and invited me out for the evening."

"When she believed you living in the squats?" Kia said with a frown. "Or did you admit to your background?"

Jonas shrugged. "We chatted for a while. I believe she understood enough not to expect me to attend the ball in messenger-garb." Well, she hadn't, if only because she'd been ready to dress him herself.

"Well," Kia said, pursing her lips. "House Fereno. You could do worse."

Jonas blinked. "Marcia – what? No. I do not – we have barely met! We are merely friends, I assure you."

"As you say," Kia said, shrugging. "She is a pleasant enough young woman, though, and from one of the Thirteen Houses." She looked sharply at him. "So Marek has not gained your loyalty from Salina, then?"

This conversation kept taking unexpected turns. "Loyalty? No. No, I do not intend to become Mareker, if that is your meaning. I am hoping to take passage when the ships leave after Year-end."

It was true. Wasn't it? And what if he hadn't solved his little problem by then? But he could hardly mention that to Kia.

"So soon?" Kia said. "Well. Very wise. The climate here doesn't grow on one, I have to say. I miss the open sea." She sounded wistful. "Still. Fereno-Heir is a useful person to know. I am acquainted with the family myself."

Slowly, too slowly Jonas caught up with her meaning. Diplomacy. House Fereno must be involved in something that Kia, and Salina in general, had an interest in.

"You wanted to speak to her," he remembered.

"And she may well hold to that agreement anyway," Kia agreed. "But it might not hurt if her young Salinas friend was involved." She nodded at Jonas. "Ne?"

"I... Of course," Jonas said, helplessly. "If it would be of assistance."

Kia nodded briskly. "My thanks." She hesitated again, obviously thinking something over. "In fact, someone else involved in this particular issue will be here later today. Perhaps you should meet him."

Jonas blinked at her, feeling trapped. His mother would have his hide if Kia asked for assistance and he didn't provide. But neither did he want to be embroiled in some complicated matter of diplomacy that kept him from his purpose here. The purpose he'd already been neglecting for entirely long enough. If he really meant to leave in the next week... He narrowly restrained himself from grimacing. A week. Put like that, it seemed rather unlikely; but if Beckett held the key, it could be done by tomorrow. Still. This kind of involvement was *exactly* why he had been avoiding the embassy, damn Kia's hide. He sought for a way to refuse.

"Although," Kia added, "perhaps I should warn you... The young man – Urso, his name is – has quite the interest in magic." She wrinkled her nose. "I have traded some of my own ocean experiences with spirits with him – one must fulfil one's diplomatic obligations. And he has been a good friend, a good trading partner, over the years I have been here. One is more prepared to discuss these things with friends, ne? And to forgive a friend the odd strange interest. But if you would react badly, perhaps... Well, I would not wish to insult him."

Jonas' heart leapt. "He's not a sorcerer himself, is he?" he asked, playing up the doubt Kia would expect to see.

"No, no," she assured him. "There are scarce any sorcerers in Marek now. I suppose one must regret any loss of life, but with an illness quite as focussed as that plague was, well, it is hard not to conclude that magic *does* have consequences, ne?

But in any case – no, Urso has an academic interest, is all. A collector of tales."

And one who collected tales might have collected tales of interest to Jonas.

"Well," Jonas said, trying to keep his tone light. "I have been six months in Marek. I am sure I can manage not to embarrass you."

"Excellent," Kia said with a smile.

Perhaps this visit would pay off, after all, in more than just bread wraps. Reminded, he took another wrap.

Just as he was swallowing his mouthful, a flicker hit. Three figures on a hill. He recognised Daril's height and half-shaved head; with him, forming a loose circle, stood a man with red-brown hair, posture indolent but power fairly crackling from him, and someone else who Jonas could see only from behind. Marcia sprawled flat on grass, her head to one side and her eyes closed. Then the flicker switched location with a lurch that nearly brought Jonas' bread wrap back up; to Reb in a small room with a scalpel, head bent down over her arm. Beckett's tall gangly silhouette, still against a wall. Something rang in Jonas' head, like a cracked bell, and his mental vision went entirely blank, pure white across the inside of his eyelids. The air felt different, wrong, around him. Another flicker pasted over the white, Beckett in Reb's room, staggering and falling, Reb's startled face, a broken bowl...

The cityangel. There was a new cityangel. That wasn't a flicker; it wasn't a flash of the future. That was, Jonas knew down to his bones as undeniable truth, *now*.

He was coughing on the mouthful of wrap, and Kia was on her feet, thumping his back and looking concerned.

"Jonas? Are you all right?"

"'M fine," he wheezed, reaching for water. "Just – went down the wrong way. Really. Fine."

He should go and find Reb and Beckett and Marcia. Even if it was all too late.

"Well. This fellow Urso is due at sixteen hours. You're welcome to stay here until then, use the library, have a rest."

"No, no," Jonas said hastily, deeply though he wished he could just stay peacefully here, just for a few hours. "Things to do. I'll be back before then."

He couldn't just leave them to it. He had to go to Reb's.

Kia was looking him up and down. "We've some spare Salinas wear, not quite the formal you had last night, but for afternoon…"

He could be insulted by the suggestion that he couldn't dress himself; but it saved a return to his rooms, and if he was to visit Reb *and* get some jobs in, before sixteen hours… And he still hadn't asked Beckett about his flickers. Could Beckett even answer, now? What would Beckett *do* with themselves, if there was now a cityangel again?

"That would be helpful," he said. "I promise, I'll be back with time to spare."

He couldn't get out of the embassy fast enough.

☉ ☉

Despite the hurry he'd been in leaving the embassy, as he walked over Old Bridge, Jonas' steps began to slow. It had happened now, after all. Was it all that urgent? Was he really all that keen to go running into what would doubtless be a scene of regret and perhaps recrimination?

He did very much want to speak to Beckett. But perhaps it would make more sense to get a job or two in on the way there.

"Hey! Jonas!"

He turned to find Tam running up behind him.

"Someone asking for you over by the market."

He gave the address. Reb.

"Dunno why she'd pay me to tell you to get over there rather than just give the job to me. Mind you, sorcerers – you knew she was a sorcerer, right? – always a bit weird." He peered more closely at Jonas. "Hey, friend, you don't look so good. Late night last night?"

"Yeah," Jonas said, rubbing the heels of his hands against his eyes.

"Not like you, friend," Tam said. "Never seen you drink more than one or two, hey?"

Jonas opened his mouth to say that it wasn't the beer, then

closed it again. "Met an old friend," he said instead, which had the advantage of being true.

"Down in the docks?" Tam asked, nodding away. Jonas didn't bother correcting him. "They drink hard down there, true. Hope you had a good one, anyway. You sure you'll take this job, hey?"

"Got to pay for the beer somehow, right?" Jonas asked, and turned away from Tam's grin to start towards the old market.

If Reb was asking for him, that solved the question of what he should do when. And it made sense to ask Beckett as soon as he could, now, anyway, in case Beckett's memories of their past were about to change. Jonas shivered slightly. Three hundred years, and now, suddenly, everything different. He didn't care to imagine how Beckett was feeling.

Marcia opened the door when he got there. She was clad in an incongruously down-at-heel tunic and trousers, with a blanket round her shoulders. There were dark rings under her eyes.

Jonas was about to say something about the new cityangel, then remembered that none of this lot knew about his flickers, and he had no intention of letting them know. Although if everyone had felt what he did – had they? Or was that just a sort of a flicker? He didn't want to risk it.

"Got a message," he said instead. "Reb's after me?"

He followed Marcia into the house. Reb sat on a stool next to the fireplace. She had a cracking bruise coming up across her cheekbone, deep scratches across her right arm with some kind of unguent smeared on them, and from the splint and bandages on the table and the ginger way she was holding her arm, a broken wrist. She looked bad, but not nearly as bad as the apparently un-injured Beckett. Beckett's face was gaunt and hollow, and there was something dark burning behind their eyes. Jonas repressed another shiver.

"What in the seas has been going on here?" he asked, trying to sound innocent and ignorant.

"They replaced the cityangel," Reb said succinctly.

"What, there's another one now? Not Beckett?" Jonas avoided looking at Beckett. He wasn't sure he could bear to.

"That's about the size of it."

They didn't expect him to have noticed, obviously, which

meant that that feeling of absence, of the world turning around him – that must have been a flicker. Even if it had felt different from any other flicker he'd ever had. But then, he'd never been around when something like that had happened.

"Apparently, one wouldn't have wanted to be halfway through doing magic at the time," Marcia said, with a lift of her eyebrows. She came over to kneel in front of Reb, and her voice gentled. "Are you sure you don't want a proper healer?"

"No," Reb said. "It's a clean break. It'll be fine. Just do what I told you. Splint it, bind it nice and tight, ignore me swearing."

Marcia looked a little doubtful but she picked up the splints and laid them carefully along Reb's arm.

"So – do you know who did it?" Jonas asked, trying not to think about Reb doing magic. Actual real magic. The idea made him feel a bit sick.

"Daril. Cato. Some other sorcerer."

Marcia's words were clipped and precise. She didn't stop wrapping bandages around Reb's arm. Reb hissed as Marcia pulled the bandage up to tighten it before wrapping again.

"Some other sorcerer I didn't *know* of," Reb grumbled. "Someone who's been *hiding*. And I didn't notice." She didn't seem to be expecting anyone to answer.

"How do you know?" Jonas asked Marcia.

"I was there," Marcia said. "Followed them from House Leandra, up to Marekhill Park, and the monument. Technically I didn't *see* them, what with Cato knocking me out and all, but I saw enough. And Beckett felt it."

For a moment, Jonas thought of admitting that he had, too. The idea of sharing his burden – maybe they could help, if he explained properly, maybe Reb would think of something. He thrust the idea away. He couldn't tell people. He couldn't tell *anyone*. He'd always known that.

He wandered around the room, and felt a sudden shock as he passed the inner door into Reb's workshop. A shadow of what he'd felt at Cato's, when Reb was performing sorcery... He swallowed. He didn't want his flickers to mean that he could feel sorcery. He didn't want to feel sorcery. He wanted *rid* of this.

Marcia had finished binding up Reb's arm. But it was Reb who put her good hand on Marcia's shoulder, as if to comfort her, and Marcia leaned very slightly into her. Well. It must be a shock, to be clipped over the head by your brother, sorcerously or otherwise.

"So then," Jonas said. "Is that it, then? Does that mean your magic is working again, Reb? If there's a cityangel again."

Beckett's shoulders flinched, and Jonas realised he could probably have put that better, or at least more gently.

"Haven't tried it yet," Reb said, scowling down at her arm, then wincing and touching the bruise on her face. "Ought to, I suppose."

"But I don't understand what he *wants*," Marcia said.

"Your brother?" Jonas asked.

"Daril," Marcia said, her lips tightening. "This must be in aid of something. What does he want?"

"What did he want last time?" Reb asked.

Marcia shook her head irritably. "That was – we were children. Foolish children. Even Daril was barely twenty-one."

Jonas, just turned nineteen, closed his mouth on his response.

"This time – he wouldn't do this for, I don't know, just for a laugh. He must *want* something."

"Can't be money," Reb said. "Can't be power, not the heir of Leandra."

"He's not Heir," Marcia and Jonas both said together.

"What?" Reb frowned.

"He's not Leandra-Heir," Marcia said. "It's been a, well, a bit of a joke for a long time. Gavin Leandra is a bitter old man, and Daril won't dance to his tune." Marcia snorted. "The more he shows off his independence, the more the old man baulks. Everyone's constantly expecting him to be disinherited altogether, but it's been going on for years now." Her eyes were suddenly bleak, and Jonas wondered what had happened to Cato and his own House inheritance, when he left Marekhill. "He makes light of it, Daril does, in public, and," she hesitated, "he mostly did from the start, but – I know he feels something about it."

"I thought he'd have it automatically," Reb said.

Marcia shook her head. "That's not how it works." She frowned. "Didn't you know that?"

Reb shrugged. "Can't say I give much of a shit about Marekhill politics, truth be told. Doesn't really matter which high-born idiot takes over from which other high-born idiot, does it?" She eyed Marcia sideways, looking a little guilty. "Saving your presence, and all that."

Marcia shrugged in turn. "I know enough high-born idiots, thank you. In any case. It's not automatic. Heir is usually the eldest child, but it doesn't have to be. It's down to the Head. It doesn't happen so often, if there is an eldest child, that someone else is named, but Gavin Leandra would certainly do it, if he felt it were best." She paused, staring into space. "Power. Daril always wanted power." She was fiddling with her bracelet. "If he were finally to believe that he'd never be Head, and he went looking for other options…"

"Could he?" Reb asked.

Marcia and Reb were looking at each other, wide-eyed.

"Could he what?" Jonas asked, impatient.

"Overthrow the Council," Reb said.

"He's been talking to my generation," Marcia said. "About the way that the Heads aren't handing over their power. I was wondering what he was up to, but… You wouldn't need that much, if it came down to it. Enough to swing the balance behind you. The Council have a good eye for the main chance, and then there's the Guilds. Get them onside, get rid of a few of the older Heads, replace them with younger ones who think Daril got them their chance…"

"But is it anything to do with Beckett?" Jonas asked. "As I recall, that's where you and I, Reb, came in in the first place."

It came out blunter than he'd intended.

"Why does Daril care who the cityangel is, you mean?" Marcia asked.

It wasn't quite what he'd intended, but he let that slide.

"Can the cityangel make any political moves?" Reb asked.

"No magic in the Council," Marcia said, automatically, then paused. "But Daril wouldn't give a shit about that rule, if there's no enforcement of it."

"The covenant." It was the first thing Beckett had said

since Jonas arrived, and they all jumped. "The covenant prevents interference with the political rule of the city." Beckett was looking at the floor, not at any of them.

"So that can't be it," Marcia said, irritably. "Except – wait. The covenant." A sick look was creeping over her face. "It applied to you, because you made it, with Rufus Marek and Eli Beckett, that's what you said. So – would it apply to the new one?"

"I do not know," Beckett said, still without looking up.

"Possibly not," Reb said. "They might have put something in place when they did the ritual, of course."

"But it might not have been the same as before," Marcia said. She swallowed. "It would make a lot of sense, if that's what's happened. Daril would be prepared to do – a lot, to get that sort of backup." She took a deep breath. "So. Can we do anything about it?"

Reb looked over at Marcia, her expression unreadable. "What has this done to the magic? That would be my question, first."

Marcia stared at her.

"I mean – politics. Does it matter, to us, if one person or another is in charge? I've never noticed a damn difference. My job is magic. Looking after the magic needn't mean looking after the Council."

Jonas, despite himself, was impressed at her hard-headedness.

"But what about Beckett?" Marcia demanded. "Are you just abandoning them, too?"

Reb looked over at Beckett.

"I don't know if I can do anything," she said, after a moment, quietly. "I don't know if what was done today can be undone."

"I do not know either," Beckett said, their head bowed. "I cannot – I still cannot return to the other plane. If that is relevant. But I cannot... I do not know who I *am*." Their voice was very quiet.

"But –" Reb hesitated. "If I can do anything, without risking the city, I will. This is not *right*. I don't care about the politics of it, but it is not *right*."

Marcia had a mutinous look on her face, but Reb didn't let

her start talking.

"So. Before anything else, we need to find out whether Beckett's place truly is taken. Whether there is a Marek cityangel again, and whether it is acting as Beckett did."

"Which means magic?" Jonas asked.

"Yes," Reb said, fingers tapping irritably against her thigh. "I'm not sure there's much I can do alone, though."

Jonas shifted uncomfortably in his chair. There was no way on this earth he was about to offer to help with anything magical. He wondered if it would be better just to find a pretext to clear out right now, before he found himself engaging in some sorcery or other the same way he'd found himself at a posh Marekhill party. But no one else in the room seemed to be paying much attention to him, and he relaxed a little.

"Any you can do *with* help?" Marcia asked Reb.

Reb jerked upright and stared at her. "Is that an offer?"

Marcia flushed slightly. "If needed."

"You said you've no magic." Reb sounded suspicious.

"And I have not," Marcia said, her chin going up. "I assure you on my honour. But I used to help Cato."

"Well, thank you," Reb started, just as the market clock chimed the hour.

Marcia's eyes widened, counting the chimes. "Oh no," she said. "I must... I promised my mother. I need to go home, right away. But I promise I will return as soon as I can."

She dumped the blanket off her shoulders and was out of the door in seconds.

"Well," said Reb, after a moment, still staring after Marcia. "I suppose perhaps I shall see what I can do on my own."

Jonas, looking at her splinted wrist, wanted to ask if that was wise, but he didn't want to risk being recruited to help in Marcia's absence. What he did want to do was to talk to Beckett, and that just might be possible if Reb locked herself away to do sorcery.

☙ ❧

Jonas shifted on the wooden chair again. Reb had

disappeared into the other room, muttering to herself, and he'd heard the sound of a bolt being thrown on the door. Did that mean she was going to try magic even without help? Jonas preferred not to think about it. Or about anything else to do with magic. In fact, he would prefer to be out of here altogether. But it was just him and Beckett, now, in the room, and this was the perfect opportunity to talk to Beckett about his flickers without anyone else overhearing.

Or, not exactly talk *about* his flickers. That didn't feel like a good idea at all. He wasn't sure how reliable Beckett would be about keeping secrets. Did they have any idea about that sort of thing? About human notions of privacy? Jonas couldn't quite work out how to ask that, either.

He took a deep breath, and looked over at the cityangel. Former cityangel. They weren't looking at the floor any more; they were looking at the wall across the room, instead. There was no real expression on Beckett's face; yet somehow they looked austere, distant. Then Beckett turned to meet Jonas' eyes and Jonas rocked back on his chair, hit by the depths of the distress in Beckett's gaze.

Hundreds of years as Marek's cityangel? Spirits had similar emotional experiences to humans, in Jonas' limited experience. But the spirits he'd met, or heard of other ships meeting, had been engaging directly in the world. Beckett – hadn't been. Not for three hundred years. They had been elsewhere, part of the city, or maybe everywhere in the city, doing something else. Watching humans live their lives, without exactly living a life of their own. And now that was all gone.

Three hundred years.

Jonas swallowed, and reminded himself of his priorities right now. That was three hundred years in which Beckett might have heard or seen something about flickers, or something, anything like them. *Any* information would be more than he had currently, and if he was lucky it might be a lot more than that. If he got on and asked, he could also get on and get *out* of here, and away from all of this.

"So," he asked, going for brightly and falling a fair ways short. How could he possibly bring this up? "Asa was telling me, the other day, about how Rufus Marek and Eli Beckett discovered this place. Which, I'm guessing, you were there?"

Beckett didn't exactly flinch, but something happened in their eyes, and Jonas felt even more like a shit. But he forged onwards. No point in backing out now.

"But she was telling me that Eli Beckett had some kind of vision or something that they were following. I reckoned that was bullshit. Has to be, right? Visions, that's got to be a myth. But Asa was pretty insistent. And then I thought, maybe you would know."

Beckett was silent. Jonas began to wonder if they were even listening. He'd run out of other things to say, though, and while he was wondering, Beckett shifted slightly where they were leaning against the wall, and Jonas realised that they were thinking.

"If Eli Beckett had a vision, it was not of my doing," Beckett said, eventually. "Certainly they, both of them, knew where it was they were going. And they knew what to do when they got here." Beckett's gaze was even more distant, now. "I did not expect… Well. It was a deal with advantages on both sides, in the end."

A deal which, according to the stories, had either cost Eli Beckett's life, or which he had purely coincidentally not lived beyond seeing, depending on which version you heard. Jonas wasn't particularly tempted to ask about that. He didn't think he wanted to know.

"So the vision thing, that's horseshit, then?"

"I did not send any visions. I was not, before then, particularly interested in humans. I did not say the visions did not exist."

Jonas' heart rate quickened. "Prophecies and things like that? They're real?" He tried to sound scathing, disbelieving.

"What is and is not real?" Beckett said. "I sent ideas to humans, sometimes, myself. When I needed something from them."

"What, you put things into their minds?"

Beckett shrugged. "You could say that. Ideas. Images. In all truth I do not know how they seemed to the receivers. And the effects varied."

"Ideas of the future? Do *you* know the future, then?" Despite himself Jonas was a little awestruck. Yes, sometimes he saw a little bit of the future – though he tried not to think of his flickers that way more often than he could help – but it never felt like *knowing*. It was rather more uncomfortable than that.

"No," Beckett said, definitively. "I know the future no more than anyone else. But I could create an image of something I *wished* to come about, and that – sometimes, not always – had the desired effect. Encouragement. Encouragement to seek something or to create something. Something to strive towards." Their face was almost animated. "Something to make Marek better, more as it should be."

But Jonas' images weren't of things that he could endeavour to create or to achieve or to seek out. They were more like warnings.

"So you couldn't warn people, like if something bad was coming?"

Beckett shrugged. "I could, indeed, if I saw possibilities arising that I did not like. But I did not foretell the future, any more than anyone else who sees something and sees what it may lead to. Perhaps my knowledge was more complete, is all."

None of this, how Beckett was talking about their own future-sight, and how they were talking about sending ideas to others, quite matched Jonas' experience. But then, his flickers had been happening since he was a kid, and he'd only been in Marek six months. So it couldn't be Beckett having anything to do with them anyway. It was just information he wanted, and it didn't sound like Beckett had any useful information for him. But then, Beckett was still spirit, and if this was a spirit thing, not a cityangel thing…

"Can all spirits do this, then?"

"I cannot – I believe I could not, now," Beckett said, and that aching sorrow was back in their voice. "Other spirits – I do not know. Spirits have only very occasionally been in Marek, ever, until now. And I have always been in Marek. And I do not remember, before. But perhaps."

Perhaps. Well, that was a bit further on than he'd been before. Jonas tried to swallow down his disappointment. Perhaps, then, he needed another spirit to talk to, but how the hell was he going to do that?

Of course, there was one other spirit who was definitely around Marek now, according to the flicker he'd had back at the embassy. But trying to get in touch with the new cityangel without knowing anything about it – in all honesty, trying deliberately to get in touch with it at all – felt like lunacy. And Reb had already said she didn't know much about spirits. That's why they'd gone to find Cato.

Cato knew about spirits. And Cato was just a sorcerer, not a spirit himself. Cato had disappeared, so Jonas could hardly speak to him, either. Dammit. This was just one dead-end after another. He bit the inside of his cheek, hard.

"Why, then, do you ask?" Beckett said, looking very directly at him.

Jonas hadn't expected Beckett to ask. He hadn't expected Beckett to be paying enough attention to the ways in which human minds operated to *think* to ask. Not only that, but... from Beckett's expression, they had something in mind. Jonas felt a lurch of panic.

"I just – something someone said to me," he said, trying to look innocent. What had he said in the first place? "My friend Asa was telling me stories, like I said."

Beckett tipped their head to one side slightly, looking almost birdlike with their thin narrow face. "It seems to me that there might be more to you than you have admitted."

Jonas' stomach dropped.

"In Cato's rooms," Beckett said. They made half a gesture, then stopped. "I could have found out, for myself, once. I could feel sorcery." And shit, that wasn't at all creeping Jonas out, no. "In this place, in this body..." Beckett continued. "Are you too a sorcerer, Jonas?"

"No!" Jonas said. His flickers didn't make him a sorcerer. Salinas folk weren't sorcerers. Whatever had happened in Cato's room was just weird, or coincidence, or... Beckett was still looking at him. Shit.

The door of the inner room opened, and Reb came out, looking mildly frustrated.

"Simple charms work, as far as I can tell. But that's – that's just the basics. If someone scattered milkseed and called on the cityangel for a blessing, that kind of thing. Nothing that's really *sorcery*. There's a response, that's all I can tell. It feels a bit off, but I can't pin that down, and I certainly don't know if anything more specific will work. I daren't try without someone to ground me."

She eyed both of them thoughtfully. "I can't use a spirit…"

Jonas jumped to his feet, alarmed. "I gotta go. Work. Been off a whole day now. Dinner to pay for. I'll be back, yeah?"

He slid out of the door before Reb could marshal any objection. No way was he getting involved in any magic. Not after what Beckett had just said about what had gone down in Cato's room. It must have been Beckett, whatever they said. It had to have been.

Another dead end. Dammit. At this rate he'd be in Marek for another year.

Would that really be so bad?

He was supposed to be going home. He'd promised his mother he'd be home. And he wanted rid of these bloody flickers. He needed a solution, and he wasn't getting anywhere.

He took off at a run for the market, hoping to shake answers out from the pounding of his feet against the street; or at least to find a couple of good jobs and something to eat.

TEN

Marcia raced down to the ferry-dock, but when she got there, she saw with frustration that it had just left, already halfway over towards the foot of Marekhill. If she waited, she'd be even later. She'd have to go round by Old Bridge. And run. This was absolutely the last thing she needed. What she needed was to keep hold of this project, as part of the process of gaining more responsibility and proving to Madeleine that she was capable of being a more useful part of the House. That Madeleine could start *letting go*. Being late to a meeting was an utter disaster as far as all of that went. She gritted her teeth and started along the riverside path at speed.

She was hot, sweaty, and out of breath by the time she reached the House; and she still had to change into appropriate clothes. Which did at least give her a chance to splash some cold water on her face and catch her breath. In an ideal world she would have notes to review. Then again, in an ideal world she wouldn't be late already.

When she finally made it into the receiving room, both Gavin Leandra, and a younger man she didn't know, facing away from the door, were already there with Madeleine.

Madeleine's knee-length day tunic and loose trousers were in a pale blue with the House colours along the bottom of the tunic; the colour brought out her blue eyes and brown skin.

Madeleine's face tightened slightly as she turned to face Marcia, but she showed no other outward signs of annoyance. Marcia suppressed her own wince. She was going to hear about this later.

"Marcia. At last."

"I am so sorry, Mama. Head Leandra. I was unavoidably detained."

"Well, we are all here now," Madeleine said graciously, though Marcia could hear the bite underlying her voice. "This is Urso Leanvit, a cousin of House Leandra."

The other guest turned and Marcia's stomach flipped. Urso.

Urso who she'd last seen on top of Marekhill, with Daril and Cato. Did he know she'd been there? She pasted her social smile on and murmured the appropriate pleasantries. Urso returned them. There was no indication in his eyes, none at all, that he knew. Had Cato kept it secret that she'd been there? And what did that mean, in terms of Cato's involvement with all of this?

And what about the political implications? Why was this cousin here with Gavin Leandra? Madeleine had invited no secretary to this meeting; which didn't mean that Gavin wouldn't, but did rather suggest that Urso had a more prominent role. In any other House, Marcia would have expected the Heir to come, to match her own House's attendance. She blinked. Or, perhaps, one being groomed for Heirship. Had Gavin Leandra finally given up altogether on Daril? Was he out for a replacement?

"So," Madeleine said. "To business."

She seated herself, and the others followed suit. Marcia was at one end of a sofa from Urso Leanvit. Madeleine preferred to conduct her business meetings in cushioned comfort, rather than at office tables, but it didn't make her any the less sharp.

"We are all aware that Salinas shipping rates went up significantly in the last two years," Madeleine began.

Marcia nodded. "There was the big storm, that must have cost them a lot. And the poor trade year before that."

"Which cost all of us," Madeleine said, with an edge to her voice. "And yet they continue to squeeze more out of us."

Marcia frowned. "Shipping costs, though, no? I haven't seen the charges as excessive." She didn't see what Madeleine was getting at. For certain, trading without Salinas rates would be more profitable, but they'd just demonstrated with that wretched expedition that there was no alternative. Leandra and Fereno working together might be able to negotiate a better rate with Salina, or some other kind of deal, she could see that; but whipping themselves into irritation about the situation was hardly going to make anyone a better negotiator, nor help them find the best options to offer, nor yet squeezes they might be able to put on.

"Salina makes too much of its monopoly of transport,"

Gavin Leandra said, leaning forwards. "They charge what they like, simply because there is no one else."

"For a trading city, a city that relies so strongly on trade, it passes understanding that we are reliant on another nation for all of our transport," Urso put in, nodding.

Marcia frowned, baffled. "But this has been the case for time out of mind, no? The Salinas take the burden and risk of the transport. We can focus on the trade, and on bringing goods here from Teren to trade around the Oval Sea, and vice versa." And Marek had been doing very nicely on that, and on other exchanges, since its founding.

"The fact that it has always been the case does not mean that it always needs to continue," Urso said, with a slight smirk. "We could realise far more of the profit if we were conducting that trade for ourselves. As a trader myself, I can assure you that there is scope for this."

Ah, so that was his angle. Individual traders were not quite House-status, even though the Houses themselves traded, but in the circumstances Gavin might value the expertise enough to overlook that, if Urso was prepared to roll his own operation into that of the House. Madeleine was frowning almost imperceptibly; was she chasing the same chain of thought?

"Marek's trade goods are renowned for their quality, and yet the city's income decreases year on year," Urso continued. "Of course, the market pays what it will. And yet my information is that prices for Marek-made goods have not fallen elsewhere – in the Kingdoms, for example."

"No," Madeleine said, the syllable dropping sharply. "It is the overheads which increase."

"Now, it is true, as Fereno-Heir says, that the Salinas have had a difficult year," Urso said. "And they do provide a very reliable service. But if there were to be an *alternative*, well." He sat back a little and spread his hands. "In due course, costs would have to fall. And one might consider the fact that an alternative shipping service that handled only the shorter routes would not need to subsidise the longer ones."

"But who is to provide this alternative?" Marcia asked, restraining herself from rolling her eyes. This was all very well, but it was simply idle speculation. For this she had raced back across the city? "We are not a seafaring city."

Marek had fishing boats, but nothing that could do even the shorter routes across the Oval Sea. "Hence the attempt to find an overland route, but we now know that is not feasible. I have been considering further negotiations with the Salinas…" Should she mention her discussion with Kia the night before? Perhaps not yet.

"Which," Gavin Leandra said, "is why we must seek *further* alternatives. Ships that are not under Salinas control. Ships of our own."

Madeleine was nodding. Marcia opened her mouth to argue, then thought better of it and closed it again. Clearly she was the least-informed person in the room. Equally clearly, Madeleine would expect her daughter to back her – especially in front of House Leandra.

Instead, she said, "Hm. So, we are to build a shipyard? An ambitious plan. And expensive." Did they even have shipwrights here who could build ocean-going vessels?

"Too slow," Gavin Leandra said, with an impatient wave of his hand.

Marcia frowned.

"One of the initial steps will be to confiscate a proportion of the ships currently in dock," Madeleine said, as casually as if that were something she might propose every day.

Marcia sat forward, horrified. "Confiscate Salinas ships? Under what pretext?" And with what reaction?

Madeleine shrugged. "I am sure we can come up with some appropriate way of tightening docking regulations. Salina has been bleeding us dry for far too long."

Marcia bit back the immediate response that rose to her lips. This was insanity! But there must be something she was missing. Madeleine could hardly be so cavalier if she didn't believe that there was a way to do this without Salina treating it as an act of war.

"You think the Council will vote for this?" she asked. Surely the Council would not be so foolish? Even if many of them were annoyed with Salina currently?

Madeleine shrugged. "They will agree with our action once the advantages are clear."

Urso smiled knowingly. "And it is always better to get forgiveness than permission, am I not correct? Who at the dockyards will doubt the authority of Houses Fereno and Leandra, especially backed up by the City Guard?"

The Guard was involved? Well. The Guard, doubtless, would take the word of Leandra-Head and Fereno-Head. More so, given their customary and well-known antipathy; surely they would not both be involved in anything that did not have the backing of the full Council. Marcia bit the inside of her cheek.

"Once it has happened, well, what is the Council to do but agree?" Gavin Leandra said. "They will benefit as much as we do; and we both," he nodded at Madeleine, "have a sufficiency of allies in the Chamber."

It was true, as well. That antipathy again. It was all Marcia could do not to curse aloud. This was *stupid*.

"And the Salinas reaction..." she said, trying for a tone of interest wrapped with practical concern.

"It is nearly Mid-Year. The ships are about to leave," Urso said. "We wait until the majority have left, then confiscate the remainder in one fell swoop. There will be no one to take the news to Salina; they will know only that some of their ships are missing. We can then fortify the harbour before their return, and allow them in only when they agree to our terms."

"Well, if we must do it, that is sensible timing, I suppose," Marcia said, slightly reluctantly, and Madeleine smiled at her for the first time. It took everything Marcia had not to react.

Gavin Leandra was nodding, looking satisfied. "They need our trade," he said. "And we will not be able to take it all over, not all at once, so we will allow them to continue with some of it."

They wouldn't be able to take it all over at *all*, Marcia thought, fighting hysteria. Marek had no direct trading partnerships elsewhere – and the easiest option for the Salinas would not be to hang around asking for entry to Marek's harbour. It would be for them to demand that the other cities and nations around the Oval Sea boycott any direct trade with Marek; and they would have the power to do that.

She tried, gently, to say as much.

"Marcia," Madeleine said. "Marek trade is important to everyone. Why would they choose to spite themselves in this way?"

"Because the alternative..." Marcia started.

"You underestimate our importance," Urso Leanvit said, kindly.

Or he over-estimated it, especially in comparison to Salina, who traded all the way around the Oval Sea and beyond, with rather more goods and clout than one single city, even if you included the Teren goods that all came through Marek.

"We would need to think also about training," she said instead, trying for a different angle. "We can hardly confiscate the crews with their ships."

"The advantage of beginning with the lucrative shorter routes," Urso said, "is that local fishers already have many of the required skills."

Smugglers, he meant. If the Salinas didn't come back and sink every ship, in preference – or in addition – to instituting a boycott.

Madeleine was frowning at her. She hated it when Marcia disagreed with her publicly. Marcia needed to back off now, if she was going to have any impact on this at all. What could Gavin and Madeleine be *thinking*? Were they *wilfully* blind to all the ways in which this was a disastrous idea?

"And some of the younger children of the Houses and their offshoots might find the sea a rewarding option," Urso added.

"It will strengthen Marek to manage more of our own trading," Madeleine said. "A highly suitable pursuit for the lesser Houses."

The other two were nodding. Marcia thought of what Daril had been saying at that party, of her fed-up generation. This was another way for the older ones to hold power for longer, wasn't it? Send more of the younger generation off to sea, to trade directly. No wonder Madeleine thought it would be popular with the Council.

Marcia took a long breath and summoned up a smile. Fighting further at this point clearly wasn't going to get her anywhere, other than excluded from this plan. She maintained it while further details of the absurdity were discussed, nodding along as though she was convinced, until Gavin and Urso finally left, and she could talk to her mother alone.

"Mother," she said, the moment the door was safely shut

behind the departing visitors. "You cannot seriously think that this is a good idea? We are not a shipping city! We have no ships. Even if you take a handful of Salinas ships, we have no *crew* for them. If we have ships and train crew – which itself can hardly happen overnight – we will be exposed directly to the risk of shipping rather than outsourcing it to the Salinas."

"Greater risk, perhaps, but greater profit along with it," Madeleine said. "And it is simply not *suitable* that we should be indebted to the Salinas in this way."

"But we've been doing things this way since – since the founding of the city!"

"We had overland routes as well, once," Madeleine said. "This total dependence is much more recent, and it is time that we removed ourselves from it. As for the rest, well, there is time to work through it. You recall, we do not anticipate ceasing all dealings with the Salinas. At least not immediately. We will find a trade balance which is agreeable to everyone."

"But if their ships are confiscated then I can promise you that they will cease all dealings with us immediately," Marcia said. "And then they will come back and attack the stolen ships. Mother, I have a meeting arranged with the Salinas ambassador tomorrow. I am sure I can negotiate improved charges, perhaps even for our House alone…"

"Silence," Madeleine said.

Marcia blinked in surprise.

"I believe I did not speak clearly." Madeleine's voice was crisp. "House Fereno has taken its decision. I require you to pursue it. And you will cancel your meeting with the ambassador."

Marcia opened her mouth, then closed it again. There was no purpose arguing with Madeleine in this mood. This was *stupid*, a stupid, foolish decision, and she had no way of arguing against it short of resigning her position altogether. She tasted blood, metallic in her mouth, and realised that she'd bitten straight through the inside of her lip.

"Mother," she said instead, and bowed her way out of the door, barely holding herself in check.

ELEVEN

Jonas managed to fit in three jobs between running away from Reb's place, and being due back at the embassy to meet Kia's Mareker friend. He wasn't particularly enthusiastic about that, but a promise was a promise; and who knew, maybe it would even be useful with solving his little *problem*. Since Beckett had been no bloody use, and Cato was still missing, he was reduced now to clutching at any opportunity. At least, with the three jobs, and the free lunch at the embassy – and with luck there would be some kind of food available at this meeting too – he was more or less even financially for the day, which was enough to get by for now.

He presented himself at the embassy in good time to get changed again into Kia's idea of respectable; which turned out to be a slightly dulled-down version of Salinas formal.

"It's awkward," Kia explained as Xera handed him a pile of clothes. "These Marekers have a far more complicated dress code than we do – many more levels. It ought to be possible simply to stick to our own standards, but experience suggests that we get under-rated if we do." She pursed her lips thoughtfully. "Of course, that can be handy, on occasion."

"So what is this meeting about, then?" Jonas asked, once he was decently dressed. He might as well have some idea what he was stepping into.

"Trading fees," Kia said. "Urso is related to House Leandra, but more importantly is directly involved in trade, rather than working through agents like the full Houses do. Mind you, I was surprised by how willing Fereno-Heir was to meet with me; I do wonder whether this is beginning to change." She tapped a finger thoughtfully against her leg. "Assuming Fereno-Heir does in fact honour her promise, that is. In any case, Urso Leanvit is a very useful contact. We've worked with him before – excellent goods, good prices, profit for both sides. But it's been a bad year, and we do need to renegotiate."

The start of the meeting went more or less as Jonas had expected. Urso Leanvit was a stocky man, hair and skin both mid-brown. He was maybe ten years older than Jonas, with a narrow face and calculating eyes. Kia greeted him cheerfully, their friendship clear.

"Jonas and I were on the Lion t'Riseri together, Urso," Kia said, introducing the two of them. "His mother is Captain t'Riseri, and he is spending a little while in Marek."

"The famous Captain t'Riseri?" Urso asked, giving a Salinas-style double handshake. "Well, it is an honour to meet you. Kia has told me many stories of her days on the Lion. Sadly I have never yet run a cargo on a t'Riseri ship, but I do have hope. What brings you to Marek, then?"

"It's always interesting to find out about other cultures," Jonas temporised. "I am likely to return soon, but it has been an interesting six months." He paused, then decided that he might as well risk the question. If he was going to have to sit through this meeting, he needed to make some use of it. And Kia evidently considered Urso a friend, rather than a diplomatic connection to be kept at arms length. It would be acceptable to be a little more blunt. "In fact, one of the things that has most interested me about Marek is its magical history, but sadly I have been unable to speak to any practitioners."

"The plague," Urso said, his face sombre. "Of course."

Kia's eyebrows had shot up at Jonas' apparent desire to speak to a sorcerer, but she didn't interrupt.

"It must have been very distressing for Marek. But Kia tells me that magic is an interest of yours, as well? Of course, Marek has long been the place to be for those interested in magic." Unless one wished the risks of blood-magic, of course; but that wasn't something to mention in polite circles, in Marek or anywhere else.

Urso nodded slowly, his eyes alight with interest. Too much interest, maybe, Jonas wondered with a sudden lurch. He reminded himself that Kia trusted the man. An eye for the main chance was part and parcel of being a trader, not something to be ashamed of.

"Well now. Kia is correct, I do indeed have an interest in magic. In fact, I have put myself to some effort to gather a number of books on the matter from various parts of the world. You would be very welcome to visit and take a look at them, should that be appealing to you."

Jonas blinked. A library. Of books on magic. And not just Marek magic. Surely there might be something useful there. He wondered, briefly, whether Urso's interest included actual practice – but no, there had been the plague. Reb had said there was only herself and Cato left. She would hardly be mistaken.

"I would love to," he said.

"Then I look forward to seeing you," Urso said. "Do please come to visit." He named an address a few streets up and around the Hill from the embassy.

"How delightful," Kia said. "It is always rewarding to bring two people with a shared interest together." She smiled. "Even if it is an interest which I myself cannot share, as you are aware, Urso, my friend." The look with which she regarded Jonas was appraising.

Well. Whatever Kia might think, even if she did disapprove, he wasn't going to pass up this opportunity. He was no longer a child, being looked after by his adult ship-mates.

"Indeed," Urso agreed. "And a pleasing way to start our own meeting of shared interest."

"On which note," Kia said. "What do you have for our ships this season? It would be good to load up for the final run before the storms blow up."

Urso and Kia began a detailed conversation about trading goods, which Jonas paid next to no attention to, until his attention was caught again.

"I hesitate a little to mention this," Urso said, delicately, "but I have heard rumours, from other Marekers, that there may be *alternatives* to Salinas ships available soon."

"The Council's secret exploratory trip to the mountains?" Kia said. She waved a hand. "Not, in fact, as secret as they would have liked. And at any rate, the report back was public within half a day of the expedition's return. I'm afraid your rumour-mongering friends are wrong; there is no route over the mountains, so no alternative."

Urso shook his head. "No, indeed, you are correct. What I *heard*," he laid heavy emphasis on *heard*, "from, ahem, *reliable* sources, was that there are some persons who seek to explore the possibilities of Marek taking up seafaring." He sat back a little. "Of course, I'm sure there is nothing in such gossip, and I wouldn't bring it here were it not for our long history of friendship. As we both know, sometimes a small hint can be a surprising amount."

This was absurd. How could Marek seek to outmatch the Salinas on the sea. The best they had were fisherboats which barely went out of sight of land. The Salinas had been sailing the Oval Sea for hundreds of years before Marek was even established.

Kia's eyebrows raised. "Building shipyards takes time, and could hardly be done without anyone noticing. It's not like the local vessels would be up to much. Even the smugglers are land-huggers at best." Her tone was slightly mocking, as befit someone who had sailed on a ship like the Lion. Or any other Salinas ship.

"There is a whole dockyard full of ships," Urso said. There was something in his face that Jonas couldn't quite read.

Kia's eyes widened. "But you cannot mean…"

Urso shrugged. "I am sure that, as you say, my rumour-mongering friends are wrong. It would be an absurd step to take, after so many years, so many centuries, of successful collaboration. And indeed," he smiled at Kia, "who could think to outmatch the Salinas on the sea? A rumour, nothing more, for certain. I should not have mentioned it to my honoured friend."

There was an undercurrent in his voice that Jonas couldn't quite read. Kia was frowning very slightly, a crease between her brows.

"So," Urso said, tone brisk again. He wrote down another string of numbers and pushed it across to Kia. "I think this reflects our deliberations to date?"

Kia's frown smoothed, and she pursed her lips at the paper. Another couple of rounds of haggling, and they were done, both seeming satisfied, though Kia's frown had returned, and a slightly distant look.

"Do please indeed come to visit my library," Urso urged Jonas, as they were all bidding one another farewell. "I am always delighted to talk to someone who shares my interest."

He turned to Kia. "Oh, and I gather that you have a meeting planned with Fereno-Heir? I trust you are able to come to equitable terms with her as well; though of course I will also hope that they are not quite as good as those you and I have agreed." He smiled, and Kia smiled back at him, making a joke about trade secrecy as she did.

After Urso had gone, Kia stood, tapping her fingers on the table, and staring at nothing. "The ships in the docks... No. I cannot believe that is more than rumour-mongering. And certainly, Fereno-Heir, your Marcia, Jonas..."

"What about her?" Jonas asked, when Kia tailed off.

"Well, Fereno and Leandra were the funders of that mountain expedition, although both tried to hide it. Urso Leanvit is not exactly Leandra, but close, and we have a deal with him. I would not expect him to do that if he truly thought that... Well. And if we come to a deal also with House Fereno, it would seem clear that all is well." She nodded decisively. "At any rate, Jonas, do you wish to stay for dinner?"

Reluctantly – free food! – Jonas shook his head. He'd had about enough of Salinas-politicking as he could take for now. Still. This meeting had been more useful than he'd expected, though he wasn't sure what Kia had got out of having him there. Not his problem.

He left Kia still staring thoughtfully at the walls.

☻ ☻

"So, where've you been today?" Asa asked, sliding onto the bench next to him in the Dog's Tail. It was warm again, even late in the evening, the doors and windows flung open. "I haven't seen you around much."

Messengers tended to pass one another, throughout the day, so it was notable if one didn't see someone for the duration.

Jonas grimaced. "It's been a bit hit and miss today. Had some other stuff to do."

He'd done a couple more jobs after leaving the embassy, but he was fed up and his skin felt like there was something itching underneath it. He'd stopped sooner than he'd meant to. He shouldn't really have come here and bought the beer, but the last thing he wanted was to sit in his room and have time to think.

It hadn't been his most lucrative evening, even before he'd stopped. Just as he'd been about to cut his losses, he'd been signalled by someone who wanted him to run a small unidentified package all the way across to halfway up Marekhill. Jonas had been pretty sure that the package wasn't strictly legal, but he wasn't really that bothered either way; and he was confident that he wouldn't get caught. He didn't; and the receiver had doubled the agreed payment, which had been a very pleasant surprise.

"I'll stand you the next one then," Asa said cheerfully. "I had a pretty good day today." They waved aside his attempt to protest. "That's how it goes, right? We help each other out. You'll have a good day sometime when I don't. It all balances out."

There was a sudden hot feeling in Jonas' chest. The way they said it made him feel that he was part of something, just like when he'd been on board a ship. And just like he hadn't felt at all at the embassy, when he'd had instead the feeling that whyever it was that Kia had wanted him along, it wasn't wholly why she'd said it was. And that the conversation Kia and Urso were having had undercurrents that he didn't understand.

"Where were you, then?" Asa asked. "If you weren't working." They grinned. "Do tell me to sod off if I'm being too nosy."

Jonas was surprised into a smile. "No, it's fine. I was – seeing someone from home."

"*Seeing* someone?" Asa asked, raising an eyebrow. "A sweetheart, you mean?"

"Angels, no," Jonas said, horrified at the idea. "A friend of my mother's; someone I was shipmates with, when I travelled with my mother when I was younger."

"Ah, checking up on you to report back home, huh?" Asa said. "Sympathies. I hope at least they fed you while they were interrogating you."

"Yes," Jonas admitted. "Plenty of food. Plenty of checking up, too, you're right." He tilted his head slightly, looking at

Asa. "Do your family live here, then?"

"Down in the fishing village, out by the marsh," Asa said. "I moved into the city when I was twelve, picking up around the market. Sweeping and that. Started doing a bit of messenger work when I got fed up with that, and it worked out a lot better." They shrugged. "But my parents don't exactly check up on me. I go back to visit once in a while, but mostly they were glad to have me out of the house and feeding myself. Plenty of us and not so much money or food, you know?"

Jonas didn't know. It wasn't a thing that happened in Salina. But he'd seen enough since coming to Marek to nod with a sympathetic look.

"I like messengering partly because of the people, you know?" Asa went on, half-shyly. "The thing I said before, about looking out for one another, you know? I mean, I know you've not been here long, but... Well, angels, I hope we've all been doing that for you, too."

"You have," Jonas said, and it was true, although he half-surprised himself with his own certainty. "I know what you mean."

It was that shipboard sense of camaraderie, again, and he hadn't expected to find it in Marek, but it was there.

His spine tingled, and *Asa was standing up and leaving the table, walking towards the bar.*

"I'll get the next one," Asa said, and stood up, leaving the table and walking towards the bar. Jonas scowled. He hated those sorts of flickers, the ones that nearly overlapped reality. Even on the occasions that they helped him win at dice or cards, they were unsettling, like double vision.

He stared down at the table, and pushed a puddle of beer around with his finger, thinking again about camaraderie.

As a child, he'd been wrapped in that sense of shipboard unity. But the reason he was here, when it came down to it, was that he was excluded from that now unless he changed something about himself. Unless he got rid of his flickers.

He hadn't mentioned his flickers to Asa or Tam or any other of the messengers or his neighbours in the squats. But – Marek was comfortable, more or less, with magic. If he did mention them, maybe, just maybe, unlike his mother, Asa and Tam and the others wouldn't mind. Wouldn't expect him to change in order to fit in with them.

It was a curious thought. He'd never questioned, before, whether it was *right* for his mother to make that demand.

"You know," he said, once Asa had sat down again, "I might go back home, in a couple of weeks."

"Back to Salina?" Asa asked, their eyebrows high. "You – I didn't know you were thinking of it." They looked downcast. "I mean, well, I guess it's your home and all that, so... But I'll miss you, you know? We'll miss you."

Come back when and only when you have fixed this problem, his mother said in his mind, and Jonas swallowed. Asa didn't know about the flickers. Maybe they would be more like that if they did.

"I'd miss you too," he said, honestly. "I don't – I don't know if I definitely will leave."

"The ships come and go all the time," Asa said. "You can always just leave it a while longer."

Jonas laughed. "Well, they'll not be here for a few weeks after Mid-Year, but I take your point."

Asa nudged him with their shoulder. "Stay with us, Jonas!"

They were laughing, half-teasing, but obviously also meaning it. That warm feeling inside him was there again. But – it was absurd. He couldn't just accept his flickers and stay here. He had to fix them, and go back home, as soon as maybe. That had always been the plan. He had to go back to the life that was waiting for him, once he'd fixed his little *problem*. Not indulge himself by ignoring it.

He swallowed down the lump in his throat, and did his best to smile back at Asa.

TWELVE

The ritual on Marekhill had been far more exhausting than Daril had expected. Even Cato had looked pale and drawn afterwards, and hadn't made any of his usual snide remarks on the way back to House Leandra.

"But did it *work*?" Daril had demanded, frustrated, after a while of silence. He hated that he had no way of telling for himself.

"It worked," Cato said. "Marek has a cityangel again. Lucky Marek."

"But the *deal*? What about the *deal*?" Daril demanded.

Cato shrugged. "It agreed when I asked before. It agreed again just now. So there you go. Next question – when do I get paid?"

"We can't test it yet," Urso said. "If that's what you mean. And I don't know how much raw power there will be, yet." He frowned. "It ought to be... the old one would have, I mean..."

"*When*?" Daril demanded through his teeth.

"Impatient much?" Cato drawled.

Daril and Urso ignored him. Urso rubbed at his eyes.

"Later," Urso said. "Later today. I have – responsibilities, first, and we need to allow, as it were, settling-in time. I will send a messenger, later."

Those 'responsibilities', Daril was gnawingly aware, included a meeting with Gavin, as part of this absurd competition, or whatever it was, for the Heirship. Not that that mattered any more, of course, given what they had – probably – just achieved. And the meeting in question fitted in nicely with the rest of their plans. He was not in the slightest bit bothered about it.

"Is that when I get paid, as well?" Cato asked.

"You get paid when we decide you're done," Daril said, turning on him. "Which isn't yet."

Cato, scowling, retired straight to his room the moment they got back to House Leandra. Daril had paced, and fretted, and gone obsessively over the plans. Early evening brought a message from Urso.

My place, eight hours. U.

Daril glanced at the clock. It was just after seven, but Urso's house further down the Hill was not a long walk.

"The messenger awaits a response," Roberts said.

Daril scribbled "Yes. DL" underneath the note, resealed it with a dab of wax from the dish on the dresser, and handed it to Roberts.

He wouldn't bring Cato. If everything had gone according to plan, they wouldn't need him any more. And if it hadn't, Daril didn't want Cato around until he and Urso had decided what to do next. Cato would stay here, with Roberts put to watch him.

The sea-fog was rolling in over from the swamp on the far side of Marekhill when Daril, wrapped in a muffler, walked briskly down the hill towards Urso's house. He made his way along the network of small side streets, only wide enough for a couple of pedestrians, that linked the main roads.

Urso lived above the middle class district of the Hill, but only just. Whilst his branch of House Leandra was acknowledged, or Gavin wouldn't be even pretending to consider him as Heir, it was minor, and he had never previously had any apparent interest in politics. Which, Daril thought with no little frustration, surely meant that his candidacy couldn't be *serious*. Not that it mattered. Urso's income was almost entirely from trade; his scholarly interest in magic was known, and considered slightly odd but not actually objectionable. His sorcerous ability, of course, was secret. Gavin Leandra would not have tolerated it in an acknowledged relative.

Urso's man-of-all-work bowed Daril silently into the house. The place was small, as they all were at this level of the Hill, but well appointed. Urso's business office was at the front of the house, its door closed and locked at this hour. His personal reception room was at the back, looking out onto the tiny garden. The drapes were drawn now against the encroaching dark, and against curious eyes.

The room was decorated in shades of blue, with a very comfortable set of new padded chairs. Far more comfortable,

Daril could never avoid reflecting when he visited, than any of the venerable Leandra furniture. They could replace it, of course, if they chose, but his father would never have thought of it, nor sanction the expense if he had, and Daril could not abide giving the old man the impression that he cared. One day. Soon. He would be able to rip the whole lot out and start again, if he wished, and his father would have to put up with it, and stop playing these absurd games with Daril's rights.

Urso was standing warming himself at the fire as Daril came in and shut the door.

"Greetings," Daril said pleasantly, and Urso nodded at him.

Daril settled into an armchair, sinking comfortably into it. Urso left the fire for the chair opposite.

"My meetings this afternoon were most successful," Urso said. "Though Fereno-Heir was less convinced."

"If Madeleine Fereno has made her decision you need not worry about Marcia," Daril said, with a shrug.

"Not even when she's been poking around after Cato?" Urso asked.

Daril suppressed a flash of annoyance that the other man had heard about that encounter – but of course it would be gossip, and Urso kept tabs on gossip as much as anyone else did – and shrugged. "She can poke around all she likes; she's hardly going to search House Leandra for him. And he is with us, at any rate."

At least while they were paying him. Daril didn't harbour any illusions about Cato's commitment to the cause.

"If you say so," Urso said, with a tiny quirk of his mouth. "In any case. I dropped some helpful hints to the Salinas ambassador. They'll be prepared. The whole thing is shaping to go up like tinder."

"But will it be *enough*?" Daril asked. "Is the cityangel truly in place?"

Urso scowled. "That's the bad news. It is indeed in place, but with nothing like the power we will need. As things stand, we could start the war at any point, but we would have no certainty of causing things to fall out as we intend. The Council might survive regardless. It would depend more on your abilities to talk yourself into position than we had planned."

Which wasn't the *point*. The point was to have the cityangel's power behind him, ensuring co-operation. Daril was halfway up out of the armchair before he even realised he'd moved.

"Then we must *fix* it! We can fix it?"

"That's what I have been researching, these last hours," Urso said. His face looked weary, in the candlelight. "And I have a solution. We don't have much time, though, to put everything in place. We will need to move faster than we originally intended. And it will mean revealing the rest of it to Cato."

"Can we trust him?" Daril asked.

"We can't do it without him," Urso said, flatly. "I'm not strong enough. Cato and I together – yes. Probably."

Daril chose to ignore the caveat.

"Very well," Daril said. "Explain, and I will address the issue of managing Cato."

Urso sat back. "Firstly – I think we can no longer leave this until Marek and Salina are actually at war. Which may be for the best; the war was only ever a means to an end."

"But without that, what is our reason for taking over the Council?" Daril said. "That was surely the whole point – chaos and mismanagement, the clear failure of the Council as it currently stands, backed up with the power of the cityangel to create change."

Urso shrugged. "Broadly speaking – we use raw power, instead. There's a ritual."

"But you just *said* that the cityangel doesn't *have* power," Daril said, his teeth clenching.

"That is the purpose of the ritual," Urso said, patiently. "Mid-Year is coming."

Daril rolled his eyes. "Yes. And?"

"I understand – my research tells me – that the festival generates a great deal of raw power in the city," Urso said. "It's fallen out of common knowledge among sorcerers, but I've found reference in older books. And that raw power, the cityangel can take advantage of it. But it will need help, to make the most of it. We will need first to focus that power, both into the cityangel, and then, with the cityangel's aid, to direct it back out again to you. The Council will be in session." He spread his hands. "With the power surge behind you, you don't need the excuse of the war. They will fall into place. The war would itself have generated power, and given us certain opportunities, it is true. But this is likely a safer option. And a quicker one, there is that."

"We are certain that the cityangel is no longer bound as the old one was?" Daril demanded. "Politically bound?"

Urso nodded. "Certain."

"Very well," Daril said, sitting back. "Tell me more about this ritual. Tomorrow? On Mid-Year?"

"Yes. And for the strongest effects, we will need to be at Marek Square."

Marek Square, which at Mid-Year would be full of people and celebration.

"You don't mean we're to conduct a sorcerous ceremony in the middle of Marek Square at Mid-Year," Daril said, his heart dropping.

"No. Of course not. We'll have to use the Salinas," Urso said.

Daril saw it immediately. The Salinas Embassy overlooked Marek Square, very near the centre of the square's Mid-Year festivities. The problem being...

"The Salinas? But everyone knows how they feel about magic! And it is *tomorrow*, Urso, surely there isn't enough time..."

"I believe I can, ah, leverage our existing plans to work around the matter of the Salinas and magic. I have already dropped a couple of hints to the Salinas ambassador about what may be coming. She is primed to believe me, when I go to her in great concern and some urgency tomorrow morning. What the Salinas are above all, you understand, is *pragmatic*. Once the ambassador is fully informed of what Madeleine Fereno and your father plan, she will fall in with us."

"We will need to promise her something, surely," Daril said. Although, most likely there would be something that they could give to the Salinas; unlike his father and Madeleine Fereno, Daril saw the relationship with the Salinas as broadly successful for both parties. He had no intention of damaging it.

"The whole point is that this idea of your father's is foolish and could never succeed," Urso said. "But in the process of demonstrating that, there would be a great deal of damage to both Marek and Salina. Merely promising that we will prevent that should be enough."

It was true enough. Daril had always known that the war would be costly, and hoped to stop it as soon as possible after it had done its job. He merely believed that it was worthwhile. If they could get away without it... It was a far neater plan, if it worked.

It would work. Daril had to believe that it would work. If Urso said they could be ready tomorrow, then, well, he was the one who knew about the magic, wasn't he?

"Very well," Daril said, sitting forwards. "Give me the details."

☉ ☉

Cato's allocated room in House Leandra was next to Daril's. This was, clearly, because Daril wanted Cato under his eye, but it also meant that Cato had that same view out over Marek that Daril so visibly relished. A prison cell with a view, Cato thought, cynically, as he sat on the wide windowledge, his back propped against the wall and his feet up in front of him. He looked out over the city. The sun had just set, and torches were beginning to be lit, speckles of light visible lower down the hill and in the Square, where they weren't obscured by buildings.

To call it a prison cell was, of course, overstating the case. Whatever Daril b'Leandra might think, if Cato really wanted to walk out, he had absolutely no doubt that he could. There might be collateral damage on the way, but if that was the better option, well, so be it.

Just at the moment, it wasn't worth it. For a start, he wouldn't get paid. And whilst the restrictions on his freedom of movement were faintly irritating, and Daril's sense of his own importance somewhat more so, House Leandra was comfortable enough. It was quiet, the food was good, and he didn't have to deal with idiots trying to hire him. Other than the idiot who had already hired him.

But that was unfair. Daril b'Leandra was no idiot. A little short-sighted occasionally, even perhaps slightly ignorant, but not a fool.

Cato sighed, and propped his shoulder against the window, leaning into the glass. He could see the dark curve of the river, the torches outlining the shape of the Old Bridge and the New Bridge beyond it, and north of the river, the imposing bulk of the squats, mostly dark with the odd pinprick of light outside a pub or coffee-house around the edges. He thought of the Purple Heart, his preferred drinking establishment, and wondered whether anyone there was concerned that he was missing, other than in terms of the relationship between his absence and the dip in their nightly takings. Doubtless not. It was a long time since anyone other than Marcia had worried about him.

And it was a long time since he'd had a view like this, too. He was aware, as he had been since he got here, of House Fereno down the street. He could swear that he could feel it, through the stone of the wings of House Leandra and the three other Houses that stood between them and blocked his view. Was Marcia at home, tonight, looking out?

Marcia. He sighed. If only she could have the good sense to stay out of this. Hopefully he'd convinced her now that he didn't need rescuing. Marcia was stubborn, always had been, but surely being knocked out was enough of a hint even for her. He'd have to apologise, once it was all over. She'd forgive him. Marcia always forgave him, in the end.

And it should be over, soon, surely. He'd done what they hired him for. He was only waiting on the irritating Urso – and Cato was kicking himself that he'd missed that there was another sorcerer in Marek, he really shouldn't have been blindsided by that – to confirm that everything was suitably fixed. That their deal, whatever it was, was being adhered to.

Of course, if they'd told him what the deal *was*, rather than demanding that he keep himself outside of the communication channel he'd opened, he could have told them immediately. He was, after all, much more experienced, and stronger, than Urso. He could tell already that the new cityangel wasn't as strong as the old one, which it seemed Urso hadn't been immediately aware of. But then, half a day of support set against three hundred years – what would you expect? Surely they couldn't have anticipated anything else? He scowled. People expected the most unreasonable things, sometimes.

What was really bothering him was the sense that he was missing something. Whatever this deal was, it meant that there was something that Daril and Urso wanted, something they weren't telling him. Something they were very deliberately not telling him. Cato hated not knowing things, especially when they were things he was directly involved in. He'd considered jiggering the communication channel, to listen in, but even if Urso wouldn't have noticed, the prospective cityangel would have, and Cato had no idea whether or not it would have given him away. Wasn't worth the risk.

After all, in this situation, he *was* the hired help. He couldn't expect to be given every detail, annoying though that might be. He might be back up on Marekhill for a few days, but he wasn't Cato b'Fereno any more, hadn't been for ten years. He was a sorcerer from the squats with a reputation for negotiable morals. (And, of course, he was alive, which these days was a strong qualification by itself if you needed a sorcerer. You could choose him, or Reb, or to go down to the boneyards and see what you could get there.) But time in the squats hadn't dampened the political sense that his sixteen years growing up in Marekhill had gifted him. And his political sense was telling him that something was wrong.

Cato *really* hated not knowing what was going on.

He dug his teeth into his lip, thinking about the cityangel. When it came right down to it, yes, he *wanted* to know what Daril was after, but whatever it was, it was going to be politics of some sort, and, tingling political senses or not, Cato didn't care that much about politics. Marek itself would be fine whoever was in charge, and Marekhill would never care that much about the rest of the city, so why should Cato or anyone else he knew – yes, fine, other than his sister – care who was in the hot seat? But the cityangel – the cityangel mattered. Mattered, he knew in his bones, in a way that was deeper than just how it affected sorcerers. And he wasn't at all sure how the new cityangel was going to settle into the city.

Cato didn't care about politics. He did care about Marek.

If he'd been involved earlier – well, he wouldn't have been involved earlier. He wouldn't have been part of removing the old cityangel. He could admit that, even if it was slightly discomfiting to acknowledge the limits of his moral flexibility. But they'd done that already when they brought him in. Too late. Might as well get paid for fixing their fuckup, and no reason to believe that any other spirit couldn't do the same job.

He hoped.

He heard footsteps in the corridor outside. Daril, unless he missed his guess. Roberts didn't stride that way. The lock rattled with the insertion of a key, and Cato experienced his customary pulse of irritation that Daril never *knocked*. Prison cell. Just like being a teenager again, before he'd left.

He didn't bother to get off the windowsill.

"Cato?" Daril said. "Are you asleep?"

"No."

"Why have you not lit the lamp?"

Cato ignored this in favour of watching while Daril found and lit the lamp. Daril had just been out, and he was visibly tense. Was this where Daril was going to let him in on what happened next?

"So," Daril said. "The cityangel isn't as powerful as we need."

"Need? Now there's an interesting word."

Daril ignored him. "Urso has a fix. It requires your help."

"Well, let us discuss that, and then we can discuss my fee," Cato said, and settled himself more comfortably to listen.

He interrupted only once, while Daril was speaking. "But the cityangel can't interfere in the Chamber. In politics at all."

"The old one couldn't," Daril agreed. "This one isn't bound by the old contract. That's the point."

Cato blinked, slowly, then nodded. "I see. A smart move, yes."

He slumped down even further onto the windowsill, propping his feet against the other side of the frame, while Daril continued.

"This will avoid war, then?" he asked, once Daril had finished.

Daril shrugged. "Should do. Which is probably better, as it happens."

Cato clenched his teeth so hard his jaw spasmed. Of course, why should *Daril* care about the impacts of war? It wouldn't be his house that'd be fired if the Salinas came sweeping into the Marek docks to get their revenge. It wouldn't be him being conscripted to wave weapons around. Of course, it wouldn't be Cato either, but it most certainly would be his friends and neighbours.

He took a slow breath, until he was able to reply with some semblance of his customary lazy disinterest. "Yes, in general I prefer my home city in its more peaceful times."

"Well, then," Daril said. "Urso is working on the details. If we wish to do this tomorrow, we haven't much time to delay."

Once Daril had left, Cato put out the lamp, and let the expression of sardonic half-interest slide off his face as the darkness wrapped itself back around him. He took another look out of the window at Marek, then padded over to the bed and lay down on his back, staring up as if he could see straight through the stone to the starry sky above. His face was bleak. What now, then?

He hadn't thought about the political part of the contract. Which was a real fucking oversight on his part, and he could kick himself for it. It seemed obvious now why his political sense had been bothering him. Fine, he didn't care about politics, but he cared about stability, and keeping magic out of politics was pretty necessary for that stability. That was sufficiently obvious that it hadn't occurred to him to worry about it, and it *should* have occurred to him, because fuck knew you could never overestimate the ability of people to totally screw something over in pursuit of their own selfish interests.

This was going to be a total bloody disaster. If Daril and Urso could do it, so could someone else, in a year or five years or ten years.

On the other hand, if he just ran, right now, to avoid helping them with their stupid plan, they'd come after him, and he wouldn't be that hard to find. Unless he left Marek, which was just as unthinkable. Blood magic wasn't his style.

Also, if he ran, he wouldn't get paid. And it wasn't even as if there was another option, any more. The old cityangel was *gone*. The new one was in place. Surely there wasn't anything more to be done about that? In which case, well, perhaps the political situation had changed already, and it was too late to do anything other than go along with it, and learn to deal with the new arrangements. Even if they were inferior to the old arrangements.

It wasn't as if he was particularly in favour of the Thirteen Houses or any of the Marekhill swamp-slime. If Daril was knocking them over – well, so be it. Maybe. Especially if Daril's alternative was this war that Urso was trying to set up.

What would Marcia think of all this? Cato felt his shoulders tense, and dismissed the thought. He and Marcia didn't see eye to eye on everything, anyway.

The old cityangel was gone. Was it, though? It was evicted, not killed, from what Urso had said. Could it, maybe, be out there somewhere? Was there a way of finding it?

Mid-Year. Tomorrow. He had until tomorrow to decide whether there was anything he could – and would – do about all of this.

☉ ☉

There were doubtless things that Marcia could – should – have been doing. Working on this absurd project of her mother's, for example, though the thought brought bile to her mouth. She wouldn't do that – and she couldn't settle to anything else despite her best efforts. Instead, she took herself out of the house, down to the baths on Third Street.

She fumed as she walked. She was supposed to be *Heir*. If it weren't for that change ten years back, she would be about to be Head, not waiting on Madeleine's pleasure. She remembered being named Heir, the ceremony in the Chamber. She remembered feeling proud, and ready to take on responsibility.

During the Heir-ceremony, she'd kept thinking of Daril, despite her best efforts. Partly it had been that Gavin Leandra was, of course, present in the Chamber, scowling down at her and Madeleine and the Speaker in the centre of the room. Marcia hadn't taken it personally; Gavin Leandra rarely did anything but scowl. But she knew, of course, as everyone knew, that Daril still hadn't been named Heir. Everyone knew, too, how much at odds he and Gavin were, and that Daril was by all accounts pursuing a dissipation that his father abhorred as hard as he could go.

She remembered looking around at the other Heads and Heirs arrayed around the Chamber. The Guild members hadn't been present; the Heir-ceremony was for the Houses alone. One of the ways in which the Houses indicated to the Guild that they were subordinate.

As Marcia turned the corner onto Third Street, her steps slowed a little. She'd been thinking, back then, of the Inner Council, too. Thinking about the fact that it had been meeting more often than it once did. At the time she'd decided that she must be wrong, that she was just misremembering from a time when she was less involved in politics, although Madeleine had been encouraging her to take an interest for some time before her Heir-ceremony. But now, four years since that day, she was certain that much of Madeleine's Council business time was spent at the Inner Council; which was made up only of the thirteen Heads, excluding both Heirs and Guild. Back then she'd wondered just how much sway she would have over the Council's, and the House's business, even once she was formally Heir.

Well. Ha. Now she knew.

And how much say, then, did the Guilds have?

Did Daril still think that way, as he had when he was twenty-one and she was sixteen? Perhaps not. Perhaps he no longer cared.

Did she care?

She reached the bathhouse and paid her way in. Inside, the atmosphere was warm from the hot water pipes that ran under the floor from the furnace towards the steam pool. Marcia accepted a wrap from the attendant, stripped her clothes off, and handed them over to the attendant in exchange for a ceramic token. She hung the token round her neck, threw the wrap around her shoulders, and left the changing room.

The cold showers were between her and the baths, and she rubbed herself briskly down under them, shivering. The patrons up here, unlike, say, those at the baths on the north of the city, were unlikely to truly need that first wash to remove surface dirt, but it was still part of the bathing ritual. And the shock of the cold water felt good, almost calming. It took her out of her head, just a little, and she badly needed that.

Once through the showers, she put the wrap back on, and stepped gratefully into the steam room. She let herself sink into peaceful quiet in the damp heat. A couple of people over the other side of the small room, shadows in the steam, were gossiping about a mutual friend, but Marcia didn't recognise either them or the name they mentioned. She let herself drift for a while, deliberately blanking her mind, pushing away thoughts of Madeleine and politics every time they intruded.

She roused herself after a while, stepped outside, and asked one of the attendants to scrape her down, before going into the big soaking pool.

"Marcia!" someone hailed her.

It was Nisha, soaking in the pool with Aden.

Marcia hesitated for just a moment – she hadn't intended to be sociable, today. But nor did she want to beg off, and she was remembering, now, what Nisha had said at the party, about Daril. Perhaps now was a good time to talk about it. Despite the openness of the soaking pool, it was possible to have a surprisingly private conversation. The slight echo of the tiled walls and floor, and the size of the pool, amplified voices but also confused them, as soon as more than a couple of groups were present. It was next to impossible to overhear someone unless you were right next to them.

Aden and Nisha had a pot of tea on the side of the pool next to them, and Marcia signalled for another cup. They sipped at their tea as they chatted idly for a few minutes. Marcia was fairly sure that Aden had spotted that she wasn't entirely calm, but he had evidently chosen not to bring it up.

"Oh hey," Marcia said, "what happened about when you were going to join the Embroiderers Guild, Aden? Didn't you say you thought you could join as a journeyman, if they let you?"

"Well," Aden said, after a moment. "That didn't happen."

His tone was repressive.

Marcia deliberated for a moment, then decided to ignore his signals.

"What, did they want you to do the full apprenticeship?"

Aden narrowed his eyes at her for a moment, then shook his head and turned away slightly. "Nothing like that," he said. "They agreed that my work was entirely up to standard, and I had the fee needed. They just – made it clear that I wouldn't be voted in."

"But why on earth not?" Marcia asked. She'd seen Aden's work, and it was excellent. It had seemed like a fine idea, to actually use his skills, and he'd seemed keen about it, and she'd been surprised when nothing had seemed to materialise.

"Because he's of a House, Marcia," Nisha said impatiently. "It's not official, of course not, but they won't allow anyone with a verifiable House lineage into any of the Guilds."

"But that went out ten years ago," Marcia objected. "That was part of the negotiations when the Guilder seats on the Council were finally approved, that junior House members would be allowed into the Guilds again."

"Indeed, the rule is no longer there," Aden said, sounding so supremely bored that Marcia knew he must be faking it. "And yet, you still cannot get voted in."

"Ten seats," Nisha said. "They're still annoyed. And what with the way the Inner Council works now – one could say, who could blame them."

"And thus you have it. I remain in blissful sloth," Aden said. "Arguably I got the better of it. Journeymen do work tremendously hard, you know, Marcia. Now the initial excitement of the idea has worn off, I'm far from sure that I would have suited the job."

"He's lying," Nisha said. "He's bored as hell, just like I am. But I haven't bothered trying to join one of the Guilds, because I had already spotted how there *aren't* any junior House members in any Guild, rule or not. And I'm not cut out for trading on my own cognisance, and unlike your brother I don't fancy the squats nor yet have sorcerous talent, so..." She shrugged. "Living on someone else's money it is. At least Kilzan-Head is happy to support us. Kilzan-Heir is an idiot, but even if I bumped the wretched woman off I wouldn't be in line for Heir, so…"

Marcia looked at her curiously. "Would you care to be in politics?"

"Gods yes," Nisha said with feeling. "So interesting. But there are only so many places, aren't there? And I have no access to any of them. So it goes." She didn't sound resigned, the way her words pretended to be.

"Unless Daril achieves his brave new world," Aden said.

"Daril is all mouth and no breeches," Nisha said. "He talks a good talk, but if you get right down to it, he's talking revolution. Not just that, a revolution that would, I suspect, leave him in charge." She shrugged. "Although I agree it is superficially appealing."

"What is?" Marcia asked, feeling slightly cold.

"Bring down the Council, install a better system, one which doesn't rely on inheritance nor yet on the microscopic voting pool of the Guild masters," Aden said. "Blah blah revolution. He might be right, but like Nisha, I don't see it happening and I don't fancy Daril as Head of Heads, either. At least we don't have a single anyone in charge, at the moment. I don't fancy the setup they have in the Allied Cities, with a single governor making all the decisions."

"Much more scope for coming up through the ranks, there, though," Nisha said.

The conversation turned aside into a discussion of life in the Allied Cities, and Marcia let it go. But that cold feeling remained in her stomach. Were Daril's plans more realistic than Aden or Nisha realised? And she couldn't help but notice that, whatever they'd said, both of them were tempted by his vision. If he acted, would they follow? She couldn't rule it out.

Worse: was he right? Had he always been right?

She kept thinking of it once she'd taken her leave of Aden and Nisha. Thinking of it, and remembering conversations she'd had with Daril, ten years ago when he had that catastrophic row with Gavin; and with Cato, when he was recovering from the plague.

She kept coming to the same conclusion: that Daril was right. The current system didn't work.

But he was talking about not just replacing it – with

anything better? Anything that set Daril up as Governor in place of the Council couldn't possibly be an improvement. But it wasn't just that. He would be using sorcery, and the cityangel, to replace it. That was... a box she couldn't possibly want to see opened. There were very good reasons for the provisions against using sorcery or involving the cityangel in politics. Breaking that covenant, and allowing thereby for it to be broken in the future – that would be a disaster.

She had to stop Daril. But she couldn't pretend that she was doing so to defend a system that worked, for itself.

If she was going to stop Daril, she had to do something else herself. Maybe not immediately; but she had to accept that responsibility. She was stopping Daril's revolution; but that meant she had to commit to one of her own.

The terror was tinged with just an edge of a bubbling inner joy she hadn't felt since she was sixteen.

THIRTEEN

Jonas woke up just after sunrise the next morning, feeling better than he ought to have for an afternoon running messages back-to-back, a couple of evening hours of his usual nighttime-folk run, and drinking with Asa. But it had felt *good* to forget all this nonsense for a while.

He rolled over onto his back and stared at the ceiling. What of today, then? Reb and Beckett were a dead end, as far as his flickers went. They might, he supposed, be expecting him back again; but it wasn't like he'd promised to help. This Marek business wasn't any affair of his. His business was to get on with the matter of his flickers.

His spine tingled, and *he was looking at Urso, saying something to him, Urso listening intently and nodding, nodding like he understood, turning away towards a bookshelf…*

His head was pounding, and it took him a moment to remember where he was. He could feel his pulse pounding in his ears. Well. If he'd been in any doubt, that settled it. He needed to get on with the flickers, which meant visiting the trader-or-maybe-sorcerer, Urso; and since that was what the flicker had shown him, that went double. It was too early for the usual Marekhill type to be about, but Urso was a trader, and they rose early. He'd run a couple of early messages, and then he'd go along, see if the man was about.

He wanted like a physical ache to be on a ship, out in the middle of the sea, with nothing around but water and sky. Soon. Urso would, surely, be the person he needed. Soon, he could go home, with the fleet at New Year. A few days more. Urso's library would make it all work out. There would be, there must be, something there.

Once outside, he put his head back for a moment, watching the seagulls swoop and circle around the square, high in the blue sky. He badly wanted to talk all of this through with someone, finally admit the flickers, but he couldn't think of anyone he could do that with. Urso? Maybe? If the man seemed trustworthy? Maybe. He sighed, and started off towards the wholesale market. Bound to be a job or two there, even if it did smell of horses.

A couple of jobs later, when he reached Urso's house, halfway down Marekhill, Jonas realised he might have done better to have changed into his respectable Salinas clothes before he came here. The servant who answered the door clearly had no intention of admitting some messenger lad to see her boss.

"You should come back later," the servant said firmly.

Jonas stuck his foot pre-emptively in the door. "Truly," he said. "I was invited, by your master. Jonas t'Riseri. We met yesterday at the Salinas embassy. Just go and ask, I promise you."

Very reluctantly, she let him in to wait in the hall. But after a few moments, she returned, and, with poorly disguised reluctance, showed him in properly, to a reception room where Urso stood with a smile. His coat lay on the table beside him.

"Sr Leanvit," Jonas said, bowing formally. "I am sorry, were you just going out?"

"No, no, indeed the opposite," Urso said, greeting him with a Salinas double handshake. "I have just come in from an early appointment. And truly, just Urso is fine." He nodded, looking satisfied about something. Perhaps the meeting he had just come from.

"Now, Sr t'Riseri, I did not expect to see you again so soon."

"Jonas, really," he said, flushing. "I didn't... I mean, you said... But probably you are busy now."

Urso was eyeing him a little speculatively, but then broke into a cheerful, open smile. Jonas relaxed a little.

"Not at all," Urso said. "What is it that I can do for you?"

"The books. The magic," Jonas said, then cursed himself for being so incoherent and tried again. "You said, you had books on magic. Not just Marek-magic, but other magics."

"Indeed I do. Perhaps you would like to see my library?"

"It's probably an imposition," Jonas said hastily, beginning to regret this, but Urso shook his head.

"No, no. I have a turn or two before my next appointment, and I am always delighted to share my enthusiasm. If anything I fear I will end up imposing on you – do stop me if you become bored."

Urso led Jonas up the staircase to the library on the first floor. The place was full of books. More books than Jonas had ever seen together in one place. His vague notion that he would be able to look at everything and find whatever was useful crumbled away. Thinking hopefully of a useful flicker didn't produce anything, either. Stupid ability, showing up only when it wasn't wanted.

Urso stood back, smiling a little, as Jonas peered at the shelves. Was *all* of this stuff on magic? Some of the shelves had labels on: Geography, Languages, Novels and Stories. No, then. Where then was the Magic shelf?

"What exactly is it that you're interested in?" Urso asked. "Perhaps I can direct your search. I admit that I'm a little surprised – I know the Salinas take little account of magic."

Jonas did his best to look nonchalant. "As I said before – I've been interested in it since I was small. Maybe because it's not known at home. Different, you know?"

All of which, strictly speaking, was true.

"It's foretelling that I'm most interested in," he went on, a little cautiously. "Prophecies and that sort of thing. My Mareker friends don't seem to think much of that, other than a few stories about Eli Beckett."

For some reason, that made Urso's smile twitch a little.

"Hm," he said. "It's not strictly speaking magic, of course."

Jonas must have looked disappointed, because he laughed a little. "Well, most magicians and sorcerers would tell you that, anyway. Your Mareker friends... Have you spoken to a Marek sorcerer, then?"

Should he mention Reb? She was public enough, but something tugged at him, telling him to be cautious. He shrugged. "Are there any left? I heard about that plague."

Urso turned away to the shelves. "One or two, but in obscurity. A great loss. Marek magic has been famous since the city's founding. There's a story about some deal that one of them did, Marek or Beckett, at the founding, that has established it that way. The details aren't clear, but you're right that several versions of it include a vision or prophecy."

He poked around on one of the shelves, and pulled a book off it. "Here you are. If you're interested. This is one of the stories told about Marek and Beckett's expedition. It's rather more esoteric than the usual pragmatic discovery-story that the Council and the Thirteen Houses prefer. And is all most likely nonsense, of course, if interesting nonsense."

And in any case, Beckett had already said it was nonsense. Jonas tried not to let his disappointment show.

"Here's something about prophecy from Exuria." Urso handed him a book from another shelf. "They have a tradition of that, in their mountain ranges. I believe the Teren mountains have similar traditions, but I don't have anything about that. You're welcome to sit for a turn or so and look at them."

Jonas was opening one of the books, when he heard Urso take a long breath, the sort that indicated an attempt to broach a difficult subject.

"It is – a great shame, the situation with Marek's magic," Urso said. "There was a great deal of lore here." He hesitated. "I have been doing my best to track down more information about Marek's former magics, so it is not all lost."

Jonas looked up at him, suddenly alert. Might he be in contact with Reb? Or – he blinked. *Cato*? He seemed to be waiting for Jonas to say something. He couldn't be a sorcerer himself. Reb had said there were only the two of them left.

"But I have never heard of a Mareker sorcerer with the gift of prophecy," Urso went on, after a long pause. "It is rude of me, but I do find myself wondering why it is *here* that has your interest. And, ah, if you did have access to any Mareker information about any magics, of any sort at all, I would be most grateful."

He was offering payment, Jonas realised. For information on Marek sorcerers. Well. Reb was public enough, right? Information on her couldn't hurt anyone. Except that just at the moment, telling Urso about Reb might mean him finding Beckett as well, and for some unexamined reason, Jonas was less keen on that. And at any rate – he'd already said that he knew no Mareker sorcerers. He didn't want to give himself the lie.

"Only wish I could help you," Jonas said, shrugging. "As to why I came here – well, I'm Salinas, you remember? We don't know much about any magics. But Marek is famous for magic, right? I figured people would know stuff, here. Seems not." He pulled a rueful face, and sought about for a distraction.

Then his vision went black, and he staggered.

A large room, almost entirely empty. Urso standing in the middle of it, and a sense of other people around him but it was Urso's face which filled almost all of his vision. Urso's face with gold sparkles turning in his eyes, his hands up in invocation of something... Urso performing sorcery. Unmistakable.

His head ached like it was caught in a vice, and he was down on his knees on the floor. For a moment he blinked down at the soft woven rug, unable to remember where he was or what he was doing. They were getting worse. More immersive. More *painful*.

"Jonas?"

The voice from above him was enough to bring him back. He was at Urso's. In the library. Looking at books about prophecy.

Someone – Urso, presumably – was helping him up, a hand supporting his elbow. His head still ached.

"You're a sorcerer," he blurted, and the pressure in his head went away. "You are."

Urso was looking him in the eyes, and there was a moment where Jonas could see him about to deny it, then another moment where he could see Urso putting something together, then...

"And you have the gift of prophecy," Urso said, just as bluntly.

He hadn't contradicted Jonas' claim. That was a tacit admission. Jonas balanced on the knife-edge of denying his flickers... but they both had something on each other now, and Urso had these books, this might be the nearest he had come yet to an answer, and Mid-Year was *tomorrow*...

He'd waited too long to answer. Urso's eyes widened.

"Oh my," Urso breathed, his eyes wide. "But you're Salinas."

"Why d'you think I'm here?" Jonas said, bitterly, giving up on secrecy. "I want *rid* of it."

"You want rid of it? It is true prophecy, and you wish to lose it?"

"I don't know about 'true' prophecy," Jonas said.

It was a relief suddenly, such a relief, to *tell* someone. Someone who didn't look at him in disgust. Someone who was honestly interested. It felt like a breath of sea-air, the first touch of wind when you were becalmed. His hands were shaking with it.

"What is it like, then?" Urso asked, intently.

"Just a, a little picture. A few heartbeats. Like – I call it a flicker. That's all it is."

"But then it comes true?"

"Always," Jonas said. "So far," honesty compelled him to add.

"Can you bring them on at all?" Urso asked. "Deliberately, I mean. Can you *try* to see something?"

Jonas shook his head. "Never tried. I told you. I want *rid* of them."

Urso was paging through one of the books, muttering to himself. "There. That's a description by someone in old Teren of one of her visions. Does that sound like yours?"

The language was archaic, but... "Yes," Jonas said, wonderingly. "Yes, it does."

"Eli Beckett got visions, back in Teren," Urso said. "Or so they said. And then they got here, and... You've heard the legend of the Marek cityangel."

Jonas nodded.

"Well. Not such a legend, in fact. As sorcerers know, but largely choose not to talk about. The lower city accepts the cityangel, Marekhill not so much, but then Marekhill has far less to do with magic, you see." Urso's words were tumbling out over themselves now. "It's the Marek cityangel allowed us to work magic without the blood-price," Urso said.

But Beckett had denied visions... Jonas couldn't say that.

Urso stopped pacing and turned to Jonas. "I think I can help you. I think I can take you to someone who can help. But this is – has to be – a secret. I think we can do a deal, if you'll let me use – share with me – your magical ability. Just for one thing."

"Magical ability? I'm not a sorcerer," Jonas protested.

Urso shook his head. "You don't need to be. It's – I can handle that. It won't do you any damage, I promise."

"What do you want me to do?"

Urso looked downwards, blinking. Calculating. Deciding what to tell, unless Jonas missed his guess.

"There is a new cityangel," Urso said, finally, looking up. "But – it lacks the power, of the old one."

It fell, with a sudden weight, into place. Urso had got rid of Beckett. Urso was working with Daril b'Leandra. They were the ones who had done that to Beckett. Jonas' stomach turned over.

"We need – we have to help the new cityangel find its power," Urso said. "To support it. There is – well, there is a lot of political nonsense going on as well, that there's no need for you to burden yourself with. I will say this though – when I warned of the possibility of danger, to Salina, yesterday? That was flat truth. There is risk of war, and I can help avoid that. Your ambassador is already helping us."

Kia was helping? With magic?

Urso nodded, and Jonas realised that he'd said that aloud.

"Exactly so. This is important enough. That is what I need your help with. You will help Salina, and you will help Marek as well. And afterwards – you can meet the new Marek cityangel, and it can help you. I'm sure it can. What do you say?"

This was the person who had thrown Beckett out. But – but he was fixing it, now. And Beckett couldn't help Jonas. Jonas couldn't help Beckett, either, when it came to that. It was too late for that. The new cityangel might not be able to, either, if Beckett had told the truth, when they said they knew nothing helpful about visions. But it might. It might.

Urso was offering him the best opportunity yet to fix his problem. And he'd be helping Salina as well.

"Yes," Jonas said, and felt his stomach tilt.

☺ ☺

Reb leant in the doorway, and looked out at the morning bustle of the street. Everyone was busy preparing for the Mid-Year festivities later this afternoon and evening, when most of Marek would come to a standstill. The Council did something official up on the hill, but the big celebration was the public one, in Marek Square, with tumblers and fire-swallowers and musicians to keep the crowd entertained until the fireworks as night fell. Along with an extensive array of people selling alcohol – lots of alcohol – and street food.

Marcia had sent a message, the evening before, apologising that family – by which, presumably, she meant political – responsibilities meant that she would not be able to return until the next morning. Which meant this morning, by now. It was fair enough. The urgency was gone; Beckett's place was filled, and anything left was, more or less, damage limitation. Reb would still like to know what magic there was now to draw on, and she might still be *curious* about what Daril b'Leandra was up to, but that didn't make for *urgent*.

Realistically, Marcia when saying this morning had probably meant late this morning, hadn't she?

Yet here Reb was, looking out at the street. Waiting. She rolled her eyes at herself, and sat down on the step. She massaged the tops of her cheekbones with the fingers of her good hand, closing her eyes. She felt wrung out in a way she hadn't in years. And her broken wrist ached vilely despite dosing herself up with the healing recipes she'd learnt as a child.

What *was* Daril b'Leandra doing? And what was Cato doing with him? Being paid, presumably, but contrary to the image Cato liked to project, he did have *some* moral scruples, especially around magic. He wouldn't necessarily fall meekly in line with any plans of Daril's, even for money. And what of this other sorcerer, Urso, that Marcia had mentioned? How had Reb missed him?

Was Marek magic still there? She hadn't dared try. Couldn't even think about trying. Her own failure still rubbed too raw at her. But maybe, perhaps, the new cityangel was doing exactly as the old one had. Maybe. What would happen if she tried it out?

She shook her head, still rubbing at her cheekbones. Too

many questions. Too few answers. What she needed now was a nice calming infusion, and then she could think about the whole thing more clearly.

Beckett was sitting on a chair inside, bolt upright.

"Marcia's not here yet," Reb said, unnecessarily.

"I remember Marcia," Beckett said, suddenly.

"You do?" Reb said.

"She – I was not permitted to engage with the politics of the city, but it forms a part of the city, it," Beckett was gesturing now, trying to suggest something, "it shapes the city. It shapes the way that people are in the city. All of that is part of mine. Or was."

"So you knew the people who are involved in that?" Reb asked.

"I knew everyone in Marek, to a greater or lesser extent," Beckett said, simply. "But often – not until I needed to. Marcia I remember noticing." They looked aside for a moment, eyes slightly unfocussed. "She will be more, I think, in due course."

"She'll be Fereno-Head," Reb said. Her voice came out drier than she intended it to.

Beckett looked back at her. Their eyes were penetrating. "Does that perturb you?"

"Why should it?" Reb said, her shoulders hunching slightly despite her best efforts.

"Because you like her," Beckett said, as if it were obvious.

Reb stiffened. "She's certainly improved over the last ten years, that's for certain."

"It is permitted, to like people," Beckett said.

"It's dangerous," Reb said, more harshly than she meant to. "People I like tend to die."

"Zareth was not your fault," Beckett said. "Nor Marcia's."

"It wasn't Marcia's," Reb conceded. "She didn't realise what was happening, I think, until the last minute. And she did her best to help Zareth. But – if I'd been quicker, if I'd been the one in front, I could have saved him."

"That does not make it your fault," Beckett said.

Reb hunched again. "And the plague, then? Why everyone else? Why not me?"

She hadn't meant to say that either. She'd thought it, over

and over again then and in the two years since, but she'd never said it. There hadn't been anyone to say it to.

"An accident of body," Beckett said. "I know no more than that, but... Cato, too. Both of you survived. It was not a thing with intent, any more than any other disease."

I'm still dangerous, Reb thought, but didn't say. *I shouldn't get attached to people.*

"Remaining alone is – unwise," Beckett said, looking away again.

"So you have attachments, then?" Reb demanded. "The cityangel is not alone?"

Beckett looked back at her, and their eyes looked more human than they had before. "How do you think I know this, Reb?" They looked away again. "You like Marcia. That is a good thing. Do not deny yourself that."

The conversation, thankfully, seemed to be over. Beckett crossed the room and leant out of the window. It was the most casual Reb had ever seen them look, elbows resting on the windowsill, neck craning forwards between slightly hunched shoulders.

"Is there something special today?" Beckett asked, without looking around. "The street seems... different." They frowned. "Unless it is my misunderstanding."

"Mid-Year." Reb shrugged. "Doesn't make much odds to me, though. Other than that I'll have more need for a bunch of late-protection charms in the next couple of days. Good job that's almost all herbs, rather than magic, or we'd have a little population explosion in nine months. I suppose I should double-check what I've got around..."

She was turning to her workroom door, intending to check the levels of the jars she'd need, when Beckett made a peculiar noise, and she turned back.

They stood against the wall by the window, rocking backwards and forwards. Their eyes were fixed on nothing at all, and their face was distorted out of its calm expression to what she could only read as fear.

"Beckett?" she asked cautiously, then, as Beckett didn't react, "Beckett!"

They were still rocking, more and more violently. Reb got up and went over to stand in front of Beckett, and, still getting no reaction, hesitated for a moment before gently putting her hand on their shoulder. It was the first time she'd touched Beckett, and she wasn't sure what to expect. But they felt just like any other human. That was almost more disconcerting than any of the possibilities that had briefly run through her head.

Then Beckett's hand shot up to her wrist, moving inhumanly fast. For a moment Reb could feel her pulse beating hard against the imprisoning fingers and the pressure of her wrist bones grinding against each other, and wondered if she was about to break the other wrist. Almost as soon as the thought was formed, Beckett let go again. Reb took a hasty step back.

Beckett was focusing on her again, but they still didn't look normal.

"Beckett? What... is something wrong?"

Beckett swallowed. It was an oddly human gesture on a body that still didn't quite hold itself like a human one.

"The festival," Beckett said, after a moment, and stopped.

Reb frowned. "Yeah. Mid-Year. Today. So what?"

"Do you know how much *power* that generates?"

Reb shook her head. "Surely not. I mean, nothing I've ever noticed. There's, well, for certain there's an atmosphere to it, but..." She stopped. "Now I come to think of it, I don't think I've ever used a spell on Mid-Year. Other than once." That time, ten years ago – and it kept coming back to that. Exactly ten years ago, now, to the day. That had been Mid-Year, and now Reb remembered, reluctantly, the fizz of her skin as they went in. She'd put it down to the excitement, the adrenalin. But if there was more power that day...

She blinked. "How could I not know that?"

Beckett shrugged. "The power is... It goes inwards. Not outwards. You wouldn't, necessarily..." They made a frustrated gesture.

"Inwards?" Reb said. "Inwards – to you?"

"It was to me. Now..."

"To the new one," Reb said, understanding beginning to dawn.

There was a knock on the door, and Reb hurried to answer it. It was Marcia, looking slightly harried.

"Come in," Reb invited, feeling an unexpected warmth in her chest, despite her building anxiety. "Beckett is just explaining that Mid-Year is a big deal, cityangel-wise. Which – well. Come in."

"They must be planning to use it," Marcia said, her voice absolutely certain, once she understood what they were saying.

"But they wouldn't have known," Reb argued. "If I didn't know, how would they have known?"

"If it, whoever is in my place now, did not know before, then they do now," Beckett said.

"But what *for*?" Reb asked.

"I don't know," Marcia said. "But – I wonder, now, if it might have anything to do with this absurd idea of my mother and Gavin Leandra. Given that Urso is involved with both. It seems too much of a coincidence otherwise."

She explained the previous day's meeting. "But I don't understand how it could hook into the cityangel business," she finished. "Unless it truly is coincidence. But Urso, again... I can't believe it isn't linked."

"*I* can't believe I missed another sorcerer," Reb said, scowling.

"He's Marekhill," Marcia pointed out. "He'd be trying to keep it quiet. And he was never much of one, back when – back then. I suppose he must have improved. But Gavin Leandra wouldn't be hanging around with a known sorcerer. It would ruin Leandra. It's an absolute prohibition."

"Hang on," Reb said, slowly. "The prohibition. Gavin Leandra taking this Urso along to your meeting and not Daril."

"I don't know why he doesn't just get on and disown Daril, if he's going to," Marcia said, irritably.

"No," Reb said. "That's it. That's the point. Why does Daril b'Leandra wastrel around town like that? Because his father won't allow him any power, and isn't likely to. That's what you and Jonas said. What would you do, if you were him?"

"A coup," Marcia said. Her eyes were wide and horrified.

"But that's hard work, and chancy. Unless you get magic involved."

"I told him," Beckett said.

Marcia and Reb looked around at them.

"Told who?" Reb asked.

"The one who asked me, a while ago. I told him what I always tell them. Magic and politics do not mix. That is part of my deal, with Marek and Beckett. I tell them that."

"You told them no," Marcia said, her voice flat. "So they worked out how to replace you with someone who would say yes."

"Because the deal was between *you* and Marek and Beckett," Reb said. "The new one doesn't have that limitation."

"And it's about to get a whole bunch of power, today," Marcia said. "When the Council chamber will be full, for Mid-Year."

They all three looked at one another.

"A coup," Reb said. "They're planning a coup. Today."

FOURTEEN

Marcia was trying to process the idea of what Daril was intending, to fit it in with everything else that was happening, politically and otherwise. Her brains felt scrambled.

"Well," Reb said. "Now would be a good time to establish whether the cityangel is responding to magic."

Marcia blinked. "Surely it is a better time to go and warn the Council!"

"And tell them what?" Reb demanded. "Ask them to do what?"

"Daril has broken the law!"

"Can you prove it?"

Marcia opened her mouth, then shut it again. If she could find Cato... And then what? She'd hardly had much luck in persuading him of anything the last time she'd tried that, had she?

"Can you ever provide proof enough to persuade Gavin Leandra to allow them in to search?" Reb pressed.

"My word as Fereno-Heir," Marcia said. "I saw, in the Park..."

"And then you passed out. They'll say it was hallucination, imagination. We need to know what is happening with magic, before I can have any idea what to do next."

"It is *today*," Beckett said. There was urgency in their voice, rather than their usual flatness.

Marcia shut her eyes and pushed the heels of her hands against them.

"Reb. What do you need?" she asked, opening her eyes again. "You mentioned grounding, before. What does that mean?"

She couldn't quite read the emotions playing across Reb's face. Angels, she really was tired; she was good at faces. You could hardly do anything useful in the Council if you weren't; at least not when you were half the age of the rest of the vote-holders. She couldn't impose and intimidate like Gavin

Leandra, or even like her own mother, when she laid aside the gentle coaxing and drew herself up as Head of her House. Marcia had to guess and gently manipulate.

And she was *tired* of it.

"I – thank you," Reb said, eventually.

She gave Marcia a half-smile, and Marcia felt her shoulders relax just a little. "Actually, I could use you, if you think you're capable. I mean, you look a little tired." She sounded cautious.

Marcia shrugged. "I should be fine as long as you're not expecting anything very strenuous. Remember I haven't done this in ten years. Not since Cato left home."

Reb nodded, and went to unbolt the workroom door. "Beckett, best you stay out here. If the cityangel does respond – well, I don't know if it would be able to tell that you're here, or who you are, but maybe let's not find out right now?"

There was warmth in the pit of Marcia's stomach, as they entered the workroom and Reb shut the door again. Reb trusted her to help. Reb was letting her in.

Reb was muttering to herself as she moved round the small inner room, collecting bits and pieces and dumping them onto the long table. The table juddered as she slammed jars down, working one-handed. A carved wooden spoon nearly bounced off the table's edge. Reb lunged with her splinted arm, caught it with the tips of her fingers, then swore, evidently in pain. She swapped the spoon to the other hand.

"Are you…" Marcia asked tentatively.

Reb grimaced. "I can't do magic in this state of mind. Give me a moment."

She looked down at the delicately carved spoon. Gradually, Marcia saw her face relax, and heard her breathing slow. Marcia could have sworn she could hear Reb's heartbeat in the still room; and her own heart beating along with it. No sound leaked in from outside. It felt as though the world was shrinking to just this room, and the two of them in it. Marcia's skin prickled.

"You seemed – anxious," she said tentatively as Reb looked up again, after a final long exhalation.

"I seem anxious," Reb repeated, a little dryly. "I've a fallen cityangel camping out in my front room and one of the Noble Heirs stood in my workroom. Magic has stopped working the way it's done for my entire life, a very competent and completely amoral sorcerer," Marcia winced, "has decided to involve himself in politics and in particular in some plot of Daril b'Leandra, who is not famous for his patience or tolerance. Why under the skies would I feel anxious?"

She sighed, then smiled at Marcia. "Come on then. I just need an anchor, truly. Nothing too taxing at all. You said you did this for Cato?"

"A long time ago," Marcia said. "When we were sixteen or so. He used to ask me when he wanted a bit more freedom to let his mind go wandering."

"Right, yes, that's surprisingly sensible, for Cato," Reb said. "This should be easier than that. All I'm going to do is a simple guardian-spell; wouldn't dream of bothering with an anchor normally. I mean, I nearly never do anyway, these days, what with..." She trailed off, and Marcia knew they were both thinking of the plague.

"Then why now?" Marcia asked, pulling her mind back to the moment.

"It refers to the cityangel. So I'm not sure what will happen when – if – it responds. Best to be careful." She wrinkled her nose.

"What do you need me to do?" Marcia asked.

Reb knelt down and began to draw a circle with chalk on the floor around them.

"Come in here with me – yes, that's it."

She completed the circle, enclosing them both within it. Reb stood up, and took a pinch of something out of one of the little bags that hung from her belt, then turned slowly, casting it around the circle. As she came back to the beginning, Marcia felt something reverberate in her bones, a sound like a huge door shutting softly.

Reb glanced at her but didn't comment.

"Best maybe if you sit on the floor," she said, after a moment of consideration. "And we need a physical connection, to be safe." She snorted. "Seems ridiculous, doing this much for a guardian-spell. Still. Better cautious than drowned, eh? And I'm used to being able to use both hands, there is that."

She snorted.

Feeling faintly foolish, Marcia settled herself to the floor – her mother would be horrified, a little voice told her, at the lack of dignity – and, at Reb's direction, laid a light hand on the other woman's ankle.

"Skin contact," Reb said gruffly, and Marcia slid her hand under the wide cuff of Reb's trousers.

Reb's skin was warm and smooth, the little hairs on her ankles gently prickling Marcia's hand. The back of Marcia's neck prickled, too, and Marcia swallowed.

Reb took a deep breath and began the steps of the spell. Marcia watched her pinch a bit of that, and a bit of the other, and finally mutter something under her breath. For a moment, the air within the circle felt strangely empty, then Reb dropped her hands. A shiver that ran through the air around them.

"Nothing," Reb said.

"Nothing?" Marcia echoed.

"Like calling and not getting a response. Or, more, calling into an empty room, and you know that it's empty, except, you also know it's not empty at all." She scowled. "I've never known a guardian-spell not answered in *some* way. Even if you just got the echo."

"Does that mean the rules have changed?" Marcia suggested.

Reb's scowl deepened, but she didn't answer. She nibbled on her thumbnail absently for a moment, obviously considering her options. Then she cleared the circle out carefully with a fold of her tunic, dusting the floor clear to beyond the edge of the circle. She set the circle again, and again Marcia felt that soft silent reverberation in her bones. This time, the spell took longer. Goosebumps rose on Marcia's skin as Reb scattered a pinch of this, and then a pinch of that across it, as she bent and traced something through the scatterings on the floor. By the time Reb spoke the final syllables to release the spell, Marcia could barely stop herself from twitching, her tongue pressed between her teeth and her breath coming fast.

There was a pause within the circle. Reb cocked her head, as if listening, but Marcia couldn't hear anything. Then the air thickened, like a hammer blow coming from every direction at once. Reb went flying across the circle then bounced off an invisible wall at its boundary. She screamed; it looked like she'd taken the force of the blow with her bad arm. Marcia's hand was still clutching Reb's ankle, and she too was dragged across the circle with Reb, then had her own wrist painfully bent as Reb hit the floor. Reb began to shake, as though a huge hand had her by the scruff of the neck. Marcia clung grimly onto Reb's ankle, her arm flung backwards and forwards with whatever was moving the other woman. Suddenly, Reb was still, and her body began to slump forwards. Marcia relaxed her grip, just a little, then clenched her fingers hard again, desperately hard, as she felt Reb being pulled away from her. The pull got harder and harder, Reb's skin slipping under her fingers, now growing damp with sweat, yet Reb wasn't moving at all. There was no physical sign of the huge force of whatever was tugging at her. Wherever she was being pulled, it wasn't in this plane of physical existence at all.

Marcia's breathing was coming shorter, a scream rising up in her throat which she tried to push back. She could react later. Right now she had to, *had to*, keep hold of Reb. Her fingers slipped a little more, and she swallowed hard and wrapped her second hand over the first. It felt like she too now was being dragged across the floor, yet still neither of them were actually moving.

Then, abruptly, whatever was pulling them let go. Reb slumped onto the floor. Marcia's fingers were still wrapped tightly around her ankle. She didn't dare loosen them.

The room was silent, but there was no longer a sense of any presence other than the two of them. Marcia could see Reb's chest shallowly rising and falling, but she wasn't moving.

Without letting go of that ankle, she shifted herself round to check Reb's pulse with her other hand. It was fast, but steady, and easy to find. She was breathing, her heart was fine, Marcia couldn't see any blood... But she was still out cold.

Then Reb coughed, and stirred, and opened her eyes.

"Reb!" Marcia's voice cracked a little.

Reb levered herself up to a sitting position one-handed, and coughed rackingly. She looked around her, blinking a little, seeming to check everything against some inner expectation. She took a long, deep, ragged breath, and let it out again.

"Well then. Let me bring the circle down, and you can let go, Marcia."

Marcia's ears popped as Reb released the circle, and she saw Reb shake her head quickly too. Trying to conceal her reluctance, Marcia let go of Reb's ankle. Her fingers were stiff and slow to unclench.

"Thank you," Reb said quietly. "If you hadn't been able to hold on…" She swallowed. It was disconcerting, to see confident tough Reb look suddenly so pale. "Well, I suppose you'd be sweeping up little pieces of me now. Or nothing at all." She shrugged, and pasted on a grimace of a smile. "I owe you one, anyway."

"No you don't," Marcia said, then stopped, and swallowed in her turn. "We're quits now. That's all."

Reb looked at her for a long moment, and Marcia felt her breath come faster. She felt like Reb might be looking straight into her heart. Then Reb nodded, softly, once, and looked away. Marcia locked her fingers against their trembling. Reb tolerated her now. Trusted her, even, at least a little. That was all, it was enough, and she shouldn't go looking for anything else.

"So then," Reb said, more loudly. "There's something there. In case you missed that part. And it didn't like me bothering it. It may have the power of a cityangel, but it certainly doesn't have all the responsibilities. Or," she paused, "the limits. That one," she nodded out towards the other room, "would never have done that. Never."

Marcia swallowed.

"I don't know what to do," Reb said, sounding lost, and Marcia didn't know what to say.

☉ ☉

Marcia was still looking at her. Reb couldn't work out what – if anything – Marcia was expecting from her. She could still feel the imprint of Marcia's fingers around her ankle.

"I need to wash my face," Reb said, turning towards the washstand in the corner.

Her good hand was still shaking. Hell, the other one would be if it weren't strapped up. The water in the chipped enamel washstand had a few flecks of dust floating in it, but she couldn't face the idea of going out to the street tap to refresh it. She couldn't ask Marcia to do it. She splashed the water onto her face one-handed, then kept her wet hand over her face for a few moments, breathing deeply and trying to let her shoulders sink back down again, trying to ignore, just for a moment, everything that was waiting for her.

It was a long time since she had felt anything like that. But then, if she were honest, it was a long time since she'd done anything with any kind of risk to it. She'd let herself become what she looked like; a street-corner witch, performing charms and protections and small magics for a few pennies or something in trade. Working for her neighbours and the odd request from further afield.

And there was nothing wrong with street-corner magic, at that. But Reb knew she was capable of more. Zareth would have told her she was avoiding something, if Zareth were still here to say such things.

She hadn't let it slide straight away. Notionally she'd stayed part of that loose confederation who watched out for other magic-users. But she'd stepped back, and back, and back, so far that she had no longer quite known how to step forward again. And then the plague happened, and it hadn't mattered any more.

She wiped her hand on her skirt, and stared at her wet face in the brown-spotted mirror over the washstand. In the corner of it she saw Marcia, looking down at her own hands, waiting. *You've let yourself go, Reb.*

Well; now she was stepping forward again, it seemed, and perhaps that was after all for the best. Although it would be a great deal more for the best if she weren't so out of practice. Surely five years ago, she wouldn't have been blown away like that by such a small piece of magic?

She took a long breath and shook her head slowly. Out of practice she might be, but even if her magic had been small, the response hadn't been. It was as well that Marcia had been there, and had held on…

So. What next? She'd thought, if there was a new cityangel, if Marek's magic was back to normal, perhaps Beckett's situation, and whatever Daril b'Leandra was doing, was nothing of her business. But nothing was normal, neither the cityangel nor magic. And magic most certainly was her responsibility.

She didn't want to believe any of this. But she couldn't avoid it.

She grimaced in the mirror again, then took the thin towel from its hook and scrubbed her face dry. Reb turned back to Marcia, who was standing against the wall, a worried frown creasing her smooth forehead.

"Well then," Reb said, forcing a smile. "Let's go tell Beckett."

Her hands were steady again now. She pulled the door open to the main room, and stopped short on the threshold. Beckett was nowhere to be seen.

"Where… ?" Marcia asked behind her.

The front door was slightly ajar. Reb leant out of the door and looked along the street in both directions, but there was no sign of Beckett anywhere. A couple of children played tag along the street, darting from doorway to doorway. She felt Marcia, close behind her shoulder, her presence now warm and comforting.

"Could they have been *taken*?" Marcia asked, hesitantly.

Reb shook her head. "I'd have known if someone came in. I'd certainly have known if there was someone in the house. It's hardly a big house, after all."

And it was hers, and she was a sorcerer. She'd have known.

"So," Marcia said. "They went of their own accord. Or someone persuaded them out."

"And they went without telling us?" Reb screwed up her nose. "Possible. But I don't think Beckett's quite that daft."

"They went with Jonas, in the first place," Marcia said.

"They were desperate," Reb said.

"They're not desperate now?" Marcia asked quietly.

Reb sighed. "True enough. But – surely they are not *worth* abducting now? Is it not too late? Who would bother?"

"And if they have gone off alone for some reason, raising a

hue and cry would just draw attention to us all," Marcia said. "But on the other hand, if they're in trouble, we risk the trail going cold."

"Wait," Reb said, reluctantly. "A little while, at least."

They left the door open, both, without discussing it, moving the chairs to sit where they had a view of the street.

"I should have known," Reb said, after a silence. "All of this. I should have noticed what was coming."

"How?" Marcia asked. "How could you have known? It's hardly a thing to think of, replacing the cityangel."

Reb scrubbed at her face with her hands. "No, but… I haven't… I should have been watching. I used to watch, once. For problems."

"And fix them," Marcia said quietly. "We've all got things we should have done." She was speaking almost to herself.

"You were a child," Reb said.

Marcia shrugged. "I should have known better, all the same. I have a responsibility to Marek, and I knew that even back then. But," she huffed a half-laugh, "Daril was convincing, I suppose. And I was very young, you're right."

Almost, Reb reached for her hand. Almost. But Marcia wouldn't want that, she was certain of it. Marcia was younger, she was Marekhill, she had made her mistakes back when she was barely more than a child. Reb had made her own mistakes back in her own childhood, for certain; but now she was finding a whole new array of the damn things to make. She had no right to offer anything to Marcia.

But she could make a decision, here and now. She could choose to do something about the current situation. She could take responsibility for Marek magic again, regardless of what was happening to Beckett. She didn't know yet what that would actually mean, but she could damn well start working that out.

"Right," she said, standing up, but Marcia was pointing up the street.

Beckett, tall and slender and pale-haired, came around the corner of the street, walking lightly, no sign of any harm. Reb and Marcia both took a deep breath, at the same time, then caught one another's eyes and smiled, not without a hint of irritation at Beckett.

"You're back," Reb said, as Beckett loomed in the doorway.

"Yes," Beckett agreed, stepping inside and shutting the door.

She could hardly bawl them out. They had as much right as she did to walk the streets alone and without anyone's permission. Rather more, if anything. And now that they were back, it seemed somehow absurd that she had worried at all. Who could harm a cityangel?

The ones who had cast that cityangel out, perhaps. Beckett wasn't a cityangel right now, after all. That was the problem.

"We wondered where you were," Marcia said, an edge to her voice.

Beckett's head went up. They stared at both Reb and Marcia as if staring into their souls.

"I was never in any danger." Beckett sounded as if the idea was an absurdity.

"I dare say you were not," Reb agreed. "But in the circumstances, we were nonetheless concerned."

Beckett nodded, once.

"So where *were* you?" Marcia demanded, into the silence that stretched out again.

"I needed to look," Beckett said.

"At *what*?" Marcia asked impatiently.

Beckett made a flowing, expansive gesture, their hand taking in the whole city despite the size of Reb's small front room.

"It is my city, but it is not the same as before," they said. "I know it, but now I feel it differently."

They paused, and Reb took another slow, deep breath, and caught Marcia's eye in time to forestall another question.

"I know every inch of this city," Beckett said, their voice quiet. "I know how it moves, what it does, how its lifeblood flows through it in all its various ways. I have walked these streets since there were streets here. But this time, I walk the streets and I feel them fully under my feet. I can stop for a fish roll and I can speak and be spoken to, I can buy it, I can *taste* it. For myself, not just through someone else's senses. I can smell the river flowing past the docks; I can smell the tar and rope and piss of the docks. I can *exist* here." Their voice had risen, and now it sank again.

Listening, Reb felt a sudden surge both of empathy, and of deep disquiet. To know Marek for all these years and yet never to have physically experienced it.

"I want my city back," Beckett said, their voice implacable. "I know it more now than I have before, and I want it *back*. It is still mine. I can taste and smell and feel, but it is *not worth it*. I want my magic. I want my city. It is still *mine*, and I want it *back*."

Reb took a deep breath.

"Then let us sit down and talk about that, cityangel."

FIFTEEN

Jonas didn't know where he'd expected Urso to take him, when they left the house on Marek Square; but it certainly wasn't the Salinas embassy.

"*Jonas?*" Kia said, in shock, once Xera had shown them into the main reception room.

"Jonas and I have had what you might describe as a meeting of minds," Urso said cheerfully. "He has come to be of assistance to us."

Jonas glanced sideways at him, and saw calculation in his eyes. What exactly was Urso's angel in all of this, he suddenly wondered.

"I have a question, and Urso has promised to help me with it," Jonas said, hoping that this would be enough to slake Kia's curiosity; or at least that it would put her off for long enough that he could get away after... whatever it was that was going to happen here. "But I would like to know what is happening here," he added, hoping to distract Kia.

In particular, he wanted to know when he was going to meet the new cityangel, which was after all the whole point of this. But he had an uncomfortable feeling about what was happening here. Why would Kia be involved with Urso and Daril and the cityangel? This was most definitely magic. Kia had been expressing discomfort about magic only a day or two ago; it wasn't like she'd gone native or anything while she was here. But then – she was smart, and she knew her business, and Jonas knew absolutely nothing about diplomacy. He must be missing something. There must be a good reason for this.

Kia scowled, forgetting Jonas' business for the moment. "Well, and if your questions have brought you here to support your country, that is all to the good. Urso brings me news of the perfidy of the Council, the Marek Houses who seek to steal our ships! Our ships, when we have traded fairly here for so many centuries! *Our* ships!"

Jonas blinked at her, confused. "But I thought... You had an appointment, ne? To discuss trading, with Marcia..."

"Who cancelled it," Kia said, darkly. "Which indeed confirmed the word I had already had from Urso." She bowed to Urso, who returned the bow neatly.

Jonas looked between them. "But..."

"Ah, you are thinking as I did; why would this Mareker tell me what his own Council seek to do. Well, not everyone wishes to be a party to such betrayal, no?"

"And, indeed," Urso said, "I cannot but think this is a bad idea for Marek too, and I would much rather prevent it. I don't wish to see my city embroiled in a war it cannot win, for ships it cannot sail anyway." He shook his head. "I have long been a friend to Salina, too, as you well know, Kia. I see the long association between Marek and Salina as overwhelmingly positive for both of our countries, and I am truly horrified at the idea of breaking it. Truly horrified." He sounded entirely sincere. "I do not see what the Council – or at least, those Houses who are a party to this – are thinking. Fereno-Head and Leandra-Head must have lost their minds."

Urso wasn't wrong; it would be a disaster for Marek if they stole Salinas ships. The Mareker fishermen and local river-traders could no more sail a Salinas ship across the Oval Sea than they could fly to the moon; and they'd have no hope of learning before Salina came down in full force to take revenge. It was a stupid plan.

But what then was a House – Houses? – of Marek doing thinking of it? For they were not, in general, stupid; Jonas knew that well enough. If Urso was telling the truth, then something odd was happening. *If* Urso was telling the truth. But surely Kia wouldn't have just believed him, would she? Jonas thought back on Kia's references to their long history together, to Urso's references to it. If Urso had proved honest before, then how many questions would Kia ask, of an honoured friend? But would Urso necessarily treat that bond with the same honour that Kia did?

Urso knew Daril. *Urso Leanvit* – did that mean something to do with House Leandra? Were they related, not just known to one another? Daril was Marekhill. Whatever Marcia might have said about how he wasn't Heir yet, they had influence there, between them, didn't they?

Jonas realised, with a cold wash of warning up his back, that he didn't trust Urso in the slightest.

"Urso has offered his aid, in exchange for my aid," Kia interrupted his thoughts. She grimaced. "You may not like it, though."

"Urso wishes to treat with the cityangel," Jonas said, distracted, still thinking.

What did Urso want here? There was obviously something specific about here, or about Salinas help. What was it that Urso and Daril wanted to do, here, with the cityangel?

Kia blinked at him, surprised, then rallied and went on. "Yes, indeed so. And while Salina does not hold with such things, well, here we are in Marek, and Marekers have dealt well enough with their cityangel for hundreds of years, as everyone knows."

But it's not the same cityangel, Jonas thought, and was suddenly certain that Kia did not know that.

He could explain. He could explain quite a lot. Would Kia change her mind if Jonas told her that Urso had already replaced the existing cityangel – the one that had protected Marek for three hundred years – with one of his own?

But what even *was* Urso's aim, and Daril b'Leandra's? What did they want from the cityangel? And this plan, that Kia spoke of, was it true? All Jonas' instincts told him that there was something off here; that Urso was using Kia. On the other hand – they were bringing the cityangel here, and that was still his best chance to deal with the flickers. And if this nonsense of war was right – and Kia believed it could be, and she knew more about all of this than he did – then it was indeed vital to stop it.

"Urso will treat with the cityangel, and the cityangel will forbid this theft, and all will be well for us again," Kia continued. "If a Mareker – a Mareker who has been an honoured friend to me over the years – wishes to avoid the disaster that this would be to both our countries, I am equally honoured to provide this assistance, even if it would not be my choice of ways to solve the problem."

Urso was nodding soberly, expressing his thanks and assuring Kia that this would be the quickest and cleanest solution for everyone.

Jonas would bet good money – if he had any – that forbidding this theft of ships was not Urso's main aim in talking to the cityangel. But then, that didn't mean that it wasn't part of the plan. He had no *proof* that Urso was in it for himself, and even if he was, that didn't necessarily mean he wasn't trading fairly. Perhaps there really was benefit in this for both Marek and Salina. Perhaps Urso was indeed acting as the honoured friend Kia believed he was. Did Jonas really know otherwise? Wasn't Kia's trust in Urso enough to balance out his own mistrust? Kia had known the man for much longer, after all.

And he, Jonas, still wanted his own answers. (And what if the cityangel didn't hold those answers either? What then? But it was a chance, a hope...)

He shook his head slightly, trying to dislodge his thoughts, trying to come to some conclusion... A flicker hit, like a bolt of lightning. *Reb and Marcia, in an empty room, anxious looks. Where was Beckett? Then Beckett walking in, Beckett tall and powerful and shining slightly around the edges, a sense of power of purpose of...*

"Jonas? Jonas!" Kia's voice sounded as if from a great distance. Jonas realised he was kneeling on the floor, clutching at his head. Storm and wave, they were getting worse. Beckett. Marcia. Reb. They were trying to do something, they were trying to fix this... and he was here with Urso, who was doing the opposite. He might still fix the bloody flickers, but he wasn't going to be helping Salina, and he wasn't helping anyone else here either.

"I didn't – my head –" he managed, before Kia was calling to Xera, instructing her to lead him to the guest room for a rest.

"We have time yet, Jonas," Urso agreed. "Rest for a while."

He didn't know if he wanted to rest. He didn't know what he should be doing, what he should be saying, what decision he needed to make. But he couldn't think of anything to do but follow Xera where she led, the aftermath of the flicker still pounding in his head along with his scrambled thoughts.

☻ ☻

The guest room was Marek-style – bed, not hammock – and sparsely decorated. Paper and ink were arranged neatly on the desk; evidently this was intended for official visitors. Street noise drifted in, very faintly, through the window. Jonas sank down onto the bed and put his head in his hands. What was he doing here? Following Urso around for a sniff of magic? For *answers*, he told himself again. For answers and a fix and a way out, a way home. And this was Salinas business, not just him. Kia had chosen this, and he could support it in all honour.

Except: had Kia chosen right? Jonas couldn't shake off the feeling that Urso and Daril might not have the best interests of Salina at heart. That they had their own political aims. Then again, perhaps those too were for the best. Who was he to know?

And yet, and yet. Government was one thing. The cityangel was another. His flickers didn't seem to be suggesting that the new cityangel was a good and glorious thing. And Urso was lying about it to Kia. But if it could explain, if it could *take away*, his flickers...?

When it came right down to it, Jonas didn't trust what Urso was saying. It all seemed too pat. But he still didn't understand why Urso would want to be here, in the embassy, or why he would want to bring the new cityangel here.

Jonas didn't understand a lot about anything, right now. Why had he picked Beckett up in the first place? Why had he got involved at all? Because a flicker had told him to; because he looked at Beckett and saw someone who needed something. Whatever his mother might have said about the unreliability of his flickers, Jonas had never been able to bring himself to mistrust them. He remembered lying to his mother, telling her that he was ignoring them and that they were dying off. Her nod of approval had shrivelled something up inside him.

He needed to get rid of them. That was why he was here. And Urso – and the new cityangel – was the only hope he had left.

He couldn't exactly save Kia from herself. He couldn't rescue Beckett. The only thing that he could still do was to fix his own problem.

Jonas let his head fall back against the wall. He felt sick.

The door snicked, and Jonas looked up. He didn't immediately recognise the man who stood in the doorway, head tipped slightly to one side, eyes narrow. But he had a look of...

"Cato?"

"You've met Marcia, then," Cato said, and came in, closing the door behind him. "Which I'm guessing means that you are indeed the Salinas lad who Daril said was with her at that party. Good. I want to talk to you."

He leant against the door and continued to look at Jonas with a faint smile. Something inside Jonas leapt in – hope? There was something about Cato's expression... But Cato was working with Daril and Urso. There was no reason to believe he would be any help at all.

"What do you want?" Jonas said, when the silence became too much for him.

"I want to know what Urso has on you," Cato said.

"What do you mean?"

Cato lifted a shoulder. "Urso said or did something to get you here. I don't believe it's noble patriotism. It's personal. What is it?"

"Why should I tell you?" Jonas folded his arms.

"Because maybe I have another solution for it that doesn't involve screwing over Marek and Salina simultaneously." Cato frowned. "Although I don't know why he would want you here in the first place. He was awfully coy about the matter."

Jonas stared at him. "Why do you care? You're on their side."

"Well," Cato said, consideringly. "I was, I suppose. They were paying me, after all. But the thing is, it turns out, after all, that I am not all that enthusiastic about an unfettered cityangel with no tie or binding to Marek, and I'm not terribly keen on Daril as overlord either. He's started annoying the hell out of me."

"But... Then what have you been *doing*?" Jonas definitely

did not understand the direction this conversation was taking, but that little flicker of hope was growing. Cato was, after all, the other sorcerer in Marek. Maybe the new cityangel wasn't the only option after all.

"What I've been paid good money for," Cato said. "Look, mostly I don't give a flying fuck who is 'in charge'. The Council, Daril and his chums, whatever. Those at the top, whoever they are, don't give two shits about those of us over in the squats. Which is something you should probably bear in mind yourself, kid, while I'm on the subject. So. Daril was paying me. That's it." He grimaced. "Unfortunately, it turns out that I do care about Marek, and magic, and the cityangel. Foolishly, I assumed the new one would just step into the old one's shoes. Turns out it's not that simple."

He kicked a heel against the wall. "I hate being wrong. Also, I strongly suspect that Urso has been making trade bets on chaos in Marek, and chaos does not appeal. Not at that scale. I don't care who is in charge. I do care whether there's blood on the streets. And I care even more if Urso says that that's not the intention and is betting against himself." He smiled beatifically at Jonas. "Now. I've just said enough for you to go out of that door and denounce me to Urso and Daril. Or, you could tell me *your* little secret, and we'll see what arrangement we can come to."

"Why don't you just pull out?" Jonas said.

"Well. Urso might try to manage without me, at this point, and he might even do it, especially with your help. Sabotage from within is more certain. Also, if I'm convincing, I might still get paid."

"With my... Hang on," Jonas said. "I'm not a sorcerer!"

Cato eyed him. "Well. Not yet, you're not, not quite. It's in there, though. And – there's something, already. Something you know about yourself. Want to tell me what?"

"I'm not a sorcerer!" Jonas said, but he was remembering that moment in Cato's room, and the way the flickers had been getting stronger.

"You have power," Cato said. "You can deny it as much as you like, but that's just going to make life harder on yourself. Or you could tell me a bit more about what's going on with you, and maybe I can *help*. Just an idea."

Jonas couldn't think about the idea that he had any magical power, right now. Cato couldn't possibly be telling the truth. He couldn't be.

"You're talking about betraying the people you're working with. Why should I trust you?" he said, instead.

Cato flinched, very slightly, and tried to hide it. "A good point. I cannot give you better reason than to say: I vow, on the honour of my House. Even if it has disowned me."

His face was sombre. Against his best inclinations, Jonas was convinced. And anyway: Urso would probably tell Cato all about it, if Cato just asked. Jonas took a deep breath, and for the second time that day, told someone he barely knew about his flickers.

Cato heard out Jonas' halting explanation with a thoughtful frown.

"Well," he said. "I can see why Urso wanted you along. It might not be exactly what we call sorcery, but it's something, right enough. And you say it's getting stronger? Fascinating."

"Urso said the cityangel – the new one – can help," Jonas said.

Cato blinked, and his eyes went wide. "The new one. I thought you simply weren't listening just now, but – you already knew? Then Marcia already knew? Well now. I wouldn't put it past my beloved sister to show up here after all." He showed his teeth in something that approximated a smile. "But let's assume otherwise, for safety's sake. So. Urso might be correct, it's always possible, but in my professional opinion, the likelihood of the new cityangel being either willing or able to help you is slight."

"I don't want help. I want rid of them. Could it do that?" Jonas asked.

Cato looked taken aback. "Get rid… ? Ah yes. Salinas. Of course." He rolled his eyes. "Well – maybe. If it wanted to. And was patient enough not to get rid of a lot of other stuff too. I'm not sure I'd want to trust the insides of my skull to it, myself."

Jonas' heart sank.

"The good news," Cato said brightly, "is that I reckon I can. If you're really sure you want to. We could talk about it, after the dust settles."

"Could you right now?"

"Not without kit, and a bit of research, no. I'd want to double-check a few things. Also – this isn't a charity, messenger-boy. We're doing a deal. You help me screw Daril over and ditch this cityangel. I'll help you. After."

"What happens when you ditch the new cityangel?" Jonas asked. Did Daril know about Beckett?

Cato scowled. "I have to go looking for the old one in a hurry. If it's even still around. Who knows what those idiots did to it. One thing at a time, hey?"

Jonas hesitated. Should he tell Cato about Beckett, or not? He still didn't wholly trust Cato. But, on balance, he thought he trusted him more than he did Urso. And he was pretty sure that he did believe Cato about the cityangel. Cato might have other plans as well, but – he'd put himself in Jonas' power, by telling him all this.

The flicker took him by surprise. It was a tiny one this time, barely half a second, and though it rocked him backwards with its power, it didn't hurt so much this time.

Cato, winking at Reb, dropping his hands...

Cato was watching him intently. "That was one, wasn't it? What was it? What did you see?"

Jonas ignored the question. "The cityangel's with Reb and your sister," he said.

The bone-deep relief that showed on Cato's face didn't look like something he could have faked. "Oh. Marcia, bless you and your interfering ways. Of course the cityangel's with her. So if we can shove a stick into Urso and Daril's wheel, we can sort that out afterwards."

"We couldn't just – let them do whatever it is they're doing, then fix it after?" Jonas asked. Surely it would be the safer, not to mention easier, option.

Cato shook his head. "Firstly, the whole point of this exercise today is to hand over a significant amount of power to the new one. Power which, I might add, it can use entirely unhindered, which is one of the aspects of this whole thing that seriously gives me pause. Secondly, we'll then be in the throes of a coup already, and that's more than likely to get messy. Cut the whole thing off, much tidier. So. Are you with me? I'll remove your flickers, if you want that, once we've sorted this little mess out."

Jonas swallowed, and made a decision.

"You have a deal. I'm in."

☉ ☉

Cato left again after a somewhat unsatisfying discussion which seemed to Jonas to rely a lot on Cato's repeated assurance that he, Jonas, would know what to do when the time came, and that further detail was not only unnecessary but impossible.

He hoped to hell that he'd made the right decision.

But on the assumption that he had – Cato had talked about the old cityangel. There, Jonas could help – if he could get word to Reb, Marcia, and Beckett. The obvious solution would have been to ask Cato to do it. But Jonas still couldn't quite bring himself to hand *everything* over to Cato. What if it was all a setup? And in any case, was Cato all that much better placed to get a message out unseen? Jonas might be locked in, but this room had paper, ink, and a window onto the street. And he was a messenger.

Hastily, he scrawled a note to Reb, telling her about Urso and the cityangel, about Kia and the embassy; though missing out his deal with Cato. He folded it so it would stay shut, pulled his stick of charcoal out of his pocket, and scrawled his initials across the fold.

He opened the window, put his head out, and then swore viciously as he looked around. He'd assumed that it was a window out onto the street, but it gave out onto a central courtyard. If he dropped a message here, no one would see it. He pulled back a little and eyed the window thoughtfully. It was small, but he was skinny. He always had been, and he'd hardly been eating any extra while he was in Marek, on messenger earnings. He put his head out of the window again and looked upwards. The stone was pleasingly and reassuringly rough, and it was only a single storey up to the roof. A nice wide outside windowsill, too, an old style, and a helpful one.

He tucked the message into the front of his shirt, and began wriggling through the window. Hopefully no one would come into the room while he was on his way out. He got his shoulders through – that was the worst done – and turned himself round to face the wall as he got the rest of himself through. The windowsill was wide enough to back his arse onto, and as he gingerly rested his weight on it, it didn't so much as creak. From there, he could grab the top of the window-frame, lean backwards, and pull his leg through to get his foot onto the windowsill. And once he was standing on the windowsill, getting up to the roof was nearly automatic.

He made his way over the roof, towards the street, where a parapet stuck out from the roof, and he could lean over it to look into the street. He'd thought he'd just have to drop the message, but almost immediately he saw a messenger, dodging through the crowds.

"Hey!" he shouted, and the messenger turned to look up.

Storm and fire. Asa.

"Jonas?" they asked. "What are you doing up there?"

"Long story," he called down. "Family stuff. I need this…"

They were nodding already as he waved the piece of paper, and he let it fall into their hand.

"Urgently," he added.

They exchanged salutes, and Asa was off again.

That was a relief. Any messenger would have delivered it, with his mark on it. But it felt like a good omen, to see Asa.

Well then. He'd warned Reb, told her where to come to put a stop to all of this. That was all he needed, surely? He didn't know why it hadn't occurred to him, earlier, just to be out of the window and away. But he was out, now, and he could just – take himself off, out of all of this mess. No need to do what Cato wanted, nor yet what Urso wanted. No need to be involved in any of it.

And then what, for his flickers? He'd have let down both of the people who might offer him help, both at once. Then again, if he went back, he'd have to choose one of them to let down, and what if he made the wrong decision? Perhaps he should just give up this whole business. Go back aboard ship, keep his secret, tell his mother he'd dealt with it. Just – keep that secret, for the rest of his life.

He felt cold at the thought of how long he'd have to live that lie.

And Cato was right. Whatever Urso was planning wasn't a good idea for Marek or for Salina. He could walk away from that, right enough, but... And then, after, Cato would help him. Cato had promised to help him, and somewhat to his surprise, he trusted Cato rather more than he trusted Urso, whatever he'd heard of the sorcerer's reputation.

He gave one last longing look at the roofs around him – escape – then turned and began to climb back up and over the roof, back to the window of that little guest-room.

SIXTEEN

The trouble with trying to make a plan was that Reb had no idea what to do next.

The new cityangel was in place, but it wasn't keeping the magic part of the deal; and Reb very much doubted that it intended to keep the apolitical part of the deal, either. Certainly Daril thought otherwise. Beckett seemed certain that they could still do *something*, that it wasn't too late, but either wouldn't or couldn't explain to Reb exactly what that was.

Beckett was, however, absolutely certain that something was going to happen that used the festival in some way; and the festival was ramping up *right now*, building up to the festivities in Marek Square in a couple of hours.

"Marek Square, then?" Marcia said. She scowled. "I suppose the obvious place is the Guildhall, but I honestly cannot imagine how Daril could get into Guildhall on Mid-Year with enough space to do anything useful. The place will be absolutely heaving."

"Presumably anything that disrupted the official part of the celebration would also disrupt the focus of the power," Reb said, chewing at her thumbnail. "Does that rule out the Guildhall?"

Beckett, pacing up and down the room, waved an impatient hand. "The officials are not important. It is the *people*."

"Well, Marek Square will be full of people, right enough," Reb said. "And there's plenty of buildings round there. Plenty of places to hide themselves."

"Then we go there," Beckett said. "And see what we can find."

"They're not going to be stood in the middle of Marek Square invoking the cityangel," Reb said. "Not unless they intend to make a pretty show of it and put out a hat. We can hardly just break into every building around the square, either."

Beckett looked as though they might be considering doing just that. A muscle was jumping in their clenched jaw. Reb wasn't actually sure what she could do, if Beckett did just decide to storm out and start trying to solve this by main force. Beckett might not have their old powers, but if they were truly angry…

"I may be able to find them, from closer by," they said instead, after a moment, and Reb breathed a quiet sigh of relief.

Which still left the question of what to do when and if they managed to track Daril, Urso, and Cato down. Interrupt whatever they were doing, presumably, but given that Reb's magic was somewhere between unreliable and non-existent right now, and that in any case it depended on the cityangel they were trying to take down, she had no idea how to do that.

Standing around here wasn't getting them anywhere, though.

"Fine," she said. "I guess we might as well go and see what we can do."

"This isn't a *plan*," Marcia said, frustrated. "This is making it up as we go along."

Reb turned round. "If you've got any better ideas, by all means share them!"

Someone knocked on the door. They all looked at one another.

"It does not feel like a threat," Beckett said softly.

The knocking was louder the second time. "Hello?" someone called.

Reb sighed and went to open the door.

The person outside wore a messenger's armband. They had dark brown skin, and spiky-short dark brown hair, they had bare feet, and they weren't much older than Jonas.

"Message for you," they said, holding out a piece of folded paper, their Mareker accent strong.

Reb saw a smeared charcoal messenger mark on it, which she couldn't quite make out, and her own name and address. She frowned. The only messenger who would be contacting her, surely, was…

"You know a Salinas lad called Jonas?" the messenger asked.

Reb hesitated for a second, then nodded.

"He gave me this. From a window up by Marek Square." They frowned. "Look, is he in trouble?"

"Marek Square..." Beckett said from inside, slowly. "Jonas is at Marek Square? And he wishes to contact us?"

The messenger peered over Reb's shoulder. "Hey! Aren't you Tam's friend, from the other day? What're you doing here?"

"Jonas brought me here," Beckett said.

"So, let's not discuss this further on the doorstep," Reb broke in hurriedly. "Let me find..."

She tucked the message under the elbow of her bad arm, and dug in her pocket for a coin. The messenger waved it away.

"Uh-uh. I want to know what's up with Jonas."

"If Jonas needs help, we will help him," Reb said, trying again to give her the coin.

"There must be something funny going on," the messenger said. "Or he'd have delivered it himself. And he didn't look happy, not at all. I want to know what's wrong."

Their voice was rising. A couple of people turned to look as they passed, and Reb winced. The messenger spotted it, and raised their voice a bit more, their jaw set firmly. "I want to know what's happened to Jonas."

"We do not have *time* for this," Beckett said, coming to stand behind Reb.

"I can stand out here making a racket for a really long time, you know, if you don't tell me," the messenger said, their chin going up as they glanced over Reb's shoulder at Beckett. "Jonas is my friend. And every minute you put me off is a minute I get more convinced that there's something badly wrong here."

Another few curious looks from passers by. Reb weighed up the options. They didn't have time to argue this out right now. And they certainly didn't have time to deal with a ruckus in the street. They could show this person the message and then shoo them out again.

"Fine," she said, grudgingly, and stood back to let the messenger in, nearly bumping into Beckett before they took a step back as well. "Who are you, anyway?"

"Asa. I'm a friend of Jonas'. I've run messages for you, come to that, remember? And I met you," they nodded at Beckett, then looked embarrassed. ""But I'm sorry, I've forgotten your name."

Couldn't have known it, in fact, Reb realised, given that Asa must have met Beckett before Jonas brought them here, to Reb's own door. And hadn't that worked out well for her? She clenched her teeth.

"Beckett. And that is Reb, and Marcia."

Reb unfolded the message. There were only a few words. "He's at the Salinas embassy. With Daril, and Cato, and Urso. They're –" she stopped. How much of this did she want to say in front of this Asa? How soon could she get rid of them?

Asa was looking between them. "What's going on?"

If they wanted to know about Jonas, what would satisfy them?

"I was Marek's cityangel," Beckett said, and Reb looked over at them in horror. Beckett was pacing again, energy almost crackling off them. "Reb, there is no *time* to step around this matter. It is not important who knows anything, especially a friend of Jonas. Asa. Jonas is with the people who deposed me, and who are trying to make use of the new cityangel. Now we know where they are, we can stop them."

"Hang on," Asa said. "You're going to need to slow that down a bit."

Reb rubbed at her forehead. It was too late now, for sure, but she wasn't entirely convinced either that this was speeding anything up, or that Beckett was thinking clearly about risk any more. On the other hand – at this point, hopefully if Asa understood, they were less likely to try to interfere.

Beckett had already started a longer version of the story. Reb expected denial or shock or some other reaction, at least somewhere in there; but Asa just listened, and at the end, nodded.

"So Jonas is stuck with these Marekhill folks who screwed you over, for some political Marekhill aim of their own. Right. What are you going to do about it?"

"I want to know what Salina are doing involved in this." Reb said. "What could make Salina want to be involved with a coup in Marek? Especially with magic involved."

"Urso," Marcia said, in tones of enlightenment. "I met with Urso, the other day. He talked Gavin Leandra and my mother into agreeing to confiscate Salinas ships. I told them it was a bad idea, but they – well. They wouldn't listen to me. If he's with Daril, that all starts to make sense. Kia would support their takeover, magic or not, if he told her about that and promised to stop it."

"The Salinas embassy fronts onto Marek Square," Reb said.

"That's where Jonas was!" Asa said. "I'm pretty sure. It was the back street, and it was at the far corner from the door I know, but it fits."

"Marek Square," Beckett said. "The centre of power. Let us go."

"It's a good idea. I mean, technically speaking." Reb scowled. "I can't see how I *missed* this Urso."

"It is not *important* now," Beckett said. They were already at the door. "We must *go*."

"But – Beckett, wait. I can't use sorcery. You can't use sorcery." Reb said. "I don't know what we can *do* when we get there."

"Clock them all over the head hard enough and it won't matter," Asa suggested. Their grin showed their teeth.

"More to the point," Marcia said, "if we don't get there soon, it won't matter. Time's passing. This power that Beckett keeps talking about is going to be peaking. Think of something on the way. Beckett's right. We have to go."

☉ ☉

Cato wandered back through the corridors of the embassy, towards the main ballroom, feeling faintly pleased with himself. A feeling underlaid by a somewhat unfamiliar nervousness. He did not, as a rule, cheat on people who were paying him money. On the other hand, he had never previously been involved in attempting to replace the underpinnings of Marek's magic.

He scowled. He really should have thought all of this through more carefully in the first place. If they'd come to him *before* getting rid of the old one… In all honesty, he was slightly impressed by Urso pulling that part off. He wouldn't have thought Urso would have had the ability. But if they'd come to him *first*, Cato could have suggested a number of other ways, rather better thought-out, for achieving a similar end result. If what they wanted was a coup, then this was, even if it had gone wholly smoothly, somewhat overkill as an approach.

But he hadn't been there at that point. He'd been brought in to repair the damage, and at the time it had seemed like an easy enough way to resolve what was, undeniably, otherwise going to be a problem. As long as the magic *worked*, it hadn't seemed, while he was discussing the situation with a very impatient Daril, as though the detail of how they would manage it mattered. Nor yet what Daril wanted to do with it. Marekhill politics were no longer Cato's business; he'd made that decision ten years ago, and he had never yet regretted it.

But this time, he should have thought about it more carefully. Given that he knew fine well that the cityangel was real enough, he should have realised that the stories of the deal between Beckett, Marek, and the cityangel were also more than just stories. He should have thought harder about what the bond between city and cityangel actually meant. He scowled again. Power without responsibility, that was what they were in the process of setting up now; and with the sort of power that the cityangel was about to have access to, that couldn't possibly end well.

Of course, that was basically what Daril was after, on his own level. So perhaps no wonder that Daril himself hadn't thought that it might be a problem. Daril never had been all that good at thinking things through. Urso was the smart one; but Urso quite clearly didn't give a rat's arse as long as he was getting something out of it. Cato was pretty sure that Urso was set up to get more than one thing out of this. Chaos could, contrary to popular opinion, be quite good for business if you'd made the right preparations in advance.

Which left Cato himself to sort this shit out, now that he'd been foolish enough to enable it thus far. Jonas' arrival was a stroke of real luck. Cato would have backed himself, if going toe to toe with Urso, but having a little extra on hand would most certainly be an advantage, whatever Jonas might think of his own abilities (and that was something to sort out properly after the cityangel thing was dealt with). The news that the old cityangel was still around was even better; that would save Cato quite a bit of work. And finally, Jonas could now back up Cato's claim that he was doing his best to fix this, if Reb showed up at some point being all opinionated and worthy.

He scowled. Hard though it was to admit, at this point he would be quite grateful if Reb showed up being all opinionated and worthy. Jonas might have a bit of power, but Reb was a trained sorcerer, and strong with it. In her absence, he was going to have to talk Urso into including Jonas in this little ritual they had upcoming. Tempting though it was to just knock him over the back of the head, that wouldn't get rid of the new cityangel. If they ran the ritual, there would be a moment of vulnerability, and if Cato could break things down then, he could take advantage of it.

Hopefully. He thought.

He'd reached the first floor ballroom doors. He took a breath, pasted on his best careless smile, and walked in.

Urso was drawing a complicated chalk sigil in the middle of the room. More overkill, in Cato's professional opinion. Too many squiggles when a plain design did the job well enough. Clearly Urso found it reassuring, but that was because Urso was at best a mediocre talent, even if stronger than he ought by rights to be.

Daril stood at the window, looking out over the growing crowd in Marek Square. He was wearing his formal House jacket, over loose trousers. Cato found it faintly amusing that Daril had taken the trouble to put on Marekhill formal wear in order to go up and knock them all down. One might wonder whether his heart was really in the whole thing.

"Where did you find the Salinas kid?" Cato asked. "Good to have a little extra talent to draw on. Three's a much nicer number for a circle than two."

Urso carefully finished all but the final join of his circle, then looked up with a frown.

"Talent? The boy hasn't any talent. He's Salinas, Cato. They don't *have* magic. Some kind of fits he seems to have, seems to think they're prophetic, but it's hardly *magic*."

"I beg to differ," Cato said. He felt more cheerful now he was arguing with someone. "It's a bit out of the trad Marek line, but I assure you, he's talented, and the fits, as you call them, are related. Isn't that why you brought him?"

"I brought him as an extra handle on the ambassador," Urso said. "There's a family link of some sort. Same surname."

Cato knew how Salinas surnames worked, and it didn't make them family in the way Urso meant. But it was a bond, right enough, and probably a reasonable enough idea. The ambassador was clearly not entirely happy with this whole setup. Urso was lying, though. He might not have spotted Jonas' full ability, or have intended to include him in the ritual, but Cato was moderately certain that Urso was very interested in what Jonas called his 'flickers'.

"Well, he's here and he's got ability," Cato said. "Let's use him."

"No," Urso said flatly. "I'm not bringing some random Salinas kid into this."

Cato showed his teeth. "On your own head be it if it's all a bit much and you pass out again, then."

"I won't..." Urso began hotly.

"Stop it, both of you," Daril said, turning around.

He looked somewhere between tired and wired, his eyes a little too bright. And – for the love of all – he was wearing formal face paint. Cato bit the inside of his cheek, trying not to laugh. Did Daril even *realise* how much he already had invested in this stupid system?

"Urso, you've told this boy already what we're about, so it's not like we're breaking secrecy," Daril said.

"Doesn't mean he's reliable," Urso said.

"I can keep a hold on him," Cato said confidently. It was even true. If he'd wanted to do it. "He doesn't need to be reliable. It just gives me a bit more backup. I did say, already. Before. Two is not ideal, it's unstable, Daril has to be elsewhere," and was talent-free anyway, but that was a bit of a sore point and there was no advantage to poking at it right now, "and the ambassador is one hundred percent talent-free."

"You did say," Daril agreed. "And it's not like we haven't had that problem before."

"We can *manage*," Urso said.

"You thought that before," Daril said, lifting an eyebrow. "We brought Cato in for expertise, remember? If he thinks it'll work, let's do it."

Cato should probably have felt more guilt about that.

"*Thank* you," he said aloud. "It's nice to be appreciated."

Daril scowled at him. "Don't get carried away."

"You should be gone, Daril," Urso said. "We need you there in the next twenty minutes or so. Do you have the link?"

Daril raised his wrist, shaking the sleeve of his jacket down. A twisted wire gold bracelet shone on his wrist. Urso wore a similar one. The two of them would link to transfer the power that the cityangel would generate in this ritual up to Daril, in the Chamber, enabling him to conduct his takeover. It was an interesting technique, and not one Cato would have thought of. It was also slightly annoying that Urso had insisted that he would be the only one to link from down here. Anyone would think that Urso didn't wholly trust Cato.

Daril took in a long breath, then let it out in a sigh. His eyes glittered.

"Well then. Good luck, both of you. I look forward to seeing you afterwards."

He walked briskly out of the ballroom, and the door swung shut behind him. Urso and Cato looked at one another. The noise outside the window was getting louder.

"Twenty minutes," Cato said. "Right. You finish up with your candles and what-all. I'll fetch the kid."

Showtime.

☉ ☉

Beckett led Reb, Marcia, and Asa through the streets around the old market. The shops were all shut for the festival, the afternoon sun bouncing off shuttered windows. People sat on doorsteps, passing bottles around and chatting cheerfully; kids ran around playing complicated games of tag. There were a couple of street stalls out in the market itself, doing reasonably brisk business, and there were knots of people standing around in the centre of the piazza or perched on the edge of the fountain. More people were moving slowly in the same direction they were, towards Old Bridge and Marek Square, the centre of the city's festivities.

Beckett's face was set, and they walked like someone with a goal. They shouldered through the slow-moving crowds, and anyone who looked round, ready to get angry, blinked and got out of their way instead. Reb, Marcia, and Asa trailed in Beckett's wake.

The streets grew steadily more crowded as they crossed Old Bridge towards Marek Square. The bridge gave out onto the square on its north side, and the Salinas embassy was on the south side. The square was full of people, with street barrows selling food parked around the edges, and jugglers and fire-breathers and other entertainers performing in spaces carved out of the crowd. In the centre of the square there was a fountain, with a sculpture which was supposed to be an allegory for Marek's relationship with Teren and the countries and states around the Oval Sea. Reb had never been able to make head nor tail of it. Maybe she should ask Marcia. Today, its surrounding ledge was already crowded with people perching on it.

People were still coming off Old Bridge and making their way into the crowd, swelling it by the minute. The main event would begin in an hour or so, when the heads of the various Guilds appeared on the Guildhall balcony, followed by the Council procession down the hill from the Chamber, and then the fireworks as the sun went down. But Reb could already feel the power coiling in the crowd. It was the people who would make this powerful, not the official rituals, and they were here already, making the most of the day.

The buildings around the square were all three or four storeys tall, and their fronts varied between austere restraint and exuberant stone carving. Reb knew the history of it, like any other Mareker: the square had been planned out at some point in the initial settlement of Marek, at about the same time as the Thirteen Houses were establishing themselves at the top of the Hill, but initially it had been a market, with merchants and traders selling their goods around the square. Over time the Guilds had established themselves, and claimed areas of the square for their own goods, which in turn meant that the Salinas had decided to occupy a building on the square to make it easier to negotiate directly with the Guilds (something which had never been popular with the Thirteen Houses, and which contributed to the sometimes-strained three-way relationship between Guilds, Houses, and the Salinas). From there it was a short step to the Guildhalls, built by the Guilds to demonstrate their success and importance. To one side of the embassy was the Glassblowers Guild, and to the other, the Jewellers' Guild. The Spicers, the Cordwainers, the Broderers, the Haberdashers, the Vintners, the Smiths and Cutlers, and the Fishmongers, being the oldest of the Guilds, all had premises on the square as well; the other Guilds had their halls in the surrounding streets, either a little further up Marekhill, or on Guildstreet, which ran along the south side of the river.

Their destination, the Salinas embassy, was directly opposite Old Bridge across the square. It was the least architecturally enthusiastic of the buildings around the square; the Salinas weren't all that interested in competing for Marek eyeballs, given that anyone wanting to do any trading around the Oval Sea had to come to them anyway. Evidently however they hadn't quite been able to ignore the competition; the embassy was a three-storey stone building very much in Marek architectural tradition; on Salina houses were wooden, and in any case the Salinas set far more store by their ships. The architect or the builder had set a carved stone ship above the main portico as an indication, and the Salinas flag flew over it.

Reb glanced over at Marcia.

"You should be at the Chamber, shouldn't you?" she asked. Doing whatever it was the Council did up there before coming down here.

"Yes," Marcia said, without looking round at her. "I thought this was more important."

"I didn't..." Reb paused. "Thank you. I'm glad you're with us."

Marcia looked round and met Reb's eyes. She smiled, a

little tentatively, and Reb smiled back. Even here, wound up as she was, something warm curled in her stomach. Marcia blinked, opened her mouth as if she might be going to say something, then looked away again.

They were a little way into the square, now, and it looked like Beckett was going to plough straight through the crowd and up to the Marek Square entrance to the embassy, in full view of the thousands of people here celebrating. They would probably have made it, too, but just as Reb began to wonder about the wisdom of this – after all, it wasn't like they would be able simply to knock and be let in – Asa darted past her and tapped Beckett on the shoulder.

"Round the back," they said. "It'll be quicker. Follow me."

Asa led them to the west side of the square, and then through a warren of passages and alleyways that tangled out from the square and around it. This was where the work of the Guilds was largely done, and where the bulk of Guild members and shopkeepers lived and worked. There were still plenty of people here, but there was room to move, as there had not been in the square. They fetched up at the corner of the embassy.

"This is the back door," Asa said. "For messages and that."

"Right then," Reb said. "I suppose… Marcia? What's wrong?"

Marcia had stiffened and was staring up the road, through the crowds that were still coming down the hill.

"Daril," she breathed. She turned to Reb. "I just saw Daril going up the hill. In a House jacket, no less. He's going to the Chamber. I don't know what he's going to do there, but…"

"But it's probably closely related to all of this," Reb said.

If Daril had plans in the Chamber, if they failed to stop whatever was happening here… Marcia was the only one of them who could get into the Chamber.

"I have to go after him," Marcia said, obviously reaching the same conclusion.

She was already starting to move. Reb put her hand on Marcia's arm, surprising herself. Marcia stopped and looked round.

"Be – be careful," Reb said. "Look after yourself." Marcia's skin felt warm under her hand.

Marcia stared, then smiled at her, a smile that lit her face up even in their current circumstances, and Reb felt her heart constrict.

"I will. You too. See you... after." She nodded, fierce and certain, and was off up the hill, after Daril, darting through the crowd that was moving against her, running swiftly.

Asa was looking at Reb, their eyes speculatively narrowed. Reb ignored them, and pretended she couldn't feel her cheeks turning red.

"So then," she said. "How are we going to get in here? Quickly, for preference."

In theory she would have guessed that they might still have half an hour, before the moment of truth. But without knowing what exactly it was that Urso and Cato planned, there was always the risk that they would start early. It would be a damn sight easier to stop things before they'd started. Which would still leave the problem of dealing with the new cityangel, but one thing at a time.

She stepped forwards to try the door, just in case, but it was definitely locked. Beckett was sizing it up, body tensing, obviously ready just to kick it in. The former city angel's whipcord-thin frame didn't look capable of it, but that wasn't a bet Reb would have taken. The expression on Beckett's face was terrifying. It would make a hell of a racket, but it wasn't like she could risk using magic right now, either. She sighed, about to tell Beckett to go ahead.

"Wait!" Asa said. "Just – give me a moment, okay? There's an easier option, if that's the sort of lock I think it is."

They went up to the door, a little piece of wire in their hand. "Cover me a bit," they said over their shoulder. "And yell if you see a guard."

Beckett and Reb stood between Asa and the passers-by making their way along the street towards the square. A couple of people looked over at them curiously, then took stock of Beckett's expression and hastily moved away. Reb saw a couple of guard officers passing the end of the street, but they didn't look down towards the embassy. Behind them, there were some scratching noises, a couple of muffled swearwords, and then a click. They turned to see the door swinging open and Asa grinning with satisfaction.

"Is that a standard messenger skill?" Reb asked, eyebrows raised.

"I learnt it in a pub, a while back," Asa said, which wasn't entirely an answer. "Always useful to know things, right?"

Beckett was already pushing past them and through the door, into the empty hallway beyond. Reb and Asa looked at one another, and at Beckett's back.

"Determined, huh?" Asa said, quietly.

"I cannot imagine having as much to lose as Beckett does," Reb said.

She took a deep breath and followed Beckett. Asa pulled the door shut, and fell in behind.

SEVENTEEN

The corridor beyond the door was empty. This was evidently not a main entrance; the wooden floorboards were clean but the walls were plain whitewashed and no pictures or banners hung there. Reb paused, listening for footsteps, for someone noticing that they were here and rushing to investigate, but she heard nothing; and the place had an oddly deserted feel.

Beckett was already stalking down the corridor, and Reb hurried after them, Asa trailing behind her. To the left, halfway along the corridor, a big wooden door stood open, and Reb glanced through to see the kitchen, left tidy and with no one in there. Which was surprising at this time of day. Although, perhaps the servants had been cleared out for the day anyway, given that it was the festival.

Beckett pushed through the door at the end of the corridor, and they came into what was obviously part of the public area of the building. Here the floorboards were a darker wood, more thoroughly polished, and the walls were painted a pale blue. Beckett paused, looking around. They seemed to be smelling the air. Reb couldn't smell sorcery, but she could feel it, like something crawling on her skin, when she was close to someone else in the middle of a spell. She couldn't feel anything right now, but at most that only meant that they hadn't started yet.

There were stairs in the centre of the hallway, and another door stood ajar across the passage. Reb saw a few chairs and a table through the gap; a waiting-room of some sort? Again, though, it was empty. It was quiet down here, a weird hush like the building was waiting for something. Faintly, through the thick front door that faced the stairs, Reb could hear the noise of the crowd outside in the square.

Beckett looked up the stairs. They were wide, with an expensive dark blue stair-carpet running up them. More spaces for public consumption.

"There's a balcony gives onto the square, on the first floor,"

Asa said. They pointed up. "Must be whatever's up there."

Beckett's shoulders stiffened, and they started up the stairs. Reb hurried to catch up with them, though she didn't dare lay a hand on Beckett's shoulder to slow the cityangel down.

"I'm the sorcerer, right?" she reminded them. "Let me go ahead."

Not that she could do much in the way of sorcery right now; but Beckett wasn't exactly a cityangel any more, either. In any case; this was her responsibility. Illicit, dangerous sorcery in Marek, sorcery that touched on Marek's foundations, was hers to deal with. She raised her chin, and stomped up the stairs.

At the top of the stairs there was a wide landing, and another staircase, slightly less impressive, at the back right of the landing. The bedrooms must be up there. To left and right there were doors; at least one must lead into the ballroom, whose back wall was over the stairs. Both doors were shut. But now she was up here, Reb was beginning to feel that faint prickle on her skin. She took a breath, and moved to the right-hand door.

She opened it as slowly and quietly as she could. As she did, the noise of the crowd outside grew louder. They must have the doors onto the balcony open. The door was hinged on the right, so as soon as it was open a little, she was able to lean into it and see a little of the room. Beckett stood just behind her, breathing heavily over her shoulder.

Inside, there was another highly polished floor, and dining chairs lining the wall, with a table between them. It had the air of a room that had been packed away; it wasn't set up at present for the formal receptions it was so clearly designed for. To Reb's left, towards the front of the house, a folding screen wall was pulled halfway across the room, creating a smaller area which could be shut off when necessary. The space between the door and the folding wall was empty, and the wall blocked Reb's view into the rest of the room. She opened the door a little further, and stepped gently into the room. She moved towards the windows that overlooked Marek Square, until she could see through the gap between the folding screen and the wall, into the rest of the ballroom.

Cato, short and skinny, stood side-on to her, beyond the

folding wall. His shoulders were hunched in irritation, and he was saying something that she couldn't quite hear, waving a hand. She couldn't see who he was talking to. Cautiously, she stepped a little further, Beckett and Asa just behind her, until she could see more of the room.

The person Cato was talking to had their back to the folding wall, and wasn't looking towards her. Presumably that must be this Urso that Marcia had spoken of? And across from him, halfway between Cato and Urso – Jonas? She blinked in confusion. Of course Jonas was *here*, but the way he was standing, it looked like he was actively involved in this. The three of them made a circle, and – she looked down at their feet – they were standing in a chalked figure on the floor. A complicated one, too, over-complicated at that. That must be Urso's work, not Cato's. Cato wasn't given to overworking anything.

But what was Jonas doing? He had no magic. Or – angels and devils, had this all been a trap after all? Her stomach turned over, and bile rose in her mouth.

At that moment, he glanced over towards her, blinked, and swallowed. He held her eyes for a fractional moment, then looked away, swallowing again, looking back at Urso, who still hadn't noticed them.

Not a trap, then. But Jonas was involved, somehow. He'd gone over to Urso, to help Urso? Was that why they'd been let into the Salinas embassy, because of Jonas' influence? But then, in that case, why had he summoned them here? Whose side was he on? If he was betraying them then he wasn't betraying them wholeheartedly, so what *was* he doing?

Beckett growled over her shoulder, and Reb swallowed. There was no time to work this out, now. Jonas wasn't about to give them away, but he wasn't going to help them, either, that was the only reasonable conclusion. They were here, now. The only thing to do was to get on with it.

The noise from the crowd outside was still rising. Reb's gaze roamed around the room as she wondered what to do – just rush all three of them? But if they were already in the circle, and had already activated it... and how was Jonas involved, since he didn't have magic? None of this made any *sense*.

Cato shrugged hugely, threw his hands wide, and then

dropped them to his sides and squared his shoulders.

Reb had just enough time to recognise that they were starting the ritual, whatever it was, before all three of them in the circle raised their arms. Jonas was fractionally slower than the others, but he did it anyway. He looked scared, but – he had to be playing both sides, didn't he? Reb clenched her teeth against her unexpected fury and sense of betrayal.

Not important now. Deal with what was there, that was what Zareth would have told her. Look at what's in front of you, not at what you're imagining in your own head. In front of her, there was a circle, and a casting. Start with the basics.

Reb put her good hand into her pocket for a handful of salt and rosemary, and stepped forwards, towards the main room. As soon as she was close enough, she cast the salt and rosemary underhand towards the circle.

It bounced back off the invisible barrier with a rattling sound. Reb swore. Of course that would be too easy.

The roar of the crowd was still increasing. She could see the open balcony doors now, and the mass of people outside in the square.

All three of them must know she was here now, but if they said anything outside the ritual, or left their places, the whole thing would crumble. Jonas still wasn't looking at her, but his eyes were wide with what might be hope. Would he even know that he could break this just by stepping backwards? Would he dare?

Cato smiled across at her, seraphic and open. Reb narrowed her eyes, and Cato blinked at her innocently. What was his game, then? She was standing behind Urso, and he must know something was happening, but he couldn't turn around without breaking what they were building. His back stiffened, and he raised his hands a little higher and said the next words more loudly, a little faster maybe.

The air in the room was humming in time with the ebbs and flows of the crowd noise, and a column of air had begun to circle in the middle of the circle. So. Salt and rosemary hadn't worked. Could she disrupt the circle itself? Scuff a hole in it? Or would that just release that column of air. She couldn't help but remember what had happened in Cato's room; and then in her own workroom. Her arm throbbed under the bandages.

She couldn't think of anything else. She had to try it. She darted forwards, around Urso, just out of reach between both him and Jonas, and used her good hand, wrapped in her sleeve, to scrub at the floor.

The circle didn't shift, but her hand burned unbearably even through the cloth. She pulled it away, unable to repress a sob of pain. She heard a satisfied huff from Urso, but he didn't break the flow of his words.

Kneeling on the floor, cradling her hand, she heard something behind her, and turned around. Beckett was staring at the centre of the circle, their eyes wild, their hands twitching.

"Mine," Beckett said. "It is mine, *mine*, MINE."

Reb turned back to the circle just in time to see Cato's smile widen just a fraction. Jonas grunted, and Reb turned sharply to look at him. He blinked again, flicked his eyes towards her then towards Beckett, and swallowed hard. Then he staggered as if he'd been hit in the stomach, looking over at Cato as he did it, and dropped his hands. Cato swore and dropped his too, dropping to one knee. Theatrically, almost, Reb couldn't help but notice.

That should have been it. Two of them had fallen. The circle should fall with them. But the column of air was still circling, whipping round ever faster.

Urso, staggering himself, knees bent against the strain, was holding it by himself, his voice shaking as he kept speaking words Reb couldn't hear over the noise of the whirling air mixed with the road from the crowd. Reb looked back at Cato and saw a flicker of surprise and anxiety cross his face. The column of air in the middle of the room was taking on features, and shape. Urso was gasping harshly, and the noise of the crowd was peaking.

Then Beckett hurtled past her and into the centre of the circle, to hurl themself at that column of air. It shouldn't have been possible; Beckett should have burnt like Reb's hand when she'd tried to scrub the markings out. Jonas and Cato must have weakened the circle at least that much.

"MINE, you bastard," Beckett shrieked, grappling with the air.

But it wasn't working. Urso was sweating, his voice hoarse

now, but he wasn't stopping, and Beckett wasn't winning against the air. Reb could admire Urso's stamina even as she tried to think of something to break it. She dug her hand, still throbbing, into her pocket, thinking furiously. Salt again? Couldn't hurt. She looked up to see Cato, his eyes narrowed, evidently trying to make a decision. Then he looked up, behind Reb, and looked startled. Reb turned. Behind Urso she saw Asa, teeth bared, a chair in their hands. They swung it with all their might straight into the back of Urso' knees.

Urso screamed, and crashed to the floor.

There was a massive echoing crack, and Beckett and the air column both disappeared.

☉ ☉

Marcia ran up the Hill, through alleyways and passages towards that centre of Marek political and social power, the Council Chamber.

At each crossroads, she glanced in both directions along the main street. At the third one, she saw someone emerging from the next cross-street along. Her hind-brain recognised Daril before her conscious awareness did, and she dived across the street, narrowly avoiding a pair of porters trundling a large cart. She disappeared up the next alleyway with their complaints drifting behind her. She didn't pause at the next crossroads; and the one after that was the top street. She came out nearly opposite House Fereno.

She slowed to a brisk walk. A run would merely attract unwanted attention here, deserted though the street was. She couldn't see Daril ahead of her. Had she beaten him here?

When she turned through the gates of the Council onto the white marble courtyard in front of it, the doors stood slightly ajar, and there were two city guards, in full formal wear, standing beside it. Marcia frowned. They'd let her in, as Fereno-Heir. (Indeed, she should really have been here already, beside Madeleine. Who was going to be furious.) Would they let Daril in? Probably. And if not, he'd take steps to ensure his entrance. But he might be there already. Cautiously, she stepped inside, nodding at both the guards.

No Daril inside the foyer. Had he just gone straight in?

As she hesitated, she heard footsteps outside, then a muffled conversation. She turned, and Daril walked through the door. His eyes widened.

"Marcia Fereno-Heir," he said. "What could you be doing here at this hour? Shouldn't you be in there?" He gestured at the Chamber.

"I could ask the same of you. Except you're not entitled to be in there." She raised her chin. "It ends here, Daril."

They stared at one another.

"I don't know what you could be talking about," Daril said, but his tone lacked conviction. His right hand strayed to a twist of gold wire around his left wrist. Daril wasn't normally one for jewellery. There were lines of strain around his eyes.

"Oh, come on, Daril," she said. "We've known each other for a long time. Don't give me this absurdity. I could ask you what you've done with my brother, but I know now. Failure ten years ago wasn't enough for you, apparently. Now you have to try all over again."

His control cracked and he bared his teeth. "But this time, Marcia, I am not going to *fail*."

"I regret to disagree," Marcia said. "I left my friends down there to deal with Urso and my brother."

"Finally given up on him, have you?" Daril sneered. "I wondered what it would take."

That stung, just for a moment. "You leave Cato out of it. I fell for your words ten years ago. Happily I'm less credulous now."

"Fell for," Daril scoffed. "You were perfectly aware of what was going on, you just chose not to think about it."

Marcia's cheeks flamed. "You lied last time. You were defeated last time. Here we are all over again. How terribly *dull*, Daril."

To her surprise, it was the first part that he flared up at.

"I lied to no one!"

"Rubbish," Marcia said sharply. "At the very least you lied to your father."

"Ha! The old boy would have been delighted if he'd found out. I lied to *no one*. People deceived themselves, perhaps. People chose to read their own meanings into what I said…"

"Their own meanings? Deceived themselves? Daril, you deceive *yourself* speaking like that. You knew exactly what you were doing. You knew exactly what to say to bend people to your wishes."

Marcia was suddenly aware that this was the first time they had been on their own together in a room since then. Beyond the main doors into the Chamber, she could faintly hear the sound of speeches, declamations. The Chamber was designed to amplify voices. No one in there would hear them out here. Still.

"You took advantage," she said, more quietly.

"I did nothing of the sort!"

"I was sixteen, Daril! And half the rest of your little gang were barely any older. You talked us around, you convinced us…"

"You wanted to join me. All of you, you wanted what I was suggesting. You were in it too, Marcia. You can't get away by pretending that you didn't know what you were doing. You were old enough to realise what you were getting into. If you'd bothered to think about it."

Marcia shook her head, resisting. "I was deluded."

"You knew what you were about," Daril insisted. His evident conviction twined into her guilty remembrance of those days.

"So is that your excuse for winding Cato into your plans this time, then?" she demanded.

"Cato can more than look after himself," Daril said harshly.

"And what of your truth, b'Leandra?" Marcia demanded. "Can't get your father to give you power the regular way so you're taking it by force?"

Daril's face was dark with anger. "You're defending the Chamber, are you? As if this way of governing is perfection itself."

"And you'll be better?" Marcia demanded. "Don't pretend you're looking out for anyone but yourself. Daril, you removed the *cityangel*. You're trying to get us into a war with Salina. Don't claim you want what's best for Marek."

"I'm getting Marek *out* of a war. A war that your mother and my father are galloping towards. Do *they* want what's best for Marek? I am going to stop that. I don't want war any more than you do. With the cityangel's power I can denounce that idiot plan, and Houses Fereno and Leandra with it. And about bloody time too, to knock them off their pedestals."

It suddenly occurred to Marcia to wonder how it was, given the Salinas attitude to magic, that Urso was in the embassy at all? Her stomach dropped as she realised – Urso and Daril must have told Kia about the whole business with the ships. Well. That was something to deal with at a later date, if and when she was through with Daril.

"A war that Urso pushed them towards so you'd have an excuse to get into the embassy, no?" Marcia said. "Your hands are not clean."

"I notice you're not defending your mother," Daril said.

"If you want change, this is not the way to achieve it," Marcia said. "There are other ways."

"So you're happy to sit waiting for your mother to call you up, are you?" Daril said, one eyebrow raised. "Because I don't see anything changing before then. And I can't envisage you arguing all that strongly for change after that, either. You'll be part of the system, by then. You'll find a reason why it doesn't need to change after all. But happily, it's not likely you're going to be in a position to do anything at all any more."

"Wait until I get there and let me prove it," Marcia said. "Hell, Daril, comply with your father long enough to be named Heir and you can be part of that too. I'm not saying we don't need to change things. But this is not the way. And the *cityangel*."

Daril waved a hand. "I'm replacing it. One is the same as another."

There was a shiver in the air of the room, a sudden metallic taste like blood in Marcia's mouth. Daril's hand went to his wrist again, and his eyes brightened.

"Too late either way," he said. "It's happening now."

Marcia's stomach lurched. Reb and Beckett hadn't been able to stop it? But she'd left them right there, surely… She took a deep breath. The whole point of her being here was to stop Daril if they couldn't stop the ritual. Never mind that she had no idea how to do that. She had to try something. At the least, right now, she could keep trying to talk him out of it.

She shook her head, swallowing back nausea. "One is not the same as the other, Daril. I have *spoken* to the cityangel. The old one. There was a deal. Yours isn't tied by the deal."

"A deal which is out of date," Daril said. "A deal which defends the current structure, just like you're trying to do."

"The deal didn't just keep the cityangel out of politics, you idiot. It bound it to Marek's best interests," Marcia said through gritted teeth. "And it protected magic. Did Urso or Cato explain to you what's happened to magic? Are you really sure you know what the hell you're doing here?"

"Urso's magic seems just fine," Daril said, then narrowed his eyes at her. "If you've heard otherwise, you've been talking to another sorcerer – that washed-up bint over in the Old Market, then?"

Marcia fought back fury at hearing Reb referred to that way. "She defeated you last time around, Daril."

"And yet apparently not this time," Daril said. The prickling sensation in the air was growing stronger. "Funny that." His eyes were bright.

He stopped, arrested by something Marcia couldn't see, a sudden look of shocked horror sweeping across his face. He cried out, and grabbed at his wrist, going to his knees on the floor, bent over his arm in evident pain.

"What… ?" Marcia dropped to her knees beside him and grabbed at his wrist. The gold wire burnt her fingers and she snatched them away.

"That – the power, when Urso – something wrong, something wrong. Gods, it burns, Urso didn't…"

Reb must have done it. Disrupted whatever was happening.

Daril's wrist was turning red now under the wire. He didn't – whatever was going on, she couldn't just let him be burnt, not if she could avoid it. She set her teeth, wrapped her sleeves around her hands, and yanked at the wire twice, three times. Daril screamed, and it came away, stinging her fingers again. She flung it away across the floor.

She stayed there, on her knees, staring at Daril, his face now buried in his hands. They'd won. They must have won. Had they won?

And if they had – what in the name of the angel was she going to do with Daril?

EIGHTEEN

Jonas stared around the ballroom. Outside, the noise of the crowd was still going, and the light was getting on into evening. The chalk patterns were still there on the floor, but he could tell now that there was no power to them any more; they no longer had that faint not-quite-glow to them.

On the other side of the circle from him, Urso was out cold. Asa stood over him, a splintered chair in their hands. They were shaking slightly. They took a deep breath, then looked across at him, their eyes wide. He tried a tentative smile, and after a moment, Asa returned it. He didn't even know what they were doing here. He'd expected them just to deliver the message, not to come back with Reb.

He blinked, and looked over at Reb. She was still on her knees, eyes fixed on the space where Beckett had been a moment before, muttering under her breath. The hand that wasn't strapped across her body was foraging through her pockets. Sorcery. More damn sorcery. Cato, a few feet away, was also looking at the place where Beckett had disappeared. His head was cocked slightly to one side, and his eyes were thoughtful.

Something had happened, while they were in that circle. Something had changed, inside Jonas' head. It felt like a door had opened onto a part of him he'd never known about. His flickers had only been a tiny porthole onto that. His skin felt like it was vibrating, as though if he looked down it would be glowing like a night-fish.

He had no idea what he thought about any of it. He didn't dare put a label on it, although he couldn't help thinking back to what Cato had said, earlier, in that little room.

He looked over at Cato again, who seemed to have come to a decision. He backed out of the circle, keeping a careful eye on Reb, who seemed entirely engaged in whatever it was she was doing with the contents of her pockets, and walked around the edge of the room to Jonas.

"Time for me to be off, I think," Cato said quietly, eyes flicking back towards Reb. "But – look. I can still take it away, if you want. If you want to go home, and you're sure that you can't do it with this in your head. But at this point, I have to warn you, it's going to hurt like hell, and..." He exhaled, ran a hand across his face. "I don't – I think you should be very certain that that's what you want. Very certain." His gaze was serious, and sympathetic. "But if you want to stay, if you want to keep what's yours, born into you – well. I can teach you to *use* it."

He smiled that charming smile, but this time there was something real under it, something that reached his eyes. It made him look like Marcia's brother more than just superficially.

"You already have an in with the cityangel," Cato added, that smile twisting sideways a little. "The new old cityangel. You could be a very good sorcerer."

He glanced down at Reb again, and nodded sharply. He was away and out of the room before Jonas had finished processing what he'd just said.

He remembered, suddenly, the flicker he'd had back in Cato's room, when Reb had broken in, just before he met Marcia. Him and Cato discussing something – something that had to be sorcery – together. He'd assumed that it was about his flickers, Cato explaining them, about to get rid of them for him. But maybe...

He could choose. That image could be Cato introducing him to sorcery. Or it could be Cato about to take his abilities away. He could be a sorcerer. Or he could lose it.

Reb and Asa seemed to come out of their dazes almost simultaneously. Jonas wondered whether Cato could have had something to do with that. Surely not? Reb swore, shook her head, jaw clenched, and got up. She went over to Urso and prodded at him with the toe of her boot. Asa set the remains of the chair down and came over to Jonas.

"I don't – I don't think I want to stay here," they said. "Unless Reb needs us for something, I suppose. Can we just go home, Jonas? Back to the squats?" Their voice wobbled slightly.

"We should help sort that one out," Jonas said, nodding at

Urso. "But then – yes. Yes. I want out of here. And Asa – thanks."

Their grin was a bit shaky, but they slapped him on the shoulder. "Couldn't have done anything else, hey? Can't leave a fellow messenger in the lurch, you know. Or a friend."

A fellow messenger. Asa thought of him as being one of them, as belonging here.

His mother had been very clear that his flickers didn't belong on board ship. The new thing that he could feel inside his head – that would belong even less.

Cato's offer circled around his head. *I could teach you to use it.*

The ships would start leaving tomorrow. They'd all be gone in a week's time. And yes, they'd be back again, but… he knew, really, that if he stayed now, that would be a decision in itself.

☉ ☉

Marcia knelt on the floor of the Chamber foyer, the grey marble cool under her knees. Daril sat on the floor, his head down on his knees, shuddering.

She'd always thought of Daril as old, experienced. Knowing what he was doing, even if what he was doing was a terrible idea.

Looking at him now, she remembered that he was only five years older than she was, and he wasn't nearly as in control of everything as she'd always believed. Bad decisions, bad situation. What would she do, if she'd been dealing with his father instead of her mother? She let herself think of herself ten years from now, still trailing round after Madeleine and not allowed to do anything for the House, for herself. Would she, too, start making worse decisions?

Daril was right, to an extent. That was the other thing.

But that didn't solve the question of what to do with him now. The faint sounds from beyond the main Chamber doors were changing. The session was coming to an end.

She could still drag Daril in there, swear a charge of

treason against him there and then. For a moment, she could see it happening. She could envisage Gavin Leandra's reaction, the shock of the assembled Houses. Legally speaking, it was the correct thing to do. He and Urso should both pay for what they'd done. (And Cato? She swallowed. She wouldn't be able to protect Cato, and Daril would hardly be inclined to.)

But then what? What would happen after that?

She didn't know what was happening, down at the embassy. It hadn't worked as Daril had expected, that much was clear, but did that mean Reb had succeeded in whatever she was intending to do? And what did that mean for Beckett?

The she remembered, with a lurch of her stomach, how Daril had said that they'd been let into the embassy at all. He'd promised that, once he had some power, he would put a stop to it. He might even have been telling the truth. But in any case: he wouldn't be stopping it, now, yet it still had to be stopped. At present, Gavin and Madeleine were still intending to confiscate these damn ships.

Bringing that into the Council Chamber might solve the problem. Surely sense would prevail; surely the Council would shout the idea down. But that would be to the detriment of her own House, as well as House Leandra; and, worse, it would surely cause catastrophic damage to Marek's relationship with Salina, to have the whole thing publicly acknowledged. At present Kia apparently knew; but Kia had agreed to a solution which simply stopped the idea, without publicising it, suggesting that the relationship was still salvageable. If it was out in the open, formal Council business, Kia might have to react differently. Salina might have to react differently.

Worse, what if the Council *didn't* vote it down? What if there were more people who fell into the trap that Gavin and Madeleine had fallen into? There was, after all, general resentment about the increases in the trading fees. And if this whole plan came out, it would also become public knowledge that the Salinas ambassador had allowed Urso to use the Salinas embassy to attack the Council, which would be guaranteed to further inflame bad feeling. Both Gavin and Madeleine, when they chose, were gifted speakers, from powerful Houses. Could they convince their fellows to back them? Marcia wasn't sure she wanted to take that risk.

Not only that, but it seemed almost inevitable that at some point the matter of the cityangel would come up. The Upper City largely chose to believe that there was no such thing, but the Lower City would not react well. And what if Beckett hadn't been restored? How would people react to that news?

Part of her still wanted to drag everything out into the light, to point out what had happened and how; but she could see, clearly enough, that it wouldn't change anything the way she wanted to. If anything, it would solidify the current Council in their methods.

Which left the alternative. Managing this privately, behind House walls. Convincing Gavin and Madeleine to drop their idiotic ideas. She had Daril, who might not be Heir to House Leandra, but who was a candidate, and who had attempted to overthrow the Council; and the only other House Leandra candidate, Urso, was also in the whole thing up to his neck. She could use that – and her promise of secrecy about it – to put pressure on Gavin. He couldn't risk letting both treachery and involvement in sorcery taint his House.

What about Madeleine? If she got Gavin to back down first, then the fact that Madeleine would be standing alone might sway her mother. Would Cato's involvement, and the consequences if that came out, sway her at all? Marcia couldn't believe so, much though she might want to; Cato's disinheritance had been absolute, as far as Madeleine was concerned. The fact that Urso had been manipulating her, that might be relevant.

Marcia rolled a bead on her bracelet between her fingers as she thought. She had something against Kia, too. Something that she could use in negotiations. An improved deal for House Fereno with Salina. That might be enough to sway her mother. And the possibility of her Heir standing publicly against her; Fereno would look like fools, in public, if it came to that.

She sighed. It was a thin web, but she just needed to hold it together for long enough for the moment to have passed. Neither Gavin nor Madeleine could do this alone. In all honesty, Marcia couldn't see how they could have pulled it off even working together. If she could break the links apart right now, neither would be able to put it back together, at least not immediately.

She looked down at Daril, still on the floor. He'd get off without paying for his decisions, and that rankled. On the other hand – a slow smile started on her face – now he would *owe* her one. And at some point, she would be able to collect.

Well then.

Two hard thumps came from within the Chamber – the Speaker calling the session to a close. Time to move.

"Daril." He looked up, his eyes still wild. "Come on. Session's done. We need to get out of here."

She hauled him to his feet. He was still clutching his arm, but he came willingly enough, out of the Chamber and down the street to House Leandra.

"What are you going to do?" he said, halfway there. His voice was quieter than usual. "Swear treason against me?"

"I don't think that's going to help anyone," she said. "What I'm going to do right now is, I'm going to talk to your bloody father."

"He'll disown me," Daril said.

"Not if he doesn't want his warmongering to come to light, he won't," Marcia said grimly.

Daril stumbled and would have fallen if Marcia hadn't caught him. "But – why?"

"Your complaint is legitimate," Marcia said. "Your methods were not. Your father is a manipulative shithead, and always has been. And now you, and he, and House Leandra, will owe me a favour. I will be back to collect, don't worry."

Daril started to laugh. "You've grown up, Marcia."

"Something like that," Marcia agreed. "Here we are."

She steered him across the courtyard and up the steps towards the door. He was walking a little more steadily now.

"It'll be a while before your father's back from the Guildhall," she added. "I won't insist you wait with me. But you could order me an infusion."

Daril was still laughing a little. "Roberts," he said to the man who had opened the door. "Please show Fereno-Heir to the small parlour, and show my father to her when he arrives."

Roberts' eyebrows twitched very slightly. "Will you be waiting with her, sir?"

"Uh – no. No, I think best not," Daril said.

He bowed to Marcia, full formal. "No doubt we'll speak again soon," he said, and took himself, slowly, but straight-backed, towards the stairs.

Marcia sat in the parlour, sipped the infusion that Roberts brought, and ate a plate of biscuits. She was starving. While she did all of that, she thought about what to do next. It seemed all too soon that Gavin Leandra arrived.

"Urso Leanvit is a sorcerer," she said, without preamble, when Gavin saw her and began spluttering. "And he's been playing you. You've come very close to betraying Marek between you. And whilst I will leave Daril to discuss the details with you, he's been up to it in his neck as well. Abandon your absurd plans to impound Salinas ships, and I will let the whole thing disappear. Otherwise..." She shrugged. "It is up to you whether you think House Leandra can rid itself of the taint of treason, sorcery, and the intention to act without Council approval." That last one might be the kicker, now she came to think about it. The Council might have accepted something that had already happened, for their own profit and to avoid looking toothless. But to hear of it in advance, they would have to act strongly to retain their power.

"If you tell the Council about any of this, it will fall on your House as well," Gavin said, his eyes narrowing.

"On my mother," Marcia said. "And, perhaps, on my House. But not on me, and then I will be free to rebuild the House as I please. You do not have an Heir at all, and neither of your candidates have clean hands. I do not believe you are in a position to call this one, Leandra-Head."

Gavin seemed to be leaning a little more heavily on his stick as he nodded, once.

"Interesting, Fereno-Heir." He cracked a sudden smile, not a kind one. "I only wish I could see you speaking to your mother."

Marcia chose not to respond to that.

"I'll wait to see what decision you make," she said, and walked past Gavin to leave the house.

She stopped in the hall, and turned back. "One other thing.

If you name Urso Heir, I *will* tell the Council about his sorcery. If you wish this whole thing to disappear, I most strongly suggest that you stop manipulating Daril and name him Heir. The current situation is untenable, and Daril's decisions are in part your responsibility."

Her mother would have to wait until she'd got back to the Salinas embassy. She had a deal to make with Ambassador Kia t'Riseri. And she still didn't know what had actually *happened* there.

On arrival at the embassy, only Reb was still there. Urso was out cold, and a doctor, apparently on retainer to the embassy, was examining him. Reb's clothes were ripped and her unsplinted arm blistered with burns to the elbow.

"Jonas has gone home, with Asa," Reb said. She looked exhausted. "We'd have been screwed without Asa. And it was Jonas who created the hole, although... well. It was complicated."

"What about my brother?" Marcia asked.

Reb scowled. "Did a runner straight after, while I wasn't paying attention. He's not daft. He's hardly going to hang around for the fallout. I should have grabbed him before he left."

"Looks like you had enough to be dealing with," Marcia said. "But what about Beckett? Did they... ?"

"I don't *know*," Reb said, her frustration clear. "There was this, this *whirlwind*, and then Beckett walked into it and it all just – disappeared. Hopefully – well. I haven't tried a spell yet, I just did some purification stuff to get rid of the rest of the ritual markings. Maybe soon." She rubbed at her face. "I need to deal with Urso, too, once he's conscious again. He's a sorcerer, after all. I need to..." Her voice trailed off.

"You should get the doctor to look at that arm," Marcia said, fighting the urge to do it herself.

"Yeah," Reb agreed, shrugging in a way that suggested that she might or might not actually bother.

Marcia sighed. She had things to do. She couldn't look after Reb right now, much though she might want to. "Where's the ambassador? Kia t'Riseri?"

"Politics, huh?" Reb said. "Locked in her office."

The office was on the ground floor.

"So why?" Marcia said, bluntly, once she'd marched in there.

"Your poxy Council is going to steal our ships," Kia spat. She was sitting behind her desk, looking furious.

"Some idiots are trying to," Marcia corrected. "*Were* trying to."

"Your House, Fereno-Heir."

Marcia shook her head. "No. Not any more."

Kia looked confused.

"It's a bloody stupid idea," Marcia said. "You have far more experience than us, and far better contacts. You have a boat-building industry. We don't. For certain, it is possible to build all of those things. But it costs, and it's going to damage trade while we do it."

"I don't even understand why they thought of this in the first place," Kia said, but some of the heat had gone out of her voice.

"Well," Marcia said. "Partly because Urso was playing both sides to precisely this end. But he found it *easy* because of the rises in the last couple of years."

"But –"

"Yes, exactly. You and I both know that any ships would have had the same problems, and had to make the same charges. The Council are – let's say that sometimes they are a little out of touch, and sometimes they are just wilfully ignorant." Marcia sighed. "But to be honest, right now that is the least of your worries. The *other* part of Urso and Daril's plan, I am prepared to bet," she'd realised it while thinking all of it over, waiting in House Leandra, "was that by being *here*, Salina would take the fall. And Daril would have used *that* confusion – riots in the street and all that – to take over."

Kia frowned. "But Daril said – what they were doing, no one would know."

"Want to bet?" Marcia said. "If any of this gets out – the cityangel, for pity's sake, Kia! – there is nothing in the dimensions that I can say that will protect you. Salinas ships will be barred, trade be damned."

"I wasn't even there," Kia protested, weakly.

"You let them in here," Marcia said. "You were in it up to your eyeballs and we both know it. And I'm guessing that your own people won't be terribly impressed with sorcery on the premises, either. Now – I don't think either of us want a trade disaster. And I'm guessing you don't want to be stripped of your post."

Kia had gone pale.

"Now," Marcia carried on, "as a senior House member, I would like to think about both problems at once. As such, it would I think be in both of our interests to hide your involvement altogether."

Kia's eyebrows shot up. "Do go on."

Some time later, Kia had been neatly tied up in her office, ready for the guard to find. Urso could be charged with breaching diplomatic premises and kidnapping an ambassador. And Marcia was reflecting with some pleasure that she now had something on the Salinas ambassador that would be a bargaining chip for a good long time.

☉ ☉

Reb stood just inside her front door, safely closed behind her, and let her shoulders slump. She was bone-deep tired. But there was one more thing she had to try. It was foolish, given what had happened last time, to do this without someone to anchor her. But Marcia was off politicking, and Jonas had slid off back to the squats with Asa, and really there was no one else she could ask.

A sobering thought, that; that the only people she could have asked to do this, she'd known for a bare handful of days. What had she been *doing* for the last two years? Mourning was all very well, but none of the friends she'd lost would have thanked her for honouring them by this abrasive solitude.

Other sorcerers. Urso. She still had to deal with Urso, though right now he was being dealt with by the Guard for the more mundane aspects of his behaviour. Such as 'kidnapping' Kia – that had been an excellent idea of Marcia's. She could get whatever was left over once they were done with him.

Then there was the question of Cato. He'd helped Daril and

Urso, for certain, but... that smile, just as things had fallen apart. It had looked like it was down to Jonas, but perhaps...

The important thing was that Reb should have known what was happening with Urso. She should have known that there was a new sorcerer around. But neither should he have been the only one. That was her responsibility, too. Her friends wouldn't thank her for the fact that two years after the plague, she'd not been teaching a single new sorcerer. The talent had to be there. It was her job to find it. She needed to step up to the plate.

But first of all, she had to at least start to check that there would be any Marek-magic to train people up to.

She squared her shoulders and walked into her inner room. Taking a pinch of nettle weed, she invoked the guardian-spell. This time the response rang immediately, reverberating in her ears without sound, a clear pure chime. She still didn't have the first clue what had happened there, but, some way or another, all was *well*.

She washed her hands, working around the splint. (Maybe, tomorrow, a healing spell. That would be a relief. But not now.) Hands clean, she walked back into the front room and stopped dead. Beckett stood there; but Beckett subtly altered. Beckett who carried Marek with him like a cloak. You couldn't begin to doubt Beckett's nature now. Was this, even, still Beckett? The cityangel had never had a name, before.

"Reb!" the cityangel said, happily.

"Beckett?" Reb asked cautiously.

"Who else? Ah. I see. I like Beckett, yes. I will keep it."

"What happened?" Reb said. "To the other one. I mean, I take it you *are* back now?"

"Yes. The other. Well. You could say that I – ate – the other one. Not quite right, but close enough."

Reb grimaced and decided against further enquiry.

"But magic, Reb. I have realised what a terrible state Marek magic is in."

"Yes," Reb agreed, wincing.

"I stopped paying attention. The plague..." Beckett's self seemed to dim, suddenly, to shrink inwards, then they looked at her again. "I was wrong."

"We have to go on.," Reb said. "We have to – I have to –

move on, start finding sorcerers again. I know. I'm sorry it took me so long to realise."

"We both suffered," Beckett said softly. "It is past, now. We move on. I am glad that you are with me on this."

Reb's heart felt lighter, somehow. "But what of Cato? And Urso?" she asked.

"Cato is still one of mine. Twisty, but mine. I would not overlook Cato, if I were you," Beckett said. "Urso, however, you can leave to me. Urso is no longer a Marek sorcerer." Beckett bared their teeth.

"Right," Reb said. "And new talent. I was just thinking that I should be looking. Should have been looking already."

"New talent is out there, indeed," Beckett said. They seemed to be amused by something. "I am glad we agree. I will see you again, no doubt."

They flickered, and disappeared.

Reb scrubbed at her eyes. All of this, *all* of it, could wait until tomorrow. Now, she was going to sleep.

☺ ☺

Marcia walked up the stairs to her room, back straight, in case her mother was still watching. Telling Madeleine exactly why her plans had been so foolish, and what they were now going to do instead, had been… well. Perhaps the toughest thing she'd done in the last decade, including her and Reb nearly being obliterated by a rogue cityangel. The deal – the extremely favourable-to-House-Fereno deal – that Marcia had concluded with Kia had helped. And she thought – she hoped – she might have a bit more of Madeleine's respect now. It was time, after all. And Marcia was to oversee the working-out of the trade deal over the next five years.

She could, however, have done without the formal Mid-Year meal afterwards, with its twenty guests and dozen courses. She shut her door and slumped against it, eyes shut.

"Well, sister. Wasn't that delightful?"

Her eyes flew open.

Cato lounged on her bed, smiling cheerfully at her.

"Cato? What in the – you've got a nerve, showing up here."

She reached for proper anger, or at the least annoyance, but couldn't find it. Cato was Cato, when all was said and done. He was still her brother.

"What?" he asked, eyes disingenuously wide. "It all came good in the end, right? The cityangel is back, the Council remains as it ever was – lucky us – and I got the first half of my money, at least. Always get as much as you can in advance, that's my motto."

"No thanks to you, any of it," Marcia muttered.

Cato spread his hands. "Perhaps I trusted that you – or that *someone* – would be smarter than Daril b'Leandra, sister."

She looked narrowly at him. "What did you do?" she challenged him. "In the embassy, I mean. I know you what you did in the park."

Cato sighed. "In the park – Marcia, I promise you, I thought we were replacing the cityangel and all would be well. I'm sorry about that." His voice was serious for once.

"So, after all that – you suddenly thought better of it once you were in the embassy?" Marcia said.

Cato blinked at her. "Are you by any chance suggesting that I let my client down at the crucial moment? Why, Marcia, that would be *unethical*."

She knew, from extensive previous experience, that she wasn't going to get anything more explicit out of him. She rolled her eyes, and he grinned.

"So," he said. "Did you make political hay out of the whole thing?"

"Let's just say I have plans," Marcia said. She looked down at her fingers. "Daril wasn't entirely wrong, you know. His methods were appalling, but some of what he was complaining about…"

"Yes. I noticed that. I wondered if you would"

Marcia took a breath. "I've been drifting a bit, I think. Letting Mother shove me around. Letting the whole situation drift, come to that – it's not just me, after all. This – it generates an opportunity to step up, that's for certain. I just have to work out what to do with it."

"Well," Cato said. "I'd back you against anyone, for that."

She looked up at him sharply. His eyes were serious, and loving. Then he grinned, and the moment was gone. He swung his legs off the bed.

"In between all the serious politicking, though, if I were you, I'd find some time to go see the lovely Reb, hmm?"

Marcia glared at him. "What do you mean?"

"Why would I mean anything?" He blinked slowly. "I've known Reb a while, you know. Fellow sorcerers and all that."

"She doesn't think much of you."

"Very competent, Reb is," Cato said, ignoring her. "Tediously moral. No wonder you get on." He grinned at her. "Or get…"

"Oh, shut it, you." Marcia caught up a cushion from the chair, and threw it at him. He dodged, laughing, and suddenly they were fifteen again. Impulsively, she stepped forwards and hugged him. "I was going to see Reb anyway, thank you all the same. Look after yourself, you. And now shoo. I need to get to bed. I am *tired*."

He hugged her tightly, then let her go. He sauntered to the open window, sketched a vague salute, then swung his leg over the sill and was gone.

Marcia stared at the window for a moment, then shook her head. She could get rid of the creeper that climbed the wall around her window, if she ever chose to. For security.

She wouldn't.

Only Cato was Cato. And it was warded against anyone but him, ever since the night he left, ten years ago.

She really did want to see Reb. But that would have to wait for tomorrow.

NINETEEN

Marcia woke up the next morning and knew that she had to go and see Reb. Regardless of what her mother thought she should be getting on with.

She looked out of her window while she dressed, and saw the first couple of Salinas ships hoisting sail out away to the sea. The trading lull. The rest would be gone in another few days. Time to set things up for her new deal. She wondered if Jonas, in the end, had found his way onto one of those ships.

After breakfast, she took the cliff path down to the ferry. It was pleasant in the summer sunshine. She thought about Reb as the ferry crossed the river. Cato had said – but was he right? She wanted more, herself; friendship at least, beyond this thing that had temporarily brought them together. More? If Reb wanted it? She thought, just maybe, Cato was right, and Reb did want that.

Reb's face was unreadable when she opened her door to find Marcia on the doorstep.

"May I come in?" Marcia asked, politely.

"You – yes. Of course." Reb stood aside, equally politely, to let her in.

"I – I thought to see you, after I'd spoken to Kia, yesterday," Marcia said.

"Things to do," Reb said. "And you looked busy enough."

Marcia nodded, not quite in agreement. "Have you – Beckett? Have you found out about Beckett?"

Reb's face brightened. "Yes. Yes. Beckett is fine. We spoke yesterday."

"You *spoke*?" Marcia echoed.

"I don't know if their sojourn here has left them chattier," Reb said, with a half smile. "They wish to continue being known as Beckett, anyway."

They were silent for a moment. Marcia looked down at her fingers.

"What happened, then, with b'Leandra?" Reb asked. "I saw

Urso being carted off by the Guard."

"For kidnapping Kia, yes," Marcia said.

Reb raised an eyebrow. "Not for treason, then?"

"No," Marcia said, with a sigh. "And Daril will face no charges at all."

Both of Reb's eyebrows were up now. "None at all? What is this, the privileges of being a scion of one of the Thirteen Houses?" She sounded deeply disapproving.

"I suppose so, in a way," Marcia said. "But mostly because it was the only way I could think of to prevent my mother and Gavin Leandra from going ahead with this absurd plan to claim Salinas ships."

"You blackmailed him," Reb said.

"I agreed not to make the whole business public if he left Salina alone," Marcia agreed. "After which, my mother knew she most likely couldn't pull it off on her own."

Reb nodded slowly. "And why won't Urso blow that sky-high when he's tried for this 'kidnapping'?"

"Because Kia's going to refuse to press charges," Marcia said. "And Urso will then be strongly encouraged to take himself off on a nice long trip to Teren."

"Right."

She might as well admit it all at once. "And I strongly suggested that Daril should be confirmed Heir as soon as possible. Part of this mischief is down to this absurd feud Daril and his father have had."

"And also Daril will owe you something," Reb said.

Marcia, surprised, smiled over at her. "Exactly that. You're right, the whole thing is about the power of the Council and the Houses, and hiding all of this lest people get embarrassed. Because that embarrassment might cause bigger problems." Like war with Salina, for example. "But it's a bad system. Daril was right, as far as that went, even if his alternative wasn't any better. It's a bad system, and I intend to do something to change it. Daril might be able to help with that."

"I thought you wanted nothing to do with him," Reb said.

"I don't, really," Marcia said. "But neither do I want him running around loose. And he can be *useful*, if I can find a way to manage him. It's about time I started doing something useful myself, too. Like I say. Things need to change."

Reb was smiling warmly at her, and Marcia's heart gave a thump that was almost painful.

"Me too," she said. "With the things changing. Just different things. I should have been paying more attention, the last little while. The plague was awful, and I'm always going to mourn those I lost, we lost. But Marek's magic is still here. I should have spotted Urso. If I had, maybe he would have used his power differently. And there should be more sorcerers here, not just me and your brother. Beckett made that point, when I saw them, but I'd come to it myself already. I've got some work to do, on all of that."

"I suppose you'll be busy, then," Marcia said.

"Depends if I can get anything useful out of your brother."

Marcia frowned. "Cato? But just yesterday, he..."

"Funny thing, that," Reb said. "I've been thinking it over. Jonas was the one who dropped the spell, right enough. And – apparently – Cato was knocked away by that. Then Urso clung to it like a madman, and he was very nearly strong enough. But if it had been him *and* Cato... He's strong, your brother. Stronger than Urso. If Urso could hold on, well..."

"You think Cato sabotaged it?"

Reb pulled a face. "Never going to *know*. He's hard to read, that one." Reb looked at her. "Bit like his sister."

"Am I hard to read?" Marcia asked, surprised.

"Well," Reb said, considering. "Perhaps – perhaps what I need is a bit more practice."

She met Marcia's eyes, her look a question, and a hope. Marcia swallowed, and licked her lips, and saw Reb's glance flick downwards to her mouth.

"Perhaps," Marcia said. "Perhaps that would be something we could do?"

Reb's solemn face broke into a smile, and Marcia felt a bubble of happiness rise inside her. Wordlessly, she held out her hand, and Reb took it. Their fingers tangled together. Marcia met Reb's smile with her own, and it felt like a new beginning.

☺ ☺

Cato had celebrated his return by going directly to the pub; it was late morning by the time he made his way back to his rooms, and read the note pinned to his door.

I'm staying. I'll come tomorrow, to talk about your offer. Jonas.

He kicked off his boots, put all the wards back up, and collapsed onto the bed, staring at the ceiling. Well then. What with that, and the shock that the cityangel had doubtless got, and the fact that Reb seemed finally to have pulled her head out of her arse... perhaps Marek would finally get *interesting*, again, for a sorcerer. Also, he had a large quantity of cash in his pocket, for a while.

Good times, Cato thought, spreading his arms out luxuriously. Good times.

ACKNOWLEDGEMENTS

Heartfelt thanks to Peter and the lovely folks at Elsewhen Press for editorial tweaks and general publishing greatness.

Thank you to my parents, who encouraged me to make up and write down stories when I was small, and who still enthusiastically read everything I publish even when it's not really their thing.

Love and gratitude to doop for tea, chocolate, and encouragement; to Pete for gentle support; and to Leon for writing the sign on my door reminding him not to disturb me on writing-days (and then mostly abiding by it).

And finally, thank you to maia for tireless beta-reading and cheerleading across 10,000 miles and several timezones.

Juliet, May 2018

Elsewhen Press
delivering outstanding new talents in speculative fiction

Visit the Elsewhen Press website at elsewhen.press for the latest information on all of our titles, authors and events; to read our blog; find out where to buy our books and ebooks; or to place an order.

Sign up for the Elsewhen Press InFlight Newsletter at
elsewhen.press/newsletter

REBECCA HALL's *SYMPHONY OF THE CURSED* TRILOGY

INSTRUMENT OF PEACE

Raised in the world-leading Academy of magic rather than by his absentee parents, Mitch has come to see it as his home. He's spent more time with his friends than his family and the opinion of his maths teacher matters far more than that of his parents. His peaceful life is shattered when a devastating earthquake strikes and almost claims his little brother's life. But this earthquake is no natural phenomenon, it's a result of the ongoing war between Heaven and Hell. To protect the Academy, one of the teachers makes an ill-advised contract with a fallen angel, unwittingly bringing down The Twisted Curse on staff and students.

Even as they struggle to rebuild the school, things begin to go wrong. The curse starts small, with truancy, incomplete assignments, and negligent teachers over-reacting to minor transgressions, but it isn't long before the bad behaviour escalates to vandalism, rioting and attempted murder. As they succumb to the influence of the curse, Mitch's friends drift away and his girlfriend cheats on him. When the first death comes, Mitch unites with the only other students who, like him, appear to be immune to the curse; together they are determined to find the cause of the problem and stop it.

INSTRUMENT OF WAR

*"A clever update to a magical school story with a twist." – **Christopher Nuttall***

The Angels are coming.

The Host wants to know what the Academy was trying to hide and why the Fallen agreed to it. They want the Instrument of War, the one thing that can tip the Eternity War in their favour and put an end to the stalemate. Any impact on the Academy staff, students or buildings is just collateral damage.

Mitch would like to forget that the last year ever happened, but that doesn't seem likely with Little Red Riding Hood now teaching Teratology. The vampire isn't quite as terrifying as he first thought, but she's not the only monster at the Academy. The Fallen are spying on everyone, the new Principal is an angel and there's an enchanting exchange student with Faerie blood.

Angry and nervous of the angels surrounding him, Mitch tries to put the pieces together. He knows that Hayley is the Archangel Gabriel. He knows that she can determine the course of the Eternity War. He also knows that the Fallen will do anything to hide Gabriel from the Host – even allowing an innocent girl to be kidnapped.

INSTRUMENT OF CHAOS

The long hidden heart of the Twisted Curse had been found, concealed in a realm that no angel can enter, where magic runs wild and time is just another direction. The Twisted Curse is the key to ending the Eternity War and it can only be broken by someone willing to traverse the depths of Faerie.

Unfortunately, Mitch has other things on his mind. For reasons that currently escape him he's going to university, making regular trips to the Netherworld and hunting down a demon. The Academy might have prepared him for university but Netherworlds and demons were inexplicably left off the curriculum, not to mention curse breaking.

And then the Angels return, and this time they're hunting his best friend.

Visit tr.im/SymphonyCursed
Now available as audiobooks from Tantor

THE EMPTY THRONE
DAVID M ALLAN

Three thrones, one of metal, one of wood and one of stone, stand in the Citadel. Between them shimmers a gateway to a new world, created four hundred years ago by the three magicians who made the thrones. When hostile incorporeal creatures came through the gateway, the magicians attempted to close it but failed. Since that time the creatures have tried to come through the gateway at irregular intervals, but the throne room is guarded by the Company of Tectors, established to defend against them. To try to stop the creatures, expeditions have been sent through the gateway, but none has ever returned.

On each throne appears an image of one of the Custoda, heroes who have led the expeditions through the gateway. While the Custoda occupy the thrones the gateway remains quiet and there are no incursions. Today, Dhanay, the newest knight admitted to the Company, is guarding the throne room. Like all the Tectors, Dhanay looks to the images of the Custoda for guidance.

But the Throne of Stone is empty. The latest incursion has started; a creature escaping into the world, a kulun capable of possessing and controlling humans.

The provincial rulers, the oldest and most powerful families, ignore the gateway and the Tectors, concentrating on playing politics and pursuing their own petty aims. Some even question the need for the Company, as incursions have been successfully contained within the Citadel for years. Family feuds, border disputes, deep-rooted rivalries and bigotry make for a potentially unstable world, and are a perfect environment for a kulun looking to create havoc...

ISBN: 9781911409359 (epub, kindle) / ISBN: 9781911409250 (304pp paperback)
Visit tr.im/EmptyThrone

THE GHOST IN YOU BY KATRINA MOUNTFORT
A first-hand account from beyond the grave

What do you do if you're dead but haven't 'moved on'? You keep finding yourself back where you died, with very little control over when; sometimes you can be away for days, weeks or even months, and then you're back. Between times, when you're 'away', where do you go, what do you do? You've seen some other ghosts asleep at their graves, but you don't even know where your own grave is.

The living shiver if they walk through you, but they can neither see nor hear you. With practice you can pass through walls and doors, but curiously you can sit on a park bench without falling through it, climb stairs, even lie on a bed. You're stuck in the clothes you were wearing when you died, at the age you died. Waiting.

Then, after years of this intermittent existence, you realise what you have been waiting for, what it is that you have to do in order to finally move on. Just as you have found the best reason to stay.

That's what happened to Rowena...

A ghost story told from the perspective of the ghost herself, *The Ghost in You* is a first-hand account, from beyond the grave, by an innocent girl who dies before her time and tries to make sense of what is happening to her, while helping her friends and discovering her purpose.

ISBN: 9781911409328 (epub, kindle) / ISBN: 9781911409229 (184pp paperback)
Visit tr.im/GhostInYou

Resurrection Men
The first book of the Sooty Feathers
David Craig

Glasgow 1893.
Wilton Hunt, a student, and Tam Foley, a laudanum-addicted pharmacist, are pursuing extra-curricular careers as body snatchers, or 'resurrection men', under cover of darkness. They exhume a girl's corpse, only for it to disappear while their backs are turned. Confused and in need of the money the body would have earnt them, they investigate the corpse's disappearance. They discover that bodies have started to turn up in the area with ripped-out throats and severe loss of blood, although not the one they lost. The police are being encouraged by powerful people to look the other way, and the deaths are going unreported by the press. As Hunt and Foley delve beneath the veneer of respectable society, they find themselves entangled in a dangerous underworld that is protected from scrutiny by the rich and powerful members of the elite but secretive Sooty Feathers Club.

Meanwhile, a mysterious circus arrives in the middle of the night, summoned to help avenge a betrayal two centuries old...

Resurrection Men is the first book in David Craig's *Sooty Feathers* series, a masterful gothic tale about a supernatural war for control of the Second City of the British Empire, and the struggle of flawed characters of uncertain virtue who try to avert it. It is set in a late 19th century Glasgow ruled by undead – from the private clubs, town houses and country manors of the privileged to the dung-choked wynds and overcrowded slums of the poor. Undead unrest, a fallen angel, and religious zealots intent on driving out the forces of evil, set the stage for a diabolical conflict of biblical proportions.

ISBN: 9781911409366 (epub, kindle) / ISBN: 9781911409267 (400pp paperback)
Visit tr.im/ResurrectionMen

ABOUT THE AUTHOR

Juliet Kemp lives by the river in London, with their partners, child, dog, and too many fountain pens. They have had stories published in several anthologies and online magazines. Their employment history variously includes working as a cycle instructor, sysadmin, life model, researcher, permaculture designer, and journalist. When not writing or parenting, Juliet goes climbing, knits, reads way too much, and drinks a lot of tea.